BLACK CANDLE WOMEN

BLACK CANDLE WOMEN

A Novel

DIANE MARIE BROWN

THORNDIKE PRESS
A part of Gale, a Cengage Company

**LIBRARY OF CONGRESS CIP DATA ON FILE.
CATALOGUING IN PUBLICATION FOR THIS BOOK
IS AVAILABLE FROM THE LIBRARY OF CONGRESS.**

ISBN-13: 979-8-88578-568-6 (hardcover alk. paper).

Published in 2023 by arrangement with Harlequin Enterprises ULC.

Printed in Mexico
Print Number: 1   Print Year: 2023

To my dad, who read me stories.
To my mom, who encouraged me
to make up my own.

Prologue:
Augusta

The flight attendant told Augusta Montrose that she would have to remove her purse from her lap and put it on the floor before the plane took off. She realized the man wasn't joking when he stood in the aisle waiting, moving on only when her granddaughter grabbed the bag and shoved it under the seat in front of her — no place for a purse. She'd wanted to explain that it was her first time on a plane, that she was petrified. Not about the flight itself but the eventual arrival at their destination. When she'd left New Orleans all those decades ago, she'd vowed never to return.

She should have known she'd be called back one day, that the city would never let her rest, even thousands of miles away. She'd learned early on about a certain unfairness in life. Some folks struggled disproportionately, carrying things that others couldn't even lift. The Montrose women had taken on an overbalance of grief, but the way Augusta saw it, they'd been given what they were owed. And they were strong enough to endure it.

The women in her family lived solitary lives, generations of them under one roof, adapting to their isolated ways, doing fine, they all believed. They were a private kind of people, had to keep others out to keep the secrets in.

But recent events had changed them, shaking up the house, rattling the women within. And it was all because of her great-granddaughter. She didn't know yet for sure, but she sensed love was the cause of the girl's recent behavior. This, Augusta understood. She'd swapped one life for another because of love. Because of what had happened all those decades ago in New Orleans. It's what Montrose women did. And love was why she'd had to tell them her story . . . all of it, from the beginning. She'd held on to these words for years, stuck in her head, unsure how to share them, and now, she'd finally set them free.

■ ■ ■ ■

PART I
AUGUST

■ ■ ■ ■

1
VICTORIA

In her mellower days, Victoria Montrose sometimes ate two shrimp po'boys just as a snack. Good ones were hard to find near home, but lately, when she got her hands on one, it took only three bites before her stomach convulsed in protest. Hot links, the same. Crawfish étouffée, the same. In cases where she had to pause a therapy session to dash to the restroom, she blamed irritable bowel syndrome. Sometimes diverticulitis. Pain was often how her body spoke to her. A cramp or an abrupt pang forewarned of troubles to come.

But in most cases, an upset stomach simply meant that she'd overindulged. Her body wasn't as forgiving as it once was. Yet today, she'd ordered one of everything greasy and fried at the most authentic New Orleans restaurant in Long Beach. Her daughter, Nickie, had been born seventeen years ago, and an overdone meal was required. Victoria had kept careful track of the years, but the number still stunned her when the woman at the bakery asked how many candles she wanted.

"I'm sorry, seventeen? Or seven?" The woman's brow lifted as she eyed the half-sheet cake decorated with a miniature Black Barbie figurine. She had ordered it without thinking — it seemed Nickie had been seven just days go — but luckily her daughter was not hard to please.

It took Victoria four trips to bring the cake and all the food into the house. The moment she no longer needed help, her sister, Willow, joined her in the kitchen, the scent of grease filling the space as Willow took out containers from the bags, opening them as if each needed to breathe, and rating Victoria's choices. B+ for the sweet potatoes, C– for fried okra.

"You get Nanagusta's turtle soup?"

Victoria pointed to a cardboard cylinder with the letter *T* written on the lid.

"Should I wake her?"

"No. Let her sleep until we cut the cake." Their grandmother could reheat her soup, but she'd throw a book at them if they let her miss Nickie blowing out her candles.

From her purse, Victoria removed a small white box, a purple ribbon wrapped tightly around and tied into a bow. She shook it near Willow's ear, a faint jangle coming from inside. "You'll never guess what I got Nickie."

Willow withdrew a finger from her mouth, a yellow bit of macaroni and cheese on her knuckle. She closed an eye, pushed her lips to one side, and let her face harden, feigning contemplation. "Let me see . . . Oh!" She snapped her fingers. "A necklace with a painted gold talisman for Ayida Wedo."

Victoria slapped her sister's shoulder with the box. "I knew someone opened my stuff. I was going to call UPS and complain." After snooping, Willow evidently had taken the care to match the same tape that had been ripped off the original box and place the package back on the front porch, but she'd done a half-assed job of it. "Why, what'd you get her?"

"What did I get a teenage girl for her birthday? Money. It's the only right answer to that question," Willow bragged. Then she stopped to consider something, her lips twisting into a smile. "Does this mean you'll be teaching Nickie about the loa? Otherwise, she's just going to think you got her some charm from Claire's at the Lakewood Mall."

Victoria ignored Willow's dig and searched the bags for the blackened chicken salad,

13

wanting to protect it from the warm summer air that had swept into the kitchen. Victoria knew Nickie was capable of simply appreciating the beauty of the necklace, but Willow was right. Victoria hadn't done her duty to explain things. Over the years, she'd intimated at her reverence of the loa, burning through dozens of candles and keeping vigil for hours on All Saints' Day, but never had she spoken the words to Nickie: *I practice Voodoo.* She'd never admitted this directly to anyone, not even the woman who'd first taught her about the loa, her grandmother, though the woman well knew. But she could take some baby steps with Nickie tonight.

Before she could give Willow a good shove, Nickie came into the kitchen, a breeze to her walk. She noticed her daughter's lips, shiny with a hint of plum. And her eyelids dusted with a shimmery shadow. How sweet that Nickie wanted to look nice for her birthday dinner, even one spent in the company of the women with whom she dined every night.

Willow lifted her plate of carbohydrates, spilling rice on the floor as she opened her arms to invite Nickie in for a hug. "Happy Birthday, Nick. Come over here. I can't believe you're seventeen." Nickie folded herself into Willow's embrace, the two of them the same height.

The sight made Victoria's heart leap. Victoria had lived a disciplined life, a consistent life to get Nickie where she was, a straight-A student with a promising future ahead of her. One day, she would even please the loa, be blessed by their ancestor Lanora, and continue the family tradition of performing beautiful deeds for those in need.

"Nickie, we've got all your favorites here. And we're eating in the dining room," she told her daughter, still overcome with pride. "Real plates. No paper tonight."

Willow sputtered out a laugh. "Real plates? Oh, it's about to be a party up in here, I see. Your mama knows how to get things wild, Nick."

It had been years since she'd eaten fried catfish, and the nuggets on her plate were so richly seasoned, drenched, and crisp that they didn't need hot sauce. Still, Victoria sprinkled a few dashes before each bite in keeping the celebratory vibe of the afternoon. She'd been so taken by the food that she hadn't paid much attention to the conversation, tuning out once Nickie and Willow started in on some HBO show that

Nanagusta had convinced them to binge. Victoria didn't watch popular shows or have a hobby that might be interesting to discuss. But it was Nickie's birthday, and for that she had to try harder.

"Nickie," she said, picking up the small, ribboned gift from its perch on the cake box. A swift pang set in, jabbing her just beneath her ribs, and she took in a breath to clear it away. The food was worth the pain. "I am so proud of you. You never ask for anything, and you work so hard in school. You do your chores." She paused. She hated that she always came across as serious, but acting any other way felt awkward to her. "And you're seventeen now."

Before she could hand her the box, Nickie squealed, and a new joy overcame Victoria. Could she already feel the energy from the amulet inside? Perhaps. She had anointed it with a mixture of coconut oil, myrrh, a pinch of sugar, and lemongrass.

"Mom, did you get me a car?"

Victoria gripped the box. "A car?" Then she realized what her daughter assumed was inside. What Nickie probably heard as an embarrassed bit of laughter was actually incredulity. The girl thought she was getting a car? "No, not a car."

"Oh, that's fine. That's . . ." Nickie tapped

her fork on the edge of her plate.

Inside, Willow was certainly laughing at her, the scene at the table part of a reality show expressly piloted for her entertainment. She fanned herself with a short pile of napkins as she watched the interaction with those resplendent hazel eyes she'd gotten from her father, a different father than Victoria's. He'd given Willow everything beautiful about him. All the superficial things Victoria had wanted growing up, and even still.

"We can do gifts later, after Nanagusta comes down," Victoria relented, unable to stand the silence. Hopefully by then, Nickie would forget all about the car.

Victoria assumed her sister would start in on another topic, but her mouth was full of food. To stall, she'd reached for the iced tea when the doorbell rang, the surprise of the chimes causing her to spill everywhere.

"I'll get it," Nickie said, pushing back her chair.

Victoria sighed, looking around for something to sop up the mess. Willow handed her the napkins she'd been using to fan herself.

"Ayida Wedo giving you the shakes, Vic?" She'd bitten off a big piece of monkey bread and nearly choked to get the words out.

"Ha ha." Victoria bent down, getting in between her toes as best she could with the napkins.

Victoria had figured someone was dropping off a package or a neighborhood kid was selling candy, but when Nickie returned to the dining room, she had someone with her. A young man. Tall, not much meat on his frame, hair cut so low you couldn't tell the kink of it.

"Mom, Auntie, this is my friend Felix. I hope you don't mind, I invited him to my dinner. He said he hadn't eaten Southern food before."

"*Good* Southern food," the boy said, chuckling.

Victoria squinted, unable to process the scene playing out before her. Nickie had never had a friend over before, let alone a boy. She knew it wasn't okay to invite someone, especially without first asking.

"Well, welcome, Felix. Have a seat. I see you know how to get a party started," Willow said, pointing to the bottle of wine he clutched.

Felix laughed. "Are you Ms. Montrose?"

"We both are," Victoria said, folding her arms over her chest.

Nickie gestured to Willow. "Felix, this is my aunt Willow."

She waved to him with her fork. "Nice to meet you, young man. Nickie told you I drink Moscato?"

"And this is my mom, Victoria. Or Ms. Montrose."

"It's nice to meet you, Ms. Montrose. Both of you."

He and Nickie got themselves seated. Nickie explained she'd met Felix in her summer photography class. Victoria had encouraged Nickie to find a hobby, wanting to squeeze some of the sulk out of her when summer began, hoping to get her from under the covers and away from the all the videos she watched online. She'd purchased a swell little camera and then suggested the class at the rec center. Nickie hadn't seemed very interested in photography initially but, since the start of the session, had spent her days hanging out at the park, taking pictures, and editing them in the center's computer lab.

Now Victoria understood why. Her insides heated up, a sparkling sensation flying down her neck and arms. Nickie. And a boy. In their house.

"Nickie is the best model in the class. Her face is so . . . shapely. It, like, curves and goes places you wouldn't think." Nickie bent her lips into her mouth, put her hands

19

over her cheeks as she rested her elbows on the table, covering the blemishes on her skin.

Victoria believed him, believed he saw what others so far had not, though really it was all the wonderful things about Nickie she always hoped no one would notice. She shouldn't have bought that camera. She should have let the girl stay in bed, moping. Her skin prickled.

"She's modeling for you? I thought you guys just took pictures of trees and buildings and shit."

The boy turned to Willow. "That's mostly what we do. But I pretty much mastered the basic stuff the first session."

"Oh. Cocky motherfucker, aren't you?"

Nickie's hands still covered her cheeks. "My aunt Willow has a potty mouth."

"I was an English major. Can't help it," she said, flippant.

In other company and if she weren't so filled with emotion, Victoria would have pointed out how astute Willow had been with her word choice. How she'd said she was an English *major,* leaving out the absence of a *degree.* Willow had also been a theater major and premed a few years back at Long Beach City College and considered careers in environmental law and voice acting.

Victoria stewed as the three chatted on. By the time she heard her name, she felt like she'd been trapped inside a pressure cooker. She leveled her voice. "I'm sorry, can you repeat that?"

"Owning your own business. It's gotta be tough. My mom's cousin owned a restaurant in North Long Beach, but it closed after two years."

Victoria managed a short response. "I've heard that restaurants are tough. But I do pretty well." Felix waited for her to go on, but that was all he'd get.

He broke his gaze and sat up straight, focusing on Willow. "And do you enjoy being your sister's assistant?"

"*Assistant?* That's not my title. Nickie, you told him I was your mom's assistant?"

Nickie stiffened her shoulders. "I mean . . . aren't you?"

"Hell, no. I'm just as much an owner of this business as your mother. We built it together. Maybe I don't have all those letters after my name, but the people that come through that door everyday are *our* clients. Mine just as much as hers."

Victoria splayed her hands on the table, feeling the woodsy ridges, and held back

21

from correcting her sister. It didn't matter what Felix thought, anyway. He wouldn't be at their home for another dinner.

Her sister seemed to realize that she'd gotten herself worked up. "We've been sitting here talking, and you haven't eaten any food yet, Felix," Willow said. "I hope you got a big appetite. Ms. Montrose over there bought enough food to feed us until winter."

Nickie and the boy went into the kitchen, and Victoria could finally breathe again. Willow leaned over the table, wiggling her fingers to get Victoria's attention. "You better rethink that fertility amulet, Vic. I know you want Nickie to follow in your footsteps, but probably not the teen-mom part."

Felix and Nickie talked as they served themselves. Victoria couldn't help but note how blissful Nickie appeared — despite not getting a car — her smile staying put as she made recommendations on what Felix should try. Victoria tossed the crumpled napkins onto her plate, along with her utensils, and slid her glass close to her.

"You packing up to leave or something?"

"Mmm-hmm. Soon as they get back."

"Don't tell me you're tripping about Nickie having a boy over to the house."

"I'm not tripping about anything. I'm just

not feeling well. I'm going upstairs to lie down."

"And what about the cake?" Willow asked. "We need to sing Happy Birthday."

Before going upstairs, she would toss the Barbie figurine, hope the bright pink frosting wouldn't bother Nickie. Victoria shook her head. "Just do it without me. Nickie won't care. She doesn't even like cake. It's more for you and Nana."

"Now, that's a lie. If it was for me, you wouldn't have gotten chocolate."

A lie indeed, but she wouldn't admit it, just as she couldn't stick around to watch Nickie as they sang, the boy joining in as if family. She'd probably make a wish that would involve Felix. But that couldn't be a reality for Nickie. There were details of their family's history Victoria had kept from her. A critical fact that all the women had withheld.

When Nickie and the boy returned, Victoria explained as confidently as she could that she needed to go to her bedroom, using her bellyache as an excuse. "Hopefully it will go away if I rest a bit, but if I'm not back down soon, go ahead and do the cake without me."

Nickie lost her smile. "Are you sure? We can do it whenever."

"No, no. You all go on, especially if Nana comes down. You know that woman loves cake." She fixed her eyes on Felix, who had a smear of sauce at the corner of his lips. "It was nice to meet you, Felix." She stopped short of adding a polite *See you again soon*.

Victoria flipped the switch in her closet, sharp light finding the carpet between boxes and bags. In the corner sat a small table that maintained the only order in the space, a placemat on top with a few glass vials and a metal jewelry box. And candles, a hefty black one in the middle, blessed with holy water from St. Louis Cathedral. Though it served as the centerpiece to her altar, the black candle stayed preserved, used only in the most extreme of situations, like when her grandmother had suffered two strokes within a week's time. Even just standing there unlit, it held power. The black candle was Victoria's go-to stress reliever, the thing she'd clutch during severe weather or when earthquakes rattled her bed, asking the loa to intercede for her, to implore God for protection. She had the ear of many of the loa, and the hearts of a key few. They kept her from drowning, steadied her footing. She thanked them as often and as graciously as she could.

Before coming upstairs, she'd thrown a sampling of items on a new plate: a hot wing, a small filet of catfish, and a couple spoons of bread pudding. Her favorite loa had a taste for the kind of food her mother cooked back in New Orleans. She sat the plate in front of the candle and fished out a pair of scissors from a nearby basket to trim the wick as short as possible, an effort to keep the flame low and help it burn longer. Soon, the space yellowed, casting staticky shadows against the walls and clothes. She kneeled, the spiral binding of a notebook digging into one of her calves, and checked the time — 4:22.

"I believe in God, the Father Almighty. Creator of Heaven and earth," she began, following the creed with the Lord's Prayer. Both of these she would say again in exactly seven hours, then lift words to Cosmos and Damien, known in the Voodoo world as Marassa, the divine twins. As with other Voodoo loa, the Marassa twins intervened for humankind in matters of love, prosperity, power. After the seventh hour, she'd snuff the flame, and by then, the young man would lose any affections he held for Nickie and with them would go Victoria's anxiety. It was a ritual of protection. For her daughter and for them all.

Quashing things between Nickie and this Felix kid wasn't something she'd take pride in, even if it were just a temporary fix until she could explain the way of their world. Victoria had been in denial all these years, not fully convinced that she'd ever have to share their family secret. But her daughter had gotten older, had become a young woman. Which meant soon, she'd have to tell her about the curse, put into place by a bitter woman named Bela Nova — the curse that left dead any person with whom a Montrose woman fell in love.

But how would she ever explain to her daughter that, as a Montrose woman, she didn't get to fall in love?

As she sat at the altar, her belly knotted, a sharp tightening rushed her breath. She closed her eyes and exhaled, pushing the air from her abdomen the way the woman on her fitness app had instructed. Hopefully, her family didn't eat all the catfish nuggets. She knew now they weren't the cause of her bellyache. It was the boy.

2
NICKIE

Felix hadn't said anything about liking her, but Nickie had picked up something. Maybe he enjoyed her work in the classroom. Her intuition with light, the movement in her shots. But could her photographic savvy really be the reason he arrived early to the park's bungalow each morning to save her a seat in class? He would offer her a bag of Funyuns or a Twinkie — her choice. One day, she'd gone for the Funyuns, slipping them into her bag instead of opening them right away so if for some reason they happened to kiss, neither would have Funyun breath. But they hadn't kissed that day or any other. Didn't touch each other either, not even by accident. But the possibility of that kiss stayed with her.

It had been a risk, bringing Felix over when she'd never so much as mentioned a boy's name to her mother in her life. He'd wanted to meet her family, learn about her world. Hanging out with him the past few weeks was the closest she'd come to a relationship. Not that she hadn't wanted one before. She was just very selective. She recalled the poster on her third-grade teacher's wall, the one with the purple owl, bespectacled and holding a book. *Aim High,* the poster read. That she always did. If she'd known having him over for dinner would be so nice, she'd have invited him the first week they met.

"Nickie said that's your molcajete in there," Felix said to Willow, on his third helping of étouffée.

Her aunt's eyebrows squished together. "My what?"

Felix laughed. "Oh, your bowl that's in the corner on the counter. I'm guessing you must make a lot of guacamole to have such a nice set."

"Oh. Sometimes, yes."

Nickie couldn't recall her aunt ever making guacamole. She always said she wasn't a fan of it, seemed like baby food.

"Well, my godfather has an avocado tree in his yard if you ever want some. They're way bigger than the ones at the grocery store."

Willow smiled but didn't respond, which Nickie took as a sign to change the subject.

The three of them went on for another hour, her aunt's voice growing louder, her stories more hysterical with every glass of wine she poured herself. Willow had turned the conversation to her recipe for tuna fish salad when Felix's phone vibrated. He checked the screen and sprang up, saying he had to leave to do something for his mother.

"We didn't sing Happy Birthday to Nick. Hold on, I'll go upstairs and get Nana," Willow said, waving him back into his seat.

But he grabbed his plate and glass. "No, no, that's okay. You all can go ahead. I really need to get going."

"Put those down, then. We'll clean up. And Nick will save you a slice."

Nickie walked him to the foyer, disappointed. Ever since agreeing to have Felix over, she'd daydreamed of the moment she blew out her candles, of him clapping along with her family. Now, if her mother didn't come back down, her tipsy aunt would be a soloist, her voice cracking as she reached for notes out of her range while Nanagusta danced along. She wondered how they'd part ways. He wouldn't dare kiss her, not with her aunt just down the hallway. Not that he would want to kiss her at all. But just in case, she swallowed, trying to erase the earthy taste of greens, the jambalaya's garlic from her mouth.

At the door, he stopped and took her gently by the wrist, the contact giving her goose bumps. "Happy birthday," he said as he took a gift card from his back pocket. Chipotle.

Had she ever mentioned liking Chipotle? She didn't think so. Still, it was a good sign that he'd gotten her anything at all. "Thank you," she said, suppressing the grin that was sliding into place. "Next time, you can meet Nanagusta."

"Alright. Next time. Tell your mom it was nice to meet her. Wish she didn't have to bounce like that. And your aunt's cool." He narrowed his right eye, not a wink yet still intentional. "And make sure you save me that piece of cake."

Nickie didn't want to have such strong feelings for him. She just wanted to have a good time with somebody, to connect with someone outside of her family. She'd spent all these years at home studying, hanging with her aunt and Nanagusta. Until sophomore year, basketball at least had given the facade of a social life, her teammates respecting her skills, friendly enough. But then she'd injured her knee, losing the one thread she had to a community. She hadn't anticipated how hard it would be to make friends, to find belonging. Thanks to the photography class this summer, she'd met Felix, and before she knew it, the longing in her heart had taken root.

She closed the door once he left, then observed from the peephole to catch if his walk somehow hinted at any emotions. She hoped that after this visit, he'd ask about her current situation. Maybe that's what they'd discuss later — he'd mentioned calling her once he helped his mom. Though they spoke every day in class and by text afterward, she knew little about his home life, what he did in the hours between their classes and outings. He didn't have much of a presence online, only a dead TikTok account and two pictures on his Instagram — one of him holding a pet iguana, the other of Colin Kaepernick tagged *#father.*

With their rec class now finished, she'd do whatever she could to spend the last full week before school with him, even if it meant eating Chipotle. This was her final year as a kid, and she looked forward to doing all the things she should have been — chilling after classes, going to dances, even ditching to get fries at the Jack in the Box a few blocks from campus. And fine, she hadn't gotten a car. But she had a bus pass.

And an entire school year to land a kiss with Felix, though she hoped it wouldn't take nearly that long.

She smiled as she skipped back to the dining room. She was ready for her aunt's inevitable interrogation. In fact, she couldn't wait for it.

3
WILLOW

Willow had never had the desire to bring a boy home to meet her mother. She'd have been embarrassed to show her family any of the knuckleheads she tended to attract, yet just as ashamed to acknowledge her mess of a mother, Madelyn Montrose. Even if she had brought someone home back in her preteen years, before her grandmother had moved her and Victoria out West from New Orleans, her mother wouldn't have cared about her having a boyfriend, just like she hadn't cared about the straight Ds on Willow's report card or her rides up and down Canal Street on Sharkey Clark's motorcycle.

Madelyn hadn't put up much of a fight when Nanagusta had packed up their home in the Seventh Ward and driven herself and her granddaughters some nineteen hundred miles to Carson, California, a city they'd only heard of a week before. "Just make sure they call me. And don't rent no two-story house. They got earthquakes out there," Madelyn had said before hurrying out to an awaiting car, not giving Willow or her sister kisses goodbye.

Once in California, Willow still hadn't thought to bring anyone home to meet her grandmother — her goal had become devising ways to sneak boys in without Nanagusta knowing. Their grandmother had warned them to stay away from boys.

"We Montrose women weren't made for love. We're too much, you understand?" she'd said to them one day, not good at being direct. "Your grandfather died young. So did your dad, Willow. You don't want the same thing happening to some poor fool you bring home, understand?" She hadn't mentioned Victoria's dad, at times referred to by Augusta as *a sack of shit,* not worthy of discussion.

They both nodded, though Willow was apprehensive at first, figuring her dramatic, only worried about them getting pregnant out of wedlock like their own mother had. Twice. But the more she thought about it, the reality scared her. As boy crazy as she'd become, she would do what she needed not to fall in love.

Nickie entered the dining room as Willow collected their plates and glasses. "You think

Mom will be back down?" she asked.

Willow groaned softly, annoyed with her sister for leaving her with a mess, though she knew Victoria would return soon. She'd have heard the front door close, watched Felix's from Nickie's bedroom window upstairs. "You know how her stomach is. Probably took some Pepto and passed out," she said, not wanting to upset Nickie with the truth. Victoria was clearly freaked out about Felix, but that wasn't Nickie's fault.

"Oh, yeah. All this fried food."

Willow looked at the table. Did they even have enough space in the refrigerator to keep everything? Nanagusta would eat her soup and a helping of red beans and rice, but that was about it. Nickie and Victoria would go back to their regular diets — cereal and Pop-Tarts and frozen microwave meals — forcing Willow to finish off all that remained.

At least she could use the seafood from the po'boys to lure some of the neighborhood cats to the backyard, where she'd brush off clumps of their fur as they ate. She currently had no use for cat hair, but it was nice to stock up on ingredients when she had the chance. She stored an assortment of implements under her bed — blessing oils and wild sage, thin legs plucked off dead spiders, petals of jasmine, and dried berries — so that she could intervene when her services were needed.

She put the cleaning aside and sat down. Though this thing with Felix had no legs, *couldn't* have legs, the least she could do was give Nickie the chance to be excited about it for one night. "You didn't do too bad for yourself, Nick."

Nickie froze, a smile mid-bloom, and then she let the full one slip. She joined Willow at the table, tucking her feet underneath her on a chair. "Felix and I are just friends," she said matter-of-factly.

"That's fine. I got lots of friends. I don't pick 'em good as you, though." Willow smirked.

Nickie leaned in on the table. "What does that mean, Auntie?"

"Nick, that boy's what I like to call tall, dark, and ripe."

"Not handsome?"

"Well, he's handsome too. But that's the thing. He doesn't know how handsome he is yet. Doesn't realize all that art shit will be attractive as hell once he hits his mid-twenties. Plus, he's got a little bit of a chip. He's dealt with some stuff." Willow knew this from experience.

36

"Dang, I thought my mom was the therapist."

"You see there, and you wanted to label me an *assistant* a minute ago."

Nickie tilted her head to one side and pressed together her lips. "You think Mom liked him? I feel like maybe she didn't."

"Your mama isn't going to like anyone, Nickie," Willow said kindly.

"Why not? What, she expects me to be solo all my life . . . like her?" Nickie hesitated, but Willow could hear that invisible question, *Like you?*

"Nick."

"Doesn't she want grandchildren one day?"

Willow didn't know what to say. Whatever came out would be wrong. They should have anticipated this day. She stood, her movement abrupt. "You know, I'm getting worried about Nana. I should go wake her. We need to sing before it gets too late."

Their grandmother wasn't old, not in Willow's mind. But she worried about the woman having another stroke, or a heart attack, or just not waking up. to counter these possibilities, she stored a vial of youth potion in her closet, spritzing her grandmother's sheets once a week, a mixture of amethyst, lavender oil, and a couple drops of holy water from St. Lucy's. While Victoria wasted her time extolling the forces of the loa, fangirling, and buying jewelry depicting them, Willow's efforts were more practical, and she had the receipts to prove they worked.

Nanagusta napped frequently but not usually for long spells like this. Willow's heartbeat quickened as she approached the door, both in a hurry and hesitant to rouse the woman, scared she wouldn't respond to her touch. She knocked softly, sprigs of light bursting from the crack in the door. Pushing it open, she discovered Nanagusta sprawled out and bare, soft folds of skin, chest rising then collapsing with a wheeze. She typically took her mid-day nap on the living room couch but apparently had gone to her bedroom instead so she could lie naked, likely her method of combating the day's heat. Willow let her eyes linger on the woman. She hoped that once she reached her later years, her body would look as beautifully weathered as Nanagusta's. She grabbed a robe from the floor and covered her before nudging her awake.

"Nan, you gonna sleep the whole day? It's your third nap."

Her eyes blinked open, and Willow

couldn't help but feel a little relieved.

"It's time for cake," she told her grandmother. "We're going to sing for Nick, even though Victoria went and got chocolate from that bakery in Belmont Shore. Only time she leaves the house is to get that dang cake." Willow knew she was ranting, but it was fact, and Nanagusta knew it too. "You'd think she would ask me to bake or cook. Had me eating that bright yellow mac and cheese. I mean, it wasn't bad, but nothing like mine. Oh, and Nickie brought a boy over."

Her grandmother raised herself up on one elbow at this, nodding, wanting Willow to continue.

"He's gone now. Vic made him uncomfortable, said she had a stomachache."

Nanagusta pursed her lips.

"I know, right? It's like, deal with it — we have a guest. But I'm sure she's in her room, calling out to Lanora. Anyway, let me get you something to put on."

Victoria was back at the table, inserting thin candles too deeply into the shiny shellac of the cake's glaze. Once they were lit, Nanagusta clapped and swayed as the women sang the birthday song. Willow bumped up to a loud falsetto on the final refrain. She couldn't believe Nickie had almost reached adulthood, her baby, or as close to one as she'd ever have. Being a mother had never interested Willow and still didn't, especially the part about sharing her body with another human being, but she loved being Nickie's aunt.

"Make a wish," Victoria said, and Nickie closed her eyes as she sucked in air, ready to blow out her candles.

If she so desired, Willow could guarantee Nickie's birthday wish. Or steal it away. But she'd do neither. She wanted the world for her niece but had no idea what the girl might ask for. Perhaps for something romantic to happen with the Felix kid — Nickie must have liked him to ask him over. But she wasn't getting involved in that type of thorny issue. If she could go back in time, Willow would have wished for something very useful at Nickie's age. Foresight. Courage. The gumption to speak up for herself.

Willow fanned away the wispy smoke as Nickie pulled the candles from the cake, then served slices to each woman around the table.

"You aren't going to eat any, Nickie?" Victoria asked. Willow could tell she was putting on a brave face.

Nickie shook her head, leaning back in

her chair after handing Willow a plate. "My skin's broken out bad enough. Chocolate will make it worse."

Willow tried to lighten the mood. "So you're just gonna sit and watch us eat? At least open your presents." She wiggled a small envelope from her back pocket and gave it to Nickie.

"Thank you, Aunt Willow." Her niece had been trained well, pretending to be moved more by the card's cheesy words than the three hundred dollars inside.

Nanagusta slapped the table to draw Willow's attention, pointed her index finger toward her own chin.

"Oh, it's from Nanagusta too — did I forget to add her name to the card?"

Her grandmother threw a balled-up napkin, getting Willow on the nose.

"Nana, it was an oversight." Truly it had been. She wasn't one to hoard credit, even when it was warranted. "And where's the box from your mom?" Willow hoped Victoria would finally share their family history with Nickie. She couldn't fumble around another conversation like the one she and Nickie had just had.

Victoria licked her lips, clearly nervous. "Here, Nickie. Happy birthday." She slid the gift across the table.

41

Nickie pulled the end of ribbon, disentangling the bow, then removed the top. Nanagusta peered over to see what was inside.

"Oh, thank you," Nickie said. She didn't pick up the necklace to get a better look or show it off.

"It's the symbol of Ayida Wedo," Victoria explained.

Nanagusta's mouth formed an *O*, her brows perked up in surprise. She nodded her approval.

Victoria went on, a stilted explanation about Ayida Wedo, that she was in the spirit world, born from the serpent Damballa, later becoming his wife. The rainbow loa. A mother and a protector. "People will probably think you're supporting LGBTQ+ rights. But the rainbow has been Ayida Wedo's for centuries."

Willow kept quiet as her sister continued. Her words must have seemed nonsensical to Nickie, Victoria going on about Voodoo saints without using the word *Voodoo*, talking around things as if sharing about St. Francis of Assisi or Joan of Arc in a catechism lesson. Nickie had stopped feigning interest, and Nanagusta had dozed off. It no longer felt like a birthday celebration but instead a college class, the lecturer with zero self-awareness of how monotone she was.

"Here, let me help you put it on, Nickie. Stand up," Willow said to end Victoria's rambling.

She walked around to the other side of the dining room table and lifted the soft gold braid holding the amulet. Her fingers fumbled with the delicate clasp, but once it was refastened around Nickie's neck, Willow twirled her gently around. "It's lovely," she said, and she recognized that she meant it. She took in Nickie anew, tall and pretty. Her niece would have had an inch or two on her father if he'd been alive to join them.

Willow reached for the charm resting just below Nickie's collarbone and rubbed it with her thumb, hoping to stoke a warmness in the metal, but it remained unchanged. Over Nickie's shoulder, she caught Victoria's gaze. Willow wasn't a sentient being, didn't perceive things the way her sister did. The way her grandmother did.

But she had something. Something valuable. Something the rest of the family didn't give credence to, which was just as powerful for Willow because it meant she didn't have expectations on her. Someday, they would see how she'd helped their family all these years. And no one would ever call her Victoria's assistant again.

4
AUGUSTA

Each time Augusta awoke offered another battle with gravity. Earth had held onto her loosely in her youth, occasionally grabbed her by one of her belt loops or gripped a sleeve, but it had never stopped her from leaping high when her body so wanted. Never tripped her up. With age, gravity's company had become ever present. It tried to keep her in bed, shoved her back down in the mornings. She only hoped that by the time this enemy had gotten full control of her, overpowering her feet, her arms, and her head, she'd already be dead.

This recent fatigue aggravated Augusta, who had such a determined desire to carry on yet an inability to do very much. It wasn't like her inability to speak, which she'd eventually acclimated herself to after the strokes. Still, often she missed the sound of her own voice, the underhum to it like an organ.

If she had her voice, she'd use it now, as they sat around the table, to tell her granddaughter to make her another drink. Willow had stirred together a batch of tea with several shots of whiskey to perk up Nickie's birthday dinner. Augusta would also tell her to stop with the yammering.

"He was good-looking, Nan. And smart. Didn't you think so, Vic?"

Willow, ever the circulator, had started in again about the visitor who'd come and gone while Augusta had slept, a young man there for Nickie. Aside from Victoria's therapy clients, she couldn't recall the last time they'd received a guest. It had become the norm, their isolation, not even the neighbors coming over to warn them to move a car parked along the curb on street-sweeping days. Sometimes Augusta considered finding her way over to the seniors' center, how nice it might be to play cards with a group of ladies, to get lunch or even a drink with a girlfriend. But none of them had friends, not even Nickie, whose invitations to slumber parties or trips to the mall had fizzled away years ago, back when the girl was in middle school. This development had seemed fine with Victoria, who never encouraged playdates and such like other mothers. She empathized with her granddaughter, knew it had to bother her to take such an extreme stance.

Victoria stayed silent as if she hadn't heard her sister's question, but that didn't faze Willow. "Tell Nana how fine that boy is, Nickie."

"Auntie, no!" Her great-granddaughter's eyes grew big. "I mean, he's a very nice person, Nana. He's really smart. He's an artist."

Victoria cleared her throat.

"I told him that story about you meeting Madonna at your retirement party. He thought that was cool."

The singer had been at the same restaurant as they celebrated Augusta's last day as a billing clerk with South Bay Counseling Services. She'd seen the woman's photo in a magazine before, Michael Jackson's date to the Oscars one year. Someone had taken a picture of her with Augusta, the singer's lips painted a stunning red, but Augusta didn't know where it was anymore.

"He really wants to meet you, Nana. I told him that you are the most important person in our family," Nickie said earnestly.

Sometimes the way her family spoke of her worried Augusta. Her reputation approached sainthood in their home, Victoria at times even hinting at her eventual idolization as a loa, just like Lanora, a great-great-grandmother of hers. But her past knew better.

Hearing about Nickie and the boy made Augusta think back to her seventeen-year-old self in Louisiana and how infinite life had seemed then. These days, it was difficult for Augusta to recall what she'd had for breakfast sometimes or when her favorite TV shows aired, but those long-ago days were clear, almost tangible. How adventurous and confident she'd been, and how boring and unimaginative she'd believed her mother to be. There was no reason, Augusta had felt, to go to college or supposedly culture herself with haughty books or piano lessons, only to become a miniature version of her mother. On misty summer evenings, she often slipped away from the coziness of her parents' home and headed down to the club in the Quarter on Conti, the sound of hard bop filling her ears, jazz twisting itself in a swanky new way.

She'd gone to the club — the Dew Drop Inn — for the first time with a man named Clarence who was seven years her senior and father to twin girls living with their mother in what was then the Iberville. He had a narrow gap between his front teeth, always on display with his roaring hyena laugh. She liked that he took her places, showed her off. But she didn't consider him attractive. After declining his many requests for blow jobs in the bathroom, he'd given up and left her high yellow ass, as he'd said, alone. But she'd returned to the club without him one night, bribing the stubby fellow at the door to let her in with the coins she'd lifted from her father's desk drawer.

The second time without Clarence was when everything changed. It was a stormy night, the sky ripped to pieces by fingers of lightning and fists of thunder. As she entered the club, her eyes searching for a dark nook, a piece of wall to blend into, a fiery voice made her jump. "You alone tonight, pretty young girl?"

Augusta looked around for the source. Wisps of stage light floated through the dusty air, carving out a face a few feet away. A woman moving toward her, with shiny eyes, penciled-in lips, and woolly hair long enough to swing on. She came close, too close, the mint of her breath not concealing the smoke on it. She didn't smell much different than the club, its walls soaked with nights of booze, cigars, and reefer. The woman drew near enough to kiss Augusta, and for an instant, she thought the woman might do just that. But she laughed with tiny yellow teeth, then turned and beckoned for Augusta to follow. The brightness from the nearby coat-check window revealed a silky red scarf and a chaotic print of spirals on her purple dress, a pairing that might have seemed odd on anyone else. But it was right on this woman — the red, a color Augusta eventually wore every day, for it brought love and energy. Passion.

Augusta trailed the woman out of fear as much as a bizarre attraction, a magnetism pulling her along. The door in the corner where the woman sat some nights watching folks opened to a narrow set of steps leading to her workshop. Once upstairs, Augusta took off her damp jacket and sat down on a shopworn chair as instructed. The room flickered, lit by a few hundred candles, it seemed, both tall and melted down to their roots.

"Look at me," the woman said after introducing herself as Bela Nova, and Augusta did, the tiny fires all around them reflecting off the shapely bottles lined up on shelves. The walls were dark, with painted pictures of Catholic saints and snakes and odd symbols, and what looked to be a shrine in one corner. The woman's eyes widened, her lids and eyelashes smeared with makeup, blues and smoky blacks. "You know why I called you here."

She couldn't be sure if this was a question or statement, the woman's inflection oddly placed in the middle of the sentence. When Bela Nova raised one of her eyebrows and leaned in close, Augusta shook her head *no.*

The woman laughed. "Of course you do. You know why you're here. You just don't know that you know."

The young Augusta gripped the side of the chair, still not averting her eyes from the woman.

"You are Augusta Marie Laurent?"

"Yes. I am."

"I know you are." And the woman began speaking, foretelling. As she did, her hands kept busy, reaching out to touch Augusta's hair, then emptying a velvety bag onto the table: some sort of root, three dried-up peas, a playing card. She lit a candle without breaking her gaze from Augusta, poured oil over it from a tiny green bottle. She did these things naturally, effortlessly, the way fingers that know how to play the piano don't hesitate.

"You weren't born to live your own life, Augusta Marie. No. You're a daughter of Lanora. A blessed one. A special one. Not all are." The woman waved a crooked finger back and forth close to Augusta's nose.

50

"Your life, like mine, belongs to the people. For the right price, yes. But doing work for people, our people, who deserve to get a splinter of happiness in this dreadful place we call a world, you hear? Your life will be dedicated to helping them."

Against her judgment, she nodded. She could discern a sparkle of truth in the older woman's words, confirmation that what her mother desired for her was a future she'd not been intended to live.

"So you will come here. Stay with me. You'll be my student."

And right then she agreed to be Bela Nova's apprentice. That choice, to learn from Bela Nova both the religion of Voodoo and the practice of hoodoo magic, all in the name of serving their people, was one she wished she could revisit. Not the part about helping others. But everything that happened because of it. Might she have done differently with her many decades of life now behind her? Perhaps. But of course, one of the first lessons she'd been taught by her mentor was that folks didn't really have choices, just their fates. Even if she hadn't said yes that night, she would have said *yes* someday.

5
VICTORIA

A dull pain right in the center of her forehead woke Victoria. She'd forgotten to set her alarm. She tightened her grip around her pillow, longing for a few more minutes of rest and a redo of the previous night. She let a minute pass by, then sat up and stretched to get a better look at the clock, the harsh yellow light of the morning already a clue to how late she'd slept in. "Was last night a dream?" she asked the emptiness around her.

No, it was a nightmare. But it had been real, the headache told her. She only got them with stress. With too much spiked sweet tea. And with a bad hunch about someone. The reason for this morning's pain? All of the above.

Victoria pushed her hair down, brushed it back toward the band holding her strands in a messy bun, the frizzy edges framing her face like rays of sunshine. This was her attempt at freshening up, but it really didn't matter how she looked. It was her words on which she needed to concentrate. The Marassa, she was confident, were already at work, chiseling away at Felix's affections, but Victoria had to work on Nickie too to ease the burden.

The hallway was cool when she stepped out of her bedroom, air blowing from the vents above. Willow had painted the walls a light purple to harness protection and control energy, part of her belief in color symbolism. Her sister put so much faith in her hoodoo, rituals, works, magic. But Willow seemed to forget about the mysteries of the spirit world, her ancestors, and the saints, probably because Victoria had been chosen as the ostensible favored one.

"The women in our family have a gift, given to us by our grandmother from generations ago, Lanora," Nanagusta had told her and Willow when they were teenagers, sitting them down one day out of the blue. "One woman in each generation is bestowed with this blessing. One of you will learn in time that she has a unique power to help people." Victoria hadn't really listened but would come to realize in her late teens that she was the favored one, when her life took a hard turn. In the years since, Victoria had built her therapy practice by sensing her patients' needs, figuring out solutions to help them. The loa were pleased with her work and blessed her clientele accordingly. Now, she'd help Nickie understand too, talk to her about the gift that had been bestowed on her as her only daughter, as Willow vowed to never have children. Victoria originally planned to share it once Nickie turned eighteen and was ready for such a heavy responsibility. But her daughter had proven herself to be mature, and more importantly, the gift could serve as a sturdy distraction from this Felix.

Victoria didn't knock before opening Nickie's door. As she walked in, her eyes swelled with the mephitic sweetness of nail polish. Nickie was on the bed painting her fingernails the color of blackberries. She sat up straight and smiled, Ayido Wedo's rainbow flipped the wrong way on the chain. At least she was still wearing it. Victoria stepped close to turn it right, ignoring the fact that her daughter appeared indisputably happy, probably assuming she was there to gab about Felix. Which was the truth, in a way.

"So Nickie, tell me about your friend. I'm sorry I didn't get to speak with him longer." Victoria perched herself on the edge of Nickie's bed, trying her best at taking it easy. Playing therapist with your kinfolk wasn't comfortable.

"He's really cool, the best one in our class."

"Oh. That's nice." She patted the worn blanket covering Nickie's legs. "So you two are . . . dating?"

"Mom!"

"Friends?" *Fuck buddies?* She'd heard that term before but couldn't fathom saying it out loud. And more, she couldn't imagine wanting to just be friends with someone she'd been intimate with. Sex was everything or nothing to Victoria. Technically, right now it was nonexistent. But she knew that blissful promise of a new love, how it kicked aside all else. She remembered the days when she danced for no reason, sang the songs Nickie's father, Jimmie, would belt out for her when they were together, his rendition of his favorite love song by DeBarge, an R & B group he'd listened to in elementary school. *Silly,* Nanagusta called her, not yet knowing the source of her giddiness. Victoria hadn't told her after all her cockamamie warnings about boys.

Nickie suppressed a smile, looking down at her wrist, her shoulders lifting up and down. She could see that Nickie liked this boy, even if she didn't admit it.

She eased more of herself onto the bed, leaned over on a stray pillow. It was time. "Nick, there's something else I want to bring up." Victoria cleared her throat, loosened her neck as if she were about to run a hundred-meter dash. "You remember back when I used to tell you about Lanora, our ancestor from over a century ago?"

"The one in the song?"

"That's the one. You remember?"

"How can I forget? You used to sing that one part all the time when I was little, when she flipped herself inside out or something like that. Although I didn't realize she was related to us."

"Yes. On Nanagusta's side. You probably remember from the song how she helped people."

"Not really. I just remember her getting all upset over some guy — her best friend or something?"

People always recalled the drama of stories. The tragedy. But Lanora's song, in the end, held so much beauty. "Yes. She thought fate did her wrong. But that was just part of her story. One verse of it. She went on to bless people. She had a gift for doing so, something that has been passed down through our family. It's . . . well, it's how I ended up being a therapist. And I believe

56

you've got this gift too, Nickie."

Her daughter sat up slowly, letting go of the covers she'd been holding to keep her shoulders warm. "You think I have a gift?"

"That's right. For helping people. It's your calling. You have a blessing, really. I just wish I had talked to you about it sooner."

Nickie released a slow breath and hugged her body. "I don't know. This is all kind of weird. With the whole thing last night about . . . Ayana Wando?"

"Ayido Wedo."

Nickie slid the rainbow amulet back and forth along the chain. Victoria tried not to let it bother her. She got it — it was all a little strange. But if Nickie hadn't noticed in all these years that they were different, then she hadn't been paying enough attention.

"Nickie, have you ever had a certain sensation when you've met someone? Like an instinct? Maybe you got a sharp pang in your side, and you later learned the person is a real . . . a-hole?"

Nickie shrank one eye, her smile fading. "No."

"Or like . . . a flutter in your belly when you shake someone's hand, and then that person turns out to be a remarkable human being?"

"Mom, I don't really shake hands." Nickie reclined against her pillows and went to tug the covers back up, but they didn't give under Victoria's weight at the end of the bed.

"I just want you to think about what I'm saying. Think back to when you've met someone new. Try to remember what you felt."

She let Nickie contemplate this, allowing the quiet to sit.

"How about this. Who was the last person you met?"

This she answered without hesitation. "Felix."

She should have expected that one.

Victoria wasn't necessarily surprised by Nickie's skepticism. She needed to *show* the girl what she meant. A quick idea came to her, something that would give her space to consider her gift and also keep Nickie away from Felix for at least a few days. "Hey, what I really wanted to talk to you about, Nickie," she said, moving on from her question, "is that I would like some help this week. I need you to work for me at the reception desk."

"Work? Why? What about Aunt Willow?"

"Well, Willow, she . . ." Her lips had started in before her mind could figure out a story. "I'm going to give her a bit of a break this week, before you start back at school. She's having some . . . woman problems."

"Mom, I'm not six. You can just tell me what's going on."

"Willow probably should tell you herself. It's none of my business." Victoria almost couldn't hold in her chuckle, the threat of it filling her mouth. Everything that happened to everyone in her house was her business. She'd remind Willow of this if she protested after being told this plan, though Victoria couldn't imagine she would, not having had a string of days off in years. She could send her sister to the spa, on a wine-tasting trip, to a ritzy pool in downtown LA. Willow was easy to bribe, but she'd be suspicious, wanting to know what Victoria was up to. "Really, she just needs a little break. This will give you a chance to see what I do, the work with my clients. And you'll see what I mean about your gift. You were born to do this, Nickie. It's in your blood."

"I kind of had plans next week."

"With . . ."

Nickie shrugged. "With Felix."

"Well, you'll see him soon enough. You all are just friends, right?"

Nickie bit her lip. Victoria nodded.

"Anyway, school starts for you in just over a week. That's all you need to worry about. Your grades. Your academics. That's it. Although it might be smart of you to ask the basketball coach for a late tryout if your knee is feeling better." Basketball had kept Nickie out of trouble, and she'd never brought home anyone after practices or games.

Nickie didn't fight back, but the pep had left her face. Victoria scooted herself closer, patting Nickie's leg over the cover. She might have softened her tone, but that would have taken the muscle out of her stance and Nickie would see through the act. "I appreciate the help, Nickie. I really do. I know you probably want to spend more time with your friend, but there will be plenty of time for boys later. Much later, once you're done with school. Boys, men. They just get in the way of women like us." Victoria continued, spitting out clichéd phrases about men often noted in self-help books and love songs — they were from distant planets, most of them lagged a good ten years behind women in maturity, they only wanted one thing. She stopped short of mentioning the curse. Neither she nor Nickie was ready for that yet.

"We're both taking photography," Nickie

said once Victoria stood to leave.

"How's photography going to help you as a psych or a social-work major? I'd say, switch to a business administration class. You haven't taken that. Or econ." Victoria's suggestion was out of left field, and she knew it. But to propose anything else — to encourage love, to support this relationship or whatever it was — that was something she couldn't do.

She'd ignored similar words of warning from Nanagusta, and she would work triply hard to make sure that Nickie didn't fall in love, with Felix or anyone else. She would save her daughter that pain, from the guilt that all these years later still flared up in Victoria. She smoothed Nickie's hair. "I'll have you start Saturday."

"Saturday? That's tomorrow."

Victoria smiled, doing her best to ignore the concern in Nickie's tone. It didn't feel good. "Yes. You'll start tomorrow. First client's at seven thirty, but come down at seven so I can show you the ropes." She left Nickie's door open and returned to her room where she'd find some ibuprofen to help her head, though she assumed the pain would stay until she got things right.

6
WILLOW

Nearly a week had gone by since Victoria had knocked on Willow's door. Willow had steadied herself, a hollow feeling in her belly. Her sister rarely came into her room so she figured bad news was the reason for the visit. Instead, Victoria told her she had a surprise. "I'm giving you a week off. A vacation. Nickie is going to cover for you. You can do whatever you want."

Willow didn't believe her. "Whatever I want? How about Hawaii?"

"I meant whatever you want to do locally. More of a staycation. I know you haven't had time off in a long time and things have been busy for us. I think it might be good for you. And for Nickie. She wants to learn about the business."

"Fine. As long as this time off is paid, why not?" Willow said, rationalizing that, if her sister was joking, she'd had multiple opportunities to come clean.

At the time, she accepted that her sister's intentions might be genuine, with Victoria finally recognizing how hard she worked. But after her sister let slip something about Nickie being boy crazy, it occurred to her that Victoria hadn't given her the week off because she cared about her mental health. The impromptu vacation only provided a ruse, one that wouldn't work, Willow knew. She wouldn't be able to keep Nickie away from Felix.

It wasn't until she'd gotten away from home that Willow realized she *never* got away. She'd been pinned to that house, to the women in it, to her sister's business for too long. In just the last few days, she'd gotten a gel manicure (not believing the technician when she told her it was okay to reach in her purse for her wallet without her nails drying under the fan), fallen in love with tonkotsu ramen, spent two hours and three hundred dollars in a Lego store, and drunk what was called a yard of beer.

But today, she had a task to complete, one that required her to reference her trusted book, which she currently had hidden in a cabinet behind the desk in the reception area outside of Victoria's office. She needed to get Nickie away from her post. "Is Mrs. Cole in there, Nick?" Willow gestured to the office door, interrupting her niece as she read a paperback.

Nickie dog-eared her page before closing her book. "They just started."

Good. That'd give Willow some time at the desk alone. "Well, I'm back. I have to . . . check on some billing stuff. You can leave for the day. I'll wrap things up here."

"But, my mom —"

"Don't worry about your mom. You've been here all day. I bet you didn't even get lunch, did you?"

"It's okay. I wasn't that hungry. Nana brought me some cookies."

Willow smirked to herself. "We gonna have to unionize. Anyway, get on up. Let me finish so I can start some dinner for us."

Nickie stood and collected her things, then stepped around to the other side of the desk so Willow could get by. But she didn't leave. Willow adjusted her chair, lifting herself an inch, dialing up the lumbar support. Nickie drummed her fingers on the desk.

"Aunt Willow?"

"What is it, Nick?" She didn't make eye contact with her niece, trying to seem occupied as she put on her glasses and leaned in toward the screen, vigorously wiggling the mouse, quadruple-clicking the button.

"Do you think I have some kind of a gift?"

"Gift? Like another birthday present?"

"No, Auntie. A gift. Like my mom, I guess. Like . . . Lanora?"

Willow looked up and pushed the mouse aside. "So your mom's been telling stories in between clients, I see."

"Kind of. She brought it up the other morning."

Willow sighed, shaking her head. Her sister had become desperate, it seemed. First by diverting Nickie's time and attention to the practice and then filling her mind with talk about Lanora and her blessing. She knew Victoria had planned to bring up this topic with Nickie one day, but such a discussion should have been mapped out in advance and involved the whole family, not just Victoria bumbling through on her own.

"What did she tell you? That just one of us got Lanora's blessing?" Of course Victoria would have focused on *that* detail, something she long ago gloated about.

"I don't remember that part of it . . ."

"That's what we were always told. And that's what the song says. You remember the song?"

Nickie put a hand on her hip. "Some of it."

She hummed a few notes, then patted her

65

niece on her shoulder. "Of course you have a gift, baby girl. You're beautiful, you're smart. I'm sure you'll make a terrific therapist, just like your mom." Willow was bullshitting the girl, but she was anxious to move things along.

"But she said something about, like, feeling people. Or knowing things."

Willow shook her head again. Damn her sister for leaving her to fill in the mystifying details. "Your mother just needs to be patient. Hell, she didn't realize her gift until she was almost twenty years old, after she had you." She'd used her fingers to etch quotation marks in the air when she said *gift,* regretting it right away. She didn't need to confuse her niece even further. While she tried not to let it show, talk about Lanora rankled Willow. A shiv to her gut. She'd done well enough over the years not to think about their family's chronicles, but sooner or later, she knew her sister would share them with Nickie — the good, the ugly, the downright unbelievable. Victoria could at least have given her a heads-up, time to prep for Nickie's questions. She was doing okay so far, encouraging her niece to take a seat, talk low, keep an open mind. But there'd be questions, she knew, she simply couldn't answer for the girl.

Nickie shrugged. "Well, I don't feel any-thing, Auntie. I . . . can't even tell if boys like me."

Willow understood. She could remember being seventeen, feeling like she had no control, no clue, even if she gave off the op-posite vibes. All she could think to do was to have Nickie write it all down.

"Like, a journal?"

"Exactly, baby girl. Get it all out. Your frustrations, your dreams, your ideas. And sooner or later, you'll detect a pattern. You'll see what you want and what you're good at, and see how the gift works for you." She didn't know this to be true, but it seemed like a sound suggestion, maybe wisdom she could use for herself.

"You think that will help?" Nickie asked, hopeful.

Willow nodded, too emphatically. "You sit outside your mama's office long enough, you learn some things."

Having answered her questions, she waited for Nickie to head upstairs. She worked hard at pretending to scan the screen, scroll-ing up and down on a Wikipedia page about Wikipedia, the first thing she could think to type into the search box. But Nickie didn't leave. She sat down on the love seat near the reception-area window.

"What else is it, Nick? I've told you all about Lanora. You got something more to ask me?"

Nickie threw her head back and closed her eyes.

Willow was curious what her niece might ask next. If she'd told her about Lanora, could Victoria have decided to confess other family secrets? "Spit it out, baby."

Nickie blew out a breath. "I need your help."

"What do you need, some condoms?"

"Auntie, I'm serious."

Willow straightened, laced her fingers together on the desk as her niece got up and kneeled beside her chair.

Nickie rubbed the back of her neck. "Ortho Tri-Cyclen, Auntie. I need you to pretend to be my mom so I can get a prescription. It's supposed to be, like, the best thing for my skin. I read it online. But I know Mom will freak out because it's kind of like . . . birth control."

"Wait, wait. Hold up, now. Birth control? Oh, see, now I wasn't too far off asking if you needed condoms." Not only would her sister kill her for getting Nickie a birth control prescription but then she'd trash her name in the spirit world, comparing her

68

to Ti Jean Quinto, one of the most unloved loa.

"I don't need condoms. I want something to help my skin clear up. But my mom will think I just want to be on the pill."

Willow leaned back in the chair and crossed her arms. "Do you?"

"Would it be so bad if I did? The last thing we need in this house is a baby." Nickie turned toward the office door as the word *baby* bounced around the space. She glanced at Willow. "All I'm asking is that you help me out. I just want to feel better. I . . . I like Felix. I want him to like me too. I need to at least say I had a high-school boyfriend, Auntie."

"I think it's better if you talk to your mother." She hated saying this to Nickie, knowing a talk about birth control with Victoria would be unwise, but she'd panicked, not expecting Nickie to jump right to contraceptives. The girl could barely swallow a coated Tylenol without gagging.

Nickie groaned, dropping her shoulders and looking at the ceiling as if it might tell her the right thing to say. "I just have a feeling my mom will have an issue with all of this. She wants me to focus on school, you know. She keeps talking about me getting my license. Not my driver's license, Auntie.

My *therapy* license."

Willow felt for Nickie. She really did. But Willow wasn't going to get trapped in the web Victoria and Nickie were weaving around each other. "Sweetie, your mom has goals for you. That's all. And I want to help you, believe me. But I can't afford to piss off your mama. I know I made a big deal about not being her assistant, but she is my employer, you know? And my landlord. Every now and then, she accidentally does my laundry."

Despite Willow's attempt to let her down softly, Nickie's eyes glinted with hope. Maybe there was something else she could do to help, something more subtle.

Her phone vibrated just inches away from her niece, who lifted herself up to look before Willow could grab it. "Who's January?" Nickie said at the sight of the green box that had popped onto the screen.

Willow snatched the phone and let it fall into one of her shopping bags. "A friend. Just like Felix."

"Felix doesn't send me messages asking for tit pics."

Tit pics? She'd never heard the term before and didn't think January could have meant what the words implied. "He's just being silly. We joke like that. Anyway, I can buy you a pretzel from Hot Sam's. Just go on upstairs and put on something comfortable and we'll go."

Once Nickie left the reception area, Willow swiveled in her chair to the corner and reached for a sliding cabinet panel, hard to spot because the knob was missing. She pulled out the thick book, careful not to let anything fall out as she opened it on her lap and flipped to a page titled "Thursday's Attraction Spell." In the margin next to the spell's instructions, she wrote:

— For Nickie, irresistible to Felix.

Her print was small, hardly legible, but it didn't matter. Willow knew what she'd written. It wasn't her first choice, but it was a good substitute for a more potent spell since she didn't have an eyelash from Felix or anything else of his to use. With this spell, Felix would tell Nickie of his attraction to her, but only if it already existed. Unfortunately, it didn't spur attraction. Otherwise, Willow would have used it years ago with Boris Kodjoe or Lenny Kravitz. But Willow knew that Felix wouldn't have gone through the trouble of bringing over wine and having dinner with them if he didn't like Nickie. Although it wasn't a smart idea, undermining Victoria, she couldn't wait for her niece's sweet little smile when she arrived home one day, the bearer of dreamy news, that Felix had called her beautiful. Perhaps then, she would tell Nickie what she'd done. It would be Willow who could gloat — despite her sister's so-called abilities, Victoria could never show Nickie any magic like that. Would Nickie still think of her as just an *assistant* after that?

Willow recognized her sensitivity to the word, and it *was* just a word. But she'd played the same role for over a decade, consistent as her sister's accomplice, assistant, and hype woman, and she was starting to feel typecast, the loyal best friend, unswaying supporter. She had tired of it, wanted her own part. Sitting behind the desk for so long, she'd forgotten about any hopes and dreams of her own.

She'd been young when she'd gone to New Orleans under the guise of checking on the shop Nanagusta still owned in the Quarter. Tasked with signing a new tenant, she'd instead moved right into the space, selling her own perfumes and soaps and hand-dipped candles, eager to make something of herself and in no hurry to return to the situation she'd left behind in California. Nickie had just been born weeks ago. She didn't consider herself a mother type. She'd never held a baby before Nickie, never smelled that clean, fruity scent, felt the way she squirmed in her arms in search of just the right comfort. Leaving her new niece, her sister, was the hardest thing she'd ever done, but staying in California at the time had been impossible.

The club had been turned into a touristy restaurant, a wooden arrow directing folks upstairs to the shop attracting only a few customers each day. "There's a gal who used to do root work up here when I was a little girl," a woman named Teliscia told her one afternoon as she perused, sniffing sachets of potpourri. Willow figured the *gal* in question must have been her grand-mother.

By Teliscia's third visit within two weeks, Willow had readied a blessing oil she made from the instructions in the thick book she'd lugged from California, swiped from Nana-gusta's bedroom while she was busy watching baby Nickie. She'd spent a whole day on it, boiling pomegranates, searching the city for essential oil of peppermint, collecting fallen bits of tree bark from Armstrong Park. "Use it under your feet, to tell the ground what you want when you step on it."

Her next time in the shop, the woman brought feedback that filled Willow with great pride. "Ms. Willow," she said, "I'm going to need a larger bottle this time. What's it been, three days? You wouldn't believe the miraculous things that have happened to me. You got anything that can help me get rid of my boss?"

From there, word spread. For anyone who knew to ask, she could mix up a few ounces of Capricorn oil made with red pepper and sage. Or combine holy water with water from the last rain, some from the river, some she'd carried with her from the Pacific to make her version of Marie Laveau's Peace Water. It was the family business, smothering out the problems of other people, offering hope they didn't think was available to them, removing obstacles to happiness. It was a good time, her mother, Madelyn, her biggest hype woman, bringing in new clients when she was clean.

Two months into her side hustle, she phoned her grandmother with an inkling she wanted to discuss — she thought she might have Lanora's gift. She had believed this back when she was still in high school, experimenting with the spells in her grandmother's book, but she hadn't been ready to share that gut feeling with anyone else. Now, the happenings at the shop had confirmed her suspicions and increased her confidence. Willow could use the gift the same way Augusta had back when she'd run the shop in New Orleans. But she didn't get a chance to share her news.

"Willow, I have something incredible to tell you about your sister. She's got it, sweetheart. Your sister has Lanora's blessing." Willow's heart seemed to stop for a moment. She only heard a few phrases after that, something about Victoria going to school, Nanagusta paying for everything. But it had been settled. Victoria had been chosen, the torch passed to her from Augusta, Madelyn having already been deemed a lost cause.

Willow often felt alone in the house, different from the others. Even from Nickie, now. But though she'd never told her grandmother or sister, two decades later Willow still held strongly to the belief that she was indeed the gifted one.

Before putting away the book, Willow flipped to the back, drew out a small green sachet, and slipped it into her desk drawer. Satisfied with her work, she retrieved her phone from her shopping bag.

January
Send a picture of those fantastic breasts of yours. Front and side views pls.

A laughing emoji followed.

How did he know how fantastic her breasts were?

"Willow, what are you smiling about? And where's Nickie? I need her to print out a referral list and check out Mrs. Cole." Victoria stuck her head out of the office.

Willow swallowed, sliding the phone to the corner of the desk. "No problem. I'll handle it. I need to pay a couple of bills so I told Nickie she could go upstairs."

Her sister stepped aside to let Mrs. Cole pass. "Willow's here instead. She'll print the list."

Victoria said she'd be right back, and Willow quickly tugged open the drawer and handed the satchel to Mrs. Cole, who put it in her purse. Hushed, she said, "Sprinkle that around your bed, making sure to use the entire bag. Do not sweep it up or vacuum."

"Ever?" said Mrs. Cole.

"Not until your mother-in-law moves away."

The woman frowned. "You sure? It gets

dusty in our room. My husband has aller-gies."

"You want her gone? He can sleep on the couch."

Before she got a chance to say anything more, Victoria returned. "Alright, Mrs. Cole. Two weeks good? We'll send you a reminder."

Mrs. Cole looked down at Willow, who gave the woman a thumbs-up, both an agreement with Victoria on the two weeks and a *You got this, girl* for the powder in the satchel. Willow didn't doubt things would be better for Mrs. Cole very soon. She'd put her trust in the right sister, even if Victoria believed it was her work that made all the difference.

7
AUGUSTA

It rained the last Friday in August, a week after Nickie brought over a boy for the first time. According to the fancy people on Augusta's television, this rain was news. Long time ago, back home in New Orleans, talk about a summer shower might doom a conversation, make people consider you odd. Rain was what it did in the summer. But in California, folks sent text messages about the weather. Made phone calls and wrote poems. A late-summer rain hardly troubled Augusta, but it did remind her to think about the world. Made her wonder if the seasons, the sun, or the clouds were all imagined, and if she'd been a sucker to believe in it all, just like everyone else.

Propped up in her leather chair by a couple of pillows, watching the heavy mist fall, she thought of late-August days from before, when it hardly made sense to bathe, the muddiness of the day crawling over your skin even before you had a chance to wake, returning just moments after washing it off. Fans spinning in each room did nothing but push the air from one space to the next, kept the flies from settling anywhere for too long. Her last summer at her parents' home, she would sit out on the porch and read, her bare feet stretched out in front of her, drops of rain falling in spurts. When she noticed, her mother would come out to fuss, telling her she needed to be inside helping with dinner, the clothes, the ironing. And if she was going to read, it should have been something captivating. One of the classics. None of that poetry nonsense she'd gotten hold of.

The day Augusta left home for good, her mother had worn a fuzzy blue dress. Felted wool, perhaps. With it, she donned pearls and inch-high heels as she vacuumed. When she finished, she would start dinner, a pot roast or a meat loaf with potatoes and carrots. Her parents lived life straight out of the magazines, glossy and finespun.

Her father was still at work when she told her mother, clutching a large paper bag that held all the belongings she required. She'd been with Bela Nova the evening before, when the woman confirmed she had Lanora's gift, an ability to perceive people. "It's in your eyes, I know it. You can look in my eyes and feel my emotions, can't you?" She hadn't known this ability, but once Bela Nova said so, it became her truth.

Her mother shut off the chromed-covered machine and put one hand on her side.

"Young lady, your curfew is ten o'clock and not a minute later. Or didn't you learn anything from the thousand standards your father had you write about returning home at the proper time?"

The standards, she knew, had not been her father's idea. "Yes. I did."

Her mother smiled in rosy red. "Good. So I'll see you back home before ten. No later." She turned the vacuum back on, her gaze steady on Augusta for just a moment before turning it off again. "Where is it you're going this evening, anyway? And Augusta, why are you carrying that greasy bag? Is that what this is about — you want me to lend you one of my bags?"

"I don't want any of your bags. I said that I'm leaving," Augusta told her mother.

"I heard what you said." Her mother stood straighter, heels planted more firmly into the plush carpet nap. She raised her nose and rounded chin.

"I'm not coming back." She sounded confident, Bela Nova having forced her to rehearse the statement, but if she'd been honest with herself, Augusta figured she'd be gone no more than a week.

"Of course you are. You have school in the morning. You're lucky I'm letting you stay out until curfew after pulling this kind of game."

"Mother, you know what I'm trying to say." She took a step toward the door, another past her mother. "Please tell Daddy that I love him. And that I'll call soon. Don't try to find me."

"Augusta Marie, you best have yourself back here by ten, you hear?"

Making her way south in the dusty heat, she wiped away the rush of tears she hadn't thought would come, still tightly gripping her paper bag.

The door at the top of the landing opened before Augusta got a chance to knock. She marveled at the woman's ability to sense her presence, until she realized someone was exiting, a client curiously bundled up and covered in the heat.

"Come in. Excuse me for a moment," Bela Nova said, stepping out with the other woman and leaving Augusta alone in the dark blue room, filled with the smell of anise hyssop, fresh blooms that Bela Nova would later use for tea.

On the workbench, she noticed an open book, a nearby pillar candle erasing shadows from a page. The title at the top beckoned her: "Too Bad Love Hex." Beneath it, she read that the user of the spell should be ready to deal with dreadful, even violent, repercussions, that one should think not once but tens of times before employing it. At the bottom of the page were the names of two women for whom, Augusta would learn, Bela Nova had cast the spell.

"It will work, but it won't be pretty for her."

Augusta dropped her paper bag of belongings, Bela Nova's voice thwacking her from behind. She turned as the woman walked toward her, sullen moonlight from the small window finding the whites of her eyes.

Bela Nova pointed to the door with her thumb. "But she has a lot of money. She'll be fine in the end. I wouldn't advise using this one." She touched the book. "Matter of fact . . ." Bela Nova ripped the page out and halved it four times before slipping it into her cleavage. "Best to keep some distance between a strong hex and the steps to uncross it. A medic doesn't keep the venom with the antidote, does he?"

Augusta hadn't even considered that a

person stocked venom, but her naivety kept her from asking, her thoughts still stuck on the lady who'd left and the possible reasons why she might need the spell.

That first night, the two settled down to a dinner of turtle soup, dirty rice, and chicken fricassee. Before they ate, Bela Nova lifted up names of loa that Augusta would eventually come to consider family, not corporeal beings but real all the same, their bodies invisible but their spirit outlines ever present. "We bless our almighty Creator, first off, and give thanks for this abundant table. And next, to the comely and wondrous Oyá-Yansan, who has shown grace with my request, praying on my behalf to increase my influence, to double my power." Augusta tried to keep her eyes closed as Bela Nova spoke, but she couldn't stop them from fluttering free. The purple sheen on the woman's lips shone in the candlelight, her gummy mouth open wide, arms out.

"How grateful I am to you for shedding me of the burden cast by so many others. I know you spoke words in my favor, pushing YeYe off my back, reminding her of the many years I revered her, willing to offer everything I had. But now she indeed is sweet and tender, and I am in service to you, Oyá, for your intercession."

Augusta clamped down her lids again as the woman paused, less concerned about the prayer itself as she was the cooling pots and platters of food. Her mother had never been very successful in the kitchen, letting meals oversimmer or understew, adding double the salt required or forgetting to use any at all. The food would sit and wait, however. Bela Nova's routine of thanking the loa was not to be rushed or skipped for fear of pissing them off. Once she added a new loa to the lineup, the name stayed, drawing out each evening's prayer even longer: Oyá-Yansan. YeYe, also called Oshun. Papa Legba and Erzulie Freda. Erzulie Dantor when her finances needed help, and the Marrassa. In time Augusta would learn to be patient.

"And to the divine Lanora. If you are able to see, I am now raising the first of your daughters, helping her to use her gifts."

Augusta had a feeling that if she opened her eyes again, she'd catch the woman's strong stare. But she soon learned that Bela Nova kept her lids shut when petitioning the loa to show them respect, that her mind was focused only on them.

"She is well-suited for this work, and she will elevate your name in the spirit world. I pray that you will bless me accordingly, spreading far and wide my name once I am gone. That women who are desperate, who are not secure, who are not right, will call out to Bela Nova when my body leaves this world just as they seek me out now."

After dinner, Bela Nova handed Augusta two pieces of paper, a fountain pen, and a small canister of Raven's Blood ink made with a rare essential oil from Japan. "You need to learn Lanora's song. I'll sing it, and you write it down."

Augusta filled the cartridge without a problem, but when she pressed on the nib, a rush of ink flowed, a large blob soaking the sheet.

"Try again." Bela Nova picked up the second piece of paper and placed it on top of the first. "Once you can recall it without my help, you'll write it in my book, daughter of Lanora. How fortunate I am to have you to here to do it."

The woman began with a hum, long and resonant, an unexpected, beautiful sound. The lyrics haunted Augusta — she missed whole phrases trying to get the words down while absorbing the details of Lanora's tragedy, her eventual purpose, her found peace. There were more details in the song than her own family had ever spoken to her about the woman. With the exception of her father, who had told her she was related to a well-known saint but not about any kind of gift or song, the Laurents, it seemed, were ashamed of Lanora, not associating themselves with the lore about her spoken in the streets. Nickie's mother had called the woman *foul Voodoo trash.*

Once she finished to the best of her ability, Bela Nova looked over Augusta's shoulder at what she'd written. "It doesn't appear you understand the value of this song. I don't need it. And if I did, I already have it, here." She put a finger to her forehead. "Young Augusta, Lanora lived to give this story to you. You're the first daughter in her bloodline."

She began blowing out candles, gray shadows swelling to black, the room disappearing. The smoke tickled Augusta's throat. She restrained herself from coughing.

"That song's more powerful than you could imagine, especially with you coming here to join me. Singing it can thwart horrible consequences for you, young Augusta. I wish I had the same advantage, but I'm not a descendant of good Lanora. Don't disappoint her." She blew out the last candle, leaving Augusta to feel her way in the dark to the nook where she'd sleep. She lay down on the hard mattress, covered herself with a small blanket, and listened to Bela Nova's voice from a distance.

"I will make you great in her name. And for that, one day I, too, will be a mother loa."

She hadn't anticipated this sort of pressure. It scared her. But unlike the ideas her mother had for her future, her mentor's expectations also exhilarated her, even if she wasn't quite sure she was the right person for the job. How did Bela Nova know about her lineage, her relation to Lanora? She didn't dare ask. All she could do was try with all of her might and energy to believe.

The smell of garlic, onions, and simmered meat tickled Augusta awake. As routinely as she napped, she hadn't meant to doze off, wanting to catch *Judge Mathis* from the beginning. By now, she'd missed twenty minutes and so she called it a loss, refusing to rewind the show the way Nickie had taught her. On the coffee table, she noticed a packed plate, rice and a piece of shrimp having tumbled off, sauce dripped on the floor.

Willow had been in the kitchen for a couple of hours, taking a virtual cooking class. She came into the family room with a fistful of paper towels and a glass of water. "You try it, Nana? It's Puerto Rican food."

Augusta leaned forward to make out the items on the plate.

"That's mofongo right there. You'll like that, with the shrimp. And that's arroz con gandules — peas and rice, I think. *Arroz* is definitely rice. And empanadas. I'm trying to branch out, you know? I'm going to do a French bistro class next week . . ." Willow went back into the kitchen, still going on. Augusta couldn't help but note she hadn't actually cleaned up the mess she'd made.

Nickie walked in from the foyer, light on her feet. She appeared to be en route to the kitchen but stopped after glancing at Augusta. "Nana, what happened?"

Nickie picked up the bits of food that Willow had spilled, then dabbed the spots of sauce with the paper towels. She'd always been a sweet kid, but watching Nickie, Augusta noted how mature she'd become, with her lovely freckled eyes. She'd slimmed down, lost some of her musculature from her basketball days. Give it another decade, and she'd get curves like the rest of them, though Augusta wondered if the girl's feet would continue to grow; they already had difficulty finding shoes in her size. Long feet like her father, even though he hadn't been very tall.

If she had the chance, she might take Nickie aside one Saturday afternoon, come up with a way to communicate with her about love, share the things Victoria never would, not that Augusta had a lot of experience with it. If her great-granddaughter was in love, there wasn't much she or Victoria or even the loa could do about it. That first love — that young love — was resilient. Even now, Augusta hadn't shaken all the emotions ignited by the first man she had loved.

She'd apprenticed with Bela Nova for a year and a half when she stole the woman's son right from under her.

It puzzled Augusta how someone like Bela Nova had raised a man like Dudley Lee. He didn't get the business, had no clue about money, how to make it, how to get it out of strangers' wallets like his mother did. He was a heart man — he stuck it out and let it make his decisions for him. Not a very finicky heart, fond of all kinds of women. He had his pick of them too, taking Bela Nova's less interesting features and making them handsome — her square chin, her sagging thin lips, her narrow nose. These, along with his stretched-out frame and ruddy brown skin, kept Dudley Lee's little black book fully stocked with names and numbers. But he was a sweet young man, an earnest man, similar to her father. He cracked a lot of jokes, as if he was a budding stand-up comedian, and though she didn't laugh much, she always found reason to when he came around. Her favorite times in the shop always involved Dudley Lee. She was in love for the first time and had a hunch that he was attracted to her, physically and emotionally. More than a hunch, really, her body reacting, the palms of her hands tingly when she spoke to him.

But Dudley Lee was dating the only daughter of a Creole couple, up-and-comers in the local political scene. She liked the girl the moment she saw her, Bela Nova would tell folks, though Augusta recalled a grimace, a precise upturn of her nose when she first stepped inside the workshop, clinging to Dudley Lee's bicep, delicate with lanky appendages, a grasshopper of a young lady with a personality to match. When Bela Nova learned how loaded Genevieve Broussard's parents were, however, she could hear the crunch of dollar bills in her fist, and soon after, she'd urged Dudley Lee to propose with a ring that had belonged to a famous jazz singer who'd swapped it one evening for one of Bela Nova's pricey luck oils. It was a beautiful twisting of gold and cerulean gems.

Hearing that Bela Nova was a local entrepreneur, the mother and father approved of the match. With the marriage, Bela Nova's plan was to move her business out of the Dew Drop Inn to a storefront. Legitimize herself. Sell perfume and smoothed stones and lavender soaps made in her bathtub. Those more traditional pieces would pay for themselves and do the favor of bringing in clientele, people with money — no more of those light-pocketed club folks, always wanting a hex on loan.

But Augusta, ultimately, would get in the way of her grand plans.

The wedding was scheduled to happen once the weather warmed — nobody wanted a wintry wedding. Which bought Augusta time to win Dudley Lee over, not that she was sure what she'd do with it.

Change her hair, perhaps. These were the days when the earth spun slower, held on longer to rainy autumns, miserable winters. But it was muggy all the time, like the town was shoved inside a clammy locker room, and Augusta had taken to wearing her hair naturally. It never really needed all the relaxer chemicals, but her mother had seemed not to be able to get it straight enough. She preferred the edges flush with Augusta's scalp, even running a hot comb through it on Sunday mornings, weeks before a touch-up was needed. After moving to the Quarter and ditching the relaxer, she stopped worrying about her hair getting wet, walked down the streets on misty days and soaked in the city, even if it meant a frizzy do. She liked her hair the way it was, but the men, for some reason, seemed to prefer it long and straight. Maybe that's why her mother had aspired to it. It had become endemic, women with chemically treated hair. Lots of men laying their hair straight too. It was something to consider. Changing her hair and getting some new clothes, a halter dress or two, tops that flaunted her bosom, revealed more than did her collared button-ups.

With early spring came a softer, more dollish Augusta. If he did notice the changes in her appearance and the way she carried herself around him, Dudley Lee didn't acknowledge it. He even had the nerve to keep bringing the girl around the small apartment adjoined to the workshop, where they planned to move once they married, showing her where they would sleep, where she could set up her coin collection. The kitchen, where she would make his meals. How could Augusta survive sharing the wall of her small room with the two of them, forced to listen to their lovemaking?

It wasn't until a few weeks before the ceremony that Augusta made a substantial move, summoning the nerve when Bela Nova stepped out to the Marigny in need of herbs. Strange, the risks women take for a handsome face. Dudley Lee's was near immaculate, so what choice did Augusta have but to go against her better judgment and stack a stool atop a chair and climb her way up to reach the book? Never before had Augusta removed her mentor's hefty book of spells and enchantments from the shelf. She'd watched Bela Nova consult the text, hovering over it on her workbench the way a housewife might pore over a cookbook. But Augusta never dared reference it without Bela Nova's consent. Wouldn't even look at it, afraid her eyes might be plucked straight from her head if she did. The only time she'd touched it was when she'd written Lanora's song inside, two blank pages right in the middle of the book saved for the words, as if her mentor knew all along that Augusta would arrive one day and pen them there. After getting the song down, she assumed she'd be given access to the text, the act of remembering all the verses an initiation, but Bela Nova continued to withhold it. And while it had always been there for her to steal a peek at, Augusta had instead accepted things as they were and chose to believe that Bela Nova would show her what she needed to know and when. But the situation had become urgent, and now there was no way around it.

The book was weightier than she'd anticipated, and she lost her balance, fell from the stool and onto her back. It hurt, but she would be all right. As she flipped the pages in search of love spells, she could easily find something for the pain too. A healing spell using a doll, the one Bela Nova kept in her collection case that looked just like Augusta down to the small brown mole left of her chin, the wide-set rusty eyes, though it surely wasn't wise to work magic on your own doll.

When she sat at the workbench and opened the tome, it was as if her insides spun around, each and every organ inside her taking its own fun-loving rotation, reckless and fast. She tickled all over, and that made her giggle, despite being afraid — of what she'd read, about the power she'd soon have. About Bela Nova walking through the workshop's tattered wooden door, home early.

It was a leather-bound volume, its spine ribbed and worn and sprouting threads. The pages were thick and brittle. Almost burnt, but still well intact. The strip of bright light shooting down from the room's single bulb illumed long handwritten notes, an ornate typeface in squid-ink black, smudged here and there, spelling out recipes for fortune, love, revenge. It was as if anything could be had on earth, just turn to the right page.

Hours zoomed by like jet planes, whistling winds shaking the heavily draped window as she studied, her fingertips catching a prickle when they ran across a fix that suited her situation well. When the door to the shop finally opened, Bela Nova scatting her way through, Augusta had only seconds to finish scribbling down the items she needed to gather and return the book to its spot.

Arms heavy with bags, the woman called her over. "Young Augusta, come get these. I need you to find jars for the herbs from the apothecary. And label them *mandrake root, camphor,* and *rose otto.* I want the dandelion in the ice box. Same with the eucalyptus and the mint. And please toss that old, rusted kettle on the stove. I traded Mo Alarcon my malachite talisman for a new one."

Augusta got to work, stowing her teacher's goods in the cupboards and the baskets and vases at the back of the workshop. The book that day, and in the days to follow when Bela Nova left to run her daily errands, had overwhelmed Augusta. She'd learned so much from her mentor in all this time yet barely knew even a little. And that wasn't good enough anymore. Not if she would one day get from under Bela Nova's thumb. Not if she would even sooner take the woman's son for herself.

"Go on ahead and use that kettle for water. My bones are aching from the trip. Soon, you'll take over the shopping. I'm down to five stops on a good day."

Once Bela Nova rested, they began infusing oils using the herbs and plants she'd purchased from the farmers' market or picked from the yards of wealthy, white homeowners in the Garden District, tinkering with a new blessing oil steeped in frankincense. Then they polished pieces of lapis lazuli, and all the while Augusta's armpits perspired as she concentrated hard to still her nervous hands. She only hoped that Bela Nova wouldn't discover her plan, wouldn't cross it before it had even had time to ripen.

8
NICKIE

Nickie's phone buzzed right at 4:50 a.m., but her eyes had already open to her bedroom's darkness a moment before. She waited another minute, listening to the quiet to make sure it stayed, letting her eyes adjust so she could clearly see the thin outlines of the furniture, the tidy desk and white wardrobe. She'd cleaned everything off the floor the evening before to be sure not to trip and fall. If she did so now, it would be thanks to her own clumsiness. And nerves. Her hands trembled as she felt for the notebook and pen at the edge of her bed, her heart beating fast like she'd just finished a basketball game.

She'd picked the earliest slot available for a virtual session to choose her elective, the only class she hadn't finalized at the end of the previous school year, and she hoped to be first to join the queue of students with six-o'clock appointments. Nickie wanted to use the reception computer, the connection much faster than her laptop's, and this hour was also the only time she'd have privacy. She didn't hate the reception area but was certainly glad that she was almost done filling in for Willow, having mustered just about all of the customer-service pep she had in her the past week.

Though she'd told her mother that she and Felix had plans for the last week before school started, the two had more so *made plans to make plans,* ideas hatched about how they could spend the final days of summer. The morning after Felix's visit and her mother's awkward speech about men, Nickie had called him to ask about his day, thinking better of it when he answered and said he couldn't talk right then, hanging up before she could even say hello. He'd apologized later via text but hadn't offered a reason for ending the call so abruptly.

Nickie
I'm covering for my aunt, working for my mom tomorrow through next Saturday.

Felix
Got it. That's cool.

Nickie
Still want cake?

Felix
Nah, it's cool. 😉

She hadn't heard from him since but didn't dare contact him again. School would start in a few days, and she would see him there, play it cool like she hadn't been thinking about him for hours each day. She'd resigned to aligning her schedule to fit her mother's wishes, though she still didn't understand. What was the big deal about taking photography with Felix? Did she worry Nickie would get knocked up just by being in the same room as him?

Downstairs, she positioned herself behind the desktop and started a round of solitaire. She'd won her third hand in a row when the online waiting-room screen turned green and a red-headed woman appeared and asked what elective she wanted to select.

It was her nature to be first, to get things over with, but a truth glowed inside of her. She wanted to ensure that she spent time with Felix this school year. Though in her mind, she heard her mom's answer, *economics,* the counselor repeated back something different, the words that had been burning in her belly. "Advanced photography?"

Her ears warmed. "Yes."

"For that class, you need to have taken a prerequisite. Or get instructor approval," the woman said with a cheerfulness unnatural for the time of day.

She figured she could get a letter from her summer-workshop teacher, a school alumnus who knew the photography teacher well.

"I can change your schedule and put you on the waiting list for now. But it looks like you'll have to drop your AP Literature course. Both classes are only offered third period."

AP Literature with Mrs. Cofield. She'd been waiting to get a class with Mrs. Cofield since freshman year. That the class was lit and an AP course were just bonuses. The woman went on to explain more issues with her schedule.

"So what do you want to do?" she finally asked.

There wasn't much time to think, the seconds of their five-minute session ticking away. She gripped Ayida Wedo in her fist, the metal of the amulet noticeably cold to the touch. "That's fine. Go ahead and wait-list me for photography," Nickie said. She knew it wasn't a smart decision to dump a chance at AP units and the school's most beloved teacher for photography. But it felt good, even though she couldn't be sure Felix would enroll in the course or be able to get in. She'd tell her mom about the class in a month, well before progress reports came out but when it was too late to change her schedule.

Rather than going back upstairs, she stayed at the desk. She took a moment to listen for sounds, the bathroom faucet, the creak of a door. Nothing. As if she'd not already studied everything the internet had to offer about Felix, which admittedly wasn't much, she typed his full name into a search box. Just for fun, she clicked on a link that she'd scrolled past a half-dozen times before, one for an IMDb entry for a different Felix Shilling, an actor who'd been in the movie *Outbreak* and a television show called *Small Wonder.*

As she stretched her legs out, her bare heel hit something. She pulled it back and heard the soft rip of paper. Probably one of her mother's client files. Nickie bent over to retrieve it, but instead of a stack of folders, she'd torn what appeared to be an old book, its cover slanted upward, unable to lie flat to enclose the pages inside.

She placed the book on the desk, pushing aside the wireless keyboard and turning on the lamp. The leather of its spine was mealy and ripped, prior damage, not caused by her heel. She guessed it was a photo album, her aunt stashing it here to bury pictures revealing old hairstyles or bad fashion choices. It was heavier than she assumed it would be, its leather cover old but soft, the name *Delilah* pressed into it in gold. Its brittle pages creaked as she opened it near the middle and discovered a faded photo of a German shepherd taped to a page that said "Fixing a Broken Heart Spell," followed by a list of ingredients and instructions. Written below were names, with short notes.

Bette Couto, she 22, sick over Hank Riley. Amairani Dupree, fell for friend Roberta who then stopped speaking to her. Creshanne Wolfer, husband left her for best friend.

There was more about Creshanne Wolfer, but the rest of her story was covered up by the German shepherd, and the page was likely to rip if Nickie stuck a fingernail underneath to lift it. She could, however, make out the note next to the photo in faded blue calligraphy. *This here dog runs around the Dew and steals my bones.*

Printed on the opposite side was something called "Freckled Lady Oil" and, when she turned the page, a hot foot powder. In the crease of another, a crisp envelope from the Louisiana Power and Light Company, along with what looked to be a recipe for pralines scribbled in loopy cursive. On a different page, something called a "Debtor's Curse," the ingredient *rosewater* scratched out underneath. Toward the back of the book, a piece of pink folded construction paper poked out, adorned with a red heart cut freehand with scissors. Her own grade-school printing: *I love you Ant Wilow love NICKIE.*

A detail on the next page caught her eye, under something called "Thursday's Attraction Spell." Someone else may have assumed the writing was just squiggles, but Nickie knew her aunt's lettering, could decipher her pen strokes with ease.

For Nickie, irresistible to Felix

"What the fuck?" she said as her chest tightened and her stomach dropped. She glanced up. Confident that she was still alone, she spun the knob on the desk lamp, increasing the brightness to help her make out the faint text under the so-called spell.

Blend a batch of Dragon's Blood (avail. at www.PCIFarmer.com for $12.99 $13.99)
Mix with lemon rind and baking soda
Scrub a clean plate with the mixture using the afflicted's toothbrush for four minutes, four times a day
Return the toothbrush from where it came without rinsing it off, but please clean the plate

Nickie pushed her tongue against her top teeth, wondering if her aunt had really followed these instructions, a sickly feeling taking over as she tried to remember the last few times she'd brushed her teeth, unable to recall if anything seemed strange.

She wanted to check if her name or Felix's were listed elsewhere, what other items of hers her aunt might have tampered with, but she knew her mom would be up soon, or Nanagusta, and she didn't want either of them to catch her. The fact that she'd only just come across the book after all these years told Nickie they'd been hiding it from her. She snapped a picture of the page with her phone, then returned the book to its spot on the floor.

9
VICTORIA

Victoria fought back a yawn as she sat across from her last client of the day. Slumber had troubled her the last few evenings, darkness shaking her awake after a couple hours, not letting her reach deep sleep, which left her grumpy and worn. She hoped she hadn't taken it out on any clients. She'd asked Loco, the patron of healing, to free her from whatever ailment rustled her from sleep each night, but he hadn't responded. Victoria had written it off as him being busy, what with the tumultuous world they lived in. If in another day or so she still couldn't get a decent night's sleep, she'd make a batch of sweet potato fries and leave them for Gran Bwa.

Asking the loa might help her sleep better, but she knew the real issue was everything happening with Nickie. In the last week, Victoria had shared with her so much, yet barely anything at all. She could teach a graduate-level course with all the knowledge she had of the loa, lessons she'd learned from Nanagusta, and even more information she'd researched herself as she grew more confident in her abilities, more aware of how she could help others.

But it had all started with Lanora. As young children, she and Willow had learned the Song of Madame Lanora, it seemed, even before the alphabet song, before Old MacDonald and Happy Birthday. They always sang it just as Augusta had taught them, their voices first crawling and deep, a crescendo as the story moved along, the two of them shouting the chorus, out of breath and wispy.

Lanora was born a free woman of color in New Orleans in the mid-1800s, and grew up next door to her best friend, Akili. The two of them were conspirators of no good, audacious in disobeying their parents, hanging out at the Bayou St. John, watching the Voodoo rituals. As they neared adulthood, they fell in love. She with him. He with someone else.

The fateful day the truth about Akili's heart was whispered in Lanora's ear, every organ in her body deflated. Imploded. She did what she could to stop her body from reacting, pushing her fingernails into the bittersweet dirt, flipping the city inside out. Though after her death she'd become a wondrous and mighty loa in the spirit world, Lanora hadn't known of her abilities before that day, had only thought herself an ordinary young woman. Her heartache had rattled awake her senses. She pried herself out, stuffing her insides back where they belonged, and lost herself in the Bayou St. John, praying to those living and dead for Akili's love, dancing with snakes. In the metallic blue of night, you could see her chanting, shouting, stomping his love for the other woman out of him. Then she got word that the two were to marry. Forever, under God's holy covenant, her love would be someone else's.

Their grandmother always finished the ballad, slowing the tempo as she chanted the last verse. After mourning for many years, Lanora found comfort in speaking wisdom to those hurt or otherwise challenged by their lives, able to tune in to fears and wants, what others needed to hear. She'd come into her destiny, a role in which she took great honor. As foretold to her in a dream, a destined daughter in each future generation would inherit this gift. But when Lanora herself became pregnant later in life, her miracle baby was a boy, and it would take until Augusta for a daughter of Lanora to be born.

As Victoria sat in her office, she hummed the song in her head, the precise words escaping her as her mind continued to drift. How could Nickie share the gift with future generations if she couldn't even fall in love without great harm? Their family was both blessed and cursed, and the burden of one had been pitted against the other. No wonder a headache had settled in.

When she failed to keep in another yawn, Victoria's client stopped midsentence.

"I'm so sorry, Nina. I've . . . I've been having trouble sleeping at night." She hated making excuses and didn't share personal information with clients, not even as a show of commiseration. But she didn't want to come across as rude — Nina had only been meeting with her for a few weeks.

It seemed to work. The woman's face sagged with empathy. She leaned forward, hands on her knees. "Tonight, heat a cup of water and mix in bit of honey and a shot of rum. You'll be out within an hour and won't wake until the sun's up."

Everyone wanted to be a conjurer. "I'll try it. Thanks," Victoria said, knowing such a concoction would only make her tipsy and in want of another shot.

She ended her session, waited for Nickie to schedule Nina's next appointment, and then smiled, proud of her daughter's work all week. Perhaps she'd recount a funny story about an anonymous client (Willow always had a few) or something interesting she'd noticed in one of the therapy videos she'd encouraged Nickie to watch. But her daughter only sat quietly, tugging on the elastic band around her wrist.

Victoria couldn't accept defeat. "It's your last day, Nickie. Payday."

"Oh," said Nickie.

"Matter of fact, the way business is going, I could use a second person. How about you cover for Willow every day once you're home from school at four for my late sessions, and cover Saturday mornings?" Victoria could show Nickie more about the business, maybe have her create a social media account for the practice, though she hardly needed the publicity. She was already so busy.

"That's okay."

Victoria laughed. "What do you mean, 'That's okay'?"

"I just really don't want to work. It's my senior year. I want to have . . . fun. I mean, maybe in a few months. After things settle down and I feel comfortable in my classes. But I can always fill in for Aunt Willow again if she needs more time off."

Victoria fixed her gaze on Nickie. Her eyelashes were lush like Willow's. She was wearing mascara. Had Nickie been sneaking out to see Felix? Had she been sneaking Felix over to their house at night? It was not an impossibility. Even sharing a room with a nosy sister growing up, Victoria had managed to sneak Jimmie and others before him into Augusta's home in Carson.

"Nickie?" Victoria took the girl's hand and held it tightly. She hoped to get a feeling if now was the right time, if she should just spit out the truth about the curse, about Jimmie's death. But that was the thing with Nickie. She could never read the girl, Victoria's power essentially gone when she touched her daughter. If Nickie was hiding something, had a secret or her thoughts centered on something forbidden, she couldn't tell. Which, in Victoria's mind, meant Nickie's abilities might be even sharper than her own.

"Are you wearing mascara?" She'd punked out from saying what she really wanted to, but the mascara needed to be discussed as well.

"Oh. Um, yes."

"You're not supposed to be wearing makeup." This wasn't a rule she'd ever implemented, but she said it as if Nickie had been warned about it before. "What about your classes?"

"What?"

"Your elective," Victoria said, putting weight on her toes, bringing herself a smidge taller than Nickie. "Did you choose economics?"

"Oh. Yeah."

"Let me see." Though Nickie had given off nothing, she had the feeling something was working against her, some other force countering her petitions to the loa.

Nickie twisted one of her rings back and forth. "Well, it's not on there yet. I have to petition. And go the first day of class."

"Petition? You sure?" She supposed it was possible although that sounded more like a college thing. Nickie nodded and sat back down. Victoria didn't know what was going through Nickie's head, but she knew dishonesty when she heard it. When she felt it. "You know, I think I'd like to move your laptop downstairs to the dining room. Let's keep it there — we hardly use the dining room table to eat. That way, Willow can share with you. I prefer she do all her social stuff elsewhere, not on here." Victoria tapped the desktop computer on the reception desk.

Nickie seemed taken aback by this decision but didn't respond. So Victoria ramped things up, telling Nickie she'd be selling her camera — it didn't seem she would need it if she was going to take econ for her elective. Her phone snapped better photos than that clunky camera Nickie had been hauling around, anyway. She didn't say it out loud, but she would also cut off Nickie's data plan and limit the Wi-Fi, extremes the girl would have to deal with for now. Victoria and Willow had certainly found enough trouble to get into when they were younger without technology helping them out. Maybe if Victoria had discovered her gift sooner, she'd have been able to avoid it all. But she hadn't.

She knew the sooner Nickie moved past Felix, the better. There was too much at stake. Though she barely knew the boy, she didn't want Felix to become another victim of the curse. If he did, Nickie would experience a loss as immense as she once had, and Victoria would have to live with the fact that she didn't do enough to try to prevent that outcome this time.

If her grandmother had done the same

with Victoria, Jimmie Wilkes might still have
been alive today.

10
WILLOW

For her date, Willow picked a popular neighborhood diner known for its long wait. She looked nice, made-up and nails done. The curl pattern of the ponytail she'd pinned in didn't match her natural texture, but it was her favorite, called The Alyssa by the online store where she purchased her extensions, giving her the volume she'd always lacked. Nickie had walked in on her in the bathroom as she put on lipstick, a sultry red that begged for trouble. When asked where she was going, Willow said the first thing that came to mind: "Bowling." By the time she left the house, she'd made up new friends (Shay and Jay), the name of a league (Beach City Bowlers), a reason why Nickie couldn't join her (the alley had a strict eighteen-and-older policy), and an excuse should she stay out late (if they won, Shay and Jay planned to go out dancing). She left by the back door without saying goodbye to Nickie, waited for her Lyft under the streetlight at the corner. Until Victoria chilled about all this Felix business, Willow thought it best to hide her personal life from Nickie.

In the meantime, Willow had called in reinforcements. She knew Victoria wouldn't like it, but she wouldn't be able to buffer the tension between Nickie and Victoria on her own forever, and another body in the house might help. The Montroses needed new energy, and there was only one person who could bring it.

Now she was ready to relax, to have a good time, and to release the pressure in her body. It would be nice to spend a few hours with someone outside of their house. Her date this evening was with the man to whom she'd now sent half a dozen tit pics. She'd been fortunate enough to snag a pair of seats at the counter, but so far, he was fifteen minutes late. His tardiness would only add to the many strikes against the guy. His name certainly earned one — January. She'd asked him what kind of name that was, and he'd said that it was a unique one, like Willow. Another strike was his profile, in which he'd used hundreds of words to say nothing. She'd met the type before, vague in order to hide. But the more strikes, the better. Her pursuits were meant for nothing but casual sex.

She had a one-date rule, wanting nothing more from the men she met than a nice dinner, some half-decent conversation, and a single, satisfying romp. Which was why January and his tardiness, his questionable profile pictures, and his icky *Good morning, Beautiful* messages didn't bother her. She knew to stay away from the catches, the guys who might accidentally win her heart with a set of dimples, a mouth full of perfect teeth, a way with numbers, a knack at spoken word. These types she passed over to protect herself. While she pretended for Victoria and Nanagusta, Willow didn't believe in the curse. But after operating in this family for so long as if she did, if she ever did open herself up to someone, she'd hardly know how to settle in.

"Ma'am, would you like some more coffee?"

Willow shook her head at the busboy, even though she might have had another pot just to herself. She didn't want to seem strange, though, requesting the refill in a new mug. Taking a second fill of coffee in the same cup, she'd been taught, was a sure way to lose money.

She watched people come and go, with no text or phone call from January. Another few minutes and she would note herself officially stood up. That would amount to more than a strike. He'd be deleted forever from her account, and she'd throw a little left-hand magic his way, something to make his balls itch or a herpes sore erupt on his lip.

She smiled to herself. Wouldn't it be rewarding to do that for a living? Not to cause pain to random folks but to teach people how to act for themselves? The woman next to her was speaking to her friend about a podcast she was obsessed with. "I wait for it to drop every Thursday."

Willow opened the only document she'd ever created on her phone's Notes app: Ideas. To the short list, she added *Podcast: The Hex Life, with Willow Montrose.* Under that, she typed *Master Class on Conjuring, with Willow Montrose.* She wondered how else she could share her skills, her years of knowledge with the world. Even just remedies she'd learned, from the book, from Nanagusta or crafted herself — a powder rubbed on the teeth before boarding a ship to keep away seasickness, fragrant oils that helped folks relax in stressful situations, a serum for forehead burns from a pressing comb. Plenty of content existed; she just needed to figure out the best way to find an audience, while also figuring out how to get sponsors, teach herself the technical aspects, and write a business plan.

She considered herself an entrepreneur at heart, her work in New Orleans fueled by her desire to distinguish herself from her Type A sister. Her ingenuity had kept the place busy, her customers faithful for a few years. But Willow was bad at the balancing of things, the multitasking. She was great with numbers and bookkeeping but would abandon those unfulfilling tasks if, say, she thought of a unique way to infuse a tea. Or wanted to try out new foot powders or spells. After four quick years, it was all gone. Willow's poor management lost them the shop, a real estate investment that had supplemented Nanagusta's income, afforded them their Catholic school education, even with their grandmother's spotty employment as a clerk in a community clinic. Willow's only option was to return to California in silent surrender. Victoria, who'd gotten a couple of degrees and was close to obtaining her license to practice therapy by then, had certainly earned her title as the favored one.

Going out on her own again would be

risky, but now that the idea had been stoked, it wouldn't go away. She was about to note the title *Everyday Hoodoo with Victoria Montrose* when she glanced a knee bending its way between the counter and the stool next to her. Then the rest of a body in a dark gray suit, filling the space up entirely. Mad as she was at this gentleman, bold enough to sit down next to her even after saving it with an open book, she took it as a sign that January's time had run out. As she reached for her purse, she noticed the man's hands, rich and brown.

"Willow?"

She turned her head, her eyes flashing with anger, but how quickly it dissipated once she saw him. He was . . . cute. "Hi. January?"

"Where you going?"

"I'm not going anywhere." Willow twisted herself back onto her stool, a heat crawling over her skin.

"Oh. 'Cause it looked like you were about to get up."

In the flesh, January had lived up to how he'd described himself. She figured his lack of photos online meant he'd be unattractive. "You're late."

"So you *were* about to get up."

"It doesn't matter. I'm hungry, so hurry

and look at the menu so we can order. And where did you come from, anyway? I didn't see you come in."

"Maybe you weren't looking. Too busy being upset that I was late. What were you doing there? Typing up a mean text for me?"

He lifted his eyebrows, waiting for a reaction. This behavior nauseated her, the games and the *getting to know you*s. The starts of relationships were intolerable, one of the many reasons why she didn't do them. It made more sense to grab his hand and take him to his car. They could drive east a mile to a decent motel.

"I think I'm going to order breakfast. Don't you love places like this, where you can get breakfast for dinner?" He seemed comfortable with her, as if they'd done more than send messages between one another the last few weeks.

When the waitress came over, Willow followed January's lead and ordered a stack of whole wheat pancakes and seasoned hash browns.

"I wouldn't mind living near here. Being able to walk over on Sunday mornings for breakfast."

Willow unfolded her napkin, spread it across her lap. "Ain't too many of us living in this area."

"Keep up that attitude and it will stay that way." His words sounded tough, but then he winked at her, sipping his icy glass of water. "That's the problem with Black folks. Always comparing ourselves to things white. You know?"

Willow's statement had been just an observation, but she liked that he had more to say about it. He had an ability to offer insight on topics, whittling giant rocks of thoughts down to pebbles. Meaningful little stones.

"You from Louisiana, didn't you say?"

"Yes. New Orleans. Been in California just as long, though."

"Montrose, right? That Creole or something?"

Willow drew a circle on the counter with her finger. "It's everything." She hated when people asked about her ethnicity, if she was Creole. Like that had anything to do with how well you could hex someone if you knew what you were doing.

His face knotted up, and he snapped his fingers. "Like that director. Montrose. I forget his first name. Had that movie about the Voodoo lady in the French Quarter. *Madame Joelle.*"

Willow shook her head.

"From the sixties. Oh, that's right. You're

121

a young one."

"I like old movies."

"Yes, but you're no cinephile. If so, you'd know Montrose and Parks and Van Peebles."

"I guess not, since I don't even know what a cinephile is. Doesn't sound like anything I want to be, honestly."

He chuckled, leaning in closer to her. He smelled like leather and coins.

When their food arrived, she tried his omelet, ate most of his toast, and claimed his cup of coffee when, after ten minutes, he still hadn't touched it. Only syrup remained on her plate by the time she thought to ask if he wanted to taste her food, laughing at herself when she apologized.

"Don't worry about it. I'll try it the next time we come." The next time *we* come. Sleeves rolled up, he rested one arm along the back of her chair as the busboy collected their plates.

"Now, you knew that sooner or later I'd have to ask about the one who came before me," he said. There were a couple of crumbs in his beard that his napkin had missed.

"There hasn't been anyone."

His smile had no teeth; it wasn't one of his real smiles, she could already tell. "Come on, you think I believe that, fine as you are? Hasn't been anyone? Ever?"

"Not saying that. But it's been quite a while."

"Since what? Since you've hooked up with someone?"

Willow frowned all the way to her forehead.

"You know. Got with someone," said January.

"Oh. Well, yeah. I've *been* with someone."

"That's what I'm talking about. What happened with the two of you?"

Willow wasn't into making up stories. Wasn't good at it. But she'd not planned to confess to years of meaningless sex. "Don't know. Nothing important." She was looking down at her fingernails, the gel polish still a dazzling red.

"Did you love him?"

She almost choked on her giggle. "No."

"So who was the last dude you loved?"

"That's a strange question. What time is it, anyway? You think they're about to close?" Willow deflected, not comfortable with the direction this conversation was going.

His arm moved from the chair to what was considered the small of the back on some women. "Nothing strange about it. Unless you haven't been in love before."

Willow's lips shot out in front of her in

objection, blooming petals of a vibrant crimson rose. He winked at her when she tilted her face to look at him. Men who winked, that typically got noted as a strike. Wasn't so bad on him. She gave in to his charm. "I was in love. Once."

"What happened to him? He didn't mess you up, did he?"

"That's a matter of opinion."

He smiled again, a full one this time. "And where is this guy now?"

"Deep in the ground somewhere." His hand, the one that had been rubbing small circles into her back, stopped. Stiffened. She hadn't meant to be brusque. "It was a long time ago," she said, embarrassed to laugh off death.

"I'm . . . I'm sorry."

"No, no. Don't be. Really."

He took his arm back, flagged down the waitress for the bill. They waited without continuing on the subject or any subject. The fragrant air of the place was getting heavy.

"Thank you," she said when the waitress returned with his credit card and he signed the receipt, noted the total on a ledger in his phone. There weren't too many people left in the restaurant, a man paying cash at the counter, and a trio at a booth near the kitchen who seemed to be chummy with the owner. Comment about past loves aside, she wanted more of this. She wasn't ready to leave. She might have told him that right then, but her phone rang.

"I'm really sorry," she said, accepting the call once she saw the name on the screen, knowing the phone would ring again in minutes if she didn't answer.

Her gaze stayed on his as she listened, trying her best not to react. "Just check Venmo, okay?" She'd managed to squeeze any irritation from her voice, but she should have just turned off her phone altogether. Maybe calling for help hadn't been the smartest idea — why would she add discord to their already shaky home? It wasn't too late. She could say never mind, tell the woman not to come after all. But deep down, Willow still didn't believe she would actually show, move away from the only place she'd lived for nearly sixty years. And Willow had to try something. There weren't any other options. "Okay. Alright. Mmm-hmm. Do it tomorrow. That's good. Okay, bye."

The call had rattled her, the reality of what she'd done setting in. She could use a drink.

January tapped his hand on the counter. "That one of the hookups?"

She punched his shoulder softly. "I don't

have any hookups right now. What about you? You seeing anyone else?"

He'd already explained about his ex in their chats, called her a heathen, and hadn't seemed ashamed to describe her that way. The woman must have damaged him well.

"No. No, can't say I am. This online dating was just kind of a joke, really. Met you, but didn't take it too seriously. Until I *met* you. Started messaging with you." He chuckled. "Got those pictures."

She warmed, the upper parts of her thighs, and the parts above there. And more, all the way to her breasts and up her spine over her shoulders and neck. She pressed her hand into his, wondering how long it would take to get him inside her. If she didn't like the place so much, she might have grabbed him, dragged him into the bathroom just beyond the kitchen, and offered herself up on the sink.

"You think we should get out of here?" she said with a sharp nod pointing down to her lap, the layers of her summery dress drawn back. Had he touched her, put a hand just under the edge of the gauzy cotton, he would have discovered her pantyless.

He held her hand as they exited, the strawberry light at the end of the day lengthening the block in front of them. They arrived at his car, a European convertible barely used, and it occurred to her how little she knew about this man. "What is it that you do for a living, January?"

He winked, opening and closing the passenger door for her before walking around and getting in on his side. He started the ignition and drove away from the curb.

"No, really. What do you do?" They were headed downtown, toward her home, but surely he couldn't be taking her there? Had she even told him where she lived?

"Some of everything." He had worked in law enforcement up in Oakland, some PI work before getting his law degree, but then some investments had taken off and he'd launched a few online businesses that brought him down to Hollywood where he did behind-the-scenes stuff. Studio work.

"And now?"

"Now . . . I write papers."

"Papers? As in the *Los Angeles Times*? The *Sentinel*?"

"As in 'Continued Subjugation of the Black Male in Post-Assimilated Societies,' " he said, the formality of his voice exaggerated. "I didn't title that one. I was given the title and had to work with it."

"So what are you saying? You write papers?

127

For other people?"

He took them over the freeway, flipping their surroundings from suburban to industrial, sleepy oil derricks bobbing their heads into the ground. "Mostly Dominguez and Cal State Long Beach. A few LBCC students, but they've dropped off. Every now and then, I get a call from one of those USC kids. That's some big bank right there."

A hustler, but she should have known. Telling stories she wasn't good at. But hustlers? Attracting them, making love to them, giving money to them — she could write books on the topic. He'd probably sniffed her out, even over the wireless connection, knew that his occupation wouldn't worry her. He was the handsomest hustler yet.

They didn't go to her place. Or to his or a motel. Instead, he swerved into a parking garage downtown, half a block from the decaying movie theater and the empty building that had once housed an upscale furniture store. Someone had just enjoyed a joint in a nearby car, and someone else was testing the limits of his subwoofers. Another was urinating in the stairwell, even as police-radio chatter echoed from below. January apologized for these folks, explained that he just wanted to take her dancing. "You can dance, can't you?"

Of course she could dance, but she didn't tell him that. Who knew how her body might betray her, out of practice, not having been on a dance floor in years? It would come back, though, her rhythm innate. Besides, dancing together would predict their time in bed, allow them to see how their bodies responded to each other, if their movements synced well. This time, *she* took *his* hand, held it tight as they walked along the sidewalk to the club at a fast clip. After they'd sweated, bouncing song after song to hip-hop tunes with people a decade younger, a slower tune played. He held her near, her cheek finding the soothing rhythm of his heartbeat. They swayed to the music, Willow shutting her eyes, delighting in the sensation that she had drifted far away from home. "I love this."

Her own words tugged her out of her sloshy haze, and she asked God to tell her the music had been too loud for him to have heard. But January hugged his arms around her body more strongly and whispered that he loved *this* too, though she herself hadn't quite decided what *this* meant.

Willow opened her eyes and smiled, feeling empowered, brave. When she got home that night, she would start on a business proposal using Nickie's laptop in the dining room. January seemed to have a knack for writing. What a shame that she didn't plan to see him after this. If he reviewed it for her first, Victoria would be really impressed, wouldn't be able to talk her out of venturing out on her own when she decided to do so. January had his merits and would make a nice partner to some other woman one day.

Willow clasped him around his back, the two of them rocking back and forth until the song ended. She had a joint in her purse. She didn't care if he remembered her *love this* slip, but if they smoked it, maybe *she* wouldn't. And, at least for a few hours, she'd forget the mess she'd engineered. Then again, the Montrose women had been a mess for quite a long time.

11
AUGUSTA

Augusta had grown used to Willow leaving some evenings and returning at the darkest parts of night, only the moon and street-lights able to tell on her. She went on her escapades every month or so, but recently she'd been going out more often and arriving home later and later. Despite the sneaking around, the secret relations she had, Willow seemed the happiest of all the women in the house, the one who sang aloud and shook her hips when she heard a catchy jingle on TV, bid everyone good morning, afternoon, and night. Augusta only hoped Willow wasn't falling in love after all these years, thinking herself immune to it, getting careless with her heart, something especially easy for her to do. Unlike Augusta, unlike Victoria, Willow hadn't had a love of hers hexed away.

From time to time, Augusta would over-hear Willow's raucous laugh as she spoke on the phone, her flirty responses. Once, she'd walked past Willow's open door and heard her say, "You want to see my panties right now? They're black and lacy," which got Augusta's stomach to bubble, shocked that Willow had a man in her room, in this house. But when she stepped back to look inside, there was no man. Just a phone propped up on a pillow, Willow on one of those video calls she often made. Willow's self-confidence with men and her coquettish ways didn't surprise Augusta. She herself had had a flair for enticing men and tried her best not to judge.

There'd been dozens of clients at the shop for whom she'd helped lure a bedmate, a lover, a one-night stand. While yucca grew widely in the South and juniper berries worked quickly, Augusta's go-to fix for enticement had been calamus root.

An oil calling for calamus had stood out to her the day she'd flipped through Bela Nova's book, scrambling to find the right ingredients, the right words to make Dudley Lee notice her, see her in a new way. Calamus root. Such a powerful ingredient, mentioned in poems by great artists from before her time, and used by indigenous persons, who'd known its potential for centuries. The spell was really just a souped-up blessing oil, its contents written in Bela Nova's loopy script on a page of typewritten notes for love potions. Bela Nova was a masterful conjurer, and her recipe for the Test Their Heart oil required chestnuts, bay leaves, red maple flowers, and root of calamus. If her inklings were correct, once she used the oil, he'd leave Genevieve and pick Augusta instead, unable to deny his true feelings. Rather than doing so in the book, she scribbled their names on the page where she'd jotted down the spell: *Augusta M. for Dudley Lee B.*

The mixture had to be heated past its smoking point, a task Augusta did in the alley behind the Dew Drop Inn, the vapor and fumes making her eyes water, the pungency of the calamus fierce and yet delicious at the same time, smelling like something you might want to eat. What was left in the pot once the mixture cooled, she scraped away, adding fifteen drops of olive oil and a thread from Dudley Lee's clothing. She let it sit overnight in a container kept under her pillow as there weren't too many places to hide things in the shop. For nine successive mornings, she wouldn't say a word out loud before first taking the oil in the bathroom and pressing her thumb into the container, whispering Dudley Lee's name as she dabbed some on her heart, then her lips, then in the crook of her elbow. On the third morning, she'd come close to dropping to the floor when Bela Nova pointed at her. "Miss Augusta. Go on back in that bathroom and wash your face. You got some oily stuff above your eyebrows." But in the bathroom, she simply rubbed it in more. Later that afternoon, she rolled up the paper with her notes, with their names, and poked it into the flame as she boiled water on the stove.

A week passed, the oil running out exactly on the ninth day, when Dudley stopped by for lunch as he often did when his money was tight. A new and assured bravery in place, Augusta slipped her hand down his pants after Bela Nova rose from the table and excused herself to the restroom. Augusta shut her eyes and scooted toward him, fondled him. It would have been awkward to look him in the face. He hummed low, like a bear, until the sound of the commode flushing made him stiffen. Pushing himself away from her, he knocked over a glass, sending its contents across the table.

"Dudley Lee, you really need to work on yourself. Don't nobody want a clumsy husband." Bela Nova dried her hands on her moss-green dress speckled with gold, noticing the spill right away. She shook her head. "Don't go over your new in-laws' home spilling things, knocking shit down. Augusta, don't just sit there like you never seen a mess before. Go on and get a towel."

They'd both excused themselves shortly after, finding each other downstairs in the club while Bela Nova handled a customer. There was privacy backstage where the band would later set up, a little corner tucked behind a curtain. "I don't think I've ever loved anyone before. Besides my mama. Shoot, I didn't love Genevieve. She beautiful and everything, but we don't have nothing in common. I only proposed because my mama wanted me to. Not sure what it is, but I think I love you. Probably even more than I love my mama. And I could probably love you some more."

And Augusta understood what he meant. His words resonated with her, heightening the tingle she'd felt in her chest since first meeting him. She thought about her father, a man who chronically smiled, who went to work before she woke up and rarely returned before the oranges of dusk grew gray, a man she missed so much but worried about contacting, sure he'd be able to talk her out of her new life and convince her to return home. She realized what she felt for Dudley

Lee could be love as well, a different kind. "I can love you more too."

"I won't stay with Genevieve. I'll marry you instead." He kissed her, a kiss grand in its delivery, one she could still imagine clearly today, even with her eyes wide open.

She'd wanted to elope. To board the train to Chicago, DC, Los Angeles, and send a postcard to his mother telling her only once it had been done. But Dudley Lee was a proper son, despite this singular disappointment he'd cause by dismissing his prosperous fiancée and her family. He believed it better to visit the workshop, confess their decision as they stood with interlocked fingers. Bela Nova would appreciate their uprightness.

Bored with her same old television shows as she waited for Willow, Augusta got up from the couch and sat behind the laptop at the dining room table. She reached for the keyboard Victoria had purchased just for her, with large and colorful buttons. After her second stroke, she'd worked with a rehabilitation specialist to help her with speech. But when, after months, the undeniably clear words in her head left her mouth garbled, incomplete, or not at all, they worked on other methods for Augusta to communicate. The team had been so pleased when they'd given her a keyboard at the facility and she'd been able to type. But the problem with written exchange was the delay. Anger, displeasure, relief, hysteria, delirium all easily evaporated into indifference once she'd punched away with her fingers. The stress of it hurt her head, and the adaptive equipment settled in a box somewhere, dusty and likely obsolete with all the gadgets available these days. Now her family knew her shorthand, could decipher the nuanced variations of her expressions most times.

But she quite liked this new keyboard. It miraculously didn't even have to be plugged into the computer. With Nickie's help, she'd discovered websites where she could track down just about anything. She just had to be brave enough to look it up in the first place.

She hit the number *1* four times. Willow was never too secretive when entering the password Victoria had forced her to create on the now-shared laptop. The computer made its soft thinking noise and the screen grew colorful, showing the vivid lilac Willow had chosen for her background. A window popped up, just as it had when she'd watched Nickie use it. She clicked the box at the top of the page and with one finger typed a word she'd heard and seen many times: *Google.*

There appeared another box instructing her to search. She punched in the letters quickly before she could change her mind.

Bela Nova.

Her fizzy heart went flat once she saw the long list of results linking to sites about a Mexican band with the same name. It occurred to her that she might try Bela Nova's given name, and her date of birth, and as much supplementary information she could remember about the woman.

Fifteen minutes passed and nothing. But it had become a game, seeing what she could learn about anyone from the old gang. Though she struggled to recall names, she enjoyed the act of doing so, thinking about past times. The musty horn players who chewed tobacco when they weren't blowing, the gamblers, the flashy men and the women who fought over them, and the Dew Drop Inn itself, how its sticky floors kept her from slipping when she got around in heels. Augusta didn't know how the internet got answers, how so much about the past could be found online, but it could hold bits of her old life if she dared to look. She wanted to know what had become of everyone, but there weren't many answers on the computer, not for the folks she remembered. Not for Bela Nova and not for Dudley Lee.

A loud thump just beyond the dining room gave Augusta a jolt that could do damage to someone her age. When Willow flicked on the light to the family room, holding her shoes by the straps, Augusta picked up a nearby balled-up piece of aluminum foil and flung it with such ferocity that she hit her granddaughter near her temple. She hadn't known the strength she still had in her, but it could have just been adrenaline, Willow's loud entrance scaring her.

Willow's face first registered offense and confusion. It took only a moment, though, for her wide eyes to relax, for her brow to loosen. Then came a heavy laugh, and any remorse Augusta may have had for hitting the child with the foil quickly faded.

"Nan, you don't have to always wait up for me, you know. I'm not fifteen anymore." Bleary-eyed, Willow walked hard toward to the kitchen. Augusta caught the smell of reefer as she went past. "You hungry, Nana? You want some chicken pasta or maybe enchiladas?" Willow had an amazing ability to whip up dishes and would do so even in the late of night. "I'll just make us grilled cheeses."

That would be fine. She could nibble on the crust, let Willow eventually finish off the rest of the sandwich as she recounted her evening.

With her granddaughter so absorbed, Augusta turned back to the computer, half listening to her, something about the red velvet cakes at the Bake-N-Broil, that she should bring the owners a slice of the family's caramel cake.

"Alright, Nana. You want bacon on yours?"

Augusta held out her arm, lifting a thumb.

Just as she was about to close the screen, she noticed a small box in the corner. *New Notification,* it said. After closing the window where she'd been typing, she could see a picture, the person who'd sent the message, Augusta presumed. A brown-skinned woman with long, gray twists. A chill crossed her heart as she read the name. She looked up from the screen to confirm that Willow was still busy in the kitchen. Then, she clicked the box to read the message from a Ramona Decuir.

Hey there. Sorry to bother you but you wouldn't happen to be Madelyn Montrose's daughter, would you?

140

The words screamed at her at a decibel high enough to rupture her eardrums. She minimized the box, but then understood she had to figure out how to make it pop up again so that she could throw it away, make it disappear forever. Her armpits began to perspire, a phenomenon in that her body had stopped its attempts to cool itself after menopause. But beads of sweat dotted her upper lip and just above her brow now. The scrambling had done it, the clicking and typing and moving things around in search of the message. She thought about just smashing the machine with her forearm, then battering it with a potato masher from the kitchen drawer until the screen blinked dark, if that's what it took.

Finally, she clicked something that brought the message back. She was about to delete it, but then remembered that Ramona, Willow's aunt she'd never met, could be persistent, often stopping by the shop with her brother Harlowe, seeking out the most inexpensive ditty bag she could buy.

Not me

Hopefully, that would keep the woman

from reaching out to Willow again. But a worry remained. How had Ramona tracked down Willow? How had she even known her brother had a child with Madelyn? Ramona had left town before Madelyn was showing, Augusta ensuring she didn't return.

She deleted the message and closed the laptop.

12
NICKIE

Nickie didn't smile when, at two beats before the bell, Felix walked through the door of her third period, carrying no backpack, no notebook. It could have been a smile if every muscle that could twist and soften Nickie's face hadn't already been worn down, stretched to capacity. Strained and anxious as she wondered if she'd ever see Felix again. A few times, she'd even imagined her mom walking through that door, sitting in the front row, a witness to her lie. Nickie took the Ayida Wedo charm between her thumb and forefinger and held it for a few seconds. She thought she felt something different than when she'd touched it other times. She didn't know quite how to describe the sensation, but it had started to erase the specks of doubt.

Felix took the seat next to her and put his feet on the chair in front of them. "So they let you in?" His question cut the silence, an indoor voice turned up too high, prompting a girl rows ahead to turn around, get a look at who was talking.

"Yeah. Mr. Gonzalez from the park wrote a letter. Said how well I did in the class this summer," she said, trying to relax. She was proud of herself for asking Mr. Gonzalez for assistance, a sneaky email sent while completing a quick task during her rotation as receptionist, her mother only three feet away.

"What's all that shit on your face?"

The teacher, a boy-man with oodles of corkscrewed black curls, was still settling his papers from the previous period. The girl in front of them was now giving them her unabashed attention. Nickie was aware of her just as she was of Felix's eyes on her cheeks. The *shit* on her face was the two hundred dollar eyeliner, mascara, concealer, and shadow superbox her aunt had purchased for her at the mall. She'd never known of such boxes before, such shortcuts and cheats, until Aunt Willow's tour of the department-store beauty section.

If he got close enough, he might still smell the hot planks of the flat iron, the stinky burn clinging to each strand. Aunt Willow owned a salon-quality stove, calling herself *almost* licensed for how regularly she used to straighten her own hair in her youth. They'd gotten up early to press Nickie's.

She tucked her orange lips inside her mouth, licking away much of the shine. "You don't like it?" She wanted to make her lips disappear, to hide her dusted cheeks.

Felix tilted his head. "I guess. It's kind of much, right?"

She erased invisible words from a page in her notebook, wiped away the rubbery pink crumbs. "Just for today. I have my senior pictures."

"Today? I thought I was doing them. You said you were going to cancel the school picture appointment."

It hadn't been Nickie's intention to lie, but what choice did she have now? The teacher cleared his throat, and Nickie wondered if Felix would resume their conversation, start a note. Tell her he was sorry, that he was overreacting, and that she looked really pretty today.

But instead, he asked if she had a pen or pencil, then slumped and gave his attention to the teacher as she reached in her backpack pocket and pulled out a red gel roller, her favorite.

"Good morning, everyone. Apologies for the late start. It will happen again, I can assure you. So, my name's Mark, and you can call me Mark. I graduated from here five years ago." He continued his opening, a lengthy life story for someone so young. She wanted to listen, to hear more about his promise for a kick-ass semester, but her head was full of Felix. How he'd questioned her, even chided her. How he hadn't seemed glad to see her.

By the time the teacher finished, Felix had leaned over on her desk and filled up three pages in her notebook with doodles, each one worth saving, framing, just for its intricacy. He had a genius for details, spending minutes on the angled corner of an eye, the indent at the top of a lip. He drew girls, mostly. A car every now and then, but usually girls. Caucasian ones with more hair than body, and bodies that were mostly breasts. Nickie tried not to mind, tried to view them as beautiful and fascinating. But she wondered if these were the girls of his fantasies, the girls he'd choose to be with if they ever chose to be with someone like him. And since they didn't, was he just settling for her? As a good friend or someone he liked to hang with or whatever he felt for her?

The nosy girl from earlier got up from her seat, walking over a stack of photography magazines, her face softening for Felix as she passed them to him. They were to select one, keep it over the week for a homework assignment. Felix didn't hand the stack to Nickie but instead shuffled through it and gave her a *LensWork* from May–June 2000. He took for himself a *Leica Fotografie International,* then sent the stack to the guy nearest him, who hadn't removed his headphones all morning.

They were supposed to get started right away, look for two to three images that affected them, research the photographer, take shots themselves emulating the artists' styles. "I don't want a recreation, folks. I want a reinterpretation," Mark said. "Figure out the photographer's essence, their motivation. Consider what it was they needed, and ask yourself what similar need you have. Then," he said, tapping two fingers on his desk as he looked around the room, "and only then do you pick up your camera."

Her camera, which she hadn't yet figured out how to get. Aunt Willow had been great, taking her shopping, treating her to lunch, doing her hair. Nickie couldn't ask her to purchase a camera. Even a good used one would be a few hundred bucks. Between her savings and the cash stashed in her room, she could probably buy one herself, but then she'd have to hide it.

She had a week until the assignment was due. For now, she'd focus on the magazine, perhaps the only person in the room who would follow Mark's instruction to review it, rather than shooting a thousand shots as soon as class ended.

"We can work on this together if you're done avoiding me."

There. He'd said something. The dearth of communication the past couple of weeks had been just as real to him as it had been for Nickie. Her lips began to curl into a smile, but she had to play coy. She couldn't let him catch the delight in her face.

"I know you said you had to work, but you didn't even text or . . ."

"I wasn't avoiding you."

"Then straight up ignoring me? What's that shit about?" he asked, finally looking up from his magazine.

"I wasn't ignoring you either."

"So, what do you call it? I missed the exhibit at LACMA waiting for you to write me back. They were showing Hans Richter. It was supposed to be fucking brilliant."

Write her back? She hadn't received any messages from him. She'd never heard of Hans Richter and also wasn't really sure what LACMA was. She guessed it was a museum. He talked about going to museums a lot, wanted to spend his summers in New York and France and Italy and Spain and Prague inside them. She would have jumped to join him at damn near any exhibit. "That's really weird. I never got anything. I thought *you* were ignoring *me.*"

They were the only ones in the class talking. The rest were deep into their selected periodical, flipping through glossy pages. Even the girl in front of them was busy, glasses on so she could read the print, and the teacher too was distracted, back to the paperwork he'd earlier abandoned. The bell would ring in four minutes.

Nickie wiggled her phone from her pocket and opened her text messages.

"I sent it through Insta."

When she opened the app, there was indeed a new message from Friday. An embarrassed warmth washed over her face. "I didn't know I had a message."

"Did you turn your notifications off?" He took the phone from her, thumbing his way into her settings. "Yep, you turned off everything. And look, you're on airplane mode."

He tilted the phone so she could get a glimpse at the plane icon in the corner of the screen. Once he adjusted everything, he returned it to her, smiling. "Oh, Nick. I didn't realize you were so bad at tech. Good thing you have a friend like me to help you out." He was right. She'd never even been on a plane and hadn't even known there was such a thing as airplane mode. Had her mother done that?

When he lifted his pen from a new page, he'd drawn Nickie's amulet, the details remarkably accurate. She thought he might give it to her but he folded the paper up and put it in his pocket.

The bell rang and the teacher rose and clapped his hands. "Alright, everyone. Pack it up. I will see you tomorrow."

Felix dropped his feet to the floor, stood, handing Nickie her notebook and pen. Their time together had passed too quickly — she hadn't used it right. She hadn't asked about his schedule, what he had next, what period he had lunch.

He pushed his hands into his pockets, his upper body rounded, his head down as he walked Nickie to her next class. "So you want to go out Friday? Bowling or something? I can pick you up."

So this is what it felt like to be asked out on a date. If this were her movie, there'd be a close-up on her now, doe-eyed and dreamy, cartoon hearts circling her.

But then the villain appeared, her mother, sitting on her shoulder, red horns and all. *No dates for you, Nickie. You have to go to college and help the world. You have to use your gift!*

On her other shoulder, she didn't know who to imagine. Sure, her aunt was willing to help her in secret, but she didn't see Willow standing up to her mother. Would she support a date? Would any of the women in her house? Or were they all too afraid of her mom? With a solution not making itself clear, she resorted to the strategy that had seemed to keep things from imploding so far. "I don't think I can this weekend. I have to . . . go with my grandmother to San Diego." She was getting pretty good at lying. Who knew where *San Diego* came from? But it somehow sounded okay.

He took one of her hands as they strolled, squeezed it once and traced her palm with a finger. Then he inhaled. "I guess it's hard, being the one everyone depends on."

She nodded, knowing her voice would give her away. Outside her English lit class, he told her he'd meet her at lunch. He'd get them some Funyuns and some Doritos too.

"By the way, your hair looks nice. I didn't tell you earlier because I didn't want you to think I was sucking up so you'd let me borrow a pen."

Nickie sputtered out a laugh, like someone had just whacked her on the back, forcing it out.

"I'm serious. You're . . . you're very attractive. I thought I should tell you. Sometimes, us guys have a hard time saying things like that. Anyway. And that's what I meant about the makeup. You don't need it." He settled his eyes on the ground in front of her, tapping his foot.

"Oh. Um, thanks." She wondered if she should tell him that he was very attractive himself, but that seemed a stupid thing to say. Couldn't she be more original?

She didn't have a chance to respond. He started walking backward, turning around and heading off once she waved. As she entered her classroom, she wondered if the previous moment had really just happened. Three steps inside, she stopped. "Thursday's Attraction Spell?" she muttered softly, grinning to herself. In her periphery, she caught the crabby stare of a girl wearing a thin blazer and halter top in the aisle closest to her, then continued to the back corner of the room, a place where she hoped to lie low and write Felix's name a hundred times. Just maybe, her aunt's spell had actually worked.

■ ■ ■ ■

OCTOBER

■ ■ ■ ■

13
Augusta

Augusta wasn't a fan of all of Victoria's clients. Many of them ignored her, not even glancing toward the family room as they stepped inside and headed for the reception. Yet there were those who waved, blew her kisses, remembered her birthday when it came around. Her favorites went out of their way to greet her every visit, coming over to say hello despite the sign directing clients elsewhere. One of these new favorites was a man named Russell, who'd even gone so far as kissing her hand when he first introduced himself. A little old-school, even in Augusta's opinion, but still, she found it charming. Since that first meeting, she'd sneak a look at the daily schedule to make sure she was downstairs in time for his appointments. Noticing his name earlier this morning, she'd been inspired to change her hairstyle, letting it hang long over one shoulder, giving him her best side when he entered. He was a nice-looking cat — a tender face and a telegenic smile.

He'd arrived a couple of months ago for a one-time session. Just one because he didn't think much of therapists, the thorny idea of kicking around his personal sagas with a stranger, he said. But he returned weeks later, cleared by his insurance for twenty sessions annually. "Talking about things has been good for me," he'd confessed.

Augusta knew better. It was Victoria. She'd touched his hand, shook it that first meeting while he thanked her for her time. There was power in that touch. That contact had shaken him something good, just as it had Victoria, though her granddaughter would never admit it. Shaken her upside down and inside out.

Initially, it had flummoxed her — why Victoria hadn't realized that she was sick with love over this man. She had to have noticed, with her gift to discern and connect with folks. Sometimes, Augusta still considered how she might have used her abilities had they been as sharp as Victoria's. How many more clients she could have brought into the shop back in Louisiana. Though Augusta certainly couldn't feel sentiments as innately as Victoria, she had the eyes to see the girl falling in love, something that worried Augusta. As stalwart about the curse as Victoria was, even *she* could sink back down into the muddiness of love if the attraction was strong enough. When it had happened before, Augusta had been complicit, throwing up her hands once Victoria and Jimmie had eloped. Her granddaughter deserved to be in a relationship if that's what she wanted, to be caressed and doted on by someone who loved her, to enjoy all the wonders love brought, but she knew this wasn't a reality for Victoria. If Russell ever tried to make a real move, beyond their flirting, Augusta wouldn't remain idle this time. Victoria wasn't like her sister. Augusta was fairly certain Willow had had relations with men, plenty of them. Victoria, though, couldn't compartmentalize in the same way. No matter what it would mean for Russell if the two ever became intimate, for Victoria, sex would mean love. She was just like Augusta. Assured as she was that Victoria would never cross the line again after Jimmie, especially with a client, she'd keep watch on those two.

Today, Russell arrived a few minutes early, letting his hello echo a couple moments before entering. Aimed for the small reception area, he caught the tail end of Augusta's wave and turned back to return it, a mini karate chop.

"I didn't see you. Hadn't meant to be rude."

She straightened up some as he crossed the foyer to the family room.

"How you doing? It's warm outside. You're right to stay put on that couch. The air conditioning feels good," he said.

"You know she can't talk, right?" Willow had joined Russell from the reception. That was Willow, always showing up from nowhere, and probably thinking she was doing a favor by jumping in. There was a time when, in front of strangers, her granddaughters would mention her inability to speak and she'd be mortified — talk like that stirred up pity and nothing good had ever come from pity. With time, she'd appreciated her inability to speak, didn't mind the silence that encircled her. She'd learned to enjoy herself as company. But every now and then, it was nice to interact with someone new, even if in the form of nods, shrugs, and discouraging glares.

"Good afternoon, Ms. Willow." Russell bowed slightly. Augusta noticed the thinning hair on top of his head.

"Hello, Russell. And again, *Willow* is fine." Faint shadows darkened the thin lines under Willow's eyes. Too much wine and too little sleep. Her thirty-five years were catching up to her, were about to pass her up if she wasn't careful. That child always such a whip. A meddlesome one too.

"Just coming over to say hello to your grandmother," he said. "And yes, I know about Mrs. Montrose's stroke. Your sister told me what happened, back when I started."

Augusta resisted the urge to perform some kind of trick, the two of them peering down at her like she was a circus animal. Willow said she needed to go over a form with him and so he excused himself, telling Augusta he'd see her next week if not on his way out. But she wasn't ready for him to leave. She wanted him to stick around longer so she could stare at him some more, find a truth in his eyes. With force, her body became a singular muscle, all cells working together to choke out one word: *Wait.*

Willow pivoted back around at the sound, a gruff hum. "What, Gran? You want your glass of Tang?"

Augusta leaned back in her chair, very slightly shaking her head.

"I'm going to take Mr. Parker over to Victoria. After that, I'll get you anything you need." Willow's voice poured out warmly, like syrup going over pancakes. But the fake stuff made with aspartame. The sweetness left a strange aftertaste. Clients always took to Willow's affability, but sometimes she went a little too far.

Willow guided Russell away, and Augusta reached for the remote. She relaxed back against the cushions and swirled her braid around her hand, settling on a home shopping show, the volume muted so she could hear her own thoughts, let her mind drift away. But blissful memories of her younger years were chased away, replaced with Bela Nova — her cackling laugh, her glowing eyes, her cold hands.

Augusta wore a dress as purple as could be imagined, soaked in dye the night before she and Dudley Lee would meet with Bela Nova. She'd done the same to his pocket square. They needed to extract magic from wherever possible. The purple for control, summoning the woman's will. She'd tied her hair back with a red ribbon. Around her neck she'd hung a metal amulet depicting a symbol of the loa Damballa Wedo, who'd make true whatever words she would speak to Bela Nova in the dank, dark workshop. An oil infused with rosemary, basil, and lavender, which she'd been saving for a visit with her parents, whom she hadn't seen in two years, she poured over her shoulders and Dudley Lee's scalp. Could there be enough preparation? She didn't think so. Not when it came to a showdown with her teacher. She exhaled, trying not to let any of her hope seep out with her breath.

They opened the workshop door to find Bela Nova in her chair, facing her framed painting of Papa Legba, a hunched-over gray man, scuds of smoke from the pipe in his mouth circling him. Disquisitive eyes, a frown seemingly already in place, she lit a tall black candle on a table next to her and told them to come in and sit. They didn't hold hands. Didn't sit very close to one another.

"How you doing, Mama?" Dudley Lee began.

"I'm doing alright, I suppose."

Augusta stayed very still.

"I . . . I want to tell you that I've made a decision."

Bela Nova drew a cigarette from the satchel she kept wrapped around her waist, lit it from the black candle's flame. "What's that, Dudley Lee?"

He turned to Augusta, searching for the right words, asking her with his eyes for help. But she stared down at her knees.

"Must be something I'm not gonna like very much, all that purple the both of you come in here wearing. What is it, you lost some money? How much is it? Because I sure don't have anything left. Not with all the cash I'm spending on this wedding of yours."

"That's what I want to talk to you about."

Bela Nova took a drag of her cigarette, angled forward to get a better listen. Her eyes glowed in the darkness, round and shiny. Red at the edges. At that moment, Augusta believed the woman could have snapped them both in two using just her mind if she wanted to.

"Hold on, son, just a moment, now. Hold on because I've got this feeling you're about to tell me something quite ridiculous. Like you've fallen in love with missy right here." She clicked her tongue.

"Mama, just listen to me, please."

"Because if that's what you're here to tell me, you can just save your breath. You have a future with Genevieve. Understand? This is an opportunity to bring our families together. Whatever you think you got going on with Augusta, it's just a fling. You're only sprung off her pretty face. But that won't last because it's lust, not love. Genevieve, on the other hand, got roots. A Southern University gal. You can't go wrong with that." These things she said as if Augusta were downstairs instead of next to him on the couch, and in the soothing, simple voice she reserved for her most reticent clients. She went on and on until, at last, he nodded when asked again if he understood. "That's good, Dudley Lee. Now, go on. Go on over to Genevieve's. Bring her some flowers. Something yellow."

He got up without a word to Augusta or a glance in her direction. Her forehead was heavy with sweat, her hands ached from wringing as she'd listened to the woman's words.

"Did this really make sense to you, girl?" Bela Nova stood in front of her, withdrawing another cigarette. "You've been with me, what, two years? And now you know everything, don't you? Either that, or you're not as bright as I thought. And even if you're desperate enough to force a man on yourself, why choose my Dudley Lee, already betrothed? You got your pick of the men come into the Dew every night. Not all of them are sleazy, and a couple few are good-looking."

Augusta bit down gently on her bottom lip, wondering what she could do. She wondered if she'd been wrong about the spell. If he was truly meant to be with Augusta, he would have stayed.

"You used that spell I taught you last month, didn't you?"

"Which one?"

Bela Nova sat next to her, almost right on top of her. The smoke from the cigarette burned Augusta's eyes. "The one with the needles, where you break them three times and write down the names of the couple you want to break up."

As the woman explained it, she remembered bits and pieces of the spell. It had so many steps, Augusta had gotten bored. There was a part about using black, red, and green candles, hanging them upside down. Twelve of them, burning each for one hour a day. And something about putting dog shit in a paper bag on the twelfth day. She'd laughed to herself as Bela Nova talked through the spell, knowing she'd never do anything that involved dog shit.

Bela Nova had assumed it was true, that Augusta had used this particular spell, and so she dragged one of the chairs from the dinette set and climbed on top, not to reach her book but a hatbox from which she withdrew a thin stack of pages. "Now I gotta do some unhexing. Need to figure out an uncrossing potion, something to return Dudley Lee's affection back to Genevieve." Whatever it was the woman cooked up, it smelled like a solvent. Like turpentine. Like a solution that would skin you from the inside if you dared to sip it. It had to be strong, Bela Nova said. "And don't think I'm going to apologize for making you drink this. You brought this on, my sweetheart. Using magic to steal a man. Working your own hex. That's the lowest of sins. Have you not learned anything in all this time? I mean, you can follow instructions well. Just got no damn common sense. And you really thought you could outplay me? You don't know me at all. Messing with my boy."

She might have vomited the concoction right away if Bela Nova hadn't used her hands to lock Augusta's jaw shut after she drank, one arm around her head for leverage, the woman's long fingers frigid on her skin. Then, she left the workshop, abandoning Augusta on the floor, prone, her back heaving as she sobbed. For the day and a half the woman was gone, Augusta considered going back home, apologizing to her mother and hugging her father.

When Bela Nova returned, she brought with her a large trunk, secondhand, a long gash running along one side, dented in several places. From one of the bags she carried, Bela Nova took out her spell book, cackling to get Augusta's attention. She held the book high above her head, making a show of tucking it away in the trunk, latching the lid closed with a padlock, placing the key in her bosom. "To stop you from stealing, love. You can't have him, you understand?"

Augusta refused to nod, had some contentment in knowing the old woman had unhexed the wrong hex, that there might still be a chance with Dudley Lee, that she might not be tied to the shop forever. She'd have to be careful, patient, though there was not much time until the wedding.

After using what little strength the woman had in that thin, long body of hers to push the trunk to the corner next to the bookshelf, Bela Nova brewed tea, brought Augusta a cup, and placed an arm of comfort around her. "You and Dudley Lee are just not right for each other. How about this? I can see if Melvin Sharpe might want to call on you one night. That man knows how to dress. I once heard he has twenty-seven suits. Can you believe that? He's a much better catch than old Clarence, chasing anything underage." Years later, she'd find Clarence's name in the book under a spell he couldn't have possibly been able to afford. It made her wonder if she'd been set up, Bela Nova orchestrating their meeting, him bringing her to the club once the woman learned her connection to Lanora. That had been the first blow, Augusta had concluded, in their tit-for-tat relationship. After this meeting, Augusta was down again, but she wouldn't stay there. Dudley Lee returned indeed, sneaking inside, as Bela Nova slept, to whisper his intentions — it was Augusta he wanted to be with.

Both of her granddaughters thought Bela Nova was simply a woman jealous of Augusta's abilities. Augusta had taught them to believe that. She just hadn't the guts yet to let her family know the trouble she'd conjured up all those years before, how she'd wronged Bela Nova just as much as the woman had wronged her — maybe more so — and with that had hurt them all.

A car door slammed, the sound disturbing her thoughts. Outside the window, she saw a cab pulled up along the sidewalk, one of those hybrid cars, painted a vivid yellow. She recognized the passenger standing at the curb, knew her by the shape of her shoulders, the way she bent her body, as if her muscles ached. She wanted to scream, to yell a warning to Victoria, who'd be most shaken by her arrival.

After all these years, her daughter, Madelyn, had made her way to California. Augusta had figured this day would come, and leave it to her daughter to have the worst timing ever, ready to add to Victoria's stress. Madelyn had been born with a natural confidence she'd never had, standing tall, a hand on a cocked hip as she waited for the driver to make change, snapping her fingers to get him to count faster.

Augusta wanted to see Madelyn before the rest of the family did. She'd be able to tell just by the glint in her daughter's eyes whether her arrival was an earnest attempt at reconciliation or just another act of recklessness. She opened the door before Madelyn could knock.

"Mama."

A garbage bag sat on the porch at her feet, the belongings inside threatening to puncture their way through. From her shoulder hung a stuffed backpack. Madelyn's expression shifted, happiness easing into relief, as if she'd been ringing doorbells all morning, thankful to have finally landed at the right place. She sprang forward, wrapping her twiggy arms around Augusta, who didn't reciprocate the hug. Didn't move at all. She waited for her daughter to step back again so she could get a look at her, but all she could discern about Madelyn was that she'd gotten her teeth fixed. They were all there, and immaculate. She'd made herself up as best as she could, evidently inspired by the eighties, bright pink blush brushed over her cheeks, a blue powder shading her eyelids.

She walked back over to the couch and sat, Madelyn following with her bags. Her daughter asked about Victoria and Willow, wondering where they were, and little Nickie. From the side-table drawer, Augusta yanked out a crumpled pack of cigarettes and a lighter.

"Mama, what you doing? Those things will kill you."

She lit the cigarette and took a long drag, glad to feel the scratch of tobacco at the back of her throat. Her eyes closed, Augusta recited to herself the short prayer that Bela Nova used when faced with impossible circumstances.

Lift us up, St. Jude, and we won't be able to let you down.

14
VICTORIA

Russell was speaking to her in swift, abbreviated sentences and with an animation that energized the room. With him, and only with him, she mentally crept away during sessions. Pictures flashed in her head, images of the two of them, touching and laughing and embracing. Enjoying an experience together. It wasn't right to think this way about a client, someone whose insurance was writing her paycheck, but he was so engaging, the way he used his hands to illustrate what had occurred over the last week, Victoria sometimes forgot to do her job.

Willow had called her out a couple of weeks before. "Vic, I never hear you say anything when he comes in for a session. I imagine you just sitting there, staring at him all googly-eyed."

"Ain't nobody googly-anything, Willow. I would never cross that line. I could lose my license."

"What if he stopped being your client?"

"Why would he stop being my client? And anyway, there's some kind of waiting period. Like, a year or two."

"Well, shoot! We should connect him to another therapist right now. A year or two? Although, I guess you've gone all this time . . ." She squinted.

Her sister was intolerable. "Willow, stop playing. And I've told you to stay out of my sessions."

"Well, somebody needs to help the poor man out. It certainly hasn't been you."

Victoria felt like she could spit fire at her sister. "Willow, I swear, you keep it up and I'm gonna replace you with Nana. I can't keep you around here risking my license with your eavesdropping."

"I'm not eavesdropping on purpose. That man's voice shoots right through the door." For years, Victoria had neglected her self-promise for better insulation, a texture or padding to absorb sounds. She had to admit, though, it had become a pattern, she and Russell chitchatting, playing catch-up like longtime friends.

Today she was going to ask the tough questions. He'd started by mentioning the plant that sat on her window's ledge, a dracaena. After a redirect, he tried to talk about the piano in the corner of the office, then about the Lakers.

"Russell, this has to stop. We're not here to talk about me. Understand? You're paying money for these sessions."

As his eyes met hers, she saw the full hurt on his face and quickly felt bad for the tone she'd taken. She wasn't herself. Never really seemed herself when meeting with him. She didn't want to acknowledge her feelings for Russell, especially with all the speeches she'd recently given Nickie about and against men. Yet here she was dizzy in thought.

Victoria snapped back to it when Russell began speaking about his ex-wife, how he hated to admit his loneliness since she'd left him. He fumbled with all the reasons he hadn't been enough for her. He was too chatty but also boring and needy, he said. "I sit here with you once a week and something happens. I just feel . . . settled. Comfortable. Shoot, I guess I should have been doing this for years. My wife, she certainly never liked hearing me go on and on. So I apologize, Ms. Victoria. I really do. I'll try my best to focus. I know we got a lot of work to do with me."

She wondered if Willow had heard his

speech. That was poor judgment, letting her sister's words poke at her. Sometimes she regretted how she'd allowed Willow to involve herself in the business all these years and never corrected her whenever she overstepped.

"Well, thank you for sharing that with me, Russell. So, what were you saying about my . . . What did you call it?"

Russell smirked. "No wonder the plant is near dying. You don't even know the name of it. I suppose you're too busy for those sorts of things, taking such good care of your clients. And your family. All the beautiful women in this house. You must love them terribly, the way they seem so happy all the time, always friendly and smiling."

Victoria kept herself from a full-on laugh but permitted herself to smile. Did he not see the blue-black cloud hovering over the house, raining all kinds of staleness and woe? Did he not hear the gruff demands of the loa yelling for him to run? "I do love them."

"You're a nurturer. I see it. Remind me of my mother, never let herself have any fun."

Victoria tried but failed to come up with a response that wasn't trite or insincere.

"What do you do to have fun?" He'd relaxed his frame into the couch, resting his arms along its back.

"Oh, I don't know. Don't watch much TV these days. I used to read, but I need to get new glasses."

"You should try one of those audiobooks. Sometimes I listen to them on my drive."

"That's not a bad idea. Oh, and cooking."

"You can put your foot in it?"

She didn't fight her laugh. "Do you know where we're from? Shoot. When I feel like it, I can cook, bake, barbecue. I'll shuck. I'll whip. Shoot, I even used to catch fish back in the day."

Russell slapped his thigh, a glint of delight in his eyes. "We should go sometime."

"Go where?"

"Fishing."

"Oh. Well, I . . ." Victoria stood, rubbing her hands together. Her foot began to itch, so badly that she had to bend and squirm it inside her shoe. She'd had a similar itch before.

Nickie's father, Jimmie, had been one of half a dozen guys Willow went out with her junior year, each with a similar profile: athletic, confident, popular. Except Jimmie, a senior at another high school who was into comic books and presided over the chess club. The same day Willow told her that she wasn't seeing Jimmie anymore, he showed up at the house later in the afternoon, somehow knowing that Willow wouldn't be there. He asked if he could come inside.

"We're not really supposed to have company over when our grandmother is gone," Victoria had explained.

"Really? I've hung out here a bunch of times."

She wasn't sure what he wanted, what he was doing there now that he and Willow had broken up, but she could tell he liked her. And she'd *felt* it too, the itchiness along the arch of her foot signaling that he was the right kind of man to fall for.

It wasn't until weeks later, by then sprung like never before, that Victoria felt compelled to confess her new relationship to Willow. "I have to tell you something," Victoria said one day after school.

Willow didn't look up from the CD insert she held, the cardboard folded open so she could read the lyrics to the song playing on their stereo. "You're having Principal Castellanos' baby and you want me to be the godmother."

"No, Will. I'm . . . I'm going out with Jimmie. Jimmie Wilkes."

Willow put down the insert and looked

over at Victoria, seated on her bed. "Jimmie?"

"Yeah. I mean, I know you two weren't serious. He wasn't really your type, right? But he's really nice. I like him a lot."

"Oh." Willow shifted her weight, sitting back on her heels. "Hey, that's great. He is . . . Jimmie is very nice."

"I know, isn't he?"

"Just be careful. I don't want him to hurt you. Break up with you out of the blue, you know?"

Victoria laughed. "Why would he hurt me? Anyway, please don't say anything to Nana. Just like I never say anything about the guys you bring over." Victoria beamed as she sat thinking of him, tuning in to the song Willow played about the wondrous things that love could reveal.

Victoria jumped when Russell cleared his throat. She smiled, hoping she hadn't drifted off long.

"So you'll take me up on it? There's a few good spots off the bike path, near the marina."

"Oh, I don't really fish anymore. We better, uh . . ." She looked at her watchless wrist, then at the clock. They'd gone over their time. The itchiness intensified, sliding into an ache. "I'll see you next week, Russell." She did her best not to land her gaze on his as he got up, though she could tell he wanted to say more. Victoria made it to the door in just a few hurried steps, opening it to the low hum of music from the speaker on Willow's desk.

"Something this time next week, Willow."

"Um, Vic?"

"Yes." She had walked back into her office, ready to remove her shoe but anticipating the pain would dull once Russell left.

"We have a . . . visitor." Willow's voice was strained, and when Victoria looked over at her, there was an uneasiness to her face. Victoria stepped back out of her office.

"Victoria! You finally put on some good weight."

At the reception area's entrance, just beyond the foyer, stood her Nanagusta, the red of her cheeks emboldened. Latched around one of her arms was her mother.

Madelyn Montrose. She'd last come to visit over a decade ago when Nanagusta was in the hospital following her second stroke, had been in the room when the doctor gave her prognosis.

"Aphasia, which can manifest itself in a wide range of ways."

"Aphasia? What, will she have to carry one

177

of those EpiPens?" Madelyn had asked.

The doctor clarified, then furthered her explanation, telling them that, with therapy, Nanagusta would likely recover movement on her left side, but they'd have to wait to see how well she understood language, if she'd ever regain her verbal abilities.

While Willow and Victoria wrestled with this news, Madelyn shrugged, sure, she said, that Augusta would be fine — they just needed to give things time. Then she'd asked for the keys to the house and caught a cab to their home. Late that evening, after guiding a bleary-eyed Nickie up the stairs to her room, Victoria discovered that her mother had left, taking with her the cash stored in her office desk drawer, a faux-fur coat that had yet to be worn, and the leftover box of fried chicken from the day before that Victoria had planned on eating for dinner. Weeks later, she called the office number to apologize, telling Willow her probation officer had never authorized the visit. She'd abandoned them once again when they needed her most.

Any possible excuse, promise, or justification her mother could come up with now would be a lie she'd heard before. She had no problem picking up the woman's bags and walking them across the street to the park, where Madelyn could stand and wait for a ride back from wherever she came. Or to anywhere — she didn't care where her mother went. Victoria just wanted her to leave.

Her sister returned from walking Russell out and sat at the desk, a smile glued to her face. She and Madelyn had reconnected during Willow's four-year stint in New Orleans over fifteen years ago, a bond that somehow made her sister more forgiving of their mother's antics. Willow called every Mother's Day, sent her money on her birthdays. Victoria didn't even have the woman's phone number.

"Look how healthy she looks, Vic," Willow said, leaning back in her chair and studying their mother as if she could really perceive anything different about the woman aside from the wash of gray that had taken over her head.

"I have the money I borrowed last time I was here, Vic." She waved an envelope, then put it on the reception desk when Victoria didn't accept it from her.

"The money you stole?" Victoria asked.

"No, I left you a note. You didn't see it?"

Victoria clenched her jaw.

Madelyn took a step toward Victoria, trying to lock eyes with her. "I understand if you don't want me to stay. But I'm hoping you can give me just a couple of weeks. Give me a chance to get a job, someplace to live. You're my family. I need to be out here near you. I've been clean for years now. Just didn't have the nerve to show my face here until now."

She was already dealing with so much, and the idea of Madelyn in her house threatened to knock the whole place down. Her mother would say too much, would stir things up, would not mind her own damn business. While snooping, she hadn't come across any signs that something further had happened between Nickie and Felix, but things were still tenuous. She'd kept up with her petitions, but sometimes the loa took their time. While they'd surely understand Victoria's long-held frustration with her mother, it didn't seem like the right time to risk losing their favor by treating Madelyn the way she deserved. She had to show them that she could extend kindness, even when it didn't make sense to do so. Even Sousson Pannan would approve, a loa of the most terrible type, his skin specked with ulcers and rash, his mouth full of goblin teeth.

"Two weeks," Victoria said. That evening, she'd light fourteen candles on her altar, reducing the number she burned each day until it was time for her mother to leave. She picked up the envelope and counted out six hundred-dollar bills. "Willow can show you the guest room. And you still owe another twenty-five dollars." She didn't really care about the money. She'd been hurt that her mother had stolen instead of just asking for it.

The women watched her leave the reception area and round the corner to the foyer. She stopped herself from taking her offer back when, halfway up the stairs, she heard her mother say, "Boy, those long hours have done a number on her, haven't they?"

15
WILLOW

Willow's body ached. After working at the desk, she'd spent the rest of the day helping Madelyn move into her new room. Her first morning in the house, she'd located a garage sale, the Goodwill, and a Salvation Army, and had used most of what remained of the money Willow had sent her to buy furniture and have it delivered to the house. The guest room upstairs already had a bed and a dresser, but Madelyn had added to it, decorating in a bohemian motif. Willow contributed a candle, a peach one that a client had included in a Christmas basket years ago. Her mother lit it as Willow collapsed on the bed, not used to doing so much physical labor.

"It looks good in here." Willow propped herself up on her elbows, inspecting their work. "Just like that time you came over to the shop and helped me clean it up, remember?" The next day, her mother's friend had swung by to pick her up — off to speedball, the friend admitted. But Willow wouldn't remind her of that detail. Their mother had done some shitty things to them, but she was still their mother, something Victoria seemed to forget. The woman had been trying to leave her life in Louisiana, move in with them for years. This was her chance to not fuck things up for herself for once. She sat all the way up, leaning toward her mother, who was in a nearby chair. "Madelyn, listen. You need to really ramp up the charm or you'll have to say goodbye to all this stuff soon." She was thrilled her sister had so easily agreed to two weeks. Plan B had been for her mother to negotiate for one night, during which the two of them would figure out a way to make Madelyn indispensable. In comparison, two weeks was plenty of time.

"One thing you should try to do. Connect with Nickie. Vic's really worried about her right now. It's time you step up with the grandmother stuff," Willow said.

"I can try. I don't know if I'm good talking to teens."

Willow adjusted herself on the bed. "That's a good thing. They don't want you speaking to them like they're kids. Just be yourself. Talk to Nickie like you would a girlfriend."

Madelyn hooted. "You sure about that?"

Her mom had a point. "Okay, talk to her like you would one of your devout Christian girlfriends."

"Don't have too many of those in my circle, but I get you." She paused. "And how do I handle Victoria?"

That was the real question. When she'd first reunited with her mother the day before, Willow wondered again if she'd made a mistake sending for her. She knew their mother had been clean for a couple of years, but she still worried about her resorting to old behaviors — speaking out of turn, insulting Victoria. She'd had her doubts and decided to slip a ditty bag with hyssop, rock salt, clover, and crushed eggshell underneath her mother's mattress to soak up the woman's negative energy.

Her phone rang. She looked at the screen. January. She'd call him back in a bit.

"Who got you cheesing over there like that — your boyfriend?"

Willow blinked and let any reaction on her face wilt. "Ain't nobody cheesing. And he's not my boyfriend." She wasn't sure what to call January. They were just having fun, but her situation with him did make Willow think of Nickie and Felix, the brightness of early affection. She contemplated what might happen if she let herself feel that way for a man. Willow had heard for so many years, since she was even younger than Nickie, "Bela Nova made it clear that she'd take away love for us. Forever, and even some more." Indeed, after studying her book for so long, trying out hundreds of spells, she knew the powers of a hex. But a curse that killed the true loves of many generations? She couldn't believe it. Because with the exception of writers, politicians, and God, wasn't no one living or dead whose simple words could last for generations, particularly not a swindler cheat like Bela Nova. She'd heard much about her grandmother's mentor when she'd worked the shop in New Orleans. The woman had a reputation.

Willow didn't put any credence in the curse, but in doing what she had all these years to block out love, she'd essentially acted as if it were true, keeping things strictly sexual with her men, and only hooking up with them once to keep her from catching any feelings. Sometimes she wondered if what held her back had been the possibility of upsetting Victoria. But if her niece in her only seventeen years of wisdom was motivated enough to disregard Victoria, why shouldn't she? After her evening with January, she certainly wanted him, so much so that, once again, she'd put him off, letting him stick his fingers inside of her but nothing else.

"Willow!" Her mother's voice made her jump. She'd drifted off. It took her a moment to orient herself, not recognizing where she was.

"Hey."

"You ready to get into your own bed? I'd like to put on my new sheets and lie down."

Willow sat up. Looking around the room, how the two of them had transformed it in such a short period of time, she wished she would have reached out to Madelyn months ago. It was nice to have someone around who knew what she was capable of.

16
NICKIE

Her bedroom wasn't a place Nickie liked to stay anymore. The room reeked of syrupy princesses, ponies, and rainbows. Of make-believe and story time. Pink didn't even begin to describe it. It was as if she slept each night snuggled up inside a cotton-candy machine. If her mother had a choice, Nickie would stay an eternal seven years old.

She hated her room, but it had become her holding space. She stayed there most hours of the evening, on deck, waiting for the next day of school, where she went to class and counted down the minutes until advanced photography with Felix. They'd hang out at lunch and for a few minutes after school, and then she'd go home, start the cycle again. Not much had happened between them since he'd said he found her attractive that first day of school; though, technically, the two *had* spent quite a bit more time together.

She couldn't recall the house ever being so quiet, despite their lack of company all these years, and despite a whole new person having moved in. It suddenly felt so heavy, how abnormal they were — rare for them to dine out at a restaurant or go across the street to hang out at the park. And they'd not taken any vacations or even gone to Disneyland, just some twenty-five minutes away. They stayed inside, leaving everyone but her mother's clients out.

There was something about men that agitated the women in her house. All men. Her mother had nearly banished them from the house, and Aunt Willow tried to hide them.

The only one who lived out in the open was Madelyn, who seemed purely proud of her life, sharing tales that should have had her locked up for decades or dead by now. Apparently, she'd met her grandmother a few times as a kid, but Nickie didn't remember her. Strange, because Madelyn was notable for her freckled cheeks and wide-set eyes and the slow and scratchy way she spoke. "This is little Nickie?" Madelyn had asked when Victoria reintroduced them, explaining that Madelyn wouldn't be there long, just while she hunted for a place of her own. "It's nice to see you again, Nickie. Last time I saw you, you looked like who I guessed to be your father. Now that you're older, I think you look just like me. So I'd be careful if I were you." She'd laughed at herself, then told Victoria she was just kidding around.

An old Usher song played from Nickie's computer speakers, and she boosted the volume before tiptoeing to her door. She shut it behind her as she left, passed her mother's closed door and her aunt's, and knocked on the one at the end of the hallway, which was slightly ajar.

"Come in," a voice said.

In the bedroom, incense choked the air, cloying and thick. Not wanting to be rude, Nickie swallowed a cough, narrowed her eyes into slits to handle the smoke. With eight or nine lights on, the small space had been turned into a greenhouse. She hadn't visited her grandmother's room or spent much time alone with her since the woman had moved in the week before. When Nickie ran into her in the kitchen or coming out of the bathroom, her grandmother seemed rooted to the place, settled and at home. She didn't appear to be searching too hard for somewhere else to live.

Madelyn muted the TV from her spot on

an oversized wicker chair. "You can sit on the bed right there, Nickie. Just move that box, put it next to the lamp. I got that from a yard sale down the block this weekend for five bucks. That's called a bargain where I'm from." The room was full of items that had been salvaged and stowed in the short time since Madelyn had arrived.

"So, to what do I owe the pleasure of this visit from my favorite grandchild?"

Nickie humored her with a weak smile, but only because there was something she wanted. "I don't know. Just bored."

"*Just bored.* So that's the only reason you came to see me? 'Cause you're bored?"

Nickie folded her legs underneath her, accidentally knocking over a stack of clothes on the bed.

"Just leave it, just leave it. I was about to clean up, anyway."

"Oh. Well, actually, I did want to ask you something."

"Boyfriend advice? Just talked to your aunt about hers the other day."

Nickie took hold of her necklace. Had she mistakenly called Felix her boyfriend one day? "Who said I had a boyfriend?"

"Well, I don't know if you noticed, but there ain't too many people living in this house, and one of them can't talk anyway, so I think that narrows it down for you. And another one has hardly said two words to me since I've been here, so . . ."

"It's not true."

Madelyn began rocking back and forth in her chair. "What isn't?"

Nickie lifted her chin to the ceiling and closed her eyes. "I don't have a boyfriend. He's just a guy. That I like. But he's not my boyfriend. And I wasn't trying to hide him. I brought him here to meet my mom."

"And what happened?"

"She flipped out. Like totally. She told me I couldn't go out with him. Or anyone. She took away my camera — like, what's my camera got to do with anything?" Nickie wasn't sure why she'd opened up to Madelyn. Maybe because she seemed foreign, exotic even, hadn't been cooped up in this house like the rest of them. She had insight.

"Flipped out, huh? She tell you why?"

"She didn't have to. I know why. It's because she's overprotective and controlling. She wants me to be the next Lanora, like her, worried all the time about other people's problems. I wish she'd just eat a few gummies and chill out."

Madelyn laughed. "You ain't never lied. Really, we could all use a little something-something to help us out, you know what I mean?" Nickie didn't know what Madelyn meant so she just rubbed her arms, trying to make the goose bumps go away. "But it's more than that controlling spirit of hers. You need to ask her why."

Nickie sighed, tiring of Madelyn's slow-talking style, her syllables dragged out and singsongy. "I don't care why. I just want her to —"

"Your mama's worried about the curse."

Curse? She fanned herself, feeling a sudden stickiness under her arms. A tingle sprang from inside her chest. "Madelyn, are you listening to me?" She probably shouldn't call her grandmother Madelyn, but it was how everyone else addressed her.

" 'Course I am, child. You seem to be the one having trouble hearing. I told you that your mother, Victoria, probably being all uptight and scared because she thinks we got a hex on us. A crossing."

The topic seemed to tickle Madelyn, the woman sparkling with delight. She waved a hand at Nickie, as if her granddaughter had asked her to keep going. "It ain't my place to talk about it, though," she said. "You can ask your aunt, though she probably been told not to talk to you about it if you don't know by now. Willow's too occupied with all that witchy nonsense, anyway."

"What do you mean?" she asked, although she knew exactly what Madelyn was referring to.

"I mean your aunt Willow got her hands in that black magic shit." She put her fingers to her mouth. "Oh, excuse my language. Black magic *stuff.*"

It was curious to Nickie how different Madelyn was from her mother. The two were nothing alike. "What about you? Are you worried about this . . . curse?"

Madelyn flattened her lips. "I may be a lot of things, but I'm not a wack-wack. Maybe I should believe it, way things turned out. But I don't. Those needles and the drugs he put in them killed Willow's dad, not nothin' else. Harlowe Decuir did that to himself, not no curse. But I ain't saying nothing else because I need a place to stay and I don't want your mama kicking me out. Bad enough she's ignored me so far while I've been here. So please don't go running and telling her I brought this up."

"So you mean the curse makes people . . . die?"

"Apparently so. The people we love. Your daddy, for example."

Nickie swallowed hard. She felt sick, her belly cavernous like she hadn't eaten all day. Her talk with Madelyn hadn't been the help she'd thought it would be. More, it puzzled her. She'd started to accept the possibility that her mother had some special sort of talent, one that she herself might have one day. That her aunt could make things happen if she followed instructions in that book. But this curse sounded like a made-up story someone who'd lived a wild life like Madelyn's might tell. Besides, a curse hadn't taken her father. He'd died young and tragically, a late-night car accident. If he'd been cursed, wouldn't he have dropped dead in the middle of the street or spontaneously combusted?

She didn't want to be rude, but sitting there in the clutter, her grandmother staring at her like she was a shiny piece of fruit, she was becoming anxious. "Well, I need to get going. I have to finish my reading."

"Go ahead. Go on and leave me if you need to. *Your reading.*" Nickie didn't defend herself, reminded that Madelyn was a wreck, just like her mother.

She returned to her room. If there had been any reading, she would have finished it by now. So she lay down on her bed, intending to dream of Felix, hoping that he was dreaming of her too.

17
VICTORIA

The new sounds in the house since Madelyn had arrived had almost been unbearable to Victoria. Like that of her mother leaving the refrigerator door open. Too far open. Just about as open as it could get without breaking off the hinges. That sound would stir Victoria in the middle of the night, just as she'd crossed over into deep sleep. The noise would whisper in her ear, and once awakened, she'd go downstairs to find Madelyn making a sandwich, every condiment in the house set up assembly-line style. As her mother discoed up and down the line, singing a Donna Summer tune into her butter-knife microphone, the refrigerator watched, its innards exposed and warming. Victoria had said nothing. That time, it had taken her two hours to get back to sleep, even though closing her door had created silence.

Her mother brought other new sounds to

the house. There was the sound of her pressing comb, which she'd warm about as hot as it could stand on the kitchen stove and then run it down wavy wisps of hair, forcing her tresses to flat sheets, some strands breaking off, floating onto the counter, to the floor, and, somehow, into the cupboards and drawers. These sounds were nearly as loud as Madelyn doing the laundry. Her own laundry. She didn't bother waiting for her clothing to make itself into a full pile, choosing instead to wash a couple of shirts now. A pair of pants the next day. A blanket later on.

There were also the faint noises of her mother squeezing the toothpaste from the middle; of her disheveling the Sunday paper before Victoria got a chance with it; of her clipping her nails on the couch without putting a magazine or paper towel underneath, so that later when Victoria came to sit down, her thigh would be pierced by a nail sliver. And quite disturbing was the sound of that woman not saying a peep once she'd finished off the last of the fabric softener, the diet soda, the batteries, the toilet paper.

Before Madelyn's arrival, she hadn't spoken to her mother in a decade, not since Madelyn had been arrested for fraud, having impersonated Victoria and damaged her credit. And that was just the most recent offense. Willow, for some reason, seemed to forget that their mother had chosen drugs over her two young daughters, hardly caring when Augusta took them away. After vowing but failing to come out for a visit to Disneyland, to watch Victoria graduate from middle to high school, to celebrate her Sweet Sixteenth birthday, to take her Christmas shopping, Victoria had lost all faith in Madelyn, knew the woman didn't keep her word.

But tonight, Victoria could not avoid her mother. Madelyn had cooked up something garlicky and roasted — vegetables, a spicy pasta, and grilled bread — and, while she had declined the invitation each night so far, relieved to be too busy with work, she didn't have a good excuse for skipping dinner this time. If there was one positive side to having Madelyn around, it was that she had gotten the others to sit together each evening, a feat that had always seemed impossible with Augusta wanting to eat right at five, Victoria not ready to dine until after her late appointments and completing her paperwork, Willow feeding herself while she cooked between clients, and Nickie escaping to her room when she bothered to eat anything.

Victoria was not in the mood for Madelyn's stories, to witness her regaling the family. They all found her mother interesting, a good time, lots of fun. But they hadn't been burned the way Victoria had. Maybe inconvenienced or disappointed, but not wrecked. She'd only agreed to let Madelyn stay now as a show of her patience and forgiveness with the loa, wanting them to see her in a good light with all of her recent requests for Nickie, particularly Oshun, who sought beauty and peace in the world. But Madelyn's time had run out.

"So this is day fifteen, Madelyn. Have you found a place to stay?" They'd been discussing the wedding of a celebrity Victoria had never heard of, Nanagusta visibly perturbed by the change in topic.

"Well, it's been hard enough just to get settled and learn about this new city, the weather. Different people on the news. Folks drive different out here too . . ." Madelyn went on.

She didn't have a license. Willow had probably handed over her keys one day telling Madelyn to just be careful.

She put a hand on her hip. "I need another week or two, at the least."

Her mother had been on her best behavior, but Victoria knew she could only temper herself for so long. When she'd asked why Madelyn had shown up after so many years, her mother had said she wanted to start anew and to be with family again — she was lonely and getting older. And she'd changed. That's what she always said.

Nanagusta seemed to sense Victoria's hesitation, taking her hand under the table and gripping it tightly. She looked at her grandmother, but Nanagusta kept her focus across the table, on Madelyn and Nickie. Was she trying to tell Victoria to ease up or to kick the woman out? The former, she guessed.

"Madelyn, what will you do if I give you more time?"

Nanagusta relaxed her hold, then swirled the pad of her thumb on Victoria's knuckles. Her grandmother could be such a softie.

"Just what I've been doing. Calling around, searching for a rental. Looks like I have to move into a studio out here. You could get a mansion in Louisiana for what they want for an apartment. I thought this was Long Beach, not Beverly Hills. Anyway, that's what I've been doing. And I got a little flirty with the Starbucks manager the other day. I reckon I can get myself a job there. Making hot chocolates and lattos — is that what they call them?"

Nickie and Willow laughed but Victoria didn't find her amusing. Her grandmother shifted her body to face her, still rubbing her hand, expectant. Victoria closed her eyes, regretting her next words. "Fine. Two more weeks." Nanagusta released her, then clapped softly under the table, just loud enough for Victoria to hear. "I want a report every day about your job search. I know about a program for seniors that might help you with the apartment."

"Senior? I ain't nobody's senior," Madelyn said. Nanagusta relaxed her shoulders, then knocked on the table with her fist. "What, Ma?"

Victoria would bear with the woman another two weeks, in exchange for her undeniably tasty cooking. Willow had been stuck on the same rotation of menus for too long. And Madelyn would at least be another pair of eyes on Nickie. In two weeks, when she spoke to Madelyn once again about her departure, Victoria would make sure that she was sitting nowhere near Nanagusta.

The next morning, she heard the new sounds of what must have been the family at brunch. She'd slept in, forgetting to set her alarm again and missing online Mass.

The muddy aroma of newly brewed coffee had tickled her awake, and once she'd gotten herself out of bed and to the door, faint voices from downstairs tickled her ears, a tune from the Gap Band in play.

When she reached the dining room, the group quieted, the record on the player ending its spin, the arm lifting up and swinging over to rest. They watched her, each of the women in the house, waiting for her response. For they'd been joined by someone who didn't belong.

"I see you're finally up. We were being loud on purpose so you would come down," said Madelyn, who sat next to the stranger. But as much trouble as her mom could be, she knew the man was not Madelyn's guest. She hugged her arms high across her body, sure that the thin nightgown she wore didn't hide the poke of her nipples.

"Victoria, this is my friend, January," Willow said.

She slowly wiggled three fingers, stunned, as the man stood and walked over to her, offering his hand.

Victoria shook her head.

"Don't be rude, Vic."

"I'm not being rude, Willow," she finally spoke. "I'm not wearing a robe."

Madelyn pouted. "Oh, relax. You don't

have a whole lot going on up there, Vic. You're one of the lucky ones. You don't really need a bra."

The man stepped away, still smiling as he returned to Victoria's usual place at the table. The family all at once encouraged her to join. Madelyn told her to sit near Nickie, Nanagusta beckoned with her hands, Nickie told her to grab a chair, and Willow said that she was making crab cake benedict. Victoria didn't respond to any of them, her attention on the man, who kept smiling. It was dizzying, the scene in front of her, all of them sucking up the air in the room. Why did these women insist on bringing random men to her dinner table? Would Nanagusta next invite over the older man who fed feral cats at the park each morning? This would not do.

"You all look nice and cozy. I'll go upstairs and get dressed and come down again later. My stomach's cramping a bit, anyway," Victoria said, needing space. Before pivoting to leave, she caught Willow's gaze and jerked her head back, signaling her to follow.

She stopped in the foyer and waited for her sister, who was evidently taking her time.

At last Willow breezed in with a calm

Victoria didn't think she deserved to feel. "I need him out of my house now, Willow." Victoria didn't want this man there for many reasons — his name alone was suspect. But mostly, it would be a bad look in front of Nickie if she let him stay.

"Why? Just because you've decided to remain stuck in your chastity belt doesn't mean the rest of us have to," Willow said with a smirk. "Anyway, we're just eating. Everyone's having a good time."

Victoria squawked involuntarily. Why couldn't Willow just respect this one request? "I've made everything so easy for you, Willow. You have a job, a place to stay, food in the refrigerator — everything you need because of what I've built. And I've been able to care for everyone by doing what I was supposed to do. Hell, I could have gotten with a few men by now, just worried about my own needs. But no. Instead, I've sacrificed for this family, and for my clients. And you can't just do this one thing for me?"

Willow put a hand to her face as she chuckled. "What, you mean you sacrifice for us because you don't ever get any? Please, please, Vic. Don't ever sacrifice having sex on our behalf. I want you to have all the sex. Madelyn does too. I'm sure Nanagusta wants you to have sex. Shoot, Nickie would probably beg you to find someone if it meant you would leave her alone. That's all any of us want, Vic. Just let us live our lives." She pointed toward the back of the house. "Just let us have guests over to eat and laugh and have a good time. Ain't nobody gonna die from that."

Victoria scowled. "Don't say shit like that, Willow. And you don't know what might happen to him."

Willow sighed. "I'm not marrying the man, Vic." Her voice had lowered. "It's just brunch. Some eggs. Some bacon. Mimosas. Palomas, if you want."

She braced for the joke, the snarky remark. Willow always had one. But she didn't say anything else. She could hear Madelyn singing, someone clapping along, laughing. Her stomach turned.

"I'll be in my room," Victoria said and walked to the stairs, seeking refuge in her closet, where she'd call out to the warrior Changó and hope she could tune in to the wisdom he might share with her.

"Just stay and have a good time, Vic," Willow called after her.

Once she made it to her room, she slammed the door shut behind her, but she knew the women below and the man with them wouldn't hear it.

18
AUGUSTA

Augusta had known the late-morning meal would be memorable when Willow used a stool to reach for the crystal champagne flutes, which stayed shut up behind oak cabinet doors except for Thanksgiving and Christmas and All Saints' Day. The fancy glasses were in honor of their guest, January. He was a handsome man with a scruffy beard. A sharp dresser. She understood why Willow had dared to bring him over despite the curse. Augusta already knew Willow dated and probably did more than that — just as long as she didn't catch strong feelings for the man. Why shouldn't her granddaughter get to have a little fun?

She'd watched the exuberance wash right out of Victoria's face once she noticed him, but Augusta would handle her later. Right now, she had a guest at the table — a precious rarity. She'd thrown Isaac Hayes on the record player and tuned in, thrilled at the conversation January's presence had sparked. And even better, she'd used an app on Willow's iPad to voice a sentence or two, verbalizing her favorite swear words, the table quieting until the robotic "Fuck you and your stomach cramps" sounded from the gadget, Augusta giving her angriest expression as the words played. January, at first, apparently did not want to laugh but eventually joined in once it seemed acceptable to make fun of Victoria. Her audience stayed patient, sat politely as she punched in each letter with her thumb, hard thumps on the screen. Even if the routine got old when she sped up the voice and added an accent or a few more *fuck you*s and a *shizzle,* her fans were devoted, left wanting more.

Augusta had acclimated herself to single-way communication, done plenty of listening on her part. But she'd become a meaty, five-foot-one vessel filled with gripes and foul words and without an efficient way to get things out.

Madelyn pointed in Augusta's direction. "Here, let me see that thing. What is it? A *tablet,* you call it? How's that different than the computer?"

"It's a lot like a computer," said January next to her, winking at Willow each time Madelyn's chair nudged closer to his.

"Although, it's probably more like a phone."

"One of them smartphones, huh? I'm saving up for one myself. So I can take pictures of my family and send them to my old neighbor back in Louisiana."

"That's really nice, Ms. Madelyn."

"Or maybe I'll have to show them to her, with my own daughter moving me out soon and all. Ain't that something?"

"Mama." Willow frowned, and Madelyn took the warning in stride. She gave Willow a nod before turning back to January.

"Anyway, I need a picture of you. Won't no one believe I had such a handsome man over to dine," Madelyn said, patting his hand, getting him to chuckle. "Although you're not really my type."

"Don't worry, Mama. You're in California now. There's every kind of person you could ever think of out here." Willow waved her glass around as she spoke, a splash of mimosa hitting Nickie.

"Well, it would be nice if we could go someplace. I've barely been anywhere except the grocery store since I got here."

No one bothered to tell Madelyn that she had two rollers pinned to the back of her head or lipstick on her teeth. They were still getting to know this new version of Madelyn — even Willow — and seemed to be waiting for a switch to flip.

It was an odd thing, the way Madelyn had operated in their home, blending herself right in as if she'd been with them the twenty-five or so years they'd been in California. She'd acclimated herself so well that it was now Madelyn who held reign over the remote control in the evenings, turning Augusta on to *TMZ* and *Access Hollywood.* And Madelyn who chose songs for the Saturday-afternoon cleaning playlist.

Augusta's relationship with her daughter had never fully recovered from the misadventure of Madelyn's teenage years. Perhaps this time before them could be a recovery, each of them with their own regrets. But Augusta had to trust her daughter again. Relearn her and rediscover the fascinating child she'd once fallen in love with.

No one had ever accused Madelyn Montrose of being a saint. Even in kindergarten, she showed herself a scoundrel, pinching the other kids, taking pieces of bread or cheese from their cafeteria trays. She smoked before aging to double digits, had become a heavy user of reefer before her thirteenth birthday. Augusta had been so occupied at the shop, too busy concerning herself with all the other troubled folks in the bayou, that she didn't see the problems in her own kid. Her only child wasn't perfect, but Lanora's blessing would kick in eventually, and Madelyn one day would tell Augusta that she was ready to share the gift her mother knew she had. She was the only daughter in her generation — of course she had it. That's what she'd hoped, but her daughter had never seemed interested in learning about it, so Augusta didn't broach the subject again, recalling her own mother's pushiness.

Madelyn managed to make it to her twenties without any major incidents when the girl returned home high one night, arm and arm with Nicholas St. Jean, his name a dirty word as far as Augusta was concerned. He was an unlovable man known for turning hopeful young girls into exasperated, downtrodden women. "We're pregnant," Madelyn said, then laughed, almost a scream. It was clear that she wouldn't be the one to take care of the baby.

"Just stay away from her until she has this child, you hear?" This was the only sentence Augusta ever spoke to Nicholas St. Jean, knowing Madelyn would not stay sober with him around. Word came that he'd moved to Kentucky by the time Madelyn gave birth to Victoria, enamored as he'd become with a distant cousin of his who'd just come into money.

Three months after Victoria was born, Augusta heard Madelyn retching in the bathroom one morning. She opened the door to find her on the floor, chest heaving, her face against the toilet seat.

"Who is it this time?" Madelyn said.

"Harlowe Decuir."

January's eyelids struggled to stay open, what with the three bottles of champagne they'd polished off. Even Nickie had snuck in a couple of sips. They sat around the table, each trying to think of a new topic, but their minds had run out of energy.

She was going to suggest they help themselves to a slice of cake, remembering she'd baked up a spice bundt the previous afternoon. But the sound of footsteps froze her midstand, her back not yet fully erect when Victoria reappeared. By the look on her face, Augusta knew she hadn't come down to partake in the festivities.

19
WILLOW

Leave it to her sister to ruin such an intimate moment in Willow's life, one she'd kept herself from having for so many years. Though they'd made out in his car and at a booth of a 2nd Street restaurant, and had gone a step beyond outercourse at the park across the street, the exchanges she'd shared the last hour with January, Nickie, Madelyn, and Nana had been among her most cherished so far, particularly after Nan got them all laughing and January had reached one of his bulky arms around her and thumbed the skin of her shoulder. Victoria had left over an hour ago, allowing them a glimpse of the types of lives she imagined her neighbors lived. But now her sister had returned, a sinister glint in her eyes.

"Look who decided to join us," Madelyn said, scooting over so that Victoria could get herself into the seat next to her.

But Willow knew that's not what Victoria

had in mind. The fuzzy light from the chandelier cast mean shadows on her face, dating her a good ten years, her few freckles looking like age spots, silvery strands of hair doing their best to be seen among the others, the showiest of the bunch. This time, she'd tied a terry-cloth robe snug around her waist.

"What's the matter, Vic? You want someone to drive you to urgent care?" Willow asked, knowing full well that wasn't why she was there.

"Not at all. I'm fine. Would drive myself if I wasn't. I just came down to say a few words to this . . . gentleman. January, is it?"

"That's right." He straightened himself up, folding his hands. "Strange name, I know. But my mama used to remind me that many folks called their daughters April, right?"

Madelyn's forehead wrinkled. "Well, doggone, that makes some damn sense. And May. My babysitter was named May." She ignored Nana's headshaking. "And one of my best friends from junior high school. May Latchison. Or was that Dawn Latchison and May Truesdale? I forget. But yes. April. May. And —" she snapped her fingers "— June. Like June Cleaver."

Augusta slapped the table to get Madelyn's attention and then pointed to herself. "What's that, Mama? Oh — Augusta. Well, what do you know!" She leaned back in her chair with a self-satisfied grin.

"So, January," Victoria said when Madelyn was done. Despite the robe's more secure tie, she still held herself around her bosom. "I thought I would give you a little advice."

Willow sighed. She'd been planning to offer the table some of Nana's spice cake with a little ice cream, or coffee laced with rum and brown sugar, but it was clear they were about to get a Victoria lecture. "Hold on, Vic. You giving out sessions for free? Don't be trying to have me look up his insurance after he leaves so you can bill him." Humor was Willow's best coping mechanism.

Victoria didn't acknowledge Willow, nor did she laugh. "Nickie, go upstairs."

"Why?" Nickie asked to Willow's surprise. Her niece rarely questioned Victoria.

"Why? Because I said so, Nickie. And because you are a child, and this is nothing you need to hear right now."

Nickie seemed to consider resisting but eventually stood, giving a look to Willow as she left the room.

Victoria cleared her throat and focused again on January. "You into my sister? I get it. She's gorgeous, I know. Curvy. And funny sometimes, when she's not overdoing it. But falling in love with any of us comes with a price." She was stooped over the table now, a finger pressed into the wood.

Nanagusta muttered a hollow syllable, trying to interrupt, but Willow placed her hand on her grandmother's shoulder. "It's okay, Nan. Let her finish. Let's see what she has to say." Asking January over had been a bold move, one she knew would shake her sister, especially after Felix coming by a month before. Willow hadn't, however, anticipated her getting so upset that she'd start in with family secrets, but shoot — let her do the damn thing. It was inevitable, and with the rest of the women there, Willow had as much backup as she ever would.

Victoria put her fingertips to her lips, then she closed her eyes. Oh, the dramatic effect of it all. She did her best not to applaud her sister's captivating performance. Willow didn't say anything, content watching the show, letting her sister make a fool of herself. "We were not meant to fall in love." Her voice had softened now, but she had January's full attention.

"How's that?"

"We're cursed is the simplest way to explain it. Without getting into particulars, folks that we love, they die."

January nodded. "Oh, that's right. Willow said something about that to me."

She did? Willow didn't recall mentioning the curse to him in any of their conversations. Why would she have? Had she said something after drinking, as a joke? But then, she remembered: she'd told him that the man she loved had died.

"She said this to you, and you're okay with it?"

January looked at Willow, unfazed. "I mean, people die, right?"

"She's wondering if you are okay taking a risk that you might die by having relations with Willow," Madelyn said, as if he needed her explanation.

"Ms. Madelyn, I enjoy spending time with your daughter very much. I'm not too worried about losing my life over it." Willow's cheeks flushed. She hadn't ever heard a man say something like this about her. Could January really feel this way?

Madelyn's mouth puckered like she'd just taken an unpleasant bite. "I don't believe in that curse stuff, anyway."

Victoria turned to their mother. "Madelyn, can you stay out of this, please?"

"Yes, I can."

Willow's heartbeat sped up as January

clasped her hand, then cupped it with his other.

"Well, don't say I didn't warn you." Her sister turned, ducking into the brightness beyond the dining room. The electricity that had buzzed in the space went with her.

Nanagusta pushed her iPad in his direction. "I'm sorry." Her grandmother had used the app's default female voice.

"No need to be sorry, Mrs. Montrose. It ain't really a family meal if there's no drama."

She reached for the tablet and typed something again, then clicked play. "She's probably high." Nanagusta pinched together her thumb and index finger and put them up to her lips, sucking in air. At this, January laughed.

"It's okay, it's okay. Thank you, Ms. Montrose, for your hospitality and your humor. It's been really nice."

Augusta waved her hand at Madelyn, then gestured at the plates on the table.

"I know, I know. Don't worry, I'll clean up. You go on and sit down."

As the two women left for the couch and the kitchen, January still held Willow's hand. "So if this is just a Sunday, I can't wait to see what your Thanksgivings are like," he said wryly.

She smiled with all of her teeth, something she didn't usually do because, unlike her sister, Willow had never worn braces. But if he didn't flinch after that family fiasco, her gappy smile probably wouldn't make him run either. "I know. We're interesting."

He agreed, bouncing his chin up and down. "So how can I tell your sister I should have listened to her warning once I'm dead?"

"She's talking about your ghost," Willow said, matter-of-factly.

She brushed the crumbs out of his beard and kissed him. Then she kissed him again before tugging him up from his chair and leading him to her bedroom.

She lit thirteen candles around the room, including her favorite, a pillar of black wax and lavender anointed with thieves' vinegar, one of the only items from the old shop in the Quarter she'd brought back to California. Willow never played music in her room and had to open the back of the remote control and spin the batteries around a few times to change the station on the old stereo. "You think you're a hipster or something with that old tech?" he said, sitting in her bed.

"A what?"

She wished she had straightened up the night before. Luckily most of the mess in the room hid in the shadows of the flickering lights, but he might have stepped on the lid to her large container of Vaseline on their way in and knocked her cosmetics bag to the floor as he spread his arms wide to make himself comfortable.

"I truly apologize for the mess."

January rested back against the pillows. "Ain't nothing messy about this room. Just a fire hazard. You do this all the time?"

"I've done this never." In the darkness she'd managed to create by closing the blinds, she could see the rise of his cheeks as he smiled. She leaned onto the bed and squeezed his thigh. This man, who'd stood up to Victoria with such aplomb, had enraptured her. She could learn a few things from him. "I'll be right back." She wanted to brush her teeth.

In the bathroom mirror, she stared at herself. She was getting older, lines near her eyes no matter if her face moved or stayed still, the skin underneath them thin. When she finished and opened the door, she ran right into Victoria.

"Dang, Vic. What were you doing, standing here waiting for me?"

"Yes. I was."

Willow didn't understand why her sister couldn't just let her be. She'd already told her this thing with January wasn't serious. She relaxed her shoulders and smiled before stepping around her, but Victoria grabbed her forearm.

"He's nothing but a hustler, Willow."

"Oh, is he? Funny you feel comfortable telling this *hustler* our big family secret, yet you can't tell your own daughter."

"Our secret affects them differently, Willow. Anyway, I don't want him at my house ever again, you hear? I don't appreciate this shit, especially with all that I'm dealing with with Nickie. You make me look like a hypocrite, Will." The whites of Victoria's eyes were turning red.

Willow yanked her arm free. "You *are* a hypocrite," she called out and stomped to her room, half expecting her sister might tackle her from behind.

Back inside, she felt emboldened. She'd brought a man to their home, now into her bed, and what was Victoria really going to do about it?

Light danced across his naked skin, one of his hands grasping his penis. She'd been putting off sex, not ready to let him go. But a dreamy moment played in front of her, one she wouldn't deny herself. This thing with January, whatever it was, could it be more than remarkable sex? She might not ever find another man to stare down the curse like that, should Victoria decide to air their family business again. A man who didn't give a shit about the curse. Hell, who didn't give a shit about Victoria.

She inched toward the bed. "Take off my clothes," she said, straddling him.

She'd forgotten to lock her door but didn't want him to stop once he gripped her, his hands heavy and strong. If anyone walked in, she'd just have to yell at them to shut the door and apologize later. Maybe she *could* allow herself some kind of connection with a man. January had given her a reason to be brave.

■ ■ ■ ■

NOVEMBER

■ ■ ■ ■

20
AUGUSTA

Since January's visit to the house, no one dared say the b-word. Madelyn suggested a late *breakfast* one Sunday, and another weekend Willow poured several rounds of mimosas, but *brunch* had become a dirty word after Victoria's performance. Augusta had waited for Nickie to come to her with questions about the family secret they'd all heard Victoria refer to as she and Willow bickered in the hallway that day. But she hadn't. As the girl now sat next to her on the couch, nothing good on television, she contemplated what message she'd communicate should Nickie bring up the topic. Pat her on the thigh (*you'll find out soon enough*), elbow the girl in the ribs (*you misunderstood*), lean in and glower (*too dangerous for you to know*), pinch Nickie's ear (*mind your business*)? None of these responses would be right.

It was Augusta's favorite part of the day,

late dusk. Often, she lit candles as the sun set, the jumpy flames providing all the light she needed to daydream, to narrate poems to herself, to shimmy her shoulders to tunes from the Dew Drop Inn. Voices of the singers onstage big and smooth and filled with life, reminders of a good time she'd forced herself to forget. Sometimes, she even pretended to be up in Bela Nova's shop, a place that had turned beloved only once the woman left town and it had become Augusta's, though it had never quite felt entirely hers.

Even now, with Bela Nova gone for decades, Augusta still smelled her tobacco breath, felt the woman's cold touch on her shoulder. It was an irrational fear, one she'd tried but failed to will away. Many stories about Bela Nova's whereabouts had been passed around after she'd left New Orleans. One account even claimed the woman had died and was buried someplace along the Gulf. But Augusta had never seen proof, any document that would let her rest better knowing she wouldn't run into Bela Nova ever again.

She and Dudley Lee got themselves married two weeks after they'd asked Bela Nova for a blessing and after Bela Nova believed she'd broken Augusta's love spell. To be safe, in the meantime, the old woman had kept the two of them apart, though Dudley Lee had grown brave, coming by the shop the afternoon Genevieve and Bela Nova had traveled to Bogalusa to pick up the wedding dress. Bela Nova's sister had insisted on making it for the lovely Genevieve and her rich parents.

They'd devised the plan while alone in the workshop. They could get hitched and move in with Dudley Lee's cater-cousin, Charles, who lived over in Hollygrove. They wouldn't let Bela Nova get in their way. So they would marry the day before his wedding to Genevieve, which Bela Nova still assumed would go off without a hitch. She would expect Dudley Lee to be out that night with the boys, enjoying his final evening as a bachelor. But really, he'd be off, newly married to Augusta.

The day in question, Dudley Lee was so late to the church — a box of bricks off Canal Street — that Augusta came near to taking her bouquet of wild irises and her thin ring of gold and walking the mile and a half to her parents' home, and giving up, content with marrying the man they'd believed fit for her to wed. But he showed, just as her worried breaths were becoming frantic enough for the few others in the room to notice. He rubbed Augusta's hand when he said, "I do," then did his best to stifle a burp. Not so right with his social graces, but a good man — except, perhaps, in the eyes of Genevieve. Augusta had offered up a petition, asking St. Jude to provide his spurned fiancée with a new love, and they got wind just weeks later that she'd wed the eldest son of Pastor Warren Thomas Joseph of Union Bethel AME.

Neither one of them thought of the consequences, of what might happen when Dudley Lee didn't make it to his own wedding, if he didn't call Genevieve and tell her he'd changed his mind. Just for kicks, Charles had gone to the wedding, dressed in his best slacks and a starched white shirt, and reported the news. Genevieve's father was angry, said he had a shotgun and would use it to take off Dudley Lee's head if he ever saw him. "He was mad!" Charles told them, amused. "But they some classy people. Still let everyone eat and have a glass of champagne."

His eyes widened, the browns in them vivid. "What about . . . what about my mama?"

Charles's thick arms bent at the elbows and wrists to form a *W*. "Don't know. I saw her when I got to the church. Sitting in the front row, alone. Weren't too many people on that side of the aisle. And I don't think she knew any of the folks sitting behind her. If she did, maybe she fighting with them because she didn't turn around to speak. Shoot, that's why I didn't even go on over to say hello. That look on her face. Seemed unhappy about something, even before the organ started playing."

"She didn't go to the reception?"

"I didn't see her there. Figured she would be, with the food and drink and all. But maybe she embarrassed."

Augusta knew exactly where she'd been. Was certain she'd headed straight to her shop, the key to her trunk warm by the time she arrived, ready to flip through the pages of her book to see where she'd gone wrong. To figure out the best way to bring Dudley Lee back home, to get Genevieve and her family back, and to be rid of Augusta for good.

Augusta burned only one candle that evening, a green one that smelled like bergamot. Leaned against opposite armrests of the couch, she and Nickie had their legs entangled and covered with a blanket. Nickie was playing a card game on her tablet, leaving Augusta to watch the program Nickie had chosen where scantily clad single people lived on an island and tried to find a spouse. It was a strange notion to Augusta, but who was she to tell folks about relationships? Although she hoped Nickie wasn't getting any ideas. While she wanted the girl to be happy, Augusta certainly didn't want to see her great-granddaughter sitting at the pool in full makeup and a string bikini, hoping one of the other chiseled contestants would pick her for a date.

One of her feet falling asleep under Nickie's weight, Augusta adjusted herself. As she moved her body up, she caught a glimpse of the screen as Nickie typed away with one finger. She made out the face of a young man, brown-skinned with thick eyebrows. While she couldn't read the words on the screen, Nickie's beaming smile said it all.

Augusta reached over and pinched her arm. There wasn't a lot of meat on the girl. She shrieked.

"Nana, that hurt." Nickie rubbed the spot and glared at her.

She matched the girl's hard stare with one of her own. Another moment and Nickie seemed to realize what Augusta had glimpsed. She pressed around on the tablet screen in quick sequence until it went black, then handed it over. It hadn't been Augusta's intention to physically hurt the girl. She just wanted to get a message across, without using her voice app or typing it out: *Nickie, please be careful.* Victoria wasn't playing around. If she learned what Nickie was doing, she'd make her life a thousand times more miserable than Nickie probably thought it already was. But it was more than that. Right after Jimmie had died, Augusta had berated herself, ashamed of her inaction, filled with regret that she hadn't tried to stop the relationship between him and Victoria. Back then she'd had her reasons. Now she knew better. So why, she asked herself, did she keep hope that, somehow, Nickie would be able to love without loss?

21
WILLOW

When Willow returned from yet another outing with January, her third in three nights, she found Nanagusta and Nickie on the couch. She was late to her meeting with her niece, but her arrival at 1:25 a.m. was likely much earlier than her grandmother had expected her home. She hoped Nickie hadn't blabbed and confessed their plans.

Though she'd sworn that she wouldn't have January over again without Victoria's okay (which basically meant that she'd never have January over again), she'd said *yes* after he'd called to see if he could stop by on his way to work, the late shift. He'd parked in the driveway, and she'd pulled two foldable chairs from the garage so they could sit and talk, watching the dark park across the street. She hadn't counted on anyone coming outside this time of night, especially not Nickie.

But there her niece was, trash bag in hand,

just as Willow had straddled January in his chair and pressed his face into her bosom. "Excuse me one minute," she told him. She got up and pulled Nickie to the sidewalk, the girl smelling like fruity bubble gum.

"Nick, I'm sure I don't need to say this, but please keep this between us, alright?" She wished she had a twenty in her pocket to keep the girl quiet.

"Why? You afraid of Mom? You're not allowed to have boys come over either?"

Nickie yelped when Willow pinched her, taking a page from Nanagusta. Nickie hadn't witnessed the fallout from January's last visit, but clearly she knew her mom well. "I'm sorry." She could have kicked herself for letting him stop by. "But really, Nickie. I don't need your mama starting in with me. Not now. What will it take to keep you quiet?" She then regretted saying this. "And don't you dare say birth control pills."

She thought Nickie would send her off, telling her not to worry. That of course she wouldn't say anything. They were in the same boat, kindred spirits in want of a little loving. But her niece had other ideas.

"I don't need your help with those anymore," Nickie said, a smugness to her tone. "Turns out you don't need a parent's permission to get them."

"Okay."

"But can you teach me about spells and Voodoo magic stuff?" Nickie rocked back and forth on her heels.

"What are you talking about, girl?" She looked back toward the garage. January had started folding up his chair.

"Your spells. And that book."

Oh Lord, Willow thought, wondering exactly what her niece had seen. "What, my cookbook?"

Nickie leaned back in her stance, arms crossed. "I know it's not a cookbook, Auntie. I looked through it. More than once."

Willow knew someone had been rummaging through it, tearing things, moving items out of place. She'd blamed Victoria.

"Will you just please, please make Felix ask me to be his girlfriend? I know you can do it."

The attraction spell must not have worked. "That's all you want from my *Voodoo magic*?" Willow said with air quotes.

Nickie straightened, relaxing her face. "Yes, Auntie. Oh, and maybe that he asks me to the prom. And that my mom will let me go."

"You're a demanding little shit, aren't you?" She needed to wrap things up so she could wish January a good night.

Victoria had already talked to Nickie about the gift. But her explanation had surely been one-sided. Nickie's gift could manifest itself in a number of ways, including in an ability to conjure up fixes to problems, so much more effective than listening to them and giving advice. Just like Victoria had exposed the girl to therapy by having her act as receptionist, Willow could walk her through a few rudimentary spells. She wanted to show Nickie the fun stuff. Willow had been flipping through the old book since her middle-school days.

"Auntie," Nickie had said, "I think you already did something for me. You wrote my name and his under something called an attraction spell."

"And?" For the moment, she'd forgotten about January.

"Well, he did say something about me being attractive."

Willow cracked a smile. This was the best thing she'd heard in months. Her niece had borne witness to Willow's skills. She gave herself a moment to take in Nickie's words, and then just thought, *Fuck it.* "If I find out you're having sex with this Felix kid, I will indeed make a Voodoo doll and shove a dozen needles in his balls, you hear me?

Anyway, put on an old pair of sneakers and meet me downstairs at my desk tonight at one."

"Nan, why don't you go on up to bed? I'm gonna help Nickie with one of her math problems, then we'll come up," Willow told Nanagusta. "I'm sorry, Nick. I know you've been waiting on me. For help with your homework and all."

Her grandmother pursed her lips, hesitating. Perhaps the woman didn't buy their excuse, but she got up anyway, kissing Nickie on the cheek before closing her sweater and heading upstairs. Willow bid her good night, felt slighted when her grandmother passed without kissing her as well, then gestured for Nickie to follow her to the reception area.

She wouldn't offer any excuse for her tardiness or a description of where she'd been with January or what they'd done. If Nickie wanted her help, there had to be discretion all around. "Lost track of time" was all she said.

The book was stacked between boxes of manila folders, hidden in plain sight. She'd moved the book from the filing cabinet to underneath her desk to a drawer in the dining room to its current spot, and after tonight, she would take it up to her room and find a place for it there.

She had Nickie sit at the desk, set the book in front of her. "This book has been through a lot, Nick. It's been a help for us. You probably wouldn't be here without it. Your grandmother sang incantations from it to bless Madelyn when she was pregnant with your mother."

Nickie ran her middle finger over the embossed gold on the cover. "Who's Delilah?"

The truth of it was Willow didn't know. Nanagusta never answered when she'd asked. She assumed the book had been a picture album. Spots from peeled-off photo corners were a darker brown than the original pages. Her theory was that Bela Nova had held it as collateral from one of her clients, keeping their treasured moments until the woman made payment.

She continued without responding to Nickie. "Open it to the third or fourth page. You'll find something called the Quarters Bend Over spell."

Nickie followed her instructions, careful not to let any of the loose pieces fall out. "*The French Quarters Bend Over spell, for when you want to make someone do whatever you want.* Bend Over spell, Auntie? And he'll do whatever I want? Sounds a little . . . freaky."

Willow folded her arms. "Nickie, get your mind out of the gutter. It's nothing like that at all."

"So what is it? I can just say something and he'll do it? Like a Jedi mind trick?"

"Funny," Willow said, a smirk on her face. Bend Over tricks worked well, but they had their limits. As long as Nickie didn't get any crazy ideas, it would give her the results she wanted. Besides, Willow had already done a couple of tricks for Nickie, but she liked to build her spells, layering potions, powders, blessings, ditty bags. "You have to use this spell for something specific. And simple. Something you can see. Like, to have him bring you flowers."

"Have you ever used this spell to make someone bring you flowers?"

This Willow found funny. "Child, all this for some flowers? No, thanks. I'll buy my own. So you ready?"

Nickie soaked in her words, softly chewing on her lip. "Okay, fine."

"*Okay, fine?* Nickie, like I said, I'm a pro. And this is just one spell. We have time for other work. After a while. I'll have Felix writing songs about you." She widened her eyes and tilted her head toward Nickie until the girl's lips curled up. "Before we start, go ahead and write your name down underneath the others. Right after . . . Bea Ramirez."

Willow had used this spell often at the shop back in New Orleans, but it always worked best if the one who would benefit from the spell completed the steps herself. She walked Nickie through it as she cut paper into inch-wide squares, then wrote one letter of Felix's full name on each one. Nickie put them in a bowl and shook them up.

"I know it's late and dark and not too warm outside. Put on a jacket, and we'll go plant the papers in the backyard, that empty spot next to the birds-of-paradise."

"You mean bury them?" Nickie asked.

"No, I mean plant them, right at two fifteen — you got six minutes."

"Okay."

"Then at three fifteen . . ."

Nickie pouted. "There's more?"

"Yes, there's more. If these tricks were easy, everyone would do them, right?" She knew everyone wouldn't because everyone couldn't. But she didn't need to brag. Nickie would understand eventually. "You never know. Maybe your gift ain't counseling people at all but working tricks." *Like*

239

me, Willow stopped short in saying. Nickie didn't flinch.

Willow went on, having Nickie read the rest of the spell aloud to help her remember it. It was one of the first tricks she'd practiced. The instructions had been jotted down by Bela Nova herself, according to Nana, though Willow had made improvements to the spell over the years. Before closing the book, she directed Nickie to write down her name and Felix's underneath.

"Why do I have to do that?"

Willow tapped her lips with one finger. "Think of it as a contract. Between you and the spell. When the names are written down, it's basically saying the person who wants the spell done gives permission, and that it's being worked for the right person or the right reason." That's how Nanagusta had explained it to her one morning, when the two of them had played hooky from work and school because it was too cold outside. Victoria had caught a ride on the city bus, not wanting to ruin her perfect attendance or miss any classwork.

Her body quivered when she heard a scratching sound from beyond the room, what turned out to be a car driving by, not her sister coming downstairs catching them in the act. She could only imagine what Victoria would do if she learned about this. "And Nickie, no matter what, don't let your mama know what you're doing, you hear me?"

"Why not? Did she use Voodoo on my dad or something?"

Willow swallowed, her throat dry. She could tell Nickie had meant it as a joke, but Willow didn't laugh. She knew how it felt to have so many unanswered questions about a parent, but some things Nickie would have to discover on her own. Other things she prayed Nickie would never find out.

"That's enough questions for tonight. We got planting to do." It was hard to know when the timing was right for anything, which is why Willow told herself it was okay to just go for it when it felt right, and to not look back.

22
NICKIE

Nickie made her way along the sidewalk, off to meet Felix at a store north of downtown that sold used CDs, DVDs, and video games. She'd been inspired by her aunt, who seemed happier since that brunch with January, happier than Nickie had ever seen her because Willow was expanding her life, breaking the rules to do so. While she knew not to invite Felix over to the house, they could still spend a day together outside of school. Her mother thought she was at the library.

As she approached, Felix was leaning against the painted brick wall of the barbershop next door, nodding his head to the thumping beat coming from inside, the door propped open by a balled-up plastic bag. He lifted his chin, his method of saying hello.

"It won't be long," he told her, though the lineup of folks with just two guys cutting said otherwise. But she didn't mind the wait. It was just nice to hang out again like they had in the summer.

They must have been father and son, the barbers — one looked a little older than Nickie's mother, the other barely out of his teens. Light stretched over the elongated space, the walls screaming in lemon, the dinge of the white and gray tiles strong. Flipping through the magazine on her lap, she paid little attention to the words. The goings-on just feet away appealed to her senses much more. She'd never been in a barbershop before.

Above the whir of the blowing fans and the electric buzz of clippers and the warbling of an R & B singer came a husky voice bellowing greetings from just outside the door. The man walked inside and patted the back of the elder barber. Their hellos were musical, a routine the two must have performed dozens of times, slapping hands, pointing at one another and holding their bellies as they laughed, their broken phrases making the exchange difficult for Nickie to understand. Still the whole shop took notice, enjoying the show, some joining in themselves with a hand wave or a *what's-happening/how-you-doing* — old-man gibberish, although the guy wasn't old at all. It made Nickie smile, something she felt like she only did away from home these days, although her grandmother Madelyn did make her laugh every once in a while.

The man who'd caused all the commotion plopped down in the last empty seat, on the opposite side of Felix. "How you doing, young man?" he said.

"I'm cool," Felix said. He angled himself toward Nickie.

The younger barber finally called Felix to his chair. Nickie reclined, letting her head rest on the wall behind her, and closed her eyes.

After a while, she felt a tap on her arm.

"Don't I know you, young lady?" It was the guy with the lively entrance. He *had* seemed familiar to her earlier, but more in the way of a beloved character she'd seen in movies. If he wasn't a teacher or a custodian or a bus driver, she wasn't sure how she could have met him.

"You belong to Victoria Montrose, right?"

She almost laughed at his word choice, *belong to,* as if she were part of her mother's collection of antiques or jewelry. Though sometimes her mom did act that way, as if Nickie was a precious gemstone she had to keep safe from the world.

"Of course you're her daughter. You look

just like her — got those same pretty eyes she does." She wasn't sure if he meant it, both about her eyes being pretty and that she favored her mother in any way.

His voice boomed as he told her about his sessions, how helpful they were. "It's been good. Really good. You don't know how much I look forward to coming every week. Shoot, if I could afford it, I'd come every day."

Perhaps he didn't mind those in the shop being in his business. No one had ever asked her, but Nickie would hate to discuss her problems with a stranger. Not that she didn't see value in therapy, and not that she didn't think her mother's occupation important. No matter how much she and her mom disagreed, on that they were aligned. Nickie simply didn't care to be judged. She didn't understand how her mom could ever truly be objective with people, even after all her years of training and practice.

Nickie wasn't sure what she wanted to do in her future career. She liked sports. Loved to read, had written a few poems. But she hadn't yet connected how any of her interests or skills could translate into a future job. She didn't even know what she'd major in in college. But she was sure she'd never be able to do the kind of work her mother did. If she had a gift, it certainly wasn't helping people solve their problems. She was barely dealing with her own issues. She wished her mother could see that.

She pretended to be interested in the article opened on her lap, but the man was a talker. "Your mom at home?"

"I'm not sure. Maybe." There was no reason to be definitive. This dude couldn't be trusted. But something kept her from getting too anxious, a soothing sensation at the back of her neck. A thought flickered, what her mom had mentioned about perceiving things about people.

He seemed not to be able to sit still. His thumbs were busy twiddling, and he looked at them, not at her, when he asked, "She seeing anyone?"

Nickie was thrown by the question. "Like, a guy?"

"Well, yes. Yes, a guy."

"She's not into that," she said quickly. Why would this man care about her mother's dating life? Wasn't the therapist–patient relationship a one-way relationship?

"Oh, I see. She's a lesbian?"

"She's not a lesbian. She just isn't into men."

"Well, what's she into?" he asked.

The man sitting on Nickie's other side

glanced up from his phone for her reaction. She was glad to see Felix's chair had been swiveled away from them, the barber now trimming his nape. "Me. Her business. Taking care of our family." She didn't know why she was sharing so much with this man. She appreciated her mom's care for her, but it had become smothering.

After a moment's silence, he tilted his head toward Felix. "You here with your boyfriend, huh?"

A frantic heat climbed up Nickie's neck. Instantly, she was mad at herself for not lying earlier. She should have played it off like she was someone else. She hadn't thought about the connections — her, Felix, him, her mother.

"He's a friend. From school. We have a project," she said, knowing she now needed something from him. "But please, you can't tell her that you saw me today."

"I can't?"

"Please."

Felix was just about done, his guy wiping bits of hair from his neck. She wouldn't have more than a minute to convince this man to keep his mouth shut. If she begged him, she'd come across as desperate, and he'd be curious about what she was trying to hide. She returned the magazine to the table, put her backpack over her shoulder.

"Hold up," the guy said. "This is going to sound odd," he began, launching into a spiel about circumstances, God having you run into people for a reason.

As Felix paid, she stood, silently motivating the guy to hurry it up.

"What I'm trying to get at is that I hope you'll do something for me. Can I ask you to put in a good word with your mom? My name's Russell." He smiled at her as if they were dear friends now.

She blinked. Wait, so this guy actually liked her mom? Did her mom have any clue?

"Please, just like you asked me for a favor. Get me invited over for dinner or for coffee. Really, anything."

Nickie kept an eye on Felix, who was putting away his wallet as he chatted with the barber.

"I'm not some weirdo. Just dealing with some things." Russell's voice was hushed now, not the same man who'd walked in half an hour ago. "I just kind of like her, you know? And I get the sense she likes me too. But based on what you said, I'm sure she'd never act on it. I get the feeling she wouldn't want to mix business with her personal life."

He was entering territory Nickie wasn't

248

inclined to explore. Her mother was intent on living her bland, unexciting life and wanted Nickie to do exactly the same. She had enough problems with the woman already. "I don't know . . ."

"Maybe you could . . . I don't know . . . call me or text me if you think she might be open to having me stop over to bring over some coffee or dessert or something. How about you take down my number? It's the easiest number in the world — 555-1010. Like that commercial for insurance. Except that I'm 562 area code." He finally stopped, then added one last comment. "I thought about saying this to Ms. Willow but got a little embarrassed about asking. I mean, I'm embarrassed now. But hey, sometimes you just gotta go for it, you know?"

Before she could respond, Felix was by her side. "Ready?"

She could only nod, and maybe the nod was for Felix as much as it was for him.

The man waved goodbye as did the rest of the shop as Felix took her hand and led her outside to his car.

"What's wrong? You tired or something?"

"A little bit," she said, not having completely shaken off the conversation about her mother yet.

"That old dude in there, he wasn't trying

to push up, was he?"

"No. Not at all. I think he just liked to talk. Maybe he's just lonely." She began to wonder if this was in fact true, if she hadn't been kind enough to him.

Felix shrugged, quiet as he drove, the radio set to the same station that played in the shop. He parked at Tommy's Burgers, a spot near school where kids grabbed lunch or vaped before and after class. Sliding next to her on a concrete bench outside after they got their food, Felix took the gum out of his mouth and leaned in, his eyes still open. She shut hers, fast, once she caught on to what was happening, pleasantly star- tled when he pushed his tongue between her lips. It didn't last very long, their tongues in sequence going around, around, back, and around once more. Finally, her first kiss.

The Bend Over spell had worked, just like her aunt said it would, and hadn't taken any time at all.

"Better to do it now than after the chili." He picked up a fry covered in gravied bits of meat and fed it to her. She drank water from the cup they shared, wanting to cleanse her mouth as much as possible, hopeful for another kiss. He handed her one of his earbuds. "Here, listen. This is that band I went to see last weekend." He'd asked her to go with him, a place in Hollywood that was eighteen-and-over. "I'm not eighteen yet," she'd told him, happy that she didn't have to use her family as an excuse for once, though she'd worried he'd offer to get her a fake ID.

"You like it?"

The song was reminiscent of the music Willow played on Saturday afternoons when she cleaned. A real band with horns and a soulful lead singer, nearly crying by the time he got to the tag. Then, Felix hit a button on his phone, jumping to a new song. "They're influenced by a lot of the groups from the eighties. Real music. This is De-Barge. Do you know them?"

Nickie shook her head. The tune bounced around, the singer's voice bright and clear.

"Family-style. All of them talented. They had a group, but then they split off. I'd go see them if they ever got back together."

"She has a nice voice."

"He. That's El."

"Oh," Nickie said, wondering if she could ever appreciate the artistry of anything the way Felix did. Basketball she'd understood quite well, but she never studied its technicalities.

"You want to do something tomorrow?"

he asked.

She'd played around her situation pretty well over the past months, managing to hang out with Felix by making up bogus assignments, fake academic clubs that met after school. To him, she excused herself from evening phone chats and weekend outings by claiming her mother needed assistance. With the business. With her weak, fragile great-grandmother, knowing that if Nanagusta ever heard Nickie describe her as such, the woman would pinch her again. "Tomorrow's not good."

"Fine. Let's do something later tonight. I'll stop by your house, okay?"

Nickie ran her tongue over her teeth, making sure she didn't have anything stuck between them. "No, you won't."

"What if I did?"

"Then, you would have wasted your gas because I wouldn't be home."

He grinned. "So I'll just hang out with your family."

"My family won't be home either. We'll all be gone." These things she tried to say matter-of-factly, but her tone had the confidence of a gopher.

"When will you be back?"

"Late."

"Late? With your great-grandmother?

Where are you going?"

The inquisition was on, a tug-of-war she couldn't win. Felix wouldn't hear it, tired of her untruths and cop-outs. A swift breeze stirred their discarded napkins. Nickie's hair blew into her face. She let it stay, didn't want to meet Felix's eye. It didn't feel right anymore, not being honest with him. She thought back to the brunch, the scene with her mother. She'd been ordered to leave the dining room, but she'd overheard an exchange in the hallway later that day, instructions that the man never come over again.

"Look, you just can't come over my house again. Ever, okay?" Nickie brushed away her hair, looked down at her painted fingernails that needed trimming.

"Got it. But I hope it's not because you don't want me around."

"No, of course I —"

"I really like spending time with you Nickie. I . . . like you. And I hope you're not seeing someone else."

She lost control of her laugh, a little embarrassed at how loud it had come out. "I'm definitely not seeing anyone. Else."

"Good. How about we keep it that way? Officially. Does that sound alright?"

It sounded like the greatest thing in the world. And though she had to credit the

Bend Over spell for their kiss, their new official status he'd asked for on his own.

Nickie hummed aloud as she walked home, a tune she made up as she went along. The sun neared setting but still gripped the amber horizon, and the yellow-greens of the lawns were washed in shadow. Cheers from a televised football game floated out through screened windows of homes along her block, the clanging of plates. She slowed her stride, only making herself later, but not quite ready to face the consequences of arriving home at this hour.

When she reached her house, its windows were darkened. Nickie pulled her key from her pocket, but she had a feeling that she wouldn't need it.

The door was unlocked, but her mother wasn't standing there, set to pounce. The floor was gray, shadows watching her as she dumped her backpack on the floor.

At the top of the stairs, Nickie took off her shoes before stepping onto the worn hallway floor, light coming from her grandmother's propped-open door. All the other doors, closed. Tension sprang off Nickie's back and shoulders. She'd be better at defending herself after a solid sleep.

Still, it was only seven o'clock. Even if her

mother were passed out in bed, knocked down by one too many glasses of wine, she'd be up again, eventually, and in a pissier mood than before. In the meantime, Nickie wanted to do nothing more than lather in the memory of her kiss with Felix. The cushy bend of his lips around her rough, rusty ones. She could do that a hundred times more, just tonight.

Once in her room she eased shut the door behind her, darkening the already ashen space. She regretted tossing her shoes toward the closet, with the tumbling clonk they made as they hit the floor. Her hands outstretched, she found her bed, pulled off her shirt, then fell back into her pillows, finding what she recognized as her pink unicorn Miracle and wrapping her arms around it. Eyes closed, she tasted Felix again. He was squeezing her, holding her around her waist. Playing with her hair as she sang . . . DeBarge, was it?

The light flashed on. Nickie sat up, startled, then saw that her mother was in the room with her. Had been in the room all this time, standing in the corner for three minutes, not making a sound.

"What are you doing in here?" Nickie said, noticing a point to her mother's chin she hadn't seen before, a new sharpness to her face.

When her mother's eyes narrowed, moving down from Nickie to the stuffed animal, she remembered she was shirtless, wearing only a pair of frayed denim shorts and the lacy push-up bra she'd ordered from a lingerie boutique using Aunt Willow's credit card. She turned the unicorn aslant to cover up her cleavage. "I thought you were in your room. Your door was closed."

Her mother's arms were folded, and Nickie could imagine her as a bully twenty years ago, holding up the wall during recess with that tough-guy stance. "What, Mom? What do you want me to say?"

Victoria's bottom lip poked out as she shrugged. "You don't have to say anything, I suppose. Looks like you're grown now. You can come and go as you please. If you were going to be late, all you had to do was call. Why didn't you call, Nickie?"

Felix had seemed to have the afternoon mapped out for them. If she'd called her mother, it would have surely meant cutting things short, even if she'd found a good excuse. "I . . ."

"Give me your phone."

"But Mom!" She couldn't be serious. Nickie had come up with half a dozen ways to communicate with Felix without her mom figuring out, mostly using apps on her phone.

Her mom put her palm out. "Now, Nickie."

She flung it toward her mother, though nowhere close to her open hand. Her mother picked it up from where it had landed on the floor, and for a second, Nickie thought she might break it in two with her hands.

"I don't know what the big deal is. It's only, like, seven or seven thirty."

"Right. And you were supposed to be home at three thirty or four. Were you with that boy?"

"No, Mom."

Nickie lay her cheek on the unicorn's tickly mane. If Nickie weren't so frustrated with her mom, she'd be concerned that something was off. Her chemicals. That had happened to her teacher's wife one year, and he'd taken off two months to care for her. She thought about the man in the shop, Russell. If she called him, invited him over, maybe her mother would chill out. Nickie was so over her mother, she just might.

"Why don't you just lock me in the closet and throw me a bag lunch every few days?"

"Maybe I will." Her mother's eyes were wide now, wild and freaky. "And put a shirt on. Don't know what you're doing up here anyway, up in your bed naked."

"Naked? Come on."

"I'm not laughing about this, Nickie."

"Yes, I know. You don't laugh about anything." Nickie retrieved her shirt from the chair next to her desk and slid it on, not caring that it was inside-out.

"You're damn right I'm not laughing. Shit, you think this is funny, you not listening to me and you're just a child? You think you know better? Let me tell you, girl. You don't know shit. Not about life, and certainly not about boys or men. I told you to stay away for a reason. I'm sure you think I'm over-reacting, but this is for your own good. I'm trying to get you ready for life, help you learn how to use your gift. I'm setting you up for success."

It was a speech straight out of a made-for-TV movie on the women's channel. Perhaps her mother thought if she repeated herself every couple of days, Nickie would believe it, her mind washed of any of her own desires and intentions. But she couldn't let her mom get into her head.

It was then that she recalled what her grandmother Madelyn had shared, a curse on their family that had gotten her mother out of sorts lately. "Does this have something to do with that stupid curse?" She'd asked just loud enough, her voice almost failing her on the last word. But her mother had heard. Her face changed. All in one second, the color scrubbed out of it. Her hand quivered as she placed it on her belly.

It looked as though her mother might cry, something Nickie had never witnessed. The house hushed, even the murmur of Nanagusta's television disappeared. Her mother sucked in a puff of air. "Who told you that?"

Nickie could feel her pulse in her wrists and along the front of her neck.

Her mother loosened the slack on her jaw, pushed her tongue along her inner lip. When Nickie didn't respond, she came closer, running her hand along the bedspread. Abruptly, it stopped, stayed on a particular spot. Then her mother dropped her gaze, squeezed Nickie's shoulder, and backed away and out of the room, her expression stone.

Nickie replayed the whole dramatic moment for herself. She wished she could take back her question, return to ten minutes before when the idea of a curse was still laughable, some made-up story by Madelyn. Could her mother really believe a curse had killed her dad? Is that why no one ever talked about him? No wonder her grandmother hadn't wanted her to say anything. She felt flutters in her belly.

The gift was one thing, but her mother couldn't believe in curses, could she? Just like she didn't believe in tarot cards or palm readings or the daily horoscopes in the paper. Victoria Montrose believed in her priest, Father Holman, and the goblet of watery wine and the foamy host she took on Sunday mornings, back before her mother watched Mass on her phone from the house. Her mother believed in Jesus, came home and conducted her sessions with black dust on her forehead on Ash Wednesday, kept a collection of Palm Sunday fronds folded into crosses in a shoebox under her bed. True, there were those prayers to saints her mom uttered using candles and such, but Nickie always thought it more of a cultural thing, bayou Catholics more expressive and ritualistic than the standard-order Southern California versions. She'd always thought her mother was nothing like Aunt Willow, not the type to believe in magic or curses or anything like that. But perhaps she'd been wrong.

23
WILLOW

"Willow!" She'd heard her name three or four times in a dreamy space, but now it came with the hot sound of a hand clap. When she opened her eyes her sister stood over her, chest heaving. Something had upset her. Had Nickie told Victoria about January's visit? Her niece wouldn't do that. Maybe Victoria had just gotten the electricity bill in the mail. Willow sometimes ran both the air-conditioning and the heater downstairs in the same day, changing from one to the other rather than putting on a sweater or rolling up her sleeves.

Nanagusta was on the couch next to the lounge chair where Willow had fallen asleep, a blanket covering her body. Her head hurt. She'd returned home an hour ago, after a fast dinner and slow night at a local dive bar, a favorite of January's, where she'd lost track of the number and kinds of cocktails she'd had, pretty sure she'd mixed light and dark spirits, maybe even chugged a beer at the end of the evening. Experience told her the only remedy for feeling better would be to throw it all up, but she hoped it wouldn't come to that. She prayed time and water would do the trick.

"Hey, I need to talk to you in my office." Her sister's silhouette blended in with the darkness, the cinnamon brown of her eyes glimmering in the lamplight.

"What's this about? Just say it right here." Willow didn't have the energy to get up.

Victoria shook her head. "Nan doesn't want to hear all this."

She caught her grandmother in her periphery on the couch, nodding, leaning in close on a cushion. Willow reached behind her and flipped the switch to the recessed ceiling lights. Her sister blinked, narrowing her eyes as if Willow had clicked on the sun. She squinted herself, the brightness exacerbating the throbbing pain in her head, but she wanted to see her sister's expression.

"She's good. Whatever you have to say, just spit it out." Victoria's voice had been shaky, and Willow wondered if she was about to reveal she had a terminal illness or would be arrested for tax evasion. Something serious.

Victoria sank back into her heels, crossing

her arms and letting out a big sigh. Then she pulled what appeared to be Nickie's phone from her pocket and held it to Willow's face.

"This," Victoria shook the phone, "is a photo Nickie took of Thursday's Attraction Spell. And guess whose name is written underneath it?"

Willow's saw her own purple penmanship, the image blurry but familiar. "It's not what you think," she said impulsively. For her sister, this was as serious as terminal illness and tax evasion.

"It isn't? Well, let me tell you first what I think it is, and then maybe you'll be able to set me straight." She could tell Victoria was at least trying to stay composed. "This looks to me like you used a spell to make Nickie attractive to that little boy she brought over. The one I've been trying to keep her away from."

"Not exactly. That's not how the attraction spell works, Vic."

Willow wanted to explain, to let Victoria know that the attraction spell wasn't that powerful, more a modifier than anything. But her sister kept throwing out questions: *how could you*s, *what were you thinking*s, and *what if*s.

"You know what, I don't care. The point

is, you used it." Victoria pointed at Willow, close to jabbing her in the chest. "And not only did you use it, but you then told Nickie about it. And let her take a picture?"

"I didn't let Nickie —"

"All I've tried to do these last months — shit, Nickie's whole life — is keep her from having the same experience I had. I thought I was on the right track, having her focus on school, trying to help her admire Lanora and understand the value of her blessing. And eventually, she'd be ready to hear about the curse. By then, she'd be equipped for it. I've been speaking to Damballa Wedo about it. It was the right plan. Little did I know you were over there fucking it all up."

"Vic!" Willow looked over at Nanagusta, expecting her to be horrified at Victoria's language, but her eyes just moved back and forth from one sister to the other.

"Keep your voice down. And what else have you shared with her? I know you've been running your mouth. Damn, I can't believe you'd do this, after living in my home all this time."

Willow's head still pounded, but she did her best to ignore it, knowing she had to stick up for herself. Her sister never gave her credit for anything — not with the business, not with Nickie. Before Madelyn arrived, Willow had cooked almost every meal that came out of that kitchen. She purchased snacks for clients to eat during sessions, pitched in her own money to buy Christmas gifts curated to their specific tastes. She did these things and so much more, yet her sister appreciated nothing. And what else was she talking about? Had Nickie told her about the Bend Over spell? She doubted it. "Now, hold on. You're not about to just stand here and discount me, making me out like I'm nothing. All I was trying to do was help my niece, this poor kid who doesn't have any friends, hasn't had any fun. And the moment she tries to get a little bit of life, you come along with your ridiculous rules and your stupid chats with some snake-loving spirit and mess it all up for her."

Victoria opened her mouth, something between a gasp and a chuckle coming out.

Willow stood, a bit unbalanced. "She's not you, Victoria. Let Nickie live her own damn life. She isn't cursed. Nobody's going to die."

Victoria tipped her head to one side, baiting her. "How do you know?"

Willow couldn't tell her sister why she knew. It would destroy her and their family for good. "People die, Vic. Just get over it already. Damn."

Her sister stared her down, as if revisiting Willow's words to make sure she'd heard correctly. She took a step back. "Fuck you, Willow," she hissed. "Get your shit, and get out of here."

She shouldn't have said that. It was a low dig, especially for Willow, who hadn't stuck around to support her sister after Jimmie died. The room felt hot. "Victoria, just wait. Wait, wait, wait."

"Matter of fact, don't even take your shit. Just leave and we'll box your stuff for you and leave it on the porch for you to pick up."

She couldn't be hearing right. Victoria couldn't kick her out. She was her sister. They'd lived here together for over a decade. And how could Victoria operate the business without her? Willow just needed to defuse the situation. They could get past this. "Calm down. You're the one who started with the f-bombs. Anyway, you're taking this completely wrong."

"Am I? Then, explain right now what this is. You have ten seconds."

"You have ten seconds." It was a terrible imitation, and an even worse idea to make fun of Victoria right then, but she couldn't help it. Victoria was treating her as if she

were a child, so why not act the part?

Victoria closed her eyes and inhaled. "You're drunk."

"Barely tipsy." Willow felt the pressure of a burp at the bottom of her throat, though if she let it out, it was possible the contents of her stomach would come up too. She could imagine throwing up all over herself, and Victoria pushing her out, not even giving her a chance to wash up. She suddenly felt drained. "I'll be right back. I need to go to the bathroom."

"No. Put your shoes on, take a jacket from the coatrack, and leave." Her sister didn't seem ready to let up, but Nanagusta rose and took Victoria by the arm, a gentle tug to pull her back.

Willow dashed down the hall, shutting herself in the guest bathroom as Victoria called her to come back. She knelt on the tufted rug and lifted the toilet lid, but nothing came up. She felt feverish and wobbly. The blood in her head had plunged to her toes, and she rested her cheek on the toilet brim. When someone knocked on the door, she expected it to be Victoria, warning her she better not puke in the guest bathroom. Instead, it was Madelyn.

"You alright in there, Willow?"

She managed to say *yes,* that she'd be out soon.

An hour later, she'd packed a duffel and a backpack and walked downstairs, Madelyn, Nanagusta, and Victoria all waiting for her in the foyer. Willow had been thinking about leaving more and more lately, but she'd wanted to do so on her own terms, had envisioned herself quitting and telling Victoria about her big plans as she set a copy of her business proposal and business license on the desk. She didn't want to leave now, in the middle of the night, after being forced out. But perhaps she would just for a couple of days. Call her sister's bluff and spend the evening at a nice hotel, only to be asked to return Monday night after being missed at the reception desk. That would give her time to finagle an explanation about the spell, about why she'd helped Nickie with Felix. She could come up with something.

"Don't worry, Nana. I'll be fine." In the dim light from the family room, Nanagusta's eyes were creased. Worried.

"How long are you going to be gone?" Madelyn asked, glancing at Willow's bags.

She pushed her lips to one side of her face. "Who knows? You won't miss me, though. Maybe Vic will have you take over

268

reception duties since Nickie has school." Victoria would never do such a thing, but she had to say something to get through the moment.

She looked over at her sister by the staircase. She appeared withdrawn, tired as she locked her fingers together, settling herself down to a hush, probably hoping Nickie hadn't awakened with all the yelling, wasn't eavesdropping. "All this time, you've been working against me. You've undone everything I've put into place. All I've ever done is support you, Willow. I've taken care of you. I've loved you. And you just take me for granted."

Willow could agree with much of what Victoria said. Most of it. But Victoria hadn't been a perfect sister. She'd hurt Willow, even if she never knew it, agreeing to a date with Jimmie Wilkes all those years ago. He'd asked her out only hours after breaking up with Willow. And then she'd moved out of the house so quickly, leaving Willow behind the same way Madelyn had always left them.

Victoria stepped to the door and opened it.

Nana clutched Willow hard around her back as she hugged her, her grandmother sharing invisible words with her.

I will. I'll be fine, Willow said back in her

head, giving Nanagusta a knowing smile.

It would be an adventure. That's what she told herself to keep from crying. She hadn't slept anywhere but in that house since her time in New Orleans. Even with her escapades and dates, she always came home.

A stability returned to the house as Willow walked outside, an exchange — Madelyn's arrival for Willow's departure. But things were still off, her mother not able to offer all that Willow could. Maybe with her leaving, someone would notice.

Seated behind the wheel of her car, she turned the ignition and let it idle, pulling out her phone to check her bank balance, wondering how fancy a hotel she could afford.

Then she had a thought. She texted January, asked if she could stop by. He'd hinted before about waking up next to her, once even suggesting he could do it every morning. She'd see how things fared tonight and take it from there. At least then she wouldn't have to be alone.

In the drive-thru line for a burger and fries, she stalled as she waited for January to get home. A freckled teenager handed her a bag, a greasy splotch forming at the bottom. "You okay, ma'am?"

Willow smiled, embarrassed by how she

must have looked. She kept the window down as she sped off, a hip-hop song blasting, its bass line thundering. As she drove, Willow blamed the crisp late-night air for the tears that came. She wiped them away with the back of her hand.

24
VICTORIA

The Monday morning after Willow left, Madelyn greeted Victoria with coffee stirred with sugar, cream, and a sprinkle of nutmeg. She asked her mother what she was doing at the reception desk.

"Well, I'm filling in for Willow. You know, until she . . . is allowed back."

Victoria chuckled, incredulous. Madelyn was in over her head. While she'd peeked into Willow's bedroom first thing to make sure her sister hadn't crept back in overnight, the room empty, the bed made just like it had been the day before, she thought perhaps that her sister might have shown up for work, worried about her paycheck. Why else had Victoria smelled coffee?

Madelyn didn't move, waiting for Victoria to take her drink. "Well, if you're not going to drink this, then I certainly will. Looking at the schedule, we got a long day ahead."

Victoria reached for the cup, picked up

the folder from the edge of her desk, and went into her office. She didn't want to drink the coffee, but its rich aroma begged her to take a sip. Like every other thing her mother whipped up, it was delicious. She'd been on edge, the women in the house surely feeling it. Her belly ached when she thought back to the previous night's events — finding the spell on Nickie's phone, telling Willow to leave. She hadn't even grappled with Nickie's question about the curse. Willow must have said something about it. At least it was done. The truth was out, and if Nickie wanted to know more, she could come to her. In a way, her sister had done her a favor, telling the story that Victoria herself had been too hesitant to share with her daughter.

The mug of coffee would soon cool if she didn't drink. It wouldn't hurt to accept a kindness extended her way, even if there was a motive behind it. Her mother, no doubt, would soon be asking for another extension to her stay.

The only change she'd ever imagined to her practice in terms of personnel was Nickie joining her, a grown-up version of her daughter pushing Victoria to renovate the house, expanding the reception space and adding a second office. What she saw in front of her, Madelyn at the desk, she could never have imagined. But she'd have to accept it for now. Before her first client arrived, she popped back out to the reception area where Madelyn was sorting paperclips by color into a divided container. "We'll try this out. But you have to be on your best behavior. No talking back. No sass."

"I know how to work in an office, Ms. Montrose. You see that? I didn't even call you Victoria. Or should I call you Doctor?"

"Victoria is fine." She told Madelyn if she was going to help out, she needed her to be on time every morning at seven thirty sharp, looking neat and smelling like soap — no perfume. They'd see how it went this first week, or however long it took until Willow came crawling back, once she'd grown tired of whatever shit January was giving her.

"Don't you worry. I won't even wear deodorant if that's what you want."

She'd let Madelyn keep the room while she worked — at least she wouldn't have an excuse for not arriving on time if she was just upstairs. It wasn't the perfect plan, but she couldn't have some outsider in the house helping her out. Not now. Maybe not ever. With everything going on with Nickie, she needed her circle small and tight. There wasn't any other choice.

Their first day working together went well. Uneventful, which is how Victoria liked her days to go. She kicked off her heels, bending and flexing her feet to crack them before walking around the desk to switch places with Madelyn. She needed to show her how to use the scheduling system. The doorbell rang.

"I'll go get it," said Madelyn.

Clicking around on the screen, she absorbed all the other things she'd eventually have to teach Madelyn — corresponding with the practice's email, updating the website, setting up appointment reminders, billing, finding continuing education opportunities, ordering just the right snacks for clients. Honestly, she wasn't even sure she knew how to take care of many of these tasks herself.

Victoria still couldn't believe she'd been gutsy enough to force Willow to leave. So many times, when her sister frustrated or angered her, she'd wanted to fire Willow or ask her to move out. But the complications that would follow had never been worth it. Maybe she didn't show it enough, she could admit that, but Victoria valued all that Willow did for their family. She mopped the floors, she scrubbed the toilets. Before Madelyn's arrival, Willow cooked most of the family's meals, tackled the grocery shopping. All things Victoria didn't have time to do. But helping Nickie in a way that opposed what Victoria was trying to build for her daughter, protect her from? She could forgive Willow's harsh words, but all she could see when she closed her eyes now was that photo, Nickie's and Felix's names next to each other, Nickie returning late from the library, half-naked in her bed, surely because of that boy.

The two sisters bickered and jabbed at each other often, but she couldn't recall another time when they'd argued like they had the last couple of weeks, first about January, then their showdown the day prior. When they were younger, the two of them had agreed to always talk through their issues when they had them, particularly if a guy was involved.

Even with Jimmie, their bond had stayed solid; though, for Willow, he had been just another one of her admirers. He had been Victoria's first and only for everything romantic, sensual, sexual. He was her husband, her child's father, her partner in life, at least for many months.

Jimmie might be home right now if he hadn't decided to pick up late-night burgers and fries in Torrance for a pregnant Victoria. She'd been waiting up for him, lying on her back in their new bed, trying to remember all the words to the song he'd written about the baby, convinced they were having a girl, when someone knocked on the door. It must have been Jimmie with his hands full, she figured. Or he'd somehow lost his door key between the car and their upstairs apartment unit, with its view of Los Angeles on a clear day or so they'd been told by the manager. Instead, the person on the other side of the door was a police officer. Her first thought was that she was in trouble, perhaps for the time she'd cut school to go to the beach with Jimmie, or when they'd eaten at El Torito and left only a dollar for a tip.

"Are you the spouse of Jimmie Wilkes?" the man had asked.

When she nodded, he asked if he could come in, then told her she should sit down. She wore a satiny two-piece pajama set, the pants with a drawstring so she could adjust them to her growing bump. Victoria smiled at him, despite his uneasiness. She wanted to come across as pleasant.

"I'm afraid that there's been an accident."

"Something at the airport? What happened?" He worked in baggage. She teased him often about being a klutz, telling him not to get knocked out by a Samsonite at work.

The officer explained that a car had been driving on the 405 in the wrong direction. A drunk driver. He'd hit Jimmie's car head-on.

The man dropped his gaze to the floor, and it was only then that the scene made sense to her. He'd come to their home to deliver this news because it was the worst news possible. She hadn't listened to Nanagusta about the curse.

"But . . . but we're having a baby. I know I'm not showing yet, but we are." Her hand was on her belly.

"I'm very sorry, miss. Ma'am. Is there anyone you can call? Family? Or is there a neighbor who can come over here to help you?"

There wasn't anyone she wanted to talk to besides Jimmie. But the only people she could call were Nanagusta and Willow. And then, only two months after Nickie was born, her sister Willow — her best friend — left her, off to New Orleans.

When Willow finally returned, Victoria, Nickie, and Nanagusta had moved from

Carson to their current home, a fixer-upper bungalow across the street from a park. Having lost the shop, Willow had ingratiated herself to the family, offering to find affordable contractors to work on the house, to assist Nanagusta with her retirement, to drive Nickie anywhere she needed to be. Victoria welcomed her back, glad that Nickie would get to know the infamous Aunt Willow that Nana always spoke about, but she'd kept her distance, still hurt that her sister had hightailed it so soon after Nickie's birth. After Jimmie's death.

They settled into routines, into roles, Willow the math tutor, the baker, interior designer. She talked Victoria into bringing her on as receptionist, refining her skills over the years to the point where Willow handled just about everything in the business but counseling folks. Time also did the favor of easing the pain she'd caused, though Victoria never mentioned to Willow that she felt abandoned, that she hoped they'd parent Nickie together. Ultimately, she'd gotten her wish. Willow had helped care for Nickie most of her life. But this time, she didn't know if something would force her sister to return.

They'd be able to handle things, she and

Madelyn. What mattered most, what had built her wide clientele was Victoria's skills, her gift. The other details would fall into place. She hadn't completely forgiven her mother, wasn't sure if she ever would, but she could trust that if the woman really wanted to connect with the family again, if she really wanted to change, they would create a way. They'd be just fine.

"Vic," her mother called from under the archway connecting the foyer to the reception area. "I mean *Victoria,* it's your client, I believe."

It was indeed. Maya Ackbar.

"Hey, Ms. Victoria. So sorry to show up like this without calling first. I texted Willow a message but didn't hear back so I thought I could stop by on my way home. I know it's late."

"Willow is bad with texts. She keeps her phone in her purse and never feels it vibrating. And she's off today." As she said this, she began to wonder why Maya would have Willow's number.

"I see. I was just hoping she had more of that orange powder mixed up that I could buy from her. I accidentally broke the bottle last week before I had a chance to use it and —"

"Powder?"

"Yeah. She called it a foot powder, I think? To be honest, it smelled a lot like what I use on my brisket."

Victoria asked Madelyn if she could go to the kitchen and brew her a cup of tea. She wasn't thirsty but worried what else Maya might say in front of Madelyn.

"So what I was telling you is that I dropped it on the carpet. I scooped some of it up but had to vacuum the rest. I figured it probably lost all its power after the mess I made of it. I stopped by hoping I could buy another batch. Wasn't sure if that was something she kept around or if she put it together specifically for me."

Victoria's jaw clenched as she stood. "I'm sorry, Maya, but I don't know what you're talking about. This . . . foot powder. What was it supposed to do for you?"

Maya met Victoria's eyes, her face kidlike. "It's to use with Nelson. Willow said that if I put this on the floor at his apartment under all of his rugs and the bath mat, he'll propose to me."

Maya had shared in her session the week before that she wasn't in a hurry to get married. Had she just been telling Victoria what she wanted to hear?

Something worse occurred to Victoria.

"And did Willow have you pay money for this?"

Maya opened her palms, spreading her fingers wide, and waved them, a big *no*. "Oh, no way. Absolutely not. Ms. Willow never charges for her services."

"Her services?"

"Right. She said it was a bonus add-on. For her favorite clients. But since I'd been the one so clumsy, I figured I should offer to pay for more."

Victoria's chest rose and fell, her nostrils flaring as she measured her breaths. She didn't know how long it had been going on, but work like this didn't stay hushed. She worried about the State's ethics board. "Maya, I apologize for Willow. I do not support or endorse what she's doing. And it's not real."

Maya looked away. Victoria didn't mind shaming this grown woman, especially after all the work they'd done together, contemplating, role-playing, digging. She'd let Maya come in on Sundays, texted her messages of support, and played with strategies to help her maximize visits under her insurance plan. And for what? So she could attribute all her success to Willow's hoodoo?

"I suggest if you really are interested in marrying Nelson that you talk to him about it. And we can explore this more in our session this week." She patted Maya's upper arm, a subtle push back toward the foyer, then followed her to the front door and guided her outside without another word.

How many of her other clients had been offered an *add-on service* by Willow?

Victoria needed a release. Back inside, she looked up at the dull ceiling and screamed, forcefully enough to stir the pendant light hanging above the space. Then she stomped her foot, stomped it so hard that it hurt.

"Are you . . . okay?"

Victoria turned to find her mother, frowning, hands on her hips. Victoria covered her face, dizzy with frustration. This was not the calm mental space she wanted to be in after a long day of clients. "I'm fine." She walked past Madelyn toward the staircase, aimed for Willow's room to search for their grandmother's book. She wanted to destroy it but knew she would never do such a thing. But she could hide it away, make it disappear until it couldn't inflict any more harm. There wasn't anything she could do about the family being cursed. However, she would always do what was needed to prevent further misfortune.

■ ■ ■ ■

PART II
JANUARY

■ ■ ■ ■

25
WILLOW

So far, living with January had been less than phenomenal. She'd shifted her schedule so that she was awake while he was at his security job. She slept the same few hours he did each morning, and then they watched television in the afternoons until he left again. He still wrote papers and had recruited her into the business, mostly for English composition classes. Sometimes he used her for poetry or early-American lit. Someone once complained after getting a C− on one of the papers Willow wrote and wanted his money back. Since then, business had slowed, and she earned extra money bartending some weekends, not that she had a license or knew what she was doing. Those were the nights she most looked forward to, the few hours she could escape into the world.

A little over two months had passed since Willow had last seen her family, and

Thanksgiving, Christmas, New Year's, and Nanagusta's birthday had come and gone. She had been shocked when Victoria hadn't called after a few days, and a little hurt that no one had gotten in touch with her. She'd tried to still be part of the family from a distance, mailing greeting cards, having hot wings and cheesecakes and rum punch delivered, though Victoria probably tossed everything she sent in the trash before the others could see. Her resolution for the new year was to save money, which meant that she'd have to find cheaper — and more effective — methods to stay connected to the women.

She wasn't ready to go back with her tail between her legs, so she started calling. She hoped to catch Nickie by reaching out early in the mornings, when her niece might be downstairs near reception before school, before the office's seven thirty start time. The calls went to voice mail the first few times, but one morning, when she'd tried at 7:18, the phone picked up on the second ring. "Hello?"

On the other end, she heard nothing at first. Then, the sound of breathing. "Hello? Nana?"

The breathing grew heavier. Then she heard what sounded like snapping.

Willow put her hand to her chest, her insides fluttering. She couldn't hear her Nanagusta but certainly felt her there, on the other side of the line. "Nana, it's me. I miss you. I miss all of you. You doing okay?"

It had become their thing, the timing perfect, January falling asleep quickly after arriving home. She'd call and talk to Nana for fifteen minutes, then join him under the covers. It was nice, letting her old and new worlds overlap, but she knew she couldn't keep this up. She missed her family, and she missed helping people. She hadn't figured out a way to do that in her new life yet.

Well, except that she served as January's hype woman.

"Babe," he now called over to her from the bed, his shirt off, his legs under the covers, "I'm thinking about opening up a group home."

She buttered the bread of what would soon be his grilled cheese sandwich. "Is that right?"

"That's what you always say."

She almost repeated herself but didn't feel like bickering. January had a lot of ideas. "Sorry, babe."

"So what do you think?"

Just like most of January's plans, it didn't make sense, not without some sort of passion or experience behind it. Had he spent time in a group home before? Had he ever worked as a counselor? Did he own a house that could be used? She was certain the answer to these questions would be *no.* But what Willow admired about January was his ability to just *do.* He went for it, just figured out a way. She studied him, wondering if there were a mixture she could one day bottle up and use to spark a little ingenuity. Nothing more had progressed with her business plan. She hadn't even created a You-Tube account or added to her list of titles yet, not feeling fully herself, driven, in the months since the fight with Victoria. Though Willow deserved more from her sister, she still felt badly about the words she'd said.

"I think it makes sense. There's a lot of need out there," she said, humoring him. He still hadn't commented on the draft business plan she'd shared. She'd worked on it for hours a day when she first moved in, pumped with an important task to take care of, but she'd reworked it so much by now she was going in circles.

"Exactly. I mean, we could find us a foreclosure, maybe over in Paramount or Gardena. Get a couple of grants, hire a grad student to run sessions. Maybe your sister could supervise."

"Mmm-hmm." She did her best to sound enthusiastic, to not poke holes right away. Especially Victoria's purported role — she might have laughed, but that would have hurt his feelings.

"And you could do whatever job you want, though I know you loved that reception work, didn't you?"

That he was correct about. She absolutely wanted to do something more, but right now, being a receptionist seemed like a dream compared to her current day-to-day of watching romantic comedies and true crime shows, cooking January's keto-friendly meals, and studying a GRE test prep book she'd found in January's trunk. The first couple of weeks had been euphoric, but now she was bored as hell. Had she not appreciated her job with Victoria enough?

If only she had some of the implements she'd left at home: the jar of cotton balls soaked with Essence of Van Van stashed high atop the bookshelf behind a plant. The Hail Mary prayer that had been torn out of the book, handwritten by Bela Nova, pressed between pages thirteen and fourteen of a World Book Encyclopedia G volume. And a packet of wishing beans slipped in the cover with her pillow. Maybe having these would shake awake some motivation. She had to get her hands on them without her sister knowing.

26
AUGUSTA

In the time since Willow had been kicked out, the house had grown colder. Others might blame the wintry weather but Augusta believed their home missed Willow's warm spirit. In many ways, she'd been the heart of the place, and they'd all tried to keep operating as if they weren't missing a vital organ. From time to time, Augusta logged into Willow's Facebook account to see what she'd been up to. Thankfully, there'd been no more messages from Harlowe's sister, Ramona. She couldn't risk the truth coming out that way.

As far as she knew, Augusta was the only one who still had a lifeline to Willow. Her granddaughter called reception every couple of days to tell Augusta about how she was doing, what she'd made January for dinner, the great book January recommended, January's new custom-made suit, a story about how someone had slapped January after mistaking him for someone else. If she could speak, she'd tell Willow quite loudly that she didn't care to know anything else about January. Not that she didn't like the guy. She'd enjoyed his company that day at brunch, but by now, she knew more about him than she did any of her own family members. Still, she answered the calls when they came, pleased to hear Willow's voice.

This morning, she rang a little earlier than usual, and Augusta had to hustle over from the dining room where she'd been drinking her tea and using the laptop. Willow started in about a cocktail she'd learned how to make the night before at the bar and how she'd experimented with some of the drink ingredients, conceiving a potion that made folks with two left feet able to find rhythm and dance well. Eventually, predictably, she turned to January. "I've been trying to get him to learn how to play pickleball with me. I guess it's like the newest thing and a good way for me to get in shape so I can wear some of those dresses still back in my closet. But it takes two of us to play. Who knows? We get good enough, we can enter a tournament, play other couples. I ordered us some equipment. Maybe he'll take a hint."

Augusta had never heard of pickleball and wondered what in the world kind of equipment one needed to play it. What she did know was that her granddaughter's approach was all wrong. Not that she was encouraging it, but if Willow wanted January to do something, she'd have to talk to him about it, gently, while in bed before they drifted off to sleep. Pillow talk had been her specialty with Dudley Lee, the two of them smooshed together in the twin bed they shared. She didn't have any grand plans for him, however, content with putting her arms around him, gazing into his eyes until the two of them fell asleep, always him first.

A week into their marriage, Dudley Lee got a job as a janitor at a hotel on Canal Street. He wouldn't make much money, he'd told her, wouldn't be able to move her into a house like that of her childhood. But she didn't care. "Silly Dudley Lee. I love you for these dimples. And the way you make me feel. I love you for how you stick it to me, especially when you go in there with your tongue. I don't care about what you can buy me."

"But I want you to love me more. And if I buy you a proper house, you will."

While he was away, she spent her days baking, cooking, perfecting his most beloved dishes, things his mother would make for him — candied yams, crawfish Creole, monkey bread. The kitchen she shared with Charles's wife, Aletha, who took over the space in the afternoons, so Augusta had to hustle to get his dinners ready in the morning, rewarming them each evening. With the little room available to her in the refrigerator and the cupboards, Augusta shopped daily at the French Market. She knew Bela Nova got her produce, spices, and teas as soon as dawn hit, arriving before even some of the vendors. So she'd wait, send Dudley Lee off with chicory and a pair of warm biscuits spread with butter, then join the crowds that gathered mid-morning. Women — housekeepers, nannies, widows, and young girls in their school clothes — she made the rounds with them all, choosy with how she spent her money, knowing the modest stack of cash she'd saved working under Bela Nova wouldn't last the summer.

One Friday morning while in line to purchase buttermilk and peaches for a pie, Augusta felt herself being watched. When she turned around, she met the steely eyes of a very made-up woman, cheeks stained burnt orange and eyelashes coated with mascara. She wore pink lipstick, though she hardly had any lips on her, and Augusta could smell her department-store perfume.

The woman said nothing, just lifted an eyebrow and squished together what little lips she had, perhaps appalled by Augusta's nerve to give her the once-over. Turning back around, Augusta paid for her items and started home. Before she made it to the walkway, she heard the soft clack of heels on the hard dirt only a few feet behind her. She was sure it was the woman, though she wouldn't check this time. The click-clacks matched her own hurried footsteps, and Augusta assumed the woman would soon branch off in a different direction, splitting off into the Quarter somewhere or getting into a parked car.

But a half mile away from the house, the footsteps still followed. It could be simple coincidence, the two of them heading in the same direction, keeping the same pace, but Augusta didn't think so and wasn't surprised when, as she reached Royal Street, the footsteps doubled in time until they were right up with her. The woman grabbed hold of her arm.

Augusta stopped, not smiling, not wanting to appease or entertain her. "You need something?"

When tears began pooling in the woman's weary eyes, smearing her makeup, Augusta placed her bags on the ground, ready to offer comfort or to block a right hook. She saw despair in the lady, a bloat around her eyes. The most decent thing to do was to hand the woman her handkerchief. After blotting away tears, the woman was finally able to speak, thanking Augusta for her kindness. "You'll have to excuse me for behaving this way, but I haven't been myself lately. You see, I've got a bad husband."

Augusta steadied herself, wondering what the woman was implying.

"I'm sure this happens to you a lot. And I apologize for coming up to you in the street like this instead of at the shop."

"The shop?" asked Augusta. Did Bela Nova have eyes on her from somewhere way off and had sent this person to trap her?

"It's just that, once I recognized you, it seemed right. I ain't never believed in hoodoo all my good life. But I don't know what it is — you got some kind of energy about you. Made me think you can help me."

The scene remained vivid to Augusta even decades later. It was a purely Southern day, a mist in the air that pressed you down, the heat making you sweat soon as you woke up. Wild iris was in bloom and salt marsh pinks, abundant enough to smell, tangy and bitter. Her feet ached from walking so quickly, her soles worn thin on the gravelly road.

"You the girl that works with Delilah, right?"

Delilah was the name Bela Nova had been given by her parents, a name she stopped answering to once she opened up her shop. By now, she'd separated herself fully from the girl Delilah, a standout student when she'd been at Our Lady of Refuge High School, would no longer humor anyone who called out that name. Perhaps this woman knew Bela Nova from before. But then, how did she know about Augusta?

"I've seen you with her in the mornings. Shopping."

"I used to work for her. Bela Nova," Augusta said, and the whole of her stomach dropped just saying the name out loud. "But I don't anymore."

"Yes, I figured as much seeing you out at the market without her. That Delilah likes to keep her girls under her thumb." Augusta wouldn't dwell on those words until later, but she hadn't reckoned that there were any *girls* before her. "I'm really looking for some help, but Delilah would laugh if I ever got the nerve to step into her shop." The two had gone to school together. "I don't have a lot of money. Not anymore. But I can give you a good little wad if you'd be willing to help me." The woman, Azalea, would become her first client, asking Augusta to prevent her husband from seeing other women. Her man had said she didn't have enough meat on her, and he didn't even try to hide his gallivanting.

At the woman's home, it was a struggle to remember how to do much of anything. She'd never taken notes. Bela Nova had always insisted Augusta learn by practicing over and over, not by studying. She asked Azalea to collect any coins that her husband might have held in his hand, two bristles from their broom, a cube of sugar, and any gold jewelry she owned. From the market later that day, she purchased essence of rose, which she mixed with red ink to make what Bela Nova called Dove's Blood. She'd use it to write Azalea's name on a piece of paper seven times. Augusta would compile these items for a ditty bag to be placed under her husband's pillow to ensure his head rested there each night. "It ain't about where he's sleeping. It's what he's doing when he's *not* sleeping," Azalea had sassed. Augusta assured her that the fix would indeed fix his philandering ways.

Despite the woman's need, Augusta felt thorny about taking her money. Her home was on a good street, shined up from the outside, but it was clear better times had passed the couple by, the rooms inside stark, nothing but a small table and a stool in the front room. "Pay me when things get better."

Augusta left, wishing she hadn't indulged the woman. She'd never put together a spell outside of the shop and wasn't confident she had the chops.

She hadn't given more thought to Azalea until a couple weeks later when, while searching a pile for a ripe lemon at the market, she felt someone close behind her. She hardly recognized the woman, her face scrubbed clean of all its maquillage, the color in her cheeks natural and seemly. She'd come to the market to compensate Augusta and tell her about the accident. Augusta's pulse sped up as Azalea recounted what happened.

The husband had been on the assembly line at a meat-packing facility and for once was sober on the job. This made him in the mood to work a little more expeditiously, put a little lightning into it to speed along the day. His newfound fervor, however, brought trouble when he dropped his butcher knife, the sharp blade splitting the leather top of his shoe. Those around him hurried to get off the shoe and wrap up his foot, so much blood it soaked a towel in under a minute. They ran him to the hospital, but they'd left his toes inside the shoe.

Augusta put one hand on the stand's table, the other to her chest. "You mean he lost his toes?"

"All four of them. Dougie didn't have a pinky toe. That one got cut off when he was just a kid."

"Oh, Ms. Azalea. I'm so sorry."

She shook her head. "You don't understand. Ever since then, he ain't been going out at night. Wants me to take care of him, nurse him back to health so he can work as well as he did that day." Azalea pulled out a thin wad of folded bills. "We done it four times in one week. It'd been months since he touched me."

Augusta didn't know what to say. Again, she refused the woman's money, unwilling to welcome the responsibility for such an event, needing to prevent gossip that she'd maimed a man. Her ditty bag had been assembled wrong, obviously. She'd made some significant error, but what? If only she could refer to Bela Nova's book.

Returning home that evening, she found Dudley Lee in the kitchen drinking a tall glass of sweet tea. "I lost my job," he told her, apologetic but skipping the specifics.

As he explained his plan for finding something new and better, Augusta untied the crimson scarf from around her neck, unpacked her grocery bags. Her hand hit something coarse near the bell peppers and onions — the folded stack of bills Azalea had flashed earlier. She must have slipped the money in while Augusta was occupied. When Dudley Lee saw the cash, he wanted to know where it came from. Years later, she wished she would have just lied, said that she'd gone to visit her parents and they'd given it to her. Or that she'd picked up some work washing and folding clothes. But she told him most of the truth, omitting only the part about Dougie's missing toes.

Dudley Lee was amazed, proud of his new bride for having her own hustle.

"Dudley Lee, this was a one-time thing. A favor. I can't keep doing this."

"Of course you can. You gotta have something worth money, the way my mama put all that work into you."

"But . . . I never did things all by myself."

But he was insistent, backpedaling some, admitting now that he'd be hard pressed to get another gig soon. Later, after he was dead, she'd discover that he'd been let go for playing craps in the alley behind the hotel. "I'll get you your clients. You can meet them here. We'll fix up the front room. Or even our bedroom. Save up some money until we can get our own shop. Just like Mom's."

The concept wouldn't work if she relied on just the few snippets of spells she'd come to memorize. She couldn't risk leaving a good number of people in the parish without toes, hands, feet. So Dudley Lee would have to go steal his mother's book of spells from the workshop. Theft wasn't an easy thing for Augusta, but she rationalized it, telling herself they wouldn't be in their situation had Bela Nova just granted the two of them her blessing. Besides, Bela Nova had written that book herself, collecting hexes, chants, ingredients for powders, tinctures for years. Most of its contents the woman could recall without blinking, simply pulling down the book for good measure. The harm in taking it would be minor. And hadn't Bela Nova planned on giving it to Augusta at some point as her chosen successor of the shop and everything in it? If that was the fate she'd been ascribed according to Bela Nova, why not be assertive in chasing after it, face her future head-on? How else could she be a helper to the world, as Lanora desired of her daughters?

The next day, not soon after he'd left, Dudley Lee returned home, an impish grin on his face. It was easier than cheese to snag the book, he'd said. He'd also lifted a few dollars from his mother's tip jar. "Well, I ain't gonna put it back now," he said when Augusta protested, tucking the money in his pocket, telling her he'd be back in a few hours.

The rain outside was falling more like snow, buoyant and soft, bits of sun sneaking left and right from the clouds. By now, the best of the market pickings would be gone. And though it was late, she didn't want to chance a run-in with Bela Nova so soon after Dudley Lee had pilfered the book. She'd have to find a new place to shop. Luckily, there was still a bit of pork sausage left from the day before and some okra and corn, the makings of a sweet celebration dinner. She began to chop the vegetables, giddy and exhilarated that she'd made such an impact on Azalea's life and now could do even more.

The sizzle from working Azalea's trick remained in her body from that day forward and took hold of her like nothing else ever had, not even her love for Dudley Lee. Her fears about Bela Nova wilted away with time, and she continued pushing miracles

305

out of impossible situations, though the spark had waned as she aged. Which was fine, because Victoria had been there to step in her place.

Augusta felt a similar sizzle coming through the line as she listened to Willow, who'd miraculously stopped jabbering away about January and returned to the potion, spouting out dozens of possibilities — peeling maraschino cherries and drying the skin and crushing it into a powder, of burning sanding sugar, of macerating berries. As Willow described her work, Augusta recognized her energy, her excitement, her persistence, matching her own from decades before.

"You still there, Nana? The reason I didn't try olives is because they're stone fruits and will probably center a person's gravity, not what you want when dancing, you know?" She knew Willow still played around with recipes in the old book, studying the ingredients and processes so that she could reformulate spells, make them better. Willow had barely passed her English literature class but had years before become a student of Zora Neale Hurston's, reading and rereading both *Mules and Men* and *Tell My Horse,* texts that served as foundational for her understanding of how to craft a spell. Unlike Augusta, her granddaughter had approached the act of working tricks scientifically, grounding herself in theory so she could take hexes apart and put them back together, or rearrange them, far more than the pedestrian ways she'd remixed or altered recipes in her day.

January was clearly alive and well, and though she had dismissed Willow's feelings for the man as lust, not love, perhaps something else was at play. All these men over the years, yet the curse hadn't touched Willow. Could it be that Willow had found a way to protect herself against it? For a brief moment, Augusta wondered if maybe they'd gotten it wrong all these years. That Willow was the one who'd inherited Lanora's gift.

27
VICTORIA

Victoria could not remember a time in the last two decades when her life hadn't been nonstop. That was until recently. She no longer had to pencil clients in on Saturdays, and if someone booked a 6:00 p.m. appointment, it was only to accommodate their work schedule, not because it was the only slot left. Despite the loosening of her days, Victoria still had Madelyn report to her desk downstairs early, even when her first client wouldn't arrive until midmorning. That way, her mother could see Nickie off to school, along with Nanagusta, and answer the phone in case there were any last-minute appointments. There hadn't been in the last few weeks, but Victoria held out hope.

Today, she had only five clients to see. As she sat in her office, rearranging the books on her shelf, her mother entered, raising her new tablet high. "Vic, you have got to see these videos. They are really, really short. There's just twelve of them."

In her time there, Madelyn had developed a fondness for viral videos and consistently needed someone else to watch along with her. At first, Victoria humored the woman, knowing how badly she needed her to fill in for Willow. But after a week, Victoria had put her foot down and created a rule that Madelyn could show her a maximum of three per day.

"Three," she reminded her. "Save the others for me to watch tomorrow."

"But there will be new ones tomorrow. These kids — they so creative."

Madelyn had come quite a way in her short stint, her shirt prudently buttoned up, wispy hair settled into a low bun, yesterday's makeup washed off and replaced with new colors. She decided to be more generous. "Show me three now. If I have time later, maybe I'll let you show me three more."

"You have time. Mrs. Woodsen sent an email last night canceling."

"Anna Woodsen?"

Madelyn frowned. "You have any other Mrs. Woodsens?"

She didn't. There was an Anna Roberts and a Valerie Wood, but they'd not made appointments since the new year. "Did her message come twenty-four hours before her appointment?"

"No. But she claiming she has a fever. That's what they all say. Shoot, that's what I'd do if I was trying to get out of something without paying." Madelyn rocked in her chair, smiling to herself until she seemed to realize she'd quieted Victoria. "But I'm sure she's really sick. I hear half the city got the flu this year. Anyway, come on and see this."

The first video of the day featured a woman who falls down the steps after pretending to disappear behind a dropped blanket all for the benefit of the dog's frantic reaction. "Serves her right," Madelyn commented.

The next one was of two girls skillfully pulling off a dance segment along with their dad, who barely hit the moves a half beat behind them. "I wish y'all *would* get me looking bad, putting me out there. Then again, I always knew all the dances. *You* would have to keep up with *me.*" Madelyn's thumb swiped up to the next video.

Something about the video struck Victoria. She clasped her hands tightly in her lap as she waited for the third video to play. "Funny," she said when it finally ended. "But, Madelyn, can you go back to the other one?"

"Oh no. Don't tell me you gonna try to do that dance. Although, I can learn it for you if you want. The trick is, you play the video real, real slow. And you face the display to a big mirror to copy the moves."

The song that played was not one Victoria had heard before, but something else in it was familiar. January. She recognized his smile, beatific and cagey, lips ready to say anything you wanted to hear. Based on the name in the bottom corner of the screen, the account belonged to @apriljan, the video titled "What We Do When Mom's Asleep."

The girls in the video had January's lips, one of them closing her eyes, throwing back her head the same way he had during their brunch. Willow hadn't mentioned him having kids, surely would have wanted them to meet Nickie if she had known. The video had been posted just a few weeks ago. Without ever touching the man, her perception about him had been correct — a hustler indeed.

With this extra time she had now thanks to Mrs. Woodsen, she'd figure out what to do about this April Jan. She hadn't been able to find anything about January since Willow had brought him over. While she wanted to blame her mother for the drop in appointments, it was hard to find any supporting evidence. Clients seemed to love Madelyn, to the point where Victoria often had to interrupt their chats to get a session started. She also knew her clients had to miss Willow, who they'd known for years.

Victoria could never admit to the others how much *she* missed her sister. Madelyn had taken up space in the house but in a different way. Victoria and Willow were as different as could be, but their bond as siblings couldn't be replaced. Sometimes she thought about calling her to see how she was doing. Not that she'd forgotten what Willow did, and certainly hadn't forgiven her. Willow didn't deserve a pass on all of the things she'd done — with the business, with Nickie and the attraction spell — but she knew her sister had done what she believed was right, and she couldn't fault her for that. Some mornings, she woke up ready to call Willow and say as much, but Victoria chickened out every time.

Madelyn hovered in the doorway as Victoria clicked her computer mouse and waited for her applications to come to life. She'd start her investigative work by creating a fake Tik-Tok profile, though she could always pull out Nickie's phone from the drawer and look up the video through her account.

"Should I be worried, Vic?" Madelyn asked.

Could her mother read her mind? She hadn't seemed to notice January in the video. Victoria decided to keep that detail from her mother for now. "Worried about what?"

Madelyn took a big gulp of air and blew it out with much exaggeration. "These clients dropping off like fleas."

"Flies."

"Fleas."

"Flies."

Madelyn leaned to the side, putting weight on one elbow to square up her face with Victoria's. "That don't make sense. Fleas drop, you know, after you put the flea collar on the dog and the chemical kills them off. Anyway, flies, fleas, you know everything. But your clients," she said, pronouncing the words slowly, "are leaving."

This she knew, but having Madelyn state it made her mind spin, and if she acknowledged it to her mother, she would fall apart. She didn't want to think that Willow's departure had impacted business, that her gift of counseling people hadn't been a strong enough help for so many to stay, but she had to acknowledge the timing.

"Even that nice-looking fellow hasn't been around," Madelyn said.

"What nice-looking fellow?" Victoria was curious about whom her mother could be speaking.

"Big Russ. The one got a little crush on you."

Her smile vanished. "He doesn't have a crush on me," Victoria said sternly. But her mother was right that Russell hadn't been back for some time. While they hadn't made much progress addressing the circumstances with his ex-wife, Victoria had gotten them started during his last session, even giving him homework. He'd seemed pumped, pleased with himself that he'd finally opened up. But the following week, he canceled his appointment and had yet to reschedule. She'd stopped searching the calendar each evening, hoping to view his name listed for an upcoming visit.

"This is just how things go, especially after the holidays. It's still early in the year. People are just now returning to their normal routines."

"I suppose. But if you lose any more, I might have to get me a second gig over at Starbucks like I first was gonna do. You see that new one pop up overnight right there by the gas station?"

"It's fine, Madelyn. You don't need to get a job at Starbucks. Everything is fine." She would make sure of it. She had to.

Madelyn shrugged, still gripping her tablet. "If you say so."

Victoria put her monitor to sleep. "So what time is my first session?"

"Nothing until ten. Three more videos?"

Victoria nodded, choosing the easier route of just getting it over with, as she knew Madelyn would ask again. Then, she'd start her research. She hadn't touched January but had an inkling from meeting him that he was no good. She'd tried to warn Willow, but at least now she might have the proof she needed. She couldn't simply ignore it. Despite everything, she didn't want to see her sister get hurt.

28
NICKIE

Since her aunt had left, Nickie had gone through the five stages of grief, most of her days spent in anger. She'd now settled into acceptance. Clearly, Willow had washed her hands of their family and didn't plan to return. But what had she done to her aunt, Nickie wondered, that prevented her from saying goodbye or kept her from reaching out to her in the past two months?

Her mother had probably made Willow feel like she had to choose between January and their family. If forced, Nickie could see herself picking Felix too. His long kisses, chili fries, his eighties music — DeBarge, Klymaxx, and Shalamar. A rock group called Huey Lewis and the News. Then again, as happy as her times were with Felix, she knew she couldn't bear to be without her Nanagusta. It just sucked that her aunt had left right when her spells had seemed to be working.

With Willow's absence, she'd declared herself owner of the old, weathered book, though it still stayed hidden away in her aunt's room. While she hadn't been daring enough to direct any magic, she had tried a recipe for lemon bars in the book that turned out quite well. Another day, she'd been tempted to test out the Bend Over spell on her own, this time instead writing down the name of the man she'd met at the barbershop, Russell, willing him to ask her mother out. Who knew? Maybe a little romance would rouse her mother, kick all those curse ideas right out of her if she truly had them. Earlier in the week, the substitute in her literature class hit play on a documentary from the History Channel for the class as he scrolled on his phone. Nickie hadn't paid much attention until she heard that the show was about curses. King Tut and the Hope Diamond, Tippecanoe and several sports franchises. Was this the kind of thing her mom really subscribed to? She hadn't gotten a chance to ask her aunt about this so-called family curse before she'd left but couldn't forget her mother's face that day in her room, the look of absolute horror.

Arriving at the house, she slammed the door behind her and walked through the foyer, eager to get to Willow's room.

"Hey, Nickie. You have a good day at school?"

Madelyn had gotten herself up and around the corner from the reception area before Nickie could make it upstairs. "Yes. I, uh . . . got a hundred percent on my Spanish quiz."

"Oh, *sí*?" Madelyn put a hand on her belly and let her knees bounce with her laugh.

Nickie smiled. If she didn't, her grandmother would work hard to offer another joke or a pun, anything until she got a reaction from Nickie. "Busy evening?" She hoped she came across as polite.

"Yes, indeed. We haven't had a late night in a while but we're here until seven tonight. But don't worry, I'll put Nana's Lean Cuisine in the microwave for her. I can heat up some taquitos for you if you want. Otherwise, it's grilled cheese and sweet potato fries at seven thirty. I need to make a grocery run."

"That's fine." She didn't want to come across as suspiciously happy about dinner, but the timing was in fact great. It gave her ample opportunity to head up to Willow's room and peruse the book, as she now did most afternoons before starting her homework. Madelyn might leave her desk but wouldn't dare go upstairs while on shift. And with the promise of dinner, Nanagusta would stay put, watching her court shows, her Black millennial comedies, her K-dramas. Hopefully, none of the women would check on her. She'd already been grounded when her mom received her first semester report card a few days before, her straight As insignificant once she saw Nickie had stayed in advanced photography. But when she realized that photography was a one-semester course and confirmed that Nickie had indeed enrolled in a Felix-free econ class this semester, she seemed to forget about enforcing the punishment, though being grounded didn't look too different than her normal day-to-day.

In Willow's room, she untucked the book from its hiding spot, plopped it on the bed, and settled herself into the soft leather desk chair. That first week after Willow had left, she'd open the book, lonely, and she'd get lost in the pages. They enthralled her, let her vicariously experience the magic of the women who'd authored the book, side notes and parentheticals adding a richness to the recipes and prayers. She'd concluded that there were fifteen categories of material inside the book, some mystical, some not: powders, potions, prayers, remedies, poems, receipts, photos, greeting cards, recipes, spells, reversals, formulas and potions, rituals, blessing and anointing oils, and miscellany. She had a feeling there was a finesse to working spells, like baking. Just because someone followed a recipe didn't mean their soufflé wouldn't collapse.

She flipped to random pages, discovering a prayer of protection against Manman Brigitte.

Instructions for a blessing oil made with rose petals, almond extract, one drop of honey, lemon oil, and essential oil of lavender.

The recipe for the best fried chicken in Bunkie, Louisiana, calling for a precise eighteen-hour brine.

Willow's ninth-grade school picture. She hadn't smiled.

The remains of a pressed pink azalea.

A lipstick stain on a page with a prayer to Gran Bwa.

A Resetting and Reversing Spell written in blue ballpoint, an arrow pointing to a missing page, only the spiky roots of the paper remaining. In fact, she'd found that three or four pages were missing from the book, not taped back in or slid inside anywhere.

She turned again to the Song of Lanora,

drawn to it every time she opened the book. As her fingers ran across each line, she felt an eruption in her chest, a warmth overtaking her. It was as if seeing them had aided her understanding, got her into her mother's head. But the truth also made her anxious, especially as she read the last stanza.

Her withering heart left swollen, Lanora's
    lost love put aside
The matriarch of Eves, one of each
    generation divinely blessed with the
    foremother's gift to guide
A sweet balm on a blistering existence,
    the tenderhearted pray
This foremother bearing evermore a
    wondrous gift
Her name held high, the saint's reward by
    her daughters' arduous faith

The skin at her neckline warmed, just as a soft sound caught her attention. Looking over her shoulder, she saw her great-grandmother, all five feet of her. She let out a screech.

"Hi, Nana," Nickie said, her words breathy. She closed the book and stood, pushed the chair back to its place under the desk.

Safe in her room, she went straight to the

novel she'd picked for her English lit assignment, a classic by Bernice McFadden. She'd skip the grilled cheese and fries, avoid Nanagusta, hoping her great-grandmother wouldn't tell her mom what she'd been up to.

29
AUGUSTA

Augusta hadn't intended to startle Nickie. Or perhaps just a little, but not enough to make her squeal. She needed help with the printer and had already checked every other room in the house. When she realized what Nickie was up to, bent over the book, straining her eyes to read it in the dim light, she tightened her jaw, upturning her lips and slanting her eyebrows, her best attempt at an angry face. It worked, the girl hopping up and closing the book before scampering out of the room.

As much as Augusta had tried to warn Nickie about disregarding her mother, look how easily she'd been caught. Bold and careless, Nickie apparently didn't take her mother seriously. Or she just didn't care. At least when Willow had been around, Nickie hadn't been a risk-taker, not since she'd asked Felix over. Willow must have talked to her. While Augusta didn't approve of Willow's behavior, at least she had provided some guidance to Nickie, compared to Victoria's more distant and harsh approach. Still, if the girl wasn't careful, she'd find herself living with her aunt and Mr. January in Bellflower, calling in the mornings to listen to Augusta breathe over the phone.

Augusta hadn't seen the book in many years. She let her hand slide across its cover. Her gift wasn't as strong as Victoria's anymore, fingers not picking up heat, prickles, sparks. She pushed the book close to the headboard, then covered it with Willow's pillows, a temporary hiding spot until she could figure out someplace to stash it — she didn't want Nickie to get in trouble for lying about its whereabouts. Earlier, she'd told Victoria she had no idea where the book could be. When she laid herself down, worn out from her quest to locate Nickie, she could feel the book's edge through the down filling. She and the book were irrevocably connected, even though it never really belonged to her.

Thanks to Azalea, it had started happening on the regular. Strangers approaching Augusta in the streets, tracking her down at the house. The week after Dudley Lee stole Bela Nova's book, Augusta had avoided her usual places, using the beans, rice, flour, corn and canned goods she kept stocked on their shelf in the cupboard for meals. But they were missing the flavors they'd grown used to with Augusta shopping every other morning, Dudley Lee frowning when, each night, she offered a new angle on the same dish. Unable to fulfill her needs elsewhere, she started going back to the market, on edge the first few trips, ever on the lookout, hoping she'd be able to sense Bela Nova, notice the change in the wind if the woman came within a certain distance. Three weeks passed with no sighting, and she became complacent, forgetting to think about her. In those same weeks, she had been approached by three women, all of them referred by Ms. Azalea, each willing to pay her good money for an intervention.

She saw to them on the front porch. Dudley Lee had tracked down a set of mismatched chairs, used some of the money from Azalea to fix them up, painting them a bruised violet, reupholstering the slight squish of pad left on each. Even with the extra cotton he'd added, they weren't comfortable, but it was better than the hard stoop.

The money they'd made from just the few clients was good, more than what Dudley Lee had been bringing in from the hotel, and there should have been plenty left over after rent and food and what she gave Aletha to wash and press her hair on Thursdays. But there wasn't. She suspected Dudley Lee's gambling itch had returned, having been soothed temporarily when he was seeing Genevieve, probably fearful of what her father might think. One night, when he was out later than usual, Augusta pulled out the cigar box where they kept their cash . . . empty but for a few coins and a dented gold ring that must have belonged to Bela Nova. If she hadn't known about his previous habit, she might have thought Charles or Aletha had taken the money.

She was asleep when he returned that evening, but his smell of whiskey woke her up. The next morning, he lay stiff but snoring, one of his eyes swollen and dried with blood. He said he'd been the victim of mistaken identity, at the wrong place, but he wasn't the best liar, his tongue getting all confused when he spoke an untruth.

So her plan, in addition to purchasing greens and a meaty ham hock for dinner, was to look for some High John the Conqueror root, vanilla bean, and nutmeg to blend a Fast Luck oil. Having secured just the right bunch of parsley, she was about to head to her usual fruit stand when someone tapped her on the shoulder. She smiled as she turned, prepared to sell herself to a potential new client. Staring back at her, though, was Bela Nova, her expression menacing, like Augusta herself was the ham hock, ready to be ripped to shreds and devoured. Augusta's instinct was to run, but what difference would it make? This showdown of theirs was going to happen eventually.

"It's the thief," said Bela Nova, chewing out the words, then spitting into the hard dirt beneath them. "You're about as terrible as that thieving O'Brien, taking spells and potions that don't belong to you."

Augusta scanned her surroundings. A war was about to erupt in the square, and nobody even knew it.

A little more than two months had passed since she'd last seen her mentor, but time had made a noticeable difference, the woman's face gaunt, filled with shadows, patches of her hair gone. Her clothes hung loosely like a tablecloth. Anyone else covered with the same layers would be dripping with sweat by now. Her eyes locked on Augusta, as if trying to draw her into a trance. The woman leaned forward, and when Augusta jumped, Bela Nova laughed, and that's when Augusta saw it hadn't been a knife or a gun or a stone she'd held behind her back but a cucumber.

"After taking everything I had, the least you could do is buy your mother-in-law a few vegetables for soup, yes?"

Augusta knew that any attempt at a response or an apology would do no good. All she could do was stand there and listen to whatever it was Bela Nova wanted to say and let the woman wear herself out, at which point she might be able to walk away. But Bela Nova knew how to lure her from her quiet.

"Your mother came by the other day." She smiled. "Paid me five dollars to say a prayer of protection over her missing daughter. Someone told her she'd seen her at the Dew, in the shop."

"My mother doesn't believe in prayer."

"So perhaps that's why she asked *me* to do it. Half the miracles in life people can't do for themselves, you know." It was a verbalism Bela Nova had repeated often, as if she'd done scientific research on the topic. " 'Course, I didn't realize who she was until after I'd held her hands and spoken the words."

There was dust in Augusta's mouth when she swallowed. She couldn't even imagine her mother in the same room as Bela Nova.

"What did she want you to pray for?"

"It doesn't matter. Soon as I found out who she was, I returned her money, reversed my words right in front of her. She sat over in the corner, crying, like I'd just ripped her heart out. You sure about her not believing in prayer?"

Augusta wasn't sure about a lot, even this story — not ever had she seen her mother cry. There'd been shows of other emotions, frustration, disgust. When Bela Nova spoke, however, when she described the goings-on, it was a scene Augusta could picture.

"She wanted to know where you were. I could have told her the truth. I know about the two of you. Pathetic, not getting a place of your own. Staying over there with Charles. That's just a shame."

It didn't surprise Augusta that Bela Nova knew all this time where they'd been.

"I did tell her that you were a thieving little witch who took my son, my money, my clients. Cheated me from blessings by the loa," Bela Nova revealed. "Without my book, how could I survive? How could I please Lanora so that she'd bless me?"

Augusta was near tears, her cardinal jumpsuit dingy with sweat. All she'd wanted was to be with the person she'd grown fond of, a man she'd loved as much as her daddy, and what was so wrong with that? Why couldn't Bela Nova understand that?

"You know my memory is not what it once was. I can't recall my incantations like I used to. And you've turned my son against me, got him to take away my only source of sustenance — my book. Unfortunately for you, my little lovestruck thief, my mind got fuzzy about the Too Bad Love hex. But I remembered what I could of it and tweaked it on the spot. Spoke it right there in front of your mother. I'm calling it the True Love Always Dies curse. I reformulated it to work only on you, ten times more powerful than the Too Bad Love hex."

Augusta recalled the Too Bad Love hex from her first evening in the shop, not the words themselves but the destructive power in them. Bela Nova had paid a whole year out on her lease with the money she'd received for speaking the hex for a client.

"I spoke for you a lifetime without love, for you and your kin, if you're unfortunate enough to have any. All of you are cursed, you hear me? An ugly death for the ones with whom you fall in love. And when you hate your life, when your kinfolk want to pull out their hair in misery, you tell them about me. All the shit you done to me, you hear?"

The square had gotten loud, folks haggling, asking questions about shipments, dogs barking. Yet here were just the two of them, in a separate world from the rest. "Nothing else to say? Have I shut you up for good?" The woman took a bite from the cucumber, grinning as she chewed, green bits between her teeth. "Well, won't no one be praying to me now. To you either. See you in hell, little thief." She turned to leave but stopped herself, waving one hand as if she had already lost Augusta's attention. "Oh yes, yes. The message I was supposed to give you from your mother if I happened to see you. I almost forgot." She shifted her weight, a hip pushed out. "The funeral for your father was yesterday — she hoped you'd be able to make it. Guess I found you just a day too late. What a shame."

Augusta still to this day wasn't sure how she'd made it home that morning. Perhaps a kindly stranger had found her there, on the ground, and had carried her home. Dudley Lee wasn't around so she got into bed and slept heavily off and on, sobbing in between. When she woke the next day, he had already come and gone, and all of the money she'd earned was missing from under her pillow.

Augusta blinked a few times, back from

her memory. There were so many things going wrong with their family, and it was her fault, part of a legacy of poor choices. She'd done bad enough taking away her mentor's son, depriving the woman of her livelihood, of the extended family she'd surely pictured for Dudley Lee, lots of children birthed by Genevieve who would call her Grandmother or, even better, the wondrous loa Bela Nova, their mighty ancestor. Her father had died not knowing where she'd been, surely brokenhearted, having not seen his only child in over two years. She'd also done her own family wrong, lying all this time about how the curse had come to be, that her own miserable actions had brought it upon their family.

Bela Nova's voice in Augusta's head had been quiet for so very long that she'd almost forgotten the cackling laugh, the low burn. The voice had returned the day Nickie brought home Felix, still only whispers then. In Nickie's shouts to her mother over the months was Bela Nova. In Victoria's extreme words. She heard her old mentor in Willow's taste in men.

She had a feeling what Bela Nova was telling her now but didn't have the guts yet to do anything about it.

■ ■ ■ ■

Ever since she'd left, Willow's room had been declared communal property. Augusta tended to go in there early in the mornings, cradling a steamy mug of tea that filled the space with the scent of grass and honey. She'd place it on Willow's nightstand and then spread her body across the bed, stretching herself into an X, the silken sheets luxurious on her skin. It was as close as she could get to being romanced, to the touch of a lover, something she longed for and knew she would never feel again. Sometimes, lying there, she thought about the men whose lives she'd destroyed.

But today, she was there in the evening. After scaring off Nickie, Augusta had gone to the kitchen and returned with a mug of tea, a minty kind. She spilled some on her gown, a bit on the bed blanket, and it took her several minutes to unmake the bed, walking to each corner one by one to stretch off the linen. At the last corner near the headboard, covered by a tufted velvety cloth and nailed to the wall, she noticed a tear at the bottom, a half-dozen threads hanging loose. Had she ripped the fabric as she tugged at the sheets?

She pushed her finger up into the opening left by the rip to see how much damage she'd done when she felt something underneath the fabric where padding should have been. Rather than cotton, her nails met plastic. She was just able to reach a corner and grab hold, sliding out a compact.

She glanced up at the door, making sure it was shut securely, and then sat on the carpet, the bed a fort behind which she could hide should she be interrupted. The compact held oral contraceptive pills. She remembered the prescription she'd gotten for Willow right after Nickie was born, not wanting Willow turning up pregnant next. She popped open the container and found a third of the pills missing. Of all the things Willow should have taken with her, these pills should have been first on her list. Augusta closed the lid. Underneath, she felt the skin of a label. She turned it over and saw the name of the drug printed on the sticker: *Ortho Tri-Cyclen.* And the patient: *Nickoletta Montrose.*

The name shocked her, so much so that her fingers fumbled the plastic, sending the compact to the ground. She picked it up, read her great-granddaughter's name again, and thought of Victoria, who would surely body-slam the girl if she discovered the pills.

She lifted the lid again to check when the last one had been taken. Tuesday. Yesterday.

Her great-granddaughter had been even more nervy than Augusta had imagined. Worried about Victoria discovering the pills but not wanting to throw off Nickie, she used a nail to scrape at the corner of the label, able to unfix it completely with one pull, and crumbled it with her fist.

30
WILLOW

On a cloudy Thursday morning, Willow dozed off before daybreak hit and awoke not to the warmth of January's body next to her, home from work, but to sunlight peeking in from the blinds. It felt like she'd slept for days. She hadn't slept so much in her life, quite the opposite of when she'd first arrived, when they made love several times a day, slow-danced to songs on the radio, played checkers and Battleship, and spent his days off visiting open houses in neighborhoods they couldn't afford. He'd even gotten her to do a few workouts with him. Now, less than three months in, their relationship had gone stale.

They needed a new spark. It was too soon for their rhythm to have puttered out. It didn't require a major spell, but a nudge, a little push.

In her book was the recipe for a sweetening talc that she really wanted to get her hands on. She couldn't recall all its ingredients or how to mix it, but bringing the book with her would have been too much of a risk. While she and January had spoken about the curse, it was always in jest, and always with a jab to Victoria. "Nothing more typical than the therapist who needs therapy," Willow would say, her stomach queasy, hating to joke about mental health. She worried what he'd think if he found the book, tangible evidence of her family's weird history. There weren't too many hiding places in his apartment.

It was a little later than her usual call time, but Nana might be willing to help. They'd learned about the so-called curse on their family from her decades ago, yet Nanagusta had never stood her ground about men, about dating the way Victoria was doing with Nickie. Willow wasn't sure if it was indifference, resignation, doubt, or something else altogether that had kept her grandmother from scolding her about her love life. Maybe she just plain knew that nothing she did would ever stop her. Quickly, she washed away the trite words that occurred to her, of love making people do stupid things.

"Hello. Victoria Montrose's office." Madelyn was giving her best attempt at business friendly.

"Hi." She almost asked to speak to Augusta but doing so would give her away. She put her finger on the button to hang up but then thought of another approach.

"Hi. Can I talk to Nickie?" She'd controlled her voice, replacing her normal lilt with something pitchy and upbeat, hoping to sound like a teenager.

She could trust her niece. Nickie would be able to find the book, and if she remembered correctly, school started later on Thursdays for teacher prep.

"Willow? That you?"

She had to say, it was nice to hear her mother's voice.

"Willow?"

"Hey. Hi."

"Girl, you all right? I've been worried about you."

Willow imagined her mother sitting down, leaning back on the reception chair with her feet up, ready to spend the next hour gabbing away.

"I'm fine. I'm . . . I'm sorry I haven't checked on you."

"You sure? You sound far away."

"Well, I'm not in the house, Mama."

"I know, but you sound *very* far. Like you're in another country or something."

Willow closed her eyes. "Nope. Just over here in Bellflower."

"Well, Nickie's right here helping me file before she goes to school."

Willow nodded to herself. "So you're doing what I said? Helping out with Nickie?"

"Sure am. You know she wasn't even flossing at night? Best believe she is now. You want to talk to her?"

"Yes, if you would. I just have to ask her a question, and then I can tell you a little bit about Bellflower if you'd like." Her mother agreed.

When Nickie took over the call, Willow softened her voice just in case Madelyn could hear, then asked her if she could take the phone somewhere private, no easy feat in that house. "You alone?"

"Yes." Her one-word response was filled with curiosity. She owed Nickie a long explanation.

"Nick, sweetie. I've been trying to reach you. I really have."

Nickie didn't respond.

"I figured you didn't have your phone anymore, although I texted a couple times. Didn't get a message back. So then I started calling reception early in the morning hoping you would answer when you were downstairs getting ready to leave for school. And then Nanagusta would always pick up. Did she tell you?"

"Nope."

"Nickie, you know how much I love you."

"Well then, why did you leave without even saying bye to me or telling me you were moving out?" Nickie said.

She figured this would be the case, that Victoria hadn't been honest with Nickie about what had happened. So she explained, told Nickie about Victoria discovering the photo of the attraction spell on her phone, that they'd fought. "I promise you, Nick. I would never up and leave you like that. You're my baby — you know that."

She could hear Nickie's breath on the line, a release. "I know." Nickie had dropped the edge in her voice. They were back, the best Willow had felt in weeks. "Dang, so my mom knows about the spell?"

"Yep. But hey, if she hasn't said anything, I wouldn't worry about it." A little fib to keep her niece from stressing out. "What about the Bend Over spell? Did it work?"

"Well . . . yes, I guess so?" Her niece's response was singsongy. This made Willow happy. And proud. She did good work.

She moved on to business, asking Nickie to seek out the list of ingredients for the sweetening talc, a task she knew her niece would enjoy. And while she was at it, Nickie might as well retrieve Willow's favorite talisman and send it in the mail.

"So can I call you back this same time next Thursday for the list? Or this weekend?" Willow tried not to sound impatient and hoped Nickie didn't think she was using her.

"Um, that's fine."

She'd planned to get to work as soon as possible, but she could muster one more week, couldn't she? "Okay. Love you, Nick. I know you have to head off to school soon. You can put Madelyn on the phone."

"Aunt Willow?"

"What's up?"

"Do you believe in the . . . curse?"

The curse? How did Nickie know about that? Willow recalled Victoria's words, accusing her of running her mouth. She must have thought Willow told Nickie about the curse, which she hadn't, though her sister had to at least be a little bit relieved that Nickie finally knew. "Who told you? Nanagusta?"

"Nana knows about the curse?"

"Well, yes, Nickie. Of course Nanagusta knows. So then who told you about it?"

"Madelyn. But I didn't really take her seriously. Until I asked my mom. Then she got all weird. Madelyn said it's how my dad died. But that can't be true, right?"

Willow made a grunting sound, a flurry of words all wanting out at the same time.

"Is it true? Is there a curse that causes people to . . . die . . . if we love them?"

Willow knew her truth. "No." She shook her head, even though Nickie couldn't see her. "No, Nickie. I absolutely do not believe in the curse. But don't go telling anyone what I said, you hear me?" Willow wasn't brave enough to explain why she didn't believe in the curse, or why she didn't want the family to know. Luckily, Nickie didn't ask.

"Okay. Thanks, Auntie. I'll talk to you soon."

"Thursday, Nick. At the latest."

Madelyn coughed as she came back on the line. "You know, I think this house done gave me allergies. All these cats and possums and raccoons running around the neighborhood like street gangs. I ain't never seen nothing like it."

She missed her mother, and she longed to see Nickie again and her beloved Nanagusta. Apparently, her sister was doing fine without her. With the sweetening talc, Willow hoped that the same would be true for her. It wouldn't be her first time meddling in romantic affairs with hoodoo.

Willow was seventeen when she had first decided to use a spell on Jimmie. Something stronger than the sweetening talc, a rekindling powder. But she'd not gotten the chance to sprinkle it in his pants pockets before he and Victoria became engaged and moved in together.

This development had crushed Willow. Even though she wouldn't admit it to anyone, she'd been deeply upset that Jimmie had dumped her for Victoria, just days after she'd introduced the two of them, her sister arriving home early from her after-school activities. He'd said the words so easily: *I just don't think we're right for each other. Our time together is done.* Only days before, it seemed, he'd written her love songs, asked about her dreams. He'd been the first guy not to focus only on her looks. In the months of their relationship, he'd professed *love.* When she told him that she loved him back, Willow had meant it.

News of a baby came a few months after the wedding. Jimmie would now be permanently joined to their family. How could she stand that, watching their happy family blossom? Desperate, she again consulted the book and stumbled on something called a Bring Back a Lover elixir. It was like she'd been meant to land on that spell, like it had been custom-made for her situation, a spell she could enhance with a simple tweak.

She used the elixir because she wanted to hurt Victoria for her betrayal, for not looking closely enough to know Willow's true feelings. But she never meant for it to kill Jimmie. The potion had been more powerful than she could have known. Which was why she didn't believe in the curse. It wasn't some old hex that caused Jimmie's death. Willow had done it with her hoodoo.

31
VICTORIA

The night before last, Victoria snuck out to follow January from his and Willow's apartment to what she assumed was his job, having overheard he worked the night shift. Something about that man wasn't right, and the video had tickled her suspicions.

He was a slow driver, which made it difficult for Victoria to pace herself behind him without being noticed. She'd managed to cling close to a big rig for quite a ways, keeping in the slow lane so she could get onto the off ramp once January's car exited the freeway. She hadn't anticipated him going so far. They'd traveled north to LA and through downtown. They'd passed Silver Lake and the Hollywood Bowl and Universal Studios. Once they'd transitioned west of the 405, she prayed he wasn't headed to Ventura County. Driving wasn't her thing, and she could not recall the last time she'd ventured so far from home. When he finally pulled off the freeway, she stayed with him until he parked in the driveway of a wide ranch-style home.

Tonight, she would take the same route once again and park across the street and observe. She'd found out some things about the owner of that home. This time, she planned to confront him and didn't think it wise to travel alone.

Having confirmed Nickie was holed up in her room for the night and Nanagusta had all of her streaming services and a tray of snacks, Victoria sat in her idling car, checking the clock every twenty seconds. Finally, Madelyn walked out of the house, cautious with her body, taking her time, as if she hadn't just told Nanagusta she might sign up for a half marathon. Her mother got in and handed her a travel cup, the sweet woodsy aroma of coffee pleasing — cream and a hint of nutmeg. Her coffee skills had improved, and Victoria didn't bother telling her mother she was late.

"I put some blankets in the back seat and packed some sandwiches." She lifted a large Ziploc bag from her lap. "You said we were pulling an all-nighter."

Victoria hadn't thought about comfort or warmth or the possibility that she might get hungry. She'd been focused on one objective. The sandwiches and coffee would make it more bearable.

Madelyn had fallen asleep before they made it to the 5 freeway, but once they were close to their destination, the slow pace of the car on suburban streets stirred her. She sat up, looking around at the quiet neighborhood. "Where are we? Beverly Hills?"

"No. We're in Thousand Oaks."

As they waited at a stoplight, the gleam from a nearby gas station made Madelyn frown. "Never heard of it."

"It's not too far from where Kim Kardashian lives, like Calabasas."

"So . . . Beverly Hills?"

Victoria shook her head, decreased the volume on the radio. "I swear, this is the longest light."

"Yeah, well, I know it's late and nobody's around, but don't even think about taking it. They got people watching out for folks like us. We certainly ain't no Kardashians."

Victoria smiled, letting go of a faint chuckle. "You're right. We definitely aren't."

"What are we doing out here, anyway?"

She looked straight ahead, the road wet and glimmering in the streetlights. She wanted to tell her mother that they were saving Willow from the curse. That she'd finally found a way. But it was more than that. "Protecting Willow's heart. That January guy isn't worthy of it."

The light changed, and she turned onto a road overwhelmed with trees, one-storied houses laid flat, and wide, long walkways to the porches. After parking across from the home she'd come to surveil, she faced the window and tucked her feet underneath herself. Once Madelyn fell back asleep, she reached for one of the blankets, spreading it over the both of them before reclining a couple of inches. Not too far, though. She didn't want to risk falling asleep too. She didn't know what time January would leave.

Flits of orange began to appear in the sky. Madelyn's heavy snores had kept her up the last few hours, and she was getting tired. She regretted drinking the coffee, her bladder near full, until 6:13 a.m. when she spotted January, wearing a jacket over a polo shirt. Victoria slipped her feet into her flip flops and exited, her eyes sore from having kept her contacts in all night. She made no attempt to brush down her hair or pull up her leggings, walking quickly to the sidewalk just near the streetlight. She called out to him before he got into his car. "Thomas."

When he turned around, the red in his face spread down to his neck. "Vic . . . Victoria?" He put on a smile. "Hey, good morning. How are you? What brings you out this way?"

She held her body tightly to keep warm, asking herself why she'd not worn socks and sneakers. "What brings me out this way? Oh, I was looking for you. At your job. Isn't that where you're supposed to be right now?"

He glanced back at the house, the day's first bits of sun stenciling the outlines of brown roof tiles, the painted white bricks of a chimney. "This, uh . . . this is my job."

Victoria exaggerated her lean to take in the home behind him. "This? This is where you keep watch over priceless, exquisite art?"

"We do it remotely." His grin had slipped away.

"Oh, so I'm guessing there's a business license of some sort on the premises?"

"Well, you see —"

"Because when I looked up this address, it came up as belonging to a Thomas and Natalie January."

January crossed his arms, and Victoria was reminded how reckless it was, showing up like this. Underneath his shirt was a body that had been well invested in. When she looked back to the car, she could only see the point of Madelyn's chin through the frosty windows, her head nestled between the door and passenger seat.

"Look. Victoria —"

"Maybe Willow's told you some things about me. Whatever she said, it's mostly false. Actually, it's Willow who you probably want to know more about. Remember what I said about that curse? It's a real thing, Thomas. The people we love die. We've known this, and still, we find people to love. Innocent people. You could really call us killers, right? Because we know exactly what's at stake and, still, we pursue. I certainly did. I'm a killer. My mother is a killer. Our sweet grandmother Augusta has killed a couple of folks from what I know. And now it seems like Willow has identified a victim of her own." She let it all out in one breath.

His remained motionless, but she knew he wanted to squirm, sensed the uneasiness in his body. This only made her grow more confident.

"Deep down, subconsciously, she knows it. Maybe she's too overwhelmed to see it, too sprung off whatever you got going on in your pants to see it, but she knows the risk. The men we love die. So you can either do the smart thing and leave Willow. And I mean break it hard, so she stays wise enough to keep away from the next fool who finds her. Or you can stick around. If the curse don't kill you soon, then perhaps I'll just tell Willow about your . . . job." Victoria looked away from him and tilted her head toward the house. "And then, she'll take it upon herself to torture you in ways that are, well . . . unthinkable. Painful. And slow." She'd watched a lot of gangster movies growing up and tried to channel the brazenness she'd admired in some of the characters.

January's face finally dared to move. He probably wouldn't speak again, but she didn't want to give him the chance. "Have a nice ride to Bellflower. Your wife has a beautiful smile. The twins look just like her," she said with a grin.

As she walked away, he hurried behind her, grabbing the fleshy part of her arm, a sudden burst of spasms hitting. She spun around. "Bitch, get your fucking fingers off me. That man I killed — I loved him. What you think I'll do to you? Asshole." She rarely spoke Jimmie's name out loud and was unsettled to bring him up in this way, like she was using him. But a feeling flickered inside her, briefly, a strength she didn't know she had.

Instead of letting go easily, he gave her a

slight push, his attempt to get the last word in. She thought about her father, a man named Nicholas St. Jean whom she'd never met but had been told was a filthy, no-good human being. Once, in her twenties, she'd come across her birth certificate, touched her fingers to his name, and her arm had spasmed in the same way as it had just now when January took hold of her. If she'd had any doubts before about tracking him down, confronting him at his home, they were gone now.

She stopped short of giving herself kudos, however, shame setting in. How was it that she'd tracked this man to his house and threatened him, yet she'd still not spoken to Nickie about the curse, the girl's question about it still suspended in the cool air of her bedroom? She'd also punked out any conversation with her daughter about Jimmie. This face-off with January, in comparison, had been simple.

The slam of the car door rattled her mother awake. She opened and closed her mouth, squeezing her eyes shut before opening them again. "Good morning. You ready for me to sit for the next shift while you sleep? What is it I'm looking for?"

Her eyes hurt from being up all night, and she wanted to fit in a short nap before her first client of the day. She breathed deeply, calmed herself down for the long drive home. "It's okay, Mom. We should probably get back." Victoria started the car, turning on the defroster and lifting her seat fully upright.

"Well, dang, this must have been quite the morning for you."

Victoria looked to her, eyebrows raised.

"Well, did you hear yourself, Vic? You just called me Mom."

32
NICKIE

Nickie had made it to the front door without issue, hand on the knob, when she heard the phone ring. She wanted to ignore it, but if it kept ringing, Madelyn would hear and break her neck running to answer, and Nickie had a few minutes to spare before she needed to catch the bus. She got the phone on the second ring, hoping none of the women in the house would come downstairs and see her. One look at her made-up face or her slick hair and they would know what she was up to.

"Nickie. That you? I figured I'd get Madelyn."

"Oh, uh . . . yeah, it's me. Mom only had one client this morning."

Willow laughed. "Oh, is that right? That's . . . interesting. Anyway, I took a chance calling because it's you I wanted to reach. Did you get a chance to find the information I asked for?"

Even before her aunt had asked about the sweetening talc, Nickie had been aware of it, considered mixing it herself but hadn't been able to get some of the items required. "I think I found it."

"It's written in purple on a page with a big smudge at the top."

Actually, the ink had faded, closer to pink at this point. "Got it. But can I call you later? I'm late for something."

"Late — what kind of plans you got on a Saturday?"

The story she'd concocted had worked well enough on her mother. "I have a college expo thing." The deadlines had already passed for most schools. Her mother had watched her submit her application for Long Beach State months back. But Nickie pointed out on the flyer opportunities for academic scholarships, for networking and connecting to honor societies, and after a day thinking about it, reviewing the flyer, clicking around the event's website, her mother had nearly *insisted* that Nickie attend.

"A college expo thing? Your mom's letting you go to that?" As intuitive as her mother was, Willow seemed to be the one with a nose for picking up bullshit, her mother disconnected and distant lately. Nickie had thrown out a sentence about settling into her gift, which seemed to sell Victoria on the expo immediately. "Well, go on. Just make sure to call me this time, Nick. Otherwise, I'm gonna call you again, which I hate doing because I worry your mom's going to pick up. Please don't forget."

"I won't."

"Okay, make sure that —"

"Talk to you later." She hung up, her chest thumping a hard beat.

The bus traveled through the city carrying just a few folks. Felix had proposed a motel room — a place for them to sit back and talk. Relax. Or do whatever, as long as she was comfortable. He wanted them to meet at a little inn off of Long Beach Boulevard. She'd ridden by there scores of times. It was on the same block as her dentist's office.

Since meeting Felix last summer, she'd become a documentarian. She'd kept track of all their stats, writing in the journal Willow had encouraged her to start. There'd been eighty-five kisses, a feat she found amazing since, apart from lunches and the moments between the day's final bell and when her bus arrived, they spent most of their time away from one another. In the pretty likely case that her mother happened across the list, Nickie had used code — her categories, the titles of books, of classical music pieces, of great works of art — so that if her mother did stumble on one of these pages, she'd feel ashamed for snooping, say to herself, "Goodness, Nickie's read *The Bluest Eye* four times?" and quickly stuff the notebook back into the bag, when really that number represented how many times Felix had let his hand move under her shirt as they made out.

By day's end, there'd be a mark next to a new category, one she'd call *Brave New World,* a step she'd decided on once Aunt Willow revealed she did not believe in the curse. She'd let go of any worry for the damage that could come from loving him, not that Nickie loved Felix yet, but maybe she would very soon, especially if they did it today. She wanted to ask how many tallies he had in his *Brave New World* page, how many times he'd taken a girl to a motel, to his room, to a friend's when their parents weren't home. How many girls there'd been before her.

At the appointed time, she found him in his car parked in the small lot, legs kicked out onto the blacktop, scrolling through his phone. He stood to help with her backpack, the day's sun strumming his face, the dark stubble. It was attractive, this new shadowing, mature. She hoped he would keep it, especially if they ended up going to prom together. It would look nice in pictures.

Inside the motel room, there were incense and candles set on the side tables, ready to be lit. It had been years since she'd stayed in a motel, and she could hear the drone of the busy street beyond despite the music and the heavy curtaining. She took off her shoes, feeling the mowed-down carpet on her soles, as Felix snapped the dial on the thermostat, firing up the heater, the unit shaking the walls, spitting and sputtering.

He told her to sit and close her eyes, and when she opened them seconds later, he was in front of her holding a charcuterie tray, stacked with deli meats and cheeses along with tortilla chips and cookies. "To snack on. I got us some lunch too. I know you like Church's, but there's a Nashville hot chicken spot in North Long Beach I wanted you to try. And I have beer for later. Or now, if you want. I figure we can eat, chill out a bit, talk, watch the game. Play a game." He smiled. "Whatever. It's just nice to hang out."

As they enjoyed their chicken lunch on

the bed, they watched football, the Wild Card game, he'd said. After, he laid himself on the sheets, knees bent up, hands behind his head, studying the ceiling. She couldn't relax, worried that her mother had driven up to the college expo to give her extra cash or confirm that she'd made it. It was difficult not to think about her mother, even during beautiful moments such as this one.

"Are you kind of sad you're not really at that college thing right now?" he asked.

A tremor fluttered inside, and she had to remind herself Felix was just being curious, as he always was — he wasn't wearing a wire, a hidden camera sending transmission back to her mother's office. "No. Not at all."

Felix leaned up on his elbows, adjusting himself to match her. "You're, like, totally smart. I don't know why you didn't apply to more schools. Or why can't you now? You still have time for private schools, and out-of-state schools."

"Arizona State was at the college fair back in October. The guy I talked to helped me start an application, but I never finished it. I was going to pay for it with my aunt's credit card, but then she left. And even if I got in somewhere, my mom won't let me leave."

Felix scoffed. "I think you should submit

your application, anyway. It's only a few hours away, and they have a late admissions date. I'll pull it up on my laptop."

Her face twisted. "I don't have a way to pay for it."

"I have a credit card. Just pay me back cash."

Nickie shook her head, though her insides tingled. "I couldn't ask you to do that."

"You don't have to ask. I'm telling you I'm doing it. There. What can you say about that?"

As they drew up her account on his laptop, he admitted that he'd already applied to Arizona himself, a place far enough away from his mom that he wouldn't get called on to run errands, but could drive back in under six hours should there be an emergency.

"How can she keep you from leaving? You'll be eighteen. You can do whatever the fuck you want," he pressed.

Resigned to her fate on at least this issue, Nickie made crisscrosses in her mashed potatoes with her fork. "Yes, whatever I want."

"What do you want?"

Though it was futile, she thought briefly about his question for the first time. "My family used to have a little shop in New

Orleans. It was my grandmother's. And then my aunt moved there right after she graduated high school. She sold candles and soaps, things like that."

"It's still there?"

"I don't know. My aunt wasn't the best at managing things. We don't own it anymore. But it would be so cool to do something like that. Maybe one day I'll find it, see what it is now. If no one's there, I can start my own business."

"So that's what you want to do? Own a business? Sell soaps and shit?"

She hadn't quite articulated it that way to herself, but maybe that was the case. "That would be fun." She shrugged. "Although I applied as a psych major at Cal State."

"Because your mom said you should? Nick, you can change your major, you know. You don't even have to go to college. Just do whatever you want. You don't have to stay in that house."

"Felix, you don't get how strict my mom is." How could he understand?

"Even if we don't get in, we can enroll at Santa Monica College. Get a place together by the beach. Get jobs at a restaurant. Get a dog."

This made Nickie smile. Did he really think about these things? "Hold on now.

You're upsetting the loa Lanora with all this planning. She's going to break you in half for getting me off course." It was a funny line to herself, one she meant to keep in her own head, giddy over the words he'd said about their future.

He pulled his attention from the screen. "What are you talking about?"

She recalled that she'd not told him the entire story, only fragments here and there about her mother's beliefs. She filled in more information for him, at least what she'd gleaned from the book, her talk with Madelyn, her mom — Lanora's legacy, favored women in her lineage meant to be helpers, counselors, and then the curse, the risk of death for folks they loved. She had to acknowledge the narrative's entertainment value.

"So all this time, you didn't want me to come over because your mom didn't want you to see me?"

She nodded, feeling bad for admitting what her mom had told her after her birthday, but at least now he understood all of her maneuvering. Maybe she should have been honest with him a long time ago.

Felix got up to grab a can of beer from the cooler. "That's some deep shit."

Nickie raised her eyebrows, nodding her

agreement. She'd never been so open with another person that wasn't Willow, had never intended to share that detail. But doing so eased her breathing. Had she been holding back a little bit of breath all this time?

"You think it has something to do with your dad?"

She'd told Felix all she knew about her father — very little — but this possibility had come to her a few times, and her aunt not believing in the curse helped Nickie piece together a theory. "I think that's the excuse they're using to make sense of all these deaths. Oh, we must be cursed," Nickie's tone took on a fake-spooky effect. "All these men in the family have died." She'd said it lightly, but the words had given her an eerie tingle.

"So you know what this means, right?" Felix picked at a thread in the bedspread. "It means your mom really likes me. She's looking out for me."

"Oh, is that what it is?"

"Of course. She doesn't want anything to happen to me."

"I guess that's one way to look at it." She smiled, thinking back to her conversation with Willow. If her aunt didn't believe in the curse, then neither did she. Nothing was going to happen to Felix.

He placed his beer on the nightstand, telling her he needed to use the bathroom. She sat up cross-legged on the bed and felt around for the remote. The game was almost over, but it looked as if another might follow. Nothing wrong with football, but she was ready to watch something else, a romantic comedy or music videos.

He startled her, quietly coming up from behind, lifting her hair to press his lips to her neck, pushing her to the middle of the bed as his hands moved under her shirt. With all the care he'd put into the room, she figured they'd spend more time hanging out before turning themselves horizontal. The skin below her neck where her amulet hung felt prickly, like she was having an allergic reaction. She unclasped the thin chain, laying it on the table near the bed, not wanting Ayida Wedo to witness what she was about to do, although she hated that she'd had this concern. But just in case, removing the charm wouldn't hurt.

Their clothes were off. Not all of them, but she'd just homed in on the fact that they were making out, going at it on the bed, when the next realization hit — how quickly she had gotten down to nothing but her panties, an unfastened bra, straps loose at her shoulders, him in just boxer shorts. She could hardly wrap her head around how good it all felt and how exciting this was.

But every few seconds, she saw her mother's face, heard her mother's voice, then would wonder how painful it might be, got curious on how exactly he would put it in — would he ask? — would she have to help? — what if it didn't fit? And all the sperm, the semen that she'd learned about in health class freshman year — where would it all go? Still, she was on the pill, didn't think she'd be the two percent of users who by sheer luck got pregnant nevertheless.

"Does this feel good to you?" She said yes, only then aware that he'd slipped off one bra strap, had a whole nipple and more in his mouth. She enjoyed herself, sensations ripping from her genitals down to her knees, up her back and sides. She wandered in and out of this awareness, relaxing in their interaction, then pulled out again by her brain, her analysis of things, stress that her mother could somehow sense what was happening. She hoped she wouldn't blink and find herself forty years old, at her mother's desk, reviewing client charts, prepping for the day's sessions.

When she returned to the moment before her, they were naked. She was still a virgin, but he was ready, his strong piece of flesh bearing down into her thigh, and just that felt incredible. He slowed down, trying to catch his breath, though she wasn't really sure how what they'd done so far could have tired him out so. He lifted his body off her, rolled over. She could hardly make out his face in the pale light, but could see that his eyes were closed, and that he'd taken hold of himself, the tip of his penis poking out from his fist.

It was time, what she'd psyched herself up for the last few weeks. Just before she inched her way closer to him, he sat up, then stood, the covers sliding off of her as he did. "With all this preparation, I forgot to get the condoms," he said, now a shadowy figure in front of the bed.

"I'm on the pill, remember?"

"I know, but the pill won't stop any kind of disease."

"Oh. Yeah." Nickie felt around the bed for her bra and top.

"Not that I think you have anything. I know you don't have anything." He was hiking up his shorts. "And I don't have anything either. I just think we should be safe, you know?"

If she had nodded, he wouldn't have seen her. He'd already slid his feet back into his shoes. She'd just fastened her bra when he switched on the light. Nickie gathered the edge of the bed sheet over her thighs, up to her belly.

"I forgot to tell you I have dessert too. Cupcakes. You like SusieCakes, right?"

He didn't seem to hear her response, preoccupied as he was with trying to find his keys. She pointed to the table.

"We can watch a movie when I get back. We still have a few hours until you have to leave." She smiled, hoping she was hiding her disappointment. She hadn't wanted them to stop. "Hey, have one of the beers in the cooler before they warm up. They taste better when they're cold. There are some other fruity cider things in there too." When the door shut and his car revved away, she leaned back, listening to her own breaths.

She chose to heed his advice and have a drink to ease her anxiety. She laughed aloud when she lifted the tab, the pop of the can sending pale liquid onto her lap and the sheets. Holding the beer a ways in front of her, she craned her neck to reach it, taking a first sip with outstretched lips to keep it from dripping onto her shirt. It wasn't her first beer, but she still thought of the taste as dull. After half a can, she got up to grab a glass and added ice, which helped. Soon, the fizzy liquid made her feel electrified.

She woke in a panic, the room darker than it should have been. On TV, it was already halftime of the second game, yet still no sign of Felix. Her head dizzied with possibilities of what might have occurred, what trouble he might have met, while at the same time she reassured herself that there'd be an explanation. When fifteen more minutes passed, she turned the heater back on and got back underneath the covers to watch the ceiling. She tried her best to fall asleep so that when he came back he'd feel guilty for abandoning her there so long. But the newness of her surroundings unsettled her. She considered calling but didn't want him to hear the cry that was pushing right up against the back of her eyeballs and the top of her throat.

An hour later, her eyes puffy and red, she no longer cared how she might come off. After one ring, she got his voice mail, and the fit of crying she'd been able to quell became real, jerky and loud, and so violent she made herself throw up, all over the sheets, though she'd missed the duvet, one less thing she had to yank off the mattress and carry to the bathtub. Washing out the stinky curds, she was sober now but as empty and alone as she believed a person could be. It didn't make sense to her, how much of a turnaround the day had been.

If her aunt were home, Nickie would have trusted Willow to pick her up. Instead, she called a taxi and walked to the sidewalk in front of the motel office to wait for her ride. The neon Vacancy sign buzzed in red above her, lighting the empty space where Felix's car had been parked earlier. Across the street, voices cheered from a patio door of an apartment building — a party, people enjoying the final seconds of the game. It had started sprinkling outside, and her jacket would be soaked quickly. The taxi wouldn't arrive for ten minutes. She thought about going into the office to wait but was too ashamed to face anyone. If she hadn't been so distracted by the rain, worried about the motel staff, perhaps she would have noticed her necklace was still on the nightstand.

33
AUGUSTA

The rain hadn't stopped coming for four days. More rain was on the way, according to the anchorwoman on the evening news. Since Augusta had nowhere to go and not much to do, the rain shouldn't have bothered her. But all that accompanied it did. The slickened floors of the foyer as folks dripped in and out, no one wanting to leave their umbrellas on the stoop for fear their belongings would be blown away. Or swiped. The way the rain slowed folks, making them tardy, backing up Victoria's schedule so that dinner was late. With fewer clients, she had time to eat with the family each night, though Nickie had stopped joining them. She didn't push the issue.

This evening's storm had been strong enough to whip the power from the neighborhood, the lights going out just as Victoria was seeing off her last client. Voices had yelled from in front of her and up above telling her not to move, asking if she was okay. Augusta used a fist to pound a loud thud into the arm of the sofa, to which Nickie replied that she'd be right there with a flashlight.

The storm called to mind Mombu Mombu, a loa who showered down powerful rains. Many folks believed she sent torrents to the world when anguished, but Bela Nova said she had been a forgiving woman when alive and instead sent showers to clean and renew. Augusta tried to view storms in her life as little disruptions. Temporary challenges. But as optimistic as she'd been all of her life, the biggest battles she'd faced still impacted her today.

Dudley Lee died on a Tuesday, just months after her run-in with Bela Nova, but he wasn't put in the ground until the following Wednesday because Augusta had to work three clients to raise the funds for a proper funeral, attended only by Augusta, Charles, and the one priest she could locate who didn't care that Dudley Lee hadn't been baptized. The entire Mass she'd been on edge, waiting for Bela Nova to clomp through the door and leap at her, going for the neck. It wasn't until six months later that Augusta would fully grieve for Dudley Lee, after she learned that Bela Nova had been institutionalized in Mississippi. She didn't have to worry anymore about Bela Nova pounding on Charles and Aletha's door, demanding Augusta come out and face her. After he'd been buried, as she lay in bed, echoes of Bela Nova's cursing words kept her from finding sleep. Dudley Lee's death was her fault. He'd been so young. She'd cut his life short.

Augusta stayed with the business, establishing a regular clientele, her days filled so she only had to think about Dudley Lee at night, her broken heart beating an odd rhythm. For weeks, she wouldn't have cared if it stopped working entirely. Charles and Aletha had been kind enough right after Dudley Lee died, but it was clear they would need their room back, with Aletha soon expecting a baby and her mother coming over from Lafayette to help. Aletha, who'd brought the news back to Augusta about Bela Nova, had also told her the manager from the Dew Drop Inn was looking for a tenant for the old workshop. It was a situation just wrong enough to be right. So that same afternoon, Augusta paid Aletha five dollars for her troubles, packed her belongings, and started a lease with a deal to eventually buy the space outright.

Most of Bela Nova's goods and supplies

were in the same spot they'd been the last time Augusta had been inside. Apparently, having been kicked out for not paying rent, she'd hitched a ride to Jackson, where her mother's family lived. Between New Orleans and there, she'd been arrested for prostitution and beaten up several times before being put away. Hearing the story, Augusta felt that same rotten guilt she'd only weeks before climbed out of, feeling responsible for Dudley Lee's death. At least until, sifting through what remained in the workshop, she came across the Voodoo doll Bela Nova had made in her image, the eyes blacked out, a thick needle piercing the cloth where the doll's heart would be if she had one. Its head was cut off, threaded to the body by a few yellowed strings, and its ears were smeared in red. Paint most likely, but it wouldn't have surprised Augusta to learn the color was her own blood, that the woman had pricked her heel one night long ago as Augusta slept.

She found herself wondering how she'd become what she had, taking money to hurt people. There was healing too, and helping. Most of her conjuring benefited women who were poor, downtrodden, abused, desolate, or heartbroken. But many times, a spell worked at the expense of someone else;

to make some clients win, others had to lose.

After seeing the doll Bela Nova had made, she vowed that she would improve the woman's spells, shape them up so they did nothing but heal and help. She was a descendant of Lanora, gifted, destined to be a blessing. Rewriting the pages in the book could be the way. She spent the next several weeks editing the cures and spells, tinkering and experimenting, using herself as a guinea pig when she could. She hoped to be brave enough soon to open the doors, test the new spells out on other people. It was then that she also began her daily supplications to the loa as Bela Nova would do, building an altar, picking favorites to offer treats — Gran Bwa and Oshun.

On her father's birthday, the first after he'd passed, a leisurely walk landed her in her old neighborhood, where she glimpsed her house from down the street, the front door still painted a murky green. But the white structure didn't gleam as it had before. She didn't dare knock to check in on her mother, though she hoped to catch sight of her coming or going, confirm she was okay on her own. Even after everything, the woman had gone to look for Augusta, who was now too ashamed to even consider showing her face.

She felt queasy, standing there on her old block. If only she'd stopped to visit her father on his birthday, on Christmas. She'd never even said goodbye to him, hadn't called as she'd promised; only her mom had been home when she'd left for good. And she'd never fathomed that something bad would happen to him. Parents were eternal, weren't they?

She hurried back to the shop, then fell to the floor and wept, curled in a ball, her nose red and damp.

She must have been a sight when Benjamin Montrose let himself into the workshop. He tipped his chin. "Excuse me, miss. You alright? You need a glass of water or a handkerchief?" He had neither. He had, however, been able to get her to the tattered love seat against the wall, fanning her with the newspaper he'd picked up from the floor.

He was in town for the weekend from Chicago but had gotten into trouble and didn't have enough money to get back or pay a debt he owed. "I heard about a woman who works here at this shop who might be able to help me. I don't have much money, I have to admit. Someone suggested that, with a face like mine, well, I might do right as a payment myself." The old witch doctor was a sucker for a nice-looking man was the word. "You don't look nothing like I expected, though. You real pretty. I thought I'd find someone older. People said your hair looked like gray yarn. And that your face would be covered with moles. I see a couple freckles on you, but no moles."

When she explained the reason for the confusion, that Bela Nova was gone and she'd taken over the business, he deflated, realizing that the offer to exchange sex for a trick was likely off the table. He tried to apologize, but she put her fingers over his mouth to stop him. Dudley Lee had been her only man, but she didn't think about him when she leaned toward Benjamin Montrose and kissed him, drunk off her own despondency. He didn't hesitate, pulling her in close. The taste of sweet candy was on his tongue, which meant he'd indeed been prepared to seduce the old hag he'd expected.

After, she worked a money spell for him, but she didn't want to set precedent for herself so made him promise not to tell anyone what they'd done, that his body was the only payment he'd given her. The act had helped her forget about her sorrow, though the next morning, she wondered if Dudley Lee had watched from the heavens, if he'd heard her screaming out on his mother's furniture.

Augusta had just finished seeing a client — her first money-paying customer in the new space — when Benjamin returned with flowers, magnolias. The man standing tall in front of her was more radiant than the day before, perhaps even more handsome than her Dudley Lee.

"You gotta be patient with the money spells," she told him, as if she'd been doing them her entire twenty years.

When he replied that he only wanted to see her again, her insides tickled. And so started their ephemeral love affair, the two of them meeting up at the same time of morning and again in the evenings for a couple of months until the day came when he entered the workshop whistling, flipping a silver coin with his thumb.

"Hey, sweetie. I got lucky. Found myself a little come up. I just wanted to stop by to say goodbye and thank you. Wouldn't nothing have happened without you interceding for me." He left his address in Chicago, promising he'd be back for her once he made it big and came through on his way to Hollywood, where he hoped to get a part in a film. Augusta learned she was pregnant the following day.

■ ■ ■ ■

No one seemed to be bothered having their hoodoo performed by an expectant woman. In fact, a few of her clients asked to rub her belly while Madelyn swam around inside her.

She sent letters to Benjamin, although she didn't mention the pregnancy, worried he might not return if he found out. He didn't seem the type to run away from such a responsibility, but she didn't want to learn that he was. Checked the post daily. Finally, after five months, her belly round and hard, a note arrived. It was from Benjamin's mother. He was missing. Had never made it back to Chicago after his visit in New Orleans. She wanted to know what information Augusta had on his whereabouts and the last time they'd spoken. His mother thought he might have been on a train that crashed just outside of Chicago, and Augusta could only marvel at Bela Nova's efficiency, the curse taking out two men she loved in such a short period of time. She never wrote back and never found herself in the arms of a man again.

The lights went back on, a sweep of energy

reawakening the house. Madelyn stood quickly, returning to the kitchen to restart her abandoned cooking. Nickie rose as well, but not before Augusta got a good look at the girl's face, her eyelashes wet, her nose red. Augusta had heard Nickie sniffling in the darkness but thought she'd just caught a cold — she'd come back from a school function drenched a few nights ago.

Nickie probably didn't feel comfortable sharing the personal storms she'd been dealing with, but Augusta knew a lot had been thrown at the girl recently. The gift, Victoria's extreme helicoptering, Willow's absence. And it was clear she was dealing with love and all the complication and confusion that comes with it, just like Augusta had, just like Victoria and Willow and Madelyn had. Bela Nova's curse had impacted each of them, but they'd responded in different ways.

If their lineage was blessed enough to continue, Augusta didn't know if she'd be alive to meet the next generation. But she had an opportunity now to do something for Nickie that she'd neglected to do for the others. She could tell Nickie her story. All of it, without omission or exaggeration. From Clarence at the Dew Drop Inn to Benjamin and his fatal train ride, she would lay it all out for her great-granddaughter, scene by scene. And then, Nickie could make her own decision about love and her gift. She hadn't been honest with the other women, but if Nickie knew the full truth, she'd be more likely to listen, more prudent in her approach to love.

34
NICKIE

Nickie had declined when Nanagusta extended the phone toward her, not yet wanting to give Willow the information she requested about the sweetening talc. She had everything ready, the charm, the list of items, the instructions, but she worried that if she spoke to her aunt, she'd blurt out her plans. She, too, wanted to work some magic for herself. Felix hadn't called, had managed to avoid her at school.

The day after she'd been abandoned in the hotel, she'd distracted herself by finally following up with her aunt's task, copying the book's sweetening talc recipe down in her journal. Finding her aunt's amulet would take a little more work. According to Willow, it was sealed in a baggy, buried two inches down in the potted plant on the bookshelf. The dirt inside was cracked and hard, and Nickie had to use a butter knife to chop it into pieces. Twenty minutes in, she'd come across a small key, but no amulet. As she explored, she couldn't help but cry, fits hitting her every few minutes, her face crumbling into something sour each time she recalled moments from the night before, good and bad. But she had to compose herself if she was going to get this job done, having already missed her aunt's initial deadline the Thursday before.

She wondered if she'd misremembered her aunt's instructions when she noticed a different potted plant on another shelf, where, after just a few minutes of digging, she located a pewter charm of a woman laughing, perhaps because her thick thighs and breasts were five times wider than her waist and shoulders. The mining had left her tired and with a mess to clean up. But she'd become curious about the key from the first plant, what it opened. By the time she put all the dirt back in the pots and tidied the room, it was time for dinner, and she needed to splash some ice water on her face to reduce the swelling around her eyes. But she kept the key, and the next afternoon, while her mother and grandmother worked and her Nanagusta rested, she returned to Willow's room. On the top of the bookshelf, a small jewelry box caught her eye. The key fit perfectly. Inside were condoms and a half-smoked joint, coins from other places etched with the faces of queens and palaces. And underneath, a folded paper similar in color and texture to the pages in the book, its edge torn.

In the top corner was a handwritten prayer, a plea asking Lanora for help in gaining God's favor. But it was the words on the rest of the page that stole her attention, the perfect cure for her situation with Felix, the Bring Back a Lover elixir. Nickie didn't understand her feelings, how she could still miss Felix after what he'd done to her. How she still thought of their times together with fondness while also hating him. Could she ever forgive him? Did she really want to bring Felix back? She wasn't sure, but at least, with this spell, she had an option. It didn't mean she had to use it in the end.

The steps to make the potion seemed complicated and intricate, but that made sense to Nickie. Based on what she'd learned, why would such a task be simple? Nickie had Madelyn drive her around to several grocery stores, a farmers' market, the dollar store, and Target, an unknowing accomplice to her ingredient-gathering. "This is for the science fair, isn't it?" Nickie didn't think it hurt not to correct her.

Now, the house quiet and everyone asleep, she crept down to the kitchen and placed the torn-out page on the counter. The lettering had faded, but she could tell the writer had been someone with artful longhand. She studied the page, making sure she had all the paraphernalia she needed. Before starting in, she lit a black tea light to set the mood.

"Girl, what you doing down here?"

Nickie jumped at the sound of Madelyn's voice and wanted to scream in pain, having dropped a Pyrex cup on her foot.

"Did it break?" Madelyn asked.

Nickie shook her head as she picked it up. She winced.

"Oh, that's good. Them Pyrexes are expensive." Madelyn's robe was open, and Nickie glimpsed a crinkled slash of flesh before her grandmother caught the silky belt and tightened it. "You got the munchies too?"

"No." Nickie didn't know what to do with her body, her limbs hanging long while her fingers drummed her thighs. She hadn't expected this kind of roadblock.

"So what are you doing? You . . ." She took a step forward, her eyes cutting to slits. "You making a cake?"

Madelyn was staring at the page from the

book, vulnerable on the countertop. She should have crumpled it up.

Madelyn brought it close to her face. "Hey, where did you find this, Nickie? This is mine! This is my caramel cake." Nickie was familiar with the recipe, her family always arguing about how much buttermilk to add and whether it called for shortening or butter. She'd been so taken with the spell that she hadn't even noticed it was on the other side. "Look at that," Madelyn said, poking the paper. "I *told* them there are two cups of sugar in the frosting. I told them, I told them, I told them."

Nickie's lips quivered, a failed attempt at shushing Madelyn before she woke up the rest of the house.

Madelyn snapped her fingers as if on the dance floor. "Oooh, chile. I can't wait to show this to your Nana. And your mama. And your auntie. Especially your auntie."

"Oh no. Please, Madelyn. Can we just keep this between us?" She regretted bringing the page down with her rather than copying the instructions in the middle of her science notebook. Luckily, Madelyn did not flip the page over.

While her grandmother explained that she'd come down to make a peanut butter sandwich, Nickie pushed her ingredients aside, humoring the woman when asked if she wanted one too. Feeding folks had been Madelyn's one redeemable quality, she'd heard, when the family lived in New Orleans decades back.

"That one is yours," Madelyn said, angling her chin toward a plated PB and J once it had been assembled, then going back into the jar of grape jam with a knife. When time came for the peanut butter, she didn't wipe the sticky purple sheen off before scooping it out.

Nickie picked up half the sandwich. Beyond the kitchen, night darkened the house. Alone downstairs, she might have gotten scared by now if Madelyn hadn't joined her. She hadn't accomplished her mission of mixing the elixir, but life worked like that sometimes, she thought. Madelyn certainly was no Willow but still someone she could talk to. "Madelyn?"

"What's up — you want more?"

"No. I . . . I want to ask you something." What had transpired with Felix had been yet another reminder of the lengths Nickie had to go to live a normal life because her mother believed in a curse. She was curious how Madelyn had done it.

She stopped spreading the peanut butter and then licked the knife. "Shoot."

"Why don't you believe in the curse? If . . . if your husband . . ."

"Husband?" Madelyn puckered her face. "I ain't never had no husband."

"Or boyfriend?"

She lifted and dropped one shoulder. "I guess that's better. Had a few of those, I suppose."

"Well, if your boyfriend — Aunt Willow's dad — died."

She sucked on a finger, her forehead creasing. Then she shrugged. "Well, that whole thing is about love. Being in love, right? Well, I surely didn't love that man. Harlowe Decuir? Shoot. Barely liked him. Just another piece of ass. People die, cursed or not."

Nickie sputtered out a laugh and quickly covered her mouth, fearful of tempting fate once more with all this noise they'd been making the last five minutes. "That's his name? Harlowe?"

"Girl, they don't tell you nothing, do they?"

"I guess not."

"That's a shame. Harlowe William Decuir. I mixed his first two names up a bit and got Willow." Quiet surrounded them as they both watched Madelyn's hands slap the peanut butter side to the jammy one, then cut it into fours.

"So have you ever loved anyone?" Nickie asked, curious about the woman her family had rarely talked about in her seventeen years.

"Yes. Of course. I've been on this earth a long time, Nickie."

"My mom's dad?"

"Hell no. But someone."

"And he didn't die?"

Madelyn shook her head. "Well first off, she wasn't a he."

"Oh." Nickie dropped her gaze.

"Well, that ain't nothing to get weird about. I'm certainly not ashamed. I just don't talk about it with your mama and your auntie. Your Nana probably knows," she said. "But it's something I rarely discuss because that was in my old life. I'm too old now for any kind of romance and all that business. Just trying to do well with my family."

Nickie hadn't started in on her sandwich, turning it over in her fingers as she considered her grandmother's words. Maybe Madelyn didn't believe in the curse because the woman she loved was still alive. If she hadn't died, it would be great proof that the curse wasn't real. It would be useful information for all of them. She thought about the Russell guy, if her mother really did have feelings for him that she didn't act on, out of fear. Just when she had mustered up the words to ask about the woman's where-abouts, Madelyn spoke her name.

"Nickie?"

She looked up, the bright kitchen light drawing kind lines around Madelyn's eyes.

"I suggest you put that page back, before someone realizes it's gone. I'm guessing you found the recipe snooping around, didn't you?" Madelyn winked, a smudge of jelly on her chin.

"I'll put it back."

"Still can't believe you found it. Is that dusty old book still around? I used to write my recipes down wherever I could find paper, and that book was often in my line of fire. I wanted to make a cookbook. I whip up a mean sweet potato pie. And my gumbo probably could have won awards."

"What's in it? Do you remember?" she said to be polite.

Madelyn tutted. "Uh-uh. You aren't about to get my gumbo recipe out of me. I see what you're doing."

Nickie didn't want to tell her that she didn't like gumbo, preferred jambalaya.

"But if I ever work the recipe out again, I suppose I can share it with you. But you'd have to vow on your granddaddy's grave that you'd never tell it to anyone, not even your mama."

"Of course not. Maybe I could help you figure out how to make it again." Nickie realized she meant it.

"That would be nice. I got a bunch of prized recipes hidden away. Six or seven. I stashed the pages high up in the cabinets in the shop so no one could find them."

"You hid your own recipes?"

"Mmm-hmm, my favorite ones — when Augusta wasn't looking, of course. I tore them out and stapled them to the wall inside the cabinets at the shop. Kept them hidden behind the jars of rice and oats and beans. Couldn't be too careful. Folks would steal your evening prayers if they thought they could make money off them. Dang, I wish I still had those recipes. I would love to make that red fish again. Or my Louis Armstrong beans and rice. Anyway, your great-grandmother got to fussing at me saying I was ruining her book. I didn't see the harm. She just had some of those damn spells and what-not on the other side, stuff written down by that teacher of hers . . . I've forgotten her name."

Delilah? She wanted to ask but thought better of it, unsure how much she should let on about her secret activities. It was time to change the subject.

"Madelyn, you're not too old for romance." Nickie took the last bite of her sandwich, surprised that she'd eaten it all.

Her grandmother smiled. "You don't think so? Shoot. Maybe it's time for me to get on one of them sites. Like Willow. Get me someone named February or November."

This made Nickie laugh. For a moment she'd forgotten about the whole drama with Felix.

Nickie washed her hands, resigned to try the potion another night, at a later time so Madelyn wouldn't interrupt again. Upstairs, she'd write down the spell, return the page to its hiding space. Glancing down at it now, she noticed something she hadn't before. A word, the lettering smaller than the others: *sulfur.* Nickie sighed, upset at herself for missing the ingredient. But as her grandmother continued on, she calmed, recognizing that tonight wouldn't have worked out, anyway. Now she just had to figure out a way to get her hands on some sulfur and get it right the next try.

■ ■ ■ ■

FEBRUARY

■ ■ ■ ■

35
VICTORIA

The call came on Madelyn's two-month anniversary as receptionist. Victoria had brought her into the office for a probationary evaluation. She'd never reviewed anyone before, but she'd been able to track down sample forms used by corporations and government agencies to assess their employees' work. She'd pulled the components she most liked from these forms to build her own, even branding it with a logo she'd created herself.

Madelyn sat tall, hands on her lap, wearing a pretty floral top she must have purchased online specifically for their meeting. She had on lipstick and blush, yet had decided not to brush her hair, one side of her do still flattened from sleep, the other an untamed bundle of three-day-old curls. She could count on it, Madelyn's inconsistency.

"So how do you think you're doing, Madelyn? How would you rate yourself overall?"

"You mean if I had to give myself a grade?"

Victoria shrugged, writing her mother's first and last name at the top of the form, as if there were dozens of other employees to evaluate. The two of them hadn't spoken about their mission to confront January a couple weeks back, and she was pleased that she hadn't needed to warn Madelyn not to bring it up. No one else in the family had to know what Victoria had done. Though Madelyn had stepped up after Willow's departure, she hadn't fully redeemed herself — and maybe she couldn't from Victoria's perspective — but she sure was trying. Victoria had to give her that. "Sure. Give yourself a grade."

"Well, I'm far from perfect." Victoria bit her lip to withhold a snarky reply. "But I think I'd give myself an A–."

"A– ? Really? So, like a ninety-three percent."

"I'd say ninety-two. A ninety-two percent."

Victoria's eyebrows lifted, and she was about to probe Madelyn about her self-assessment when her phone vibrated. "I'm sorry. Let me turn this off." She recognized the number as one she'd memorized a couple years back: Nickie's school. "Actually, one second, Madelyn."

"Take your time."

It was school, all right. The vice principal, who asked Victoria to come in as soon as possible.

"Madelyn, can you call my next two clients and reschedule? Tell them I'm sorry, something came up."

A student ushered Victoria from Attendance into the vice principal's office. Nickie was already there sitting on a metal chair, her eyes bloated and dewy, mascara smeared about. She wasn't supposed to be wearing makeup. But surely, that's not what this was all about, was it?

The person Victoria presumed to be Vice Principal Logan entered right behind her with a mug of coffee and offered Victoria a shake with her free hand. "Have a seat, Ms. Montrose."

"Is this about the makeup?"

This question seemed to puzzle the woman, who moved her sharp stare to Nickie's face. "No. No, it wasn't the makeup. Nickie, why don't you go on and tell your mother what you did."

Nickie's gaze hadn't left the edge of Ms. Logan's desk. "I stole some chemicals from the lab." Her voice was raspy and weak.

Her heartbeat quickened, her mind racing with possibilities, family history repeating itself. When she'd first fallen in love with Jimmie, she too had made missteps. Her very last semester, she earned her first B, forgetting a major assignment because she'd been on the phone all evening with him. She'd hidden her relationship well from Nanagusta, the woman left to simply deal with it by the time Victoria decided that she wanted to spend the rest of her life with Jimmie. She knew she would have pilfered chemicals, held up a bank, or fled to Timbuktu for Jimmie Wilkes. Though pissed with Nickie, a bit of empathy flickered inside Victoria. And that flicker, at least, helped her feel less like a monster and more like a mother.

36
AUGUSTA

Augusta had been left alone, an occurrence almost as rare as a Halley's Comet sighting. A few minutes after Victoria had taken off, Madelyn said she'd be right back, using her sudden time off to go to the supermarket. Plenty of time for Augusta to find some kind of trouble to get into. What fun might she be able to have without the others there to witness?

Dancing seemed like a good idea. She didn't need any music, the drumbeat sounding in her head. The balls of her bare feet first struck the ground timidly, but the movement felt good. So she tapped again, switching feet, faster and faster until nearly galloping. Soon, she'd added her shoulders, and then her belly, and she was fifteen years old again, front and center in the performance of her Afro-Haitian dance troupe, parents watching from the second row. She caught a glimpse of herself in the window, her elbows arched back, feet bent in extremes — nothing but pointed or in full flex. Her ribs led any sort of body gyrations, not the hips. It seemed like the drums were just a few feet away, a rhythmic thwack on wood.

"Oooh, get it, Nana."

Augusta recoiled, almost tripping over herself, shocked to hear Willow's voice. In the foyer, her granddaughter slapped her palms onto the small oak console next to the coatrack. Her luggage sat on the floor next to her.

Willow smiled before putting her hands over her mouth, eyes crinkling. "It's so good to see you, Nana." She ran to Augusta and wrapped her arms around her. Her granddaughter held her so tightly that Augusta had to shimmy her shoulders to get Willow to loosen her grip.

"I'm sorry, Nan." When she stepped back, Willow's eyes were damp, though she kept grinning, a little too hard. "Where is everyone? Is Victoria in a session? I didn't see her car."

Augusta turned her thumb upside down and pointed it to the floor.

"You here alone, Nana?"

She flipped her thumb the other way.

"Well, I'm here now. So it's a party!"

Willow's face had thinned, her skin sallow. She looked around the room, taking it in as if there for the first time. Her arrival was a pleasant surprise, but Augusta couldn't help but be curious why she was back. Had January died?

She followed Willow up the stairs as she dragged a suitcase, then down and up again for the second one and a backpack. In her bedroom, Willow talked herself tired about her regulars at the bar where she worked and her philanderer of a boss and the game on her phone that she played for hours.

The girl still hadn't said a word about January, though if he were dead, Augusta would have been able to tell. One couldn't fake her way out of that kind of grief, the heaviness of missing someone and the guilt that you caused them to be gone.

Augusta covered Willow up with a blanket and then lay down beside her, glad to have her granddaughter back. She and Victoria were so unalike, but they complemented one another, needed each other. After all this time apart, she hoped the two of them would finally figure that out.

37
NICKIE

Nickie had visited the administration wing of Building 400 only once before. "You'll only end up here if you do something really great or if you totally fuck up," the junior leading her group on a tour for incoming students had said. Her invitation to meet with Vice Principal Logan certainly hadn't been because she deserved to receive kudos of any kind. Instead, she'd been asked to open her backpack and empty it. Another student had spotted Nickie using Mr. Love's key to enter the chemistry lab.

She thought she'd been careful, slyly picking up her teacher's keys when she excused herself to go to the bathroom. She'd slipped away while he engaged a smaller group of students, fairly sure that AP Chem was off-site on a field trip and the lab would be free (at least, that's what the bulletin said). The theft took less than two minutes, the substance she required stored in the same place it'd been last year when she was a junior in the class. Sulfur. She hadn't needed much, dumped it into an old Hydro Flask that she'd already ruined during her basketball days. On the way back to her classroom, she ran into Ed, the smallest of her school's class clowns. "Vir-gin a-lert," he said in a robotic voice as they crossed directions. But he couldn't have seen her entire route. Could he?

"Go on, Nickie. Just tell us what happened."

She faced Ms. Logan, ready to tell another untruth, as she had been doing for months to so many people. But then she paused. Maybe she could just put it all out there. She and Felix were likely done anyway, and if she told the truth, Ms. Logan might even take her side, tell her mom that she was being unreasonable. "So. There's this boy that I used to like. Still like, I guess. He . . . broke up with me." She could almost read her mother's thoughts. *You've been wearing makeup and having a relationship, one so long that there was a chance for him to break up with you?!* She tried clearing her throat, but part of it still felt clogged. "I have an aunt — Willow. She has this book with a bunch of spells. She's kind of into hoodoo."

"Voodoo?" asked Ms. Logan.

403

"Hoodoo. It's . . . related," her mother clarified. "Voodoo is the more spiritual part. Like the connection to saints in Catholicism, while hoodoo is the practice." Apparently, what her aunt Willow did wasn't completely foreign to her mother.

"Oh. Like witchcraft."

Nickie wiggled in her seat, second-guessing her decision to be honest with Ms. Logan. Her mother flared her nostrils. "My sister doesn't practice witchcraft, ma'am."

"That's fine. Tell me more about the book, Nickie."

"Well, I found something called a Bring Back a Lover elixir. One of the ingredients is sulfur. And I wasn't sure where I could get some at first, until I remembered that we used it last year in chemistry."

Ms. Logan reclined in her chair, a bony woman, and Nickie wondered if her coffee was an afternoon pick-me-up or a way to keep warm. "You weren't going to drink the potion, were you, Nickie?"

"No. No, ma'am."

"No? You've never thought of harming yourself?"

Her mom lifted her hand, blocking the road Ms. Logan wanted to go down. "Now, now. I don't know everything about my child, but I *do* know she's not suicidal.

404

Another thing you might have learned by looking in her file is that I'm a therapist."

Nickie bit her lip, embarrassed. Not in the way that teens tended to be, plagued with an uncool parent. What she hated that moment was her mom's lack of integrity, not wanting to hear out concerns about her own child, playing the ignorant parent, rattling off impossibilities. No, Nickie wasn't suicidal, but sometimes she felt lonely, especially with Willow gone.

"I know that there are some very serious implications about Nickie's behavior that I would like to figure out. Now, Nickie . . . You're a really good student." Her mother grunted, muttering under her breath as the VP talked. "You know that sulfur can be used as an explosive, correct?"

This time, her mother stood up, still holding her purse tight to her belly. "Now, you stop this shit right now, lady."

"Mom!"

"She's already told you that she stole the stuff so she can make a potion." The top of her mother's body hinged forward, and she pointed at Nickie. "Don't know what the hell she's doing because that particular mixture only works on ex-husbands if I remember correctly." Or was it ex-lovers? She didn't know the spells as well as Willow, but what did it matter? This lady didn't know any better. "But anyway, she already told you the truth, just like you asked. So yes, she needs to be suspended or punished. Or given detention after school — give her a chance to study. But you have to cut this third-degree nonsense."

"Mrs. Montrose. Please be calm." She stood too. Nickie saw the slight flitter of her blouse, the woman's heartbeat rapid. "Look, I certainly didn't intend to offend either one of you, and I know Nickie's a good kid. We just can't be too careful these days."

Her mother didn't move, and Nickie wondered if she might jump at the woman, not fully, but just enough to make her flinch. Instead, she exhaled, looking around the room and seeming to realize where she was — not in her own space but in the hot seat herself.

"Can we speak alone, Mrs. Montrose?" Ms. Logan asked.

Dismissed, Nickie took a seat in the hallway. She tried to listen in, but the wooden door kept all the sounds inside, and she was left to focus on the faded patchwork of tiles, beige and soft yellow and speckled white. She was just about to pull a book from her backpack to distract herself when the door opened.

"It was really nice to meet you, Ms. Montrose. And Nickie, come to my office first thing tomorrow morning to pick up your discipline statement. It'll be detention. Three days. I won't stop you from attending prom or graduation or any other senior events. Just don't take any more keys, okay?"

Nickie nodded. She wanted to tell Ms. Logan not to worry about the prom. Unless he made a grand gesture of an apology, she wouldn't go to the prom with Felix. Not that he would dare ask her. And even if he did, Ms. Logan had no bearing on her attending or not. That delight belonged entirely to Victoria Montrose.

Her mother didn't speak on the drive home, but Nickie could gamble on the dialogue in her head: *What else can I do to punish Nickie?* Nickie had no phone, no tablet, no computer of her very own. No camera. No car. No bicycle. She had a skateboard in her closet her mother was not aware of, but that, too, would disappear if it were discovered.

But she had something. She had her family's book. Her Nanagusta had come up with a new hiding spot after she'd caught Nickie with it, but it hadn't been a very good one. Nickie had quickly located the book and moved it to her own closet, tucking it away in a bin with her summer clothes.

She planned to reference it when they got home, in search of some sort of cure-all superspell that erased the past or could speed her along into next year, one that didn't require sulfur or anything locked up in the chem lab. Her mother had other plans. "Go get the book, and bring it to me in my office."

Nickie wasn't ready to give it up yet, and who knew what her mom would do with it? What if she decided to destroy it, or put it in a safety deposit box and swallow the key? "Can't I take a shower first? And eat something? I didn't have lunch."

Her mother creased her lips, then lifted a shoulder. "Fine. Stall all you want, Nickie. But you're gonna have to deal with this. I'm just . . ." She threw her head back and shrieked. "I don't know what else I have to do to get you to understand. I'm not doing anything to hurt you. I'm trying to protect you. Your father, Nickie —"

"Is dead."

"Exactly. He's dead. Do you know why?"

It was Nickie's turn to shriek. Her mother hadn't responded the first time she'd asked months back, but that wouldn't stop her from bringing up the topic again. "Please don't say it's because of some dang curse."

"Yes. It is, Nickie. It is because of the curse. And I should have made this clear from the beginning. The curse killed your father, your grandfather, your great-grandfather. And I guarantee, if you let yourself fall in love with Felix, he'll be next."

The two of them locked eyes, her mother's chest heaving. She didn't need a shower or food. She needed to get away. She broke her gaze with her mother and ran upstairs to her room.

"Hey, Nickie, where is your necklace?" her mom called as she made her escape.

She wanted to scream, to kick something. It was becoming too much. Nickie couldn't tell what was true anymore — if she was gifted, cursed, both, neither. What had truly happened to her father. If she'd really sensed things with that amulet, now lost forever. The only certainty was that they'd kept secrets from her, all of them, even Nanagusta. They couldn't expect her to care about some curious curse or her destiny if they wouldn't give her details.

Nickie didn't know if the curse were real or not — half her family seemed to believe in it, the other half didn't — but she knew that if she wanted to get out from under her mother's thumb, if she wanted the truth, she had to think like her mother. She had to *believe* like her.

She remembered from the History Channel documentary that there was such a thing as antihexes. Had her mother ever tried to undo the curse on their family? Nickie had flipped through the book so many times but had never found anything of the sort. She'd searched Willow's room, stumbling on odd items under her bed, like vials of spider legs and what had been labeled *Nickie's umbilical cord.* In her closet, under a cutout piece of carpet, behind a frame, she saw a baggie of eyelashes and a couple of adult teeth, but she found nothing of use.

Once in her room, she fished the book out from its hiding place to check it one more time. She decided to start in the middle, right after Lanora's song, hoping that if she searched in a different order than usual, she'd notice something different. She turned through slowly, hoping to catch a detail she'd previously missed, maybe faint words that someone had tried to erase or a message hiding in plain sight, tricking the eye.

And that's when she noticed something, the slightly frayed edge between an ode to Erzulie Freda and a listing of various hot foot powders. A missing page, the remains of the paper barely noticeable between the others. She turned past a few more entries in the book and noticed another that appeared to be missing.

Madelyn's recipes. She heard her grandmother's voice. *I tore them out and stapled them to the wall inside the cabinets at the shop.*

Could the pages still be there now in whatever had become of the shop, preserved all these years? Could those pages hold the antidote to free them all?

Desperation gnawed at her from the pit of her belly, that itch to make a move, be proactive. The odds that the cabinetry in the shop had gone unchanged over the decades were slim. So were the odds that she could get herself away from the house, all the way to New Orleans to look for them. But she had to take a risk. She had to go back to the place where it seemed their family's trouble had started.

She knew from Madelyn about the Sunset Limited, the train that ran from Los Angeles to New Orleans Wednesday, Friday, and Sunday evenings. Madelyn had boarded it to get herself to California. Today was Wednesday.

She took the binders and folders out of her backpack and threw in a few rolled-up pairs of jeans, T-shirts, sneakers, and underwear. She'd wear her heavy jacket and boots to the station. She paged through the book until she spotted the yellowed envelope from the electric company, the address on the front, she was sure, belonging to the shop, and placed it in the front pocket. The book she stashed under her bed.

The jingle for Eduardo's Auto Insurance played in her head, a trio of sopranos singing the agency's phone number, hard to forget. Russell in the barbershop that day had said to call him, his number the same as Eduardo's, just with the 562 area code. She'd become so skilled at lying that when he answered the phone, she came up with a reason why he needed to stop by on the spot. He'd be a good distraction for her family. He'd show up, and then she'd make her getaway.

As she waited for Russell to arrive, Nickie pulled the Bring Back a Lover instructions from under her mattress and laid the page flat on her bed. She used her finger to scour every bit of writing, wondering if her mom had been truthful back in Ms. Logan's office when she'd said that the spell only worked on ex-husbands. "She just makes shit up," Nickie said, not finding any evidence.

Next to the spell, she read the names she had skimmed over the other day, curious whether it had indeed brought back any of those listed.

Sandy Trafalgar for Rodney C.
K. Jackson → Gabriela V. Morales
Erika Willis for Nak Craft
Geo Forneret for Mario Castelon

There was one more line, written in such small print that Nickie couldn't read it, the pale ink smudged in a crease. She remembered the magnifying glass in her drawer, and brought the paper to the desk.

W. Decuir for J. Wilkes

The coolness she felt from time to time took hold of her, accompanied by dizziness and a pressure in her chest. She had to remind herself to breathe. The person who'd written these two names had clearly wanted to conceal her work, but Nickie saw through it. J. Wilkes was her father. W. Decuir was her aunt Willow.

Nickie closed her eyes, then let out a breath and reread the spell.

Bring Back a Lover Elixir.

413

A sprig of hyssop. Thirteen dashes of Lampante olive oil. Two squirts from two different oranges. Magnetic sand. Rainwater from a thunderstorm. Thirty grams of sulfur. Stir counterclockwise for 12 seconds with an implement used by the man to write.

To make this into an insufferable revenge oil, do not add the magnetic sand.

There were two ways to apply the Bring Back a Lover elixir. Obviously, her aunt hadn't used the spell to *bring back* Nickie's dad. He would have been her brother-in-law, not a lover. Which meant Willow had used a revenge oil against Nickie's dad.

38
WILLOW

Semisloshed from her second pour of whiskey that she'd found in a downstairs cabinet with Augusta's help, Willow propped herself up against several pillows to keep from nodding off. It would be easier to face her sister if tipsy, though in that case, she probably should have stopped after the first shot. On the ride back home from the apartment in Bellflower, she'd talked through a whole speech with the Lyft driver, who'd encouraged Willow to be apologetic but not pathetic, a mantra she kept repeating to herself. Really, that's all she could recall now sitting in her bed, the details of her speech blurred away.

Her bedroom door opened, and Willow straightened up. This was it. She'd have to sputter her way through something, which probably *would* be pathetic. Whatever, as long as Victoria allowed her to stay.

At first, Willow thought a younger version

of Victoria had entered her room, looking just like she had when they were teenagers back at the house in Carson, sharing a bedroom. But as she neared, she realized it was Nickie. "Oh my gosh. Nick, you look gorgeous." Her niece had a new vibe to her, assured and glossy. Her skin had cleared, didn't need the makeup Nickie had slathered on.

Nickie startled. Nanagusta must not have let her know she was back. Willow swung her legs over and sat on the edge of the bed, reaching out to embrace Nickie.

Nickie pulled away. "You're . . . back for good?"

Willow gestured toward the suitcases. "I am. Feels good to be home."

Nickie didn't smile. Her niece didn't seem that happy to see her. "So you're not with January anymore?"

"Nope. January and I are done." Willow knew the question was inevitable but didn't want to talk about him yet. After being gone for three months, she thought Nickie would be thrilled to see her, wanting to catch up on things.

Nickie took a step back from the bed and cleared her throat, though it stayed scratchy as she spoke. "You used a spell on my dad, didn't you?"

Willow's pulse quickened, a sudden jolt, an electric shock. She must have misheard. There's no way Nickie could know about that. She steadied herself. "Nick, what are you talking about?"

"W. Decuir. That's you. Willow Decuir, right?" Nickie pulled a folded paper from her pocket and thrust it at her, the faded rectangle immediately familiar, though Willow hadn't opened it in years. It'd been tucked under the bottom flap of her jewelry box, the potion she'd ripped from the book as a teenager, hidden from her grandmother and sister. She'd almost burned it over their stove's gas flame but ultimately couldn't do it, superstitious about destroying any of the spells in the book, not wanting to be tortured in her sleep by Bela Nova. The words on the page glowed as if it were her first time reading it. Among the names who'd had the potion worked for their benefit, Willow found her entry referencing herself and Jimmie.

She felt a sourness at the back of her throat, the sense that she might throw up, though if she did, the whiskey wouldn't be to blame. "Nickie . . ."

"So you used the revenge oil on my dad?"

Willow's stomach churned. She hesitated with her response, a mistake. She'd never admitted what she'd done to anyone, could barely acknowledge it herself. But if she learned anything from her time with January, it was that everyone deserved honesty. "I did."

Nickie bit her lip.

"But I didn't know what would happen. I didn't know he would . . . die. That was never my intention. It was a mistake."

"A mistake? Why would you even use a spell on him to begin with? Why did you need revenge?"

She'd sobered quickly. "It was stupid of me. I was young and in love and —"

"Wait a minute . . . In love? You loved my dad?" Nickie's voice cracked.

Willow nodded. "Yes, I loved him. That's why I wanted to use the potion. He was my boyfriend, but he wanted your mother instead. She didn't know how much I cared about him. Probably figured he was just another one of my flings. After he broke up with me, I thought I could get him back. But then your mom got pregnant with you, so I just hoped that he'd leave her, which was ridiculous and disgusting, I know. But at the time, I didn't think it was a big deal. We were raised by single women. So that's why I mixed the revenge oil instead of the Bring Back a Lover elixir." She wanted to drop her gaze, her cheeks aflame. But she had to take it all in, Nickie's disgust and her hate, her anger and disappointment and sadness. She had to be accountable for this mighty sin despite believing it unforgiveable. She could handle Victoria finding out, kicking her out, telling her to stay away for good this time. But the possibility that Nickie would never speak to her again terrified her like nothing else ever had.

"So then, it's real. The curse."

"The curse? No, it's not real. *I* did it, Nickie." She patted her hand on her chest. "*I* used the revenge oil. That's what killed him. Not that old woman's curse." It was so clear to her all this time that she was the one responsible. She'd simply let Bela Nova's curse take the blame for Jimmie's accident. A convenient excuse.

"But you loved him. You and mom both did. That's why he died. So the curse has to be real," Nickie concluded.

Willow wasn't sure what to think. She knew her skills, believed in her own power, her innate ability to craft and conjure magic. But if the curse had indeed caused Jimmie's death and not her use of the oil, that probably meant she wasn't the daughter who'd been blessed, that it truly had been Victoria all along. This possibility she'd refused to entertain all these years, not willing to let go of the gift, of the meaning it gave to Willow's life, even if no one else knew about it.

"How did you find this, anyway?" Willow walked over to her bookshelf, had to stand on her toes to reach her jewelry box.

"I was looking for the sweetening talc the other day . . ."

"Mm-hmm. Which was in the book, not my jewelry box. By the way, I don't need it anymore, in case you were wondering."

"Willow!" The muffled call of her name came from downstairs. Victoria. By now, Nanagusta must have let her know she was home. Did Victoria plan to put her right back out?

"One second," Willow said, hand cupped to the side of her mouth to direct her shout.

Nickie stepped closer. "So what I meant, Auntie, was that the curse must be real. Because you loved him . . . and he died."

"But *I* caused him to die, Nickie. Not the curse." She plopped down on the bed, massaging her palm with a thumb, hoping to hit a pressure point. "I made him die."

"I know you said you don't believe it, but how do you explain your dad? He died, right?"

Willow grimaced. She knew this argument but, once she killed Jimmie, she had chalked up the previous family deaths to co-incidence. "He did. And?" He had been addicted to heroin, but Willow didn't want to focus on that.

"And?" Nickie wobbled her head in exasperation. "Why can't you just be straight with me? I swear, everybody in this family lies to me," Nickie said. "Or you all just won't tell me the truth."

Willow had felt the same way growing up, Nanagusta and Madelyn sharing little with her about her own father. But she was sure Nickie wouldn't want to hear her truth, that she was the gifted sibling, not Victoria. With just her instincts, she'd tweaked the elixir and made it into something deadly. No, it was not the curse that had killed Jimmie. It was Willow.

Victoria's voice from beyond broke the quiet. "Willow! Please come down. Now."

Willow groaned. "Nickie, I'll be right back. Actually, it might take a little time, but I need to go down and talk to your mother."

Nickie nodded, her boldness from minutes before washed away. Willow squeezed her shoulder before leaving the room.

Willow was still a senior when Victoria and Jimmie wed. She didn't go to the ceremony at the courthouse. The couple had slipped off without telling family on either side except for Willow, whom Victoria informed, not realizing her sister still had feelings for him. Nanagusta hadn't listened when Willow told her she needed to leave work and stop them and, on discovering that Victoria had indeed gotten hitched that afternoon, had packed up her things, and moved in with her new husband, Nanagusta didn't scream out or cuss. She only said that she'd done her part, had done her best. And what more could she do? Willow recalled being appalled by her grandmother's indifference. Never had she seen the woman so easily defeated. "Aren't you worried that he's gonna die, Grandma?" Her grandmother shooshed her and told her to stay out of her sister's business.

In Victoria's absence, and still heartbroken, Willow devoted herself to the spell book, flipping through it on the weekends with Nanagusta, the two of them making soups and potpourri sachets. Eventually, Willow made herself a complete pupil, taking the book with her to bed, reading even the pages that Nanagusta had mentioned weren't important. When she was home alone, she'd practice money spells or a rudimentary sewing job on a voodoo doll.

One afternoon, the phone rang, and when she answered and heard Victoria's shaky voice on the other end, her muscles tensed as she anticipated the awful news that Jimmie had met his ending. The curse, it seemed, was indeed true despite their grandmother's apathy. Except that wasn't why Victoria was calling. "Will, I'm going to have a baby. Can you believe it? My God, I'm so freaked out. I mean, I knew something was off because my boobs are, like, so soft. They hurt if I just bump into something. Hello? Did you hear what I said, Willow?"

Willow said she'd call her later, then ran to the bathroom to vomit. She still loved Jimmie, or at least that's the only way she could characterize her pangs of longing. She hadn't wanted him to die, for the curse to be true, but the idea of the two of them having a child together felt worse.

That's when her intention became strong — she needed a spell to better her circumstances. There were lots of options. She could assemble a gris gris bag, fill it with an anointed talisman, patchouli, basil, and an item of clothing that belonged to him. Or she could visit their apartment, steal one of his socks or an undershirt, cut a square out of it to use in some way. She settled on the

Bring Back a Lover elixir, enhancing it by swapping out mint for hyssop and adding sulfur, a bit of it left in an old science kit high up in her closet.

In the margins, someone had noted that the elixir's magnetic sand sucked in all of the user's passions, desires, yearnings and, when stirred with the rest of the ingredients, tugged on the heart of a lover with such intensity that they had no choice but to return. The sulfur and the hyssop, she believed, would intensify the mixture's power.

What if I omit the magnetic sand? she'd asked herself. Thanks to the sulfur, the oil would exact something visceral, in opposition of love. This co-spell Willow had created alongside the original version of the elixir without the sand resulted in a murky, wrathful concoction, something that would burn and scald, the sand not there to temper things. She called it a revenge oil even though Nanagusta told her she'd rewritten all of the spells in the book so that none of them could cause harm. It was just supposed to be an experiment, her imagination getting away from her.

As much as she wanted Jimmie back, they could never have a happy ending, not with him as the father of her sister's child.

Despite the sickening feeling she had inside, she moved forward with her remixed spell, skipping the sand, assembling the rest of the ingredients to make it into the revenge oil. She stirred it with a marker she'd known Jimmie to use, then settled the mixture in a pot over low heat for twenty minutes. As it stewed, she held her face over the vapors and sang Jimmie's name thirteen times, once every ninety seconds. She thought the process would do nothing more than mess up his luck. Get him fired from his job or cause him to lose some money.

Two days later, her grandmother was the one to answer Victoria's call late in the evening. When Nanagusta clutched her robe around her neck, told Victoria to slow down, Willow was right at her elbow. Nanagusta had waved her away, motioning for her to hush, but Willow couldn't help it. Couldn't stop herself from asking what Victoria was saying. And then finally, her grandmother told her the news. "He was killed in a car accident on his way from work at LAX."

Nanagusta understood Victoria's shock, of course, but wasn't sure why it'd been Willow who stopped talking for three days, not going to school, not moving from her bed. It was during those intense hours that she changed her views of the world, decided that Bela Nova was a smart woman. She'd known the power of the book and the words inside of it. The day Jimmie died, Willow stopped worrying about the curse and became a true believer in that crumbling book of spells, the powerful hoodoo magic within it, and most of all, her own gift of conjuring.

39
VICTORIA

Following her meeting at Nickie's school, Victoria hadn't the energy to speak. She felt tapped out, limp with the realness that her efforts had been in vain. Nickie had thwarted every attempt to be shaped, molded, guided onto a smooth path. She felt heavy and hot as she rested on the love seat in her office, wanting to cry. Wanting to kick and scream.

Then, Madelyn had come into her office with the news that Willow had returned. She'd been anticipating this, wouldn't have been surprised if she came back only a couple hours after Victoria had spoken to January. But of course, Willow's timing had to be the absolute worst.

"Hey, sis. You're looking good." She let Willow belt out her story. The excuses she gave for being back were vague: tight money, incongruent schedules, different ways of living between her and January. "And I think

Nickie still needs me."

"Is that right?" Victoria had only half paid attention. The months had dulled most of her anger toward her sister, as had petitions to Erzulie Dantor at her altar. She knew Willow had been working hard all these years to make up for leaving in the wake of Jimmie's death. Maybe she had taken some wrong turns in the process, but Victoria understood how that felt, and she understood that she had *let* Willow go on that way for too long, a crutch for Victoria herself to contain her pain instead of face the past head-on. Eventually, she would bring up their fight, talk things through, but for now, she'd give her sister time. Willow carried herself like she was fine, but chances were January hadn't been kind in ending their relationship.

"Not for anything you wouldn't approve of. Just, as an aunt." Willow beamed as she walked back and forth, hands clasped as if she might break into song. "I've already spoken to the others. Madelyn says she could use some help with billing. Some of those plans can be a little tricky."

Once Willow got a look at their books, the documentation from the last couple of months, she'd surely see the challenges with the business, the loss of clients. It pained her to admit to Willow's impact on her business, mystical or otherwise. She needed her. Willow's return had already rattled away the tension of earlier, and Nickie was likely to shape up with Willow back, plus the detention. "I'd be okay with you staying here for a bit, if that's what you need," Victoria said.

Willow clapped her hands. "Oh, sis, you won't regret it. I promise you."

"Okay."

Willow cleared her throat. "And I really am sorry. I don't take you for granted. And I didn't mean to say what I did about Jimmie. That was . . . that was cruel of me."

Victoria couldn't recall the last time her sister apologized to her, not even when she'd spilled red wine on their new couch or shrunk her favorite blouse in the dryer. "It's alright. I didn't mean to yell at you. And I shouldn't have made you leave. I didn't really want to kick you out."

"I knew you didn't."

Victoria doubted this but laughed anyway. She thought about giving Willow a hug.

"Uh, Vic." They both turned around. It was Madelyn. "Someone's here to see you."

"Who?" Victoria asked.

"That handsome guy, hasn't been here in over a month. The one I used to tease you about, pretending he got a crush on you. Truth is, I think he got a little something for me, but I'm a few years older than him. I mean, I don't mind."

Victoria stood, counted backward from nine. She knew it could only be Russell, but she didn't understand why he was there after so many weeks without an appointment. She took a resounding breath and went out, Willow right behind her.

"Good to see you," Russell said with a casual wave. He was leaning against the archway that adjoined the foyer and the reception area. Willow waved back and left the two of them alone. Russell stepped closer to Victoria, who was resting her bottom on the reception desk. "I know I missed our last couple of sessions. I've had some family stuff. Nothing I need to talk to you about."

She reached for the wall to steady herself. It had been quite a while since she'd last seen him, and he looked different. Same, but different. The same eyes but a smokier brown. The same smile but with more of a sparkle. That same gutsy tone of his with a deeper richness. But those weren't observations she would share with him.

"You hungry? I brought some food. Birria tacos. And quesadillas. I thought about bringing some pupusas too — the taco spot is two doors down from my favorite stand."

Victoria folded her arms. They stood there, the two of them, each waiting for the other to speak. She wanted to ask why he'd stopped coming. There were several clients she hadn't seen in a while, but he was the only one she missed talking to.

"So why are you here, Russell? Not simply to bring me tacos, I'm sure." Her shaky voice betrayed her nerves, the shock of his unexpected presence.

Russell set the bags down, then rubbed his palms together, working himself up. "I'm just gonna come straight out and say it. I . . . I'm kind of into you, you know what I'm saying?"

Something danced in her stomach, what she could only label as delight. She thought about her speech to January months ago, about the risk that he could die. She'd never considered herself a risk-taker. Except for with Jimmie, whom she knew she loved after their first conversation, and back then, she hadn't worried about the curse anyway, too level-headed for her own good. She wanted to take a risk for Russell. But really, it wasn't a risk. If she dared cross that line, his death was inevitable. That's what Nickie didn't understand. And maybe she never would until she, too, lost someone she loved. She placed her hands on her torso to quell the sensation.

"Not really, Russell. I mean, we have a professional relationship," she finally responded, feigning ignorance to let him down more easily.

"I realize that. Which is why I've been looking for another therapist."

Victoria straightened. So he was firing her? Is that the real reason he'd missed the recent sessions?

"But I mean, you're amazing. The best therapist I've ever had."

He was surely bullshitting her now. "Russell, you told me you've never gone to therapy before."

He put his hands up, showing his teeth as he laughed. "You got me. Yes, you're correct. But I know that whoever I go to next won't even come close to you. The other day, I figured out that it didn't make sense to keep things going, not the way I was feeling. I had planned to just let things go. To move on with another therapist and, you know, just let fate take over. If I was meant to run into you again, I would. And then your daughter called and —"

"My daughter called you? Nickie?"

He came closer. "Oh. Damn. Shoot. I

wasn't supposed to say that."

Had Nickie met him any of those times she filled in for Willow? What was that girl thinking?

"It wasn't right, and I know it. I admit, I'm the one that planted the seed, but I never thought she'd go through with it. Aw, geez, now I've gone and gotten the girl in trouble."

She didn't think that Nickie would dare even fathom such a move, but with this, her antics in the chem lab, it seemed anything was plausible now. She called Willow over, knew her sister had to have been listening from the adjoining family room, telling Madelyn to hush so she could hear better.

"I'm really sorry, Ms. Victoria. You see, I ran into your daughter awhile back and told her how I felt about you. That I . . . had feelings for you," Russell continued. "But that's not why I'm here. Honest. I really did want to bring you tacos. And see if there was someone you could refer me to. I don't mind driving if you don't know anyone close."

Willow was at her side in an instant. "What do you need, Vic?"

"Willow, can you please go get Nickie?" Willow wouldn't officially come back to work for her yet, but she'd get the job done faster than Madelyn.

Once Willow left, Russell turned the conversation back to tacos, telling her about some of his favorite spots in the area, which somehow managed to make Victoria forget momentarily about what Nickie had done. Then from nowhere, Russell reached for her hand. It was both firm and soft. "This might be me thinking too much of myself, but sometimes, I get the feeling that you got a little something for me too. Like, it's mutual."

Victoria held Russell's gaze, the browns of his eyes intoxicating and warm, like long-brewed tea. On his cheek, she noticed a rusty smear of orange. He must have sampled the tacos in the car on the way over.

"Vic!"

She jumped and let go of Russell's hand, hoping her sister hadn't realized she'd just broken up an intimate moment.

"Vic."

Victoria shook her head. "What is it, Willow?"

"Nickie's gone. She's not upstairs, and her backpack isn't in her room. She must have left out the back."

Gone? But that didn't make sense. Nickie had hurried upstairs to her room right after they'd returned from the school. Victoria excused herself and signaled for Willow to handle Russell. She dashed up the stairs to the upper floor. First, she went to her own bedroom and, when she didn't find Nickie there, checked her closet, Nickie's room, Willow's room, the hall closet, the shared upstairs bathroom, Madelyn's room.

Willow was in the hallway when Victoria hustled back to the stairs, sure that the girl must be in the kitchen.

"Vic," Willow said, following her. "We've checked the whole house. She's not here."

She stayed quiet, focused on covering the first floor, knowing there had to be an explanation. Nickie had no car, no place to go, no good reason to leave. When she reached the foyer, Madelyn and Augusta had joined Russell, concern painted on their faces.

"Maybe she had a study date tonight. She's been working hard on this project with Marjorie Herrera and Alex Stevens. Perhaps she went to meet them somewhere," Madelyn said, in a pair of drawstring pants, pale pink, and a fuzzy white sweater.

A flitter of envy hit Victoria, stunned by the details her mother knew about Nickie. "She probably just went to the store. That's all."

Madelyn nodded, and so did Willow. Augusta frowned, a wave of doubt wedged into her forehead.

"We'll just wait, Nan. She's okay." Victoria turned to Russell, smiling weakly.

He smiled back, but she could tell it was just to comfort her. "Look, you guys take the food. This is probably the wrong time. I'll . . . I'll call to get that reference, Ms. Victoria."

After he took off, the four women remained in the foyer, the question on their lips: after getting caught stealing, receiving detention, and upsetting Victoria so, had Nickie left home and gone to see Felix?

40
AUGUSTA

Nights still held a chill this time of the year, but Augusta couldn't seem to cool off. It had been a perfectly good morning that had somehow twisted itself into a hell of an afternoon and a tense evening, everyone in the house on edge, including Madelyn. With all the surprises, fussing, and troubles, she hadn't gotten a chance to make dinner.

"We just gonna let those tacos sit there? They're gonna get cold. Seems like a blessing, that nice young man showing up with dinner out of the blue," Madelyn said.

"Madelyn, read the damn room. No one's thinking about food right now. We need to find Nickie," Willow chastised.

"Don't yell at me. I'm just trying to help. Most people can't concentrate on an empty stomach."

They sat around the dining room table, wringing hands, clenching jaws, worrying. Victoria didn't say much, while Madelyn could hardly stop talking, throwing out dozens of possibilities for Nickie's whereabouts. "I bet she went to study at that coffee shop on 4th Street. She always talked about going there, wanting me to drop her off. Or to Trader Joe's. I thought I heard her tell Nana she was gonna try to bake peanut butter cookies this week. The kind with the chocolate kisses in the middle."

Augusta didn't know where Nickie had gone, but she had a feeling it was her fault. She hadn't confirmed it yet, but she suspected Nickie had found the letter she'd written to her. It had taken Augusta a week to type it on the adaptive keyboard on the dining room table, her right thumb doing all the work. Her story didn't come across as the lyrical saga she spoke in her head, but it conveyed her remembrance of things, a curated collection of her memories. She then had to figure out how to print it, a feat she'd been proud to complete earlier that morning. She'd tucked the letter into the spot where Nickie hid her pills in Willow's room — just hours before Willow returned. But she hadn't thought Nickie would discover it so soon.

Of course, she *wanted* Nickie to find it. Augusta just assumed she'd have some time before this would happen. She hadn't fully mapped out the repercussions, that Nickie knowing her story would mean that they all would eventually know her story, her big lie.

Augusta and her granddaughters had come by car to California, somewhere she'd only known about from movies. And from Benjamin, who'd talked about the place like he'd lived there his entire life, painting for her scenes along the beach, people sunning themselves and driving along Pacific Coast Highway, the boundless sky only smudged by the contrails left by jets. Augusta used the hefty monthly sum she'd gotten from the workshop space to rent a four-bedroom house in Carson, right near the mall. She'd need a real career to be able to raise a pair of young ladies, the cost of living in California worse than what she'd been told. She vowed never to go back, though. New Orleans had turned sour to her. It had gotten too hard to breathe there, the memories smothering. Then there was Madelyn, who'd been the biggest challenge yet, causing chaos on either side of the Mississippi. She hadn't been an awful mother to Madelyn, but just not good enough, and so she saw a chance to redeem herself with Victoria and Willow. In California, Augusta thought she might be able to protect them in their adolescence. She could reset, obliterate old patterns.

California had been a very deliberate choice, a part of her always wanting to believe that Benjamin was still alive, that he hadn't been on that train to Chicago. She could envision him arriving at the Union Passenger Terminal in New Orleans, feeling lucky with new money in his pocket, making a last-minute decision to buy a ticket to Los Angeles instead of returning home. He'd explain to his parents later, once he was settled and had a job with one of the studios friendly to colored help. He'd play a butler or crook, the few options available to him at the time. He'd even work as a stagehand if they'd let him. Just needed a way in, and his talent, his skill at charming people would do the rest. That was the life she pictured for him, the dream he'd shared many times over their short relationship.

But she'd never had the guts to look for him. It was easier to accept Bela Nova's cursing words, to presume him dead and go on. Even now, with her recent prowess with computers, she didn't dare type his name into a search. Locating information about him would probably mean finding something about the train accident, the dozens of people killed just outside of Chicago. If she confirmed that he'd been onboard, she'd feel responsible for all the other lives lost too. It was a proof she wasn't ready to see, even after all these years.

Back then, she'd figured Bela Nova's curse had ended with her, especially when first Nicholas St. Jean and, after him, Harlowe Decuir kept right on living. She'd told Madelyn the curse killed Harlowe to try to whip her into shape. It was a lie that she'd had to perpetuate, telling the girls about his unfortunate ending when they'd first arrived in California. Chances were that Harlowe was still out there, dazzling women with his cinnamon eyes, and when it came to Victoria's father, Nicholas St. Jean, she'd told the girls he was unlovable even to his own mother. Once she'd made up the story about Harlowe's death, she couldn't go back. His ending became part of their family's history.

Having sworn off love herself, Augusta didn't think about the curse much as her granddaughters bloomed into teenagers. Until Jimmie's death. Once Victoria lost him, Augusta let go of the slim possibility that Benjamin had lived, that he hadn't boarded that train to Chicago. She concluded that Madelyn simply hadn't loved either of her children's fathers, and that was

441

why the curse hadn't touched them. What she knew then for certain was that Bela Nova's cursing words had been all too truthful, that generations would pay for what she'd done.

"You think we need to call the police?" Madelyn had retrieved the bag of tacos from the reception area and was the only one eating them. The night had grown darker, Nickie out well past a reasonable curfew, if Victoria had ever let her go out.

"No, we're not calling the police. You think I want them all up in my business?" It was the first time Victoria had spoken since sitting down at the table.

Willow bounced her fist against it. "Hell no. Besides, you have to wait twenty-four hours to declare someone a missing person."

"She's not missing," Victoria said. "I'm sure she's just gone."

"Mmm-hmm. A runaway."

"She's not a runaway either, Madelyn."

Madelyn shrugged, dipping the last bit of her taco into red consommé sauce.

As they sat, the soft whir of the refrigerator cut in from beyond. Augusta knew she had to tell them about the letter, not that that would reveal the *where,* but at least it might explain the why of Nickie's disappearance. She was about to point to the laptop, when Victoria stood up. "I'm going to call Felix."

Madelyn glanced up from her bowl. "Felix? How do you have his number?"

Victoria didn't respond as she headed for her office. Augusta snapped her fingers to get Willow's attention and pointed.

"You need the laptop, Nan?" Willow slid it her way, and Augusta jiggled the mouse back and forth, then clicked on her letter, a document in the bottom right corner of the desktop titled *my st,* as she'd somehow saved it before being able to type the rest of the word *story* and hadn't figured out how to change it. She opened it and pushed the computer back over to Willow.

"What's this, Nan?"

Augusta's face was stoic, a moment of reckoning right in front of her. She'd ignored it for too many years, telling herself that she'd share the truth one day — on her deathbed, just like in the movies. But that didn't seem fair. She'd lived out most of her years, but it was only right to stick around for the fallout of her actions. She crossed her arms and leaned back in her chair, eyes intent as she stared at Willow.

Her granddaughter seemed to understand, clearing her throat before dragging the

443

laptop close, the screen's blue light dancing in the browns of her eyes.

"What's that she's reading, Mama?" Madelyn asked her. Augusta put a finger over her lips, and Madelyn groaned, then scooted her chair toward Willow's so she could see the screen for herself. "This your story? You writing an autobiography or something?"

"Mom, I'm trying to read. Nana wrote a letter to Nickie." Willow looked up from the screen. "You gave this to her, Nan?"

Augusta nodded, her insides simmering. She wondered if this was how Lanora had felt just before she found herself inside-out.

Madelyn threw up her hands. "Alright, alright. Well, can you at least read it out loud, Will? I want to hear what she got to say about me."

As Willow read the words out loud, Augusta's mind illustrated the story with wispy animations. So many ghosts of people, places, sounds, it was hard to believe what had come and gone. When Victoria returned with her phone, Willow stopped reading, just before getting to the part that would upset her.

"Did you call him? Is Nickie with him?" Madelyn asked.

"He didn't pick up. I'll try again in a bit."

"Listen up — we're in here reading your grandmother's memoir."

Victoria's brows dug in toward her eyes. "Her memoir? What memoir? And why are you doing that now?"

Willow's attention had gone back to the computer. She waved her hand, wanting them to listen to her.

"Bela Nova wanted to punish me for what I'd done to her. By marrying her son, I kept her from aligning herself with a family with money, what she'd always wanted for Dudley Lee. Then I stole the woman's book and used it to build my own clientele. And since I was no longer her pupil, she wouldn't be looked upon favorably by Lanora, and so wouldn't become a loa herself once she died. So she created a curse just for me, just for our family, one that would keep us from love. It would either take love away . . ."

Willow stopped, the quiet letting them take in the words. It looked as if Victoria might cry, but she held it in, her chin turning rigid. "Why didn't you tell this to us before, Nan? Don't you think this would have been helpful to know?"

Augusta wanted to nod but felt too ashamed, the memory of Jimmie's death, of holding Victoria tightly, kissing the girl's forehead as she tried to calm her down,

445

soothe her cries, playing out in her mind. "Why us, Nan?" Victoria had asked after Jimmie's service. "Why did this have to happen to us?"

She'd wanted to tell them why, to tell her truth for years, but the more time went on, the easier it was not to worry about the past.

"Calm down, Vic. What difference would it have made?" Willow went back to the screen.

"I don't know. But it sucks to find this out after all this time. This is a drop, Nan. Like . . . now? We're trying to find Nickie." Victoria paced the small space between the dining area and the kitchen.

"Vic, there's a reason she's showing it to us, don't you think? *Because* of Nickie, right?"

To this, Augusta nodded.

Victoria leaned on the counter. "Well whatever it is, just tell us, Nana. All I'm hearing is that you misled us. That you . . . lied."

"Aww, come on, now, Vic. Don't be too hard on your grandmother."

"Why not? All this time, we thought that Nana's mentor just snapped and turned on her." Victoria faced Augusta, her eyes blotched red. "You made her out like she was jealous of you. That she wanted Lanora's gift and thought she deserved it more than you. You never told us the full story. And you could have."

A new hush blossomed in the room. They didn't look at one another. Augusta's insides hurt, a pain she hadn't felt before. She had intended for the letter to offer an explanation, but the words she'd written couldn't do justice to the rationale in her heart. Really, it was an indescribable mix of things: regret, hopelessness, youth, passion, terror.

"Harlowe Decuir was one of my regular clients."

Willow had started in again, her voice changed, now craggy and low. August knew that she'd read ahead, already knew the other part of her big secret. Her big lie. But Willow continued on bravely.

"More than anything, he wanted to open a tobacco shop in the Quarter. He came in to pay for foot powders and for holy water to splash on the front doors of properties he hoped to take over for his business."

"Harlowe wanted to open a business? I didn't know that. I thought he was just another pretty boy. Your father, Willow. That was a good-looking man. Sharp, I tell you," Madelyn said.

"Harlowe loved him some women. He slept with just about everyone in New Orleans."

Willow looked across the table at Augusta, a hand at her throat. *"When Madelyn was pregnant with Willow, he had at least another two women expecting children at the same time. They'd just had a fling, probably got themselves together one night at the Dew Drop Inn."*

"No, no, no. I ain't never met anyone up in the Dew. I think I met him over at Clever Charlee's. Or Scat Dog."

"After Willow was born, Madelyn started using heroin again. Heavy. She stopped coming home. I heard she was staying with her friend Felicia Tunstill over in Algiers. Best friends, always together, but up to no good."

Madelyn's chin rested on her fist.

"When she was younger, I'd shared the words Bela Nova said to me. That the people we loved would die, though when she cried about it, I told her not to worry. I figured the curse had dried up by then. It had been twenty-some years. Once she got pregnant with your aunt Willow, your mother just an infant herself, I had to act. Maybe I could scare Madelyn sober, make her come back home and stay, if I told her that Harlowe died, that I had been wrong and the curse was still in effect. So, next time Harlowe came in, I said I'd use my most powerful spell to help him out, one he'd not been able to afford. It would

448

be free, but he'd have to set up his shop over in Shreveport. He had people there, and it was far enough away that we'd never see him again. He agreed, just like I knew he would. I've never met anyone so desperate for a business. Once he left, I went over to Felicia's to find Madelyn. I brought her home, got her clean for a couple days. And I told her Harlowe was gone. Dead and gone. Told her that the curse got him, even though I knew it never would. Madelyn didn't love him, and I knew it. But she was so far gone, I knew I could make her believe she had."

Willow stopped, folding her lips inward, an attempt to keep her face from breaking. Infuriated, heartbroken, and captivated all at the same time.

"So Harlowe's still alive? That's what you're saying?" Madelyn asked.

Augusta pushed herself back in her chair and bent toward Willow, hugging her from behind, rubbing her cheek with her thumb, an apology.

"Well, I'll be damned. All this time, you think he would have reached out knowing I done had his baby." Madelyn shook her head. "Willow, I wouldn't shed a tear over that bum."

Willow sniffed, separating herself from Augusta and wiping the dampness from her eyes. "So you mean my father's alive right now?"

Augusta didn't know, honestly. The way he'd been living, he'd likely crashed into the end of his years by now, but sometimes death evaded folks. Sometimes, people changed. Maybe they could contact his sister Ramona. She'd deleted that Facebook message out of fear, but she knew the woman had reached out for a reason, and it would be up to Willow to decide what to do with it.

Augusta knew the women around the table had strong reason to be upset with her, to throw her out, stick her in an old folks' home, or just leave her on the front porch. Just like she'd stolen from Bela Nova, she'd stolen from her family too, bringing that curse upon them with her selfish behavior.

But she'd long come to accept her actions, and despite the consequences, whatever they would be, she felt a little freer. Still worried, but loosened in a way. She hadn't realized how weighty her secret had become.

Madelyn pushed her chair back and turned to Augusta, her daughter's face as serious as she'd ever seen it. "Don't nobody teach anyone how to be a mama. Especially with all that shit Bela Nova dragged you through, like keeping you from going to your own daddy's funeral." She turned to Victoria. "She wasn't perfect. Shoot, we know she was a hell of a much better mama than I ever was. But she wanted to keep us all safe. Even if she had to keep things from you."

Victoria's face relaxed. She shut her eyes, unclenched her fists. "Look, we'll figure this out. We've got a lot to deal with. But right now, I need to get away. I need to find Nickie."

"You're leaving?" said Madelyn as Victoria moved past the table toward the family room. "Vic, have a seat. Let me get you a glass of water."

"I can go with you, Vic. I could use a smoke," said Willow. She sniffled and wiped her eyes.

"You don't smoke, Willow."

"I know I don't, Mom. I said I could *use* one. Shit, I'm feeling out of sorts. I'm shook. About Nickie, about everything."

"I'll be fine by myself," Victoria said after a moment. "I'm going upstairs. If Nickie's not back by nine, I'm going to drive around to find her." She didn't wait for their reaction.

Willow watched her sister, waiting until she disappeared into the shadows before rising herself. "This has been a lot. Nanagusta," she said, not looking at her. "I know you had your reasons for handling things the way you did. But it was wrong. And I'm pretty pissed. But you also raised me, taught me all I know. So of course I'll forgive you. We're gonna be okay. For right now, though, I need some space. We're gonna locate Nickie, and then I'm gonna need some space."

Augusta moved out of Willow's way as she headed in the same direction Victoria had gone.

Augusta grabbed hold of the back post of a chair. She'd not had a lot of friends in life. Even when the girls were young, she hadn't bonded with the other moms. If she had, however, she believed she would have encountered other women who'd made questionable choices, all because they wanted to protect someone. She blew out her breath slowly.

She was left alone with Madelyn, who reached in the bag for another taco. "I'm not mad at you, Mama. I'm the last one to try to make someone feel bad for what they did. But, man, I can't help but wonder what I might have done differently without that curse in the back of my head. I never wanted to think it could be true, but sometimes, I had my doubts."

Augusta bobbed her head slowly. Harlowe wasn't the worst person in the world — nowhere as mean and awful as that Nicholas St. Jean — but their lives would have been different had he stuck around. Not better or worse, just different.

"I mean, the curse threat didn't work." Madelyn managed a laugh. "I stayed in them streets. But I did think about the curse sometimes, wondering if I really did love Harlowe. I mean, I know now that I didn't. But it made me *wonder.* Isn't that something — what just a few words can do?"

She wasn't surprised by Madelyn's wisdom. The girl had always been smart, just used it in the wrong way. It seemed she *had* really changed after all these years, had owned up and accepted her past wrongdoings. She was starting late, but she'd make a good mother now to Victoria and Willow, even if they both thought they didn't need one.

"Anyway, that Bela Nova lady can't blame you for her son running off, even if you got him whipped with a spell. Ain't she the one who wrote the spells? That's her fault for creating something that could be used against her. Just like Ironman."

She didn't understand Madelyn's reference but smiled anyway. Her daughter wasn't done.

"Anyway, if she loved Lanora so much, you'd think she'd *want* you as a daughter-in-law, wouldn't she?" They sat for a moment, Augusta considering all of Madelyn's questions, worrying about Nickie. And Willow and Victoria. She'd wanted something good to come from her story, but sharing it only seemed to have added more stress.

"Do we know what happened to that January, Willow's beau? I guess he's still alive. She say anything to you?"

Willow hadn't mentioned to anyone what had become of her and January, and no one dared to ask. Augusta shook her head.

"Well, I guess it's up to us."

Augusta didn't quite understand. Did Madelyn want the two of them to look up January?

Madelyn seemed to get her confusion. "To find Nickie. Mama, those two aren't going to be able to do anything too well after that bomb you dropped."

Despite everything, she'd missed her daughter. On this odd evening, Augusta sat in Willow's empty chair next to Madelyn and hugged her. And with her long arms, Madelyn hugged her back.

41
NICKIE

While she'd made it to the train with a blanket, a thick enough jacket, socks, and more cash than she'd ever had in her wallet, Nickie wasn't prepared for the trip, not like the riders who sat with her in the car leaving Los Angeles. They'd brought pastries and bags of apples and sandwiches wrapped in tinfoil. They wore their hair in curlers and had special pillows to keep their heads propped up for peaceful sleep. One woman had a flask, another just kept her liquor in a Clippers water bottle, no fizz to the brown liquid she poured over ice. Someone had packed smoked chicken, eating it from the comfort of his sleeping bag.

As the train chugged along, lights out, a choir of snores sounding around her, she watched the world go by through her window. She wanted to cry. In her seventeen years, she'd not done something like this.

The moon glinted down on the rugged,

dusty landscape, the train nearing its first stop of Palm Springs. Midnight had passed, but she couldn't sleep, partly because she didn't have a pillow and her blanket didn't cover both her shoulders and her feet at the same time. And also because her mind raced, thoughts pinging about where she would stay, what she would do if the shop was no longer there. What she would do if the shop still stood in the same place. Did she expect to go inside and search it as if she were some kind of inspector? She'd left without a plan, but the long trip at least gave her an opportunity to figure it all out.

Her mind went to the letter in her pocket. Once Willow had gone downstairs, Nickie went to the headboard to retrieve her birth control pills, one last item to pack. She'd fished around the padding, but after drawing out the first container, she noticed there was something blocking the second. She gripped the corner of an envelope, tearing the fabric of the headboard as she tugged. Her belly sank at the sight of her name scrawled in red ink. Someone had stashed the envelope deliberately for her, in a place she thought secret.

There hadn't been time to read it then, whatever it was. She had initially assumed it must have been from Willow, finding the hidden pills in the few hours since she'd moved back into her bedroom.

Reading might help her fall asleep. She reached up to turn on the overhead light before breaking the seal of the envelope and drawing out the stark, folded pages.

Dear Nickie,
My great-grandmother was a wondrous woman named Lanora. I was the first daughter in her bloodline. My mama wanted me to marry and be a homemaker like her. Instead, I left home when I was your age so I could begin the life that I wanted to live.

Nickie could hardly believe the words, that they'd been written by her Nanagusta, who barely knew how to use a computer. She read her great-grandmother's story. And she read it again, the pages keeping her up past the stop in Yuma, Arizona, where a woman and two children boarded, settling in the seats in front of her. The woman asked Nickie if the older kid, a girl about eleven, could sit next to her — wouldn't be a bother, she'd read or watch videos with her headphones once it was daytime. Nickie nodded, turning off the light so as not to disturb the young girl's sleep. It would be wise to try to get some rest herself.

But she couldn't. When Madelyn had told her about the curse, Nickie hadn't realized how far back it went. She hadn't known about Bela Nova or her son, Dudley Lee, or about her great-grandfather, Benjamin Montrose. If a reversal had in fact been written on the missing pages, her Nanagusta would have used it already, long before Madelyn could have haphazardly torn them out.

She didn't want to cry again, but once the tears started rolling, they were hard to stop at the recognition of her error. She used the collar of her shirt to wipe her face, pushing the cloth into the corner of her eyes as if plugging a leak. As she sniffed, she felt a hand touch her arm, the spot underneath her sleeve tingly, like someone had just worked Icy Hot into her bicep. The young girl was holding onto her, faint lighting from the aisles catching freckles on her cheeks, long lashes on her closed eyes. Nickie adjusted her body, inching nearer in case the girl needed to use her shoulder as a pillow. She sniffed one last time, sucking everything up so she could rest. Letting her eyes shut, she replayed the letter's final words.

I sometimes wonder how things would have

been if I wouldn't have left home when I did. But I believe in my heart that you were always meant to be a part of this world, Nickie. So no matter what I did, God would have figured out a way for there to be a Madelyn, a Willow, and a Victoria, so that there would be a Nickie Montrose and she would do all the things she wanted to do.

42
VICTORIA

Victoria hadn't been able to locate Nickie. She and Madelyn had driven fruitlessly around the neighborhood, then past her school, the mall, other places she thought a teenager would go. When they'd returned after midnight, she went straight to her closet and burned candles, prayed a Hail Mary and petitioned Lanora, Marie Laveau, and Papa Legba. She'd told the family if they couldn't find Nickie by the next evening, she'd go to the authorities. The distress of Nickie running away at least subdued all the anger in the house, the secrets Nanagusta shared fit to start a war, Madelyn doing her best to act as Switzerland. It had been a lot to take in, learning details about her grandmother's life that she never could have imagined. Maybe knowing what Nanagusta had done to Bela Nova wouldn't have changed anything, but that didn't excuse what *she'd* done. They were the ones impacted, and they'd deserved the truth from the very beginning.

So had Nickie.

Early the next morning, the women sat around the table again, Madelyn eating cereal, Willow the quietest she'd been in her life. Victoria's phone rang, and she sprang for it. "Hello?"

"Is it Nickie?" Willow said.

Victoria didn't answer her. "Hi. Thanks for calling me back, Felix. This is Nickie's mom, Victoria."

Madelyn put down her glass of water, and Nanagusta shuffled her chair closer to Victoria's.

"Put it on speaker, Vic."

Victoria frowned but did what Willow said, placing the phone down.

"I'm not sure if you listened to my message, but Nickie's gone. And we have no way to get in touch with her."

"Oh yeah, because you took her phone."

Madelyn winced. "He telling the truth, ain't he?" she said softly.

She couldn't disagree with either of them. Taking Nickie's phone had been foolish. Much of what she'd done these last several months had been foolish. Just plain senseless. How could she have made such bad decisions with Nickie? She'd let Bela Nova's

461

damning words hinder her parenting. And Jimmie. She'd never shared anything about him — his love for R & B, that he could blow huge bubbles with his gum, that he loved to do crossword puzzles. She'd fucked up. All the clients she'd ushered through their life's challenges, yet she couldn't fix her own family's troubles. "I did take her phone. That's correct. Anyway, I was wondering if you'd heard from her. Or perhaps if she's with you?"

"I haven't seen her this week. It's a new semester so we don't have class together." He paused. "We don't really talk anymore."

Victoria looked over to Willow. If Felix and Nickie weren't speaking, she knew it was her own fault. She tried to think of something else they could ask the boy that would offer them a clue. "Is there anyone else you can think of who we can call?"

They could hear his deep exhale on the other end. "Nah. Nickie didn't really hang out with anyone else. She's kind of independent."

Alone, in other words? Fuck. Her poor kid.

"Hey, maybe she went to Arizona to check out the campus."

Arizona? The campus? Why would she do that? She had applied to Long Beach State.

"Oh, or maybe New Orleans," he said.

"New Orleans?" asked Madelyn.

Victoria waved a hand in her direction, shushing her. "Felix, why would she go to New Orleans?"

Felix coughed a couple of times. "She said something about it before. Her aunt had run a business there, but it didn't work out."

The room was silent.

"Mrs. Montrose, will you keep me updated about Nickie? This is pretty worrying. I hope she's okay. I mean, I'm sure she is. I just want to know when she's home."

Victoria sighed, rubbing her forehead. "Yes. Yes, we'll let you know. And if you hear from her, please tell her to call me, okay?"

Victoria noticed Augusta patting Willow's arm. Their eyes matched expressions, full of grief, surely missing Nickie.

Victoria hated what she'd done to the girl. She'd been relieved, at first, when Felix said that Nickie wasn't with him, but at the same time, he was her only lead.

It seemed her daughter had lost her one friend in Felix. Would that push her to pick up and leave, to venture to a whole new city without telling anyone? Victoria thought about all she'd put Nickie through — both recently and for years. If Nanagusta had limited her world the way she'd done to Nickie, Victoria would have fled after just weeks. Nickie had put up with her nonsense for seventeen years.

"So what do we do?" Victoria said after ending the call.

"You thinking you should go to New Orleans?" There was a rustiness to Willow's voice, but also a knowingness.

"So, what — she's just going to go there and open a candle shop in the Quarter?" Victoria asked, incredulous.

Willow tilted her head. "Maybe after reading the letter, she got curious."

"Hey, hang on a second." Madelyn spoke out of nowhere, suddenly standing and saying she'd be right back. They could hear her upstairs, talking and singing loudly to herself. Madelyn soon returned with her tablet.

"I think she was on here yesterday. I saw something that I didn't remember searching for, but it was in New Orleans, so I thought that maybe I actually did, just had too much wine or something."

Victoria put up a hand, letting her mother know she'd gotten the gist. She reached for the tablet. "Let me look." She easily found the page on the browser, a map with the shop's address, which Nickie must have seen somewhere in the book. She clicked the back arrow on the window a few times and arrived at the schedule for the Sunset Limited. A train had left the night before at 10:06 p.m., arriving in New Orleans tomorrow.

She needed to step back mentally, think through the scene unfolding before her. She was a daughter of Lanora. She'd been gifted. She'd been blessed with a heightened sense. But she'd gotten lost underneath her practice and her worries about Nickie and the curse. She hadn't tuned in to herself, listened to her body. "Willow, can you please go get the book?"

Willow ran upstairs, her breaths heavy by the time she was back.

"Sorry. It took a while to find it. Nickie had it in her room."

Victoria closed her eyes, revisiting the sounds of her grandmother's now-faded voice, the lessons she'd once taught her and Willow. The tales of the loa, some of them great, some of them mischievous or cranky, some magnificently kind. The tricks and the hexes, the foot powders and healing potions. The verses written in cursive and in crayon and with calligraphy ink and with blood (though as she got older, she thought maybe Nanagusta had said that just to scare her). The old photographs and letters and recipes for muffins and pralines and crawfish. Pages smudged with dirt, with drips from cake batter. Odd items mixed in between — bookmarks, flower petals, recital programs, a laminated Hail Mary card, a cut-out *New York Times* crossword puzzle from 1972 with *AUGUSTA* written in for 38 Across (clue: *Southern home of the Masters Golf Tournament*), the waxy wrapper from a piece of saltwater taffy with a phone number in pencil.

Victoria flipped through to the place where Lanora's song had been written. She placed a palm on each page and closed her eyes, and with that, her pain and her prickles, her stings and shivers all went away, senses numb, even the drab taste in her mouth gone. But in her heart, she still felt a sharp stab. She removed her hands from the pages and opened her eyes.

"Willow, do we still have that American Express Business card?"

"We do. In the safe. Platinum."

"Go get it. We need four plane tickets to New Orleans."

Victoria looked over at Nanagusta, who took a large inhale. Slowly releasing her breath, she nodded. *Yes.*

43
AUGUSTA

Augusta had survived the flight, her purse on the floor, and now she was back in New Orleans, a place she thought she wouldn't see again. But it had welcomed her back. It took three family members and a driver to help her out of the taxi, pulled up to the curb along Conti Street. Madelyn held her dress down so as not to expose Augusta's upper thighs and poppy-colored underwear to the tourists en route to Bourbon Street, but the cool air was refreshing. She didn't mind showing a little skin. She'd spent more than a third of her life in California, and yet she'd immediately eased back into her younger self once she'd finally stood there on the damp, rust-colored sidewalk. She craved turtle soup and catfish Creole, could eat a dozen beignets if given the chance. She hadn't realized how much she missed her home.

They'd dropped their bags at a hotel, then

the same driver took them to the shop so they could ask if anyone fitting Nickie's description had stopped in. Augusta wondered if the shop still even existed, maybe now a yoga studio or boutique. Willow led, still hardly speaking to Augusta but keeping a slower pace for her. Madelyn provided the commentary as usual, pointing out sites, highlights of her wildest times. "I hate to admit it, but I used the bathroom next to that pole right there more than once." She laughed. "More than twice."

When she'd lived in the Quarter, Augusta typically spent the daytime hours cooped up in the shop, leaving at dawn to get shopping at the market out of the way, going out again late at night to run errands for Bela Nova, so she didn't know the area as well in the daytime. Still, she noticed the differences time had made, barriers blocking off Bourbon Street, the dinginess scrubbed off doors, and a lot more restaurants.

Despite the time of day, she could have located the entry to the old workshop with her eyes closed, not needing to count off the fifth door from the corner of the building as Willow did. The doors on either side of it once led to the Dew Drop Inn, which she now saw had been renovated into two different spaces — a pizza joint and a souvenir store. The door that opened to the shop's stairway still had a small symbol etched into its glass window, a serpent with a rainbow for a tail tucked into a cauldron, the loa Damballa Wedo. Above that, the sign in the window said *Rare Books.* They stopped in front of it, letting Augusta go first.

"Nana," a voice called out from across the street just as she grabbed the door handle. Nickie. The women turned. She wore a long-sleeved purple dress cut just above her knees. Augusta couldn't recall seeing Nickie in a dress, not since her collared navy uniform in elementary school, and it was obvious she wasn't used to it, slouching, her knees knobbed together. She seemed defeated, even her usual big curls slumped and heavy. She waited for a car to pass, then crossed the street.

"Nickie, I outta pop you in your head." Willow wiggled a finger as she walked up to her.

"Aunt Willow, I'm sorry. I just . . ."

"You know how I hate flying." Willow flattened her lips.

Madelyn raised her hand. "Me too."

It hadn't been as awful as Augusta had anticipated, but she planned on going back to Long Beach by bus, train, or car.

Nickie faced her mother, sullen. She opened her mouth but Victoria just reached for her hand. "Nickie, I'm sorry. I know this is my fault."

Augusta shook her head adamantly, stepping in to grab Victoria's wrist. She didn't want any of them to blame themselves or for Nickie to feel bad for leaving. None of them had anything to feel bad about. They'd all just been trying too hard to protect each other. Augusta released Victoria's wrist and hugged her instead. Victoria stayed stiff, but when Nickie joined in, Augusta felt Victoria's body relax, and soon Willow was there too, stroking Augusta's hair, holding onto her braid.

"Well, ain't that nice." Madelyn used her tablet to take a picture of them. "So are we gonna go get something to eat? Not around here. I miss Val's. Or Southern Slouch." Now Madelyn was recording, the family's official documentarian. "You already been to the shop, Nickie?"

"No. I came earlier this morning, but they weren't open yet."

"You came all the way out here to see the shop, right?" Madelyn prompted her on.

She tilted her head. "At first, yes. I thought I could find something there. And honestly, I just wanted some distance. Even for a day.

Or two."

Victoria walked back to the door, giving Nickie's dress a tug for her to follow. "Well, let's just go in. I can't have you flying off again next month upset that you missed your chance."

The stairwell was dark, just like it had always been, a weak light over the landing yellowing the new paint on the walls, the posters and framed black-and-white photos of bands and revues from the Dew Drop Inn days. Nickie held onto Augusta's back on the way up.

A tickle came to her chest as she climbed.

A woman dressed all in burgundy, a short haircut suiting her face, high cheekbones and stunning eyes, greeted them and asked if they were looking for anything in particular. They probably appeared out of place, the five of them huddled together, eyes still damp from their reunion with Nickie.

"Have a look around, and if you need anything, just holler." The woman went back to the counter, where she shooed a large gray cat. It jumped down and skittered to a pillow in the corner next to a tall wooden chair, padded and Victorian.

Nickie took Augusta by the arm, guiding her through the stacks. The living space of the shop had been opened up, making it

471

twice the size it had been before, though Augusta had moved into a proper home in Central City by the time the girls were toddlers. Candles burned, beeswax and lavender and vanilla notes filling the air, soothing aromas meant to cover up the smell of the books. There was a section on New Orleans history, another on famous women from Louisiana, and an area for Southern fiction. Nickie selected a gently used book of poetry, and they walked toward the counter. As Nickie paid, Augusta went to look for the cat when something stopped her, the painting over the register. It was Papa Legba, the same painting that had hung in the shop many decades ago.

"You okay, Nana?"

Augusta startled at Nickie's touch, the girl's hand so cold it gave Augusta a shiver. She closed her eyes hard, tuning in, listening for a familiar voice. And to her shock, it came, still husky and melodic. Still terrifying.

"That you, Augusta?"

She turned around, noting a figure in the chair on the other side of the shop, holding onto a cane.

Augusta thought she might implode as the person stood. She closed her eyes again, trying to erase the image in front of her, but when she reopened them, the scene had become even more vivid, the lines sharper. It was indeed her old mentor, now truly old. Leave it to Bela Nova to live to be 102. She'd probably forced herself to stay alive just for this moment, had somehow known it would come eventually.

Her skin had pruned, thick jowls sagging into her neck. She still had dreads, just not very many of them, large patches of her hair broken away. As Bela Nova stepped nearer, Augusta felt stuck, praying that she wouldn't tip over at her presence.

"You've gotten old like me now, haven't you?" Bela Nova laughed, shaking herself to coughing.

"You okay?" the woman shouted from behind the register.

"Estelle, come on over here." She leaned on her cane and addressed Augusta again. "I can't believe it took this long for us to have a run-in. I've been back in the city for ten or so years."

Bela Nova stopped her approach to pat the woman's arm. "Augusta, this is one of my great-grandkids, Estelle." Estelle waved and offered a pleasant smile.

Augusta bit her top lip, confused. Dudley Lee had been her only child when he died. Had she had more children after that?

"What, you think Dudley Lee didn't mess around before he met you? He had three kids already by the time you two ran off, had another on the way when he died."

Nickie held Augusta's hand. She was staring intently at Bela Nova and must have put together the story in the letter with the scene playing out before her.

Bela Nova's tone was rich enough to push down the stacks if need be, and soon Victoria, Willow, and Madelyn had come up behind them. Willow grinned, and Victoria froze and gripped her bag.

"I got eight great-grandchildren, at least nineteen great-great-grandchildren. I lost count."

"I think we're at twenty-one," said Estelle. Augusta searched for any resemblance to Dudley Lee in her face but couldn't find it.

"She would know better. And don't ask me none of their names because I would just say phooey. Except I know Billy Jr. and little Jenn." She heaved a long sigh. "Estelle, I better sit back down."

Bela Nova let the woman help her back to the chair. Once seated, she reached down and scratched the cat under its neck. "Ms. Augusta, I know I did you wrong. I took a risk laying a curse that could take my own son. Honestly, I didn't think you really loved him so I thought he'd be protected. I was incorrect. And I'm sorry. I lost a son. I wish I could take it back, what I did. I would have helped you reverse the spell, knowing how miserable you must have been after losing my Dudley Lee, but I was told you were no longer at the shop."

Victoria cleared her throat, then brushed past her toward Bela Nova. "So how do we undo the curse?"

Bela Nova's eyes seemed to jump out at Victoria, the woman amused, it appeared, to be spoken to with such authority. Augusta had never dared taken such a tone with her.

"Well, the answer's been in in the book," she said. "The one your grandmother and my son took from me."

Victoria stared back at the woman, not breaking her gaze as she then pulled the book from her tote bag. "Here's our book right here. So tell us how to undo the curse."

This wasn't a tone Victoria used with her clients, or with Nickie, or even with Madelyn or Willow when they worked her nerves. Her voice lifted the hairs on Augusta's arms.

Bela Nova chuckled. "It appears all you Laurent women are bold. This your grandchild, Ms. Augusta? I reckon she ain't Dudley Lee's, or I would have sniffed her out." She'd tilted her body to one side to help

475

her peer around Victoria, but Augusta didn't even blink in response, not wanting to give the woman the satisfaction. Of course Bela Nova wouldn't know she went by Montrose. Laurent was her maiden name, but she could at least acknowledge that Dudley Lee had shared his surname with her, even if she'd only been a Burnley for a short time, daughter-in-law to the woman born Delilah Elizabeth Burnley.

Victoria slapped the book, and Bela Nova — and really all of them — drew back. The girl meant business.

"The reversal, ma'am?"

"The reversal, it seems, you've had all along. I couldn't remember all the words, not with your grandmother and my son leaving me as they did without my book. But I couldn't unhex it for Ms. Augusta, anyway. Could only tell her how to do it for herself." Bela Nova wore a stain on her lips, which had shriveled to thin lines. "The reversal, my dear, is the Song of Lanora. All she had to do was sing it aloud with her eyes closed." Bela Nova closed her eyes and put her hand to her heart, her face tilted up toward the ceiling beams. "To untrouble the souls plagued by this hex, have one who is so blessed in her ability recount to Lanora her song," she said, with dramatic affect.

Augusta remembered the first night Bela Nova sang the song, about the power it held for her descendants. "It went something like that. You know I always loved Lanora. She's why I found you, Augusta."

Bela Nova looked again at Augusta, who bit down hard on her back teeth, her jawline rigid. These last few months, thinking back to her time at the shop and the Dew Drop Inn, she'd sometimes wondered if Bela Nova had paid Clarence to bring her in.

"So any of us can sing it?" Victoria asked.

Bela Nova pointed her bony hand at Victoria. "If she's your grandmother? Then, yes. It's your curse too. You can sing it to me." She reached down and patted the cat's head. "Though, it would make me so happy to hear it from Augusta again."

Victoria turned around, and Augusta nodded. If anyone was right for the job, it was Victoria. Such a shame that in all these years they'd been singing the story, none of them had ever done it with her eyes shut. But certainly, Victoria knew it by memory.

Victoria knelt, the book propped up on her thigh.

"What are you doing down there, love? I said with your eyes closed. You can't read with your eyes closed, now, can you?"

477

Victoria slid the book off her lap and flapped the lid over, stared down at her hands. It looked like she didn't know the song anymore. Willow came close to Augusta, keeping an eye on Bela Nova as she spoke into her ear. "Nana, does that one verse start *An innocent night . . .* or *An innocent evening . . . ?*"

It was *An innocent day,* and she knew Willow couldn't even make half a verse without flubbing. She'd never taken a strong interest in Lanora's story.

Augusta knew the lines, every one of them. Had never forgotten them since the day she'd etched the song into that very book, in this very room. When she'd first moved to California, she often whistled the tune, later sang the chorus as a lullaby to Nickie. Her Nickie, the only one of them who'd been moved to challenge the curse, to try to do something about it. Now that they had a solution, it was up to Augusta to make things right for her sake. She inhaled, conjuring the words from wherever they'd gone to hide since her strokes, determined to hear her own voice. When she parted her lips, she heard a sound.

But the voice wasn't hers. It wasn't Victoria's or Willow's or even Madelyn's. It was Nickie.

"She, of the packed cake earth. He, of the sultry moon. Lanora handed Akili her skin to peel and skipped away with a soul. And a heart, wrapped in the same hands." Nickie's voice was not bold, but it was confident. Augusta hugged herself, hoping to control everything going on inside of her body, to prevent herself from shaking with emotion.

And then she let go. Tears skied down her face, even the dips and rises not enough to stop them from dropping to her chest, onto the floor. Willow put an arm around her, the two rocking slowly as Nickie continued and Madelyn stood beside her, unusually quiet.

"Lanora sang, sang the sweetest song of love. Lanora sang, sang honey notes and nectar's start. Her blessings we keep forever to share, Lanora's sweet words leave none despaired." Nickie opened her eyes.

The cat stood, stretching itself into an arch before prancing off. Estelle held on to Bela Nova's chair, seemingly mystified at the entire scene, apparently not clued in to her great-grandmother's past. "With that, the True Love Always Dies curse is no more."

Victoria grunted as she pushed herself up. "So it's really undone now?" she asked, back to business.

Bela Nova nodded. "Indeed it is. That was impressive, young lady."

Just as Augusta hoped, Nickie didn't nod or smile at the compliment.

"I think it's probably time for your nap, Gram." Estelle had gently slipped Bela Nova's hand into her own as if the woman were fragile. Perhaps she was now, but it was hard for Augusta to think of her that way. "I can make you some tea first."

Estelle excused herself, telling the women it was nice to meet them and to come back and visit again soon.

"Let's go, Nana," Willow said, beckoning Nickie to follow.

Madelyn waved before she joined them. "Bye. That's a nice cat you have."

As Victoria opened her tote to slide the book back inside, Augusta reached for her, her fingertips just grazing her granddaughter's back.

Victoria turned. "Yes, Nana?"

Augusta folded her lips inside her mouth, wanting her expression to look stern. She pointed to the book in the crook of Victoria's arm, then shook her head. It was a moment before her granddaughter understood what she was telling her. "But, Nan . . ."

She took Victoria by the arm and tugged her back, still shaking her head.

Victoria didn't budge. "Are you sure, Nana?"

Augusta was certain. It was time. The book didn't belong entirely to her mentor anymore. So much had been added by the Montrose women since Augusta had taken it. But it was Bela Nova's turn to cherish it. To flip through and help her remember old times. To pass on to her own daughters and granddaughters and great-granddaughters.

"Wait." Victoria walked back over to where Bela Nova sat. The book still open in front of the woman, her granddaughter picked it up and tore out the pages with Lanora's song. Augusta recalled Bela Nova's words, *A medic doesn't keep the venom with the antidote.* Though the curse wasn't written in the book, it was likely still in Bela Nova's mind, even if a little fuzzy. Victoria wanted to make sure they stayed protected.

Victoria slammed the book closed again and placed it back on the woman's lap. The book had been returned to its namesake, to Delilah.

Nickie, Willow, and Madelyn had already made their way out of the shop as Bela Nova opened the book. "I wrote this," Augusta heard her mentor say to herself, probably admiring the poem scribbled on the first page.

Victoria directed Augusta toward the exit. They made it to the door when Bela Nova spoke again.

"Good-bye, Augusta. And thank you." Augusta turned around for one last look. The woman smiled. "You always was a quiet one, weren't you?" She laughed and gave her attention back to the work of art before her.

Augusta smiled herself as she turned away from Bela Nova. For decades, she'd built up disdain for the woman, blaming her for their family's history. But despite the curse, here they were. The Montrose women. The five of them had each other.

44
NICKIE

After a slow day exploring the city, the Montrose women brought beignets back to their hotel room, a bag from Café Du Monde, some from Cafe Beignet, a box from the corner stand near Madelyn's old apartment. Willow and Madelyn wanted Nickie to rank them, but she was diplomatic in her assessment that they were equally too sweet and too fried. Madelyn suggested the next day they do crawfish étouffée, but Victoria shot down the idea. They had to get back; they were not on vacation. Semantics, in Nickie's opinion — until she'd crossed the city limits into Long Beach, she was far away and in holiday mode. She had barely left Long Beach's borders in her seventeen years of life, but she found freedom in having traveled this far, even if ultimately her theory about the missing pages hadn't panned out. She was glad that she'd still been curious enough about the shop that she'd gone there, the only Montrose woman who'd never been. When she'd seen her family standing in front of it, she'd been relieved, despite wanting to get away from them only the day before. And thank goodness they'd showed up. Together, they'd managed to end the curse. She was still wrapping her head around it all, but the curse had been real indeed. And she'd helped to bring it to an end.

"We at least need to catch us a second line before we go. Nickie needs to learn about where she comes from," Madelyn said.

"Yeah, well, she'll have to do that another time. She's already missed two days of school."

Madelyn flipped a hand toward Victoria. "Big deal. You know how many days of school I missed? Dozens, and I still graduated. Besides, she's our hero. Hero, hero." It wasn't the first chant since the bookshop, her family making her feel like she'd hit a clutch shot at a championship game just as the whistle blew, when all she'd done was recite Lanora's song.

"Hey, Vic, don't forget to call Felix and let him know we found Nickie," Willow said.

Nickie turned around in her seat at the small table, her lips caked with powdered sugar, gasping as if someone had pulled her hair. "What?"

Madelyn did her best retelling of a group chat they'd had with Felix, Nickie growing more and more horrified as her grandmother spoke. To her surprise, her mother told her she could contact him the next day when they headed back.

"I don't know his number by heart," Nickie said, still stunned.

"Nick, your mom's the one who called him. She has his number. I don't know why she don't just let you call him right now. We're two hours ahead," said Willow.

Nickie's heart thudded. "That's okay." She wasn't sure she was ready for that.

Madelyn waved her hands to get Nickie's attention. "Just do it, Nick. We wouldn't have found you if it weren't for him."

This made no sense to her. How would he have known? "What do you mean?"

"I was just about to get to that part of the story," said Madelyn. It had taken her five minutes just setting the scene, describing each woman's posture, her facial expression as they gathered to talk to Felix via speakerphone.

Nickie clenched her teeth, holding in a fierce cry, trying not to be embarrassed by the whole ordeal. "Well . . . I'm glad he was helpful," she mustered with a smile. She wanted to change the subject. The events of the day had gotten her curious about something else. "Hey, Mom, can we use the laptop?" Nickie's smile deepened, knowing that her mom could no longer give her a hard time about her online activities. While Nanagusta had been the one to share the details of her life in that letter, after reading it, it was her mother whom Nicki had come to know more. She understood what was at stake, could see the sacrifices mothers were willing to take for their children.

Victoria sighed, then got up to retrieve the computer from her suitcase. Nickie scooted her chair close to Augusta, elbowing the woman to wake her. Her great-grandmother blinked to life, then used her sleeve to mop up some saliva that had escaped during her short nap.

Nickie opened a browser and typed *Benjamin Montrose.*

"What you doing, Nickie? You looking up my daddy?" Madelyn leaned over to view the screen. Willow stood behind her.

"Doggone, two million results?" Madelyn said, reporting for the benefit of Nickie's mother, who'd gotten under the covers, cold because she'd only packed her summer nightgown. "They got all kinds of Benjamin

Montroses. A dentist, an architect. A director."

Augusta balanced her weight onto Nickie as she reached for the computer, sliding it closer, just a few inches from her face.

"Nana, we can't see." Augusta shook her head that she didn't care. Nickie craned her neck. Her great-grandmother had clicked on a Wikipedia page with a picture of a handsome man on the side. "Benjamin Montrose. Nana, is that him? Is that my great-grandfather?"

Her mother sprung up from the bed, stubbing her toe as she hurried. Nickie read the page and scrolled when necessary for everyone's benefit. This guy, Benjamin, was from Chicago, born in 1938. Nothing about a life-changing visit to New Orleans in the 1950s, but it did say that he moved to Los Angeles and got small roles on the Kraft Theatre series. In the late 1960s, he wrote and produced his first movie, the story of a young man who falls in love with a Voodoo priestess in 1950s New Orleans.

This was their Benjamin Montrose, and he had not died. In fact, he was alive, owned a home in Calabasas. Had been married for forty-nine years with children and a granddaughter who acted and had just directed her first short.

"Oh damn — I've heard that name before. You mean I've got a rich grandpa and some famous cousin just thirty-some miles away from home?" Willow was on her toes, reading over Augusta's head.

"Near Kim Kardashian," Madelyn said, proud of herself.

Nickie wrinkled one side of her face, thinking. "So I guess you didn't love him, Nana."

"Or," Victoria said, "maybe he got away just in time, before she had a chance to love him enough."

"Whatever the case," Madelyn said, "I'm glad Nana took his last name. Madelyn Laurent? That just don't sound right to me."

Augusta rubbed her face, perhaps an attempt to wipe the shock from it. She kept looking to Nickie, over to Madelyn, and at her granddaughters behind her, with an expression Nickie could only describe as joy.

Willow knocked on Nickie's back with her knuckle. "You awake? You're not snoring." She spoke softly from her side of the bed they shared.

Nickie flipped herself onto the opposite hip. She didn't respond, only stared at Willow, her brown eyes picking up colorful flashes from the television.

"Nickie, tell me the truth. Did you plan on leaving out the magnetic sand in that potion you were mixing up for Felix?" Her mother must have told Aunt Willow what she'd done, how she'd gotten caught at school with the sulfur.

Her feelings about Felix ran the gamut. Nickie couldn't understand how she wanted him back after what he'd done to her, but she did, and that upset her, so much so that she had indeed planned to use the revenge oil, to omit the magnetic sand. She worried what her aunt would think of her if she told the truth. But her hesitation gave her away. She let her eyes drop, afraid to see her reaction.

Willow put her hand on Nickie's face, then moved it to behind Nickie's head. "Don't ever tell anyone, you hear?" Her voice stayed a whisper but was insistent.

When Nickie found the guts to look at her aunt again, Willow was smiling, tears in her eyes. "I don't want to keep secrets, Auntie. But . . . I'll keep yours. I know you weren't trying to harm my father the way you did . . . I was just . . . upset, betrayed. I wasn't trying to harm Felix that way either." She couldn't say the word *kill* because that didn't describe what Willow had done. In fact, Nickie had decided not to blame Willow at all for what happened to Jimmie. If Willow did kill her father, it was only because the curse caused her to do it, despite what her aunt believed.

Willow wiped Nickie's tears, smiling in return. "Hey, why don't you text Felix?"

"I don't know. I can't."

"Of course you can. You can use my phone." Willow grabbed her phone from the nightstand. "Look, I have his number too, your mom gave it to us. Here. Keep it all night, okay? It's only ten out there. I'm sure he's up."

She didn't want him to know yet that she'd reconnected with her family. With the spell, Nickie had wanted Felix to feel the crushing awfulness she'd experienced since he'd left her at the motel two weekends before, the exact opposite of how wonderful it had been to fall for him. If she could help it, she planned not to fall for him or anyone that intensely again.

Though, look at her — she'd literally come all this way, had spurred her great-grandmother to get on an airplane and helped her to face her foe. She could absolutely tell *that* to Felix, even if it was just a way for him to know that he hadn't ruined her, and that he couldn't.

Hi Felix. It's Nickie. On my aunt Willow's phone. Guess what? The shop in New Orleans now sells old books.

Seconds later, the phone vibrated and Nickie answered it quickly. "Hello?"

"Hey. It's me. Felix."

"Hi." She quieted her voice, hearing someone stir across the room.

"You're okay, sounds like."

"Yes. And thanks for helping my family."

"So you really went to New Orleans? I was right?"

She nodded, the pillowcase soft against her cheek. Willow stroked her back. She was listening, they probably all were. "Yes. You were." She swirled her feet around under the covers.

"Look, I'm sorry I was such an asshole the other night. I don't know. I guess I got scared about what you said. About that curse and all. I know it's ridiculous, but I just started thinking, *What if it's true? I'm not ready to die.* I just thought about it — me dying and my mom going through all my art projects. Who knows what she'd do with them? That just sort of freaked me out."

So he'd been a believer as well. She wanted to tell him that it was all over, their destinies reset. But she would keep this from him. If his apology was genuine, he'd find a way to make it up to her first.

"By the way, the motel called. I have your necklace. You want me to bring it by when you get back?"

She wanted to say *yes,* to have him over again as company. But for now, she thought it best to keep her distance, at least until she figured out her feelings. She simply couldn't erase how he'd treated her. "You can just give it to Mark at school. I'll get it from him." He said he would, and they ended the call.

Returning the phone to Willow, she finally felt ready to rest, sure that whatever might be next for her and Felix, for college or the prom, for her major and even this gift she had, she would get through it. She wished she hadn't gotten to the point where she wanted to use the revenge oil on Felix, but she was glad to be settled here now, trusting in herself for whatever love the future had in store for her.

45
WILLOW

For once, Willow did Victoria the favor of telling her exactly what she was doing the morning after they returned from Louisiana. "I'm gonna drive Nickie to school today. I'll bring home some chocolate croissants, and those wafer cookies from the bakery for your clients. I know Mrs. Maye loves her cookies." She hoped her sister wouldn't lecture her, give her the eye about meddling in her affairs.

She still couldn't believe her sister and grandmother had given her book away to Bela Nova, not only because of what that lady had done to their family but because so much of the book now belonged to the Montrose women. Not just the spells and instructions and concoctions inside (she knew many of them by heart, had written down as much as she could remember in a notebook on the train ride home) but also their doodles, notes, and poems. Their desires, their hopes, their loves. And most of all, their mistakes.

Mistakes. That's what she'd called Nanagusta's actions, though the hurt from her grandmother's secrets still lingered. She'd give herself time to wrestle with her emotions, but she'd already let go of her anger. After all, Willow had secrets of her own. Maybe one day she would find the courage to follow in her grandmother's footsteps, to tell the truth about what she'd done to Jimmie — even if, ultimately, the curse was what was accountable for his death. But for now, she wouldn't cause Victoria more unnecessary pain. She knew her niece wouldn't either.

Willow's belief in herself had been the boost she needed to exist as her sister's assistant, as the one who Jimmie hadn't picked all these years. But after everything that had transpired, she didn't mind relinquishing the idea that she was Lanora's chosen one. She would put that out of her mind once and for all and focus on what gifts *she* wanted to impart. Besides, that meant she could blame the curse for Jimmie's death, as Nickie had said, ease some of the guilt she'd carried about the accident. If anything, she'd been a coconspirator, the curse making her spell successful and then some.

She thought she had a picture of him tucked away in an encyclopedia on her bookshelf — volume T, the only one she had from a set. If she found it, she'd surprise Nickie with it one day, take her out for dessert and share stories about him, how great a guy he was. Sweet Jimmie. He was loved by *two* Montrose women. How could he have ever been safe from the curse?

Later that morning, Willow brewed spicy orange tea, two cups of it, and let herself into Victoria's office.

"What's up, Willow? I have a session at ten o'clock, a new client."

"I'm your ten o'clock." She'd asked Madelyn to put her down under the name Beeon Say. Madelyn told her it hadn't made Victoria the least bit suspicious.

"Oh." She sat herself down in the chair near her desk, accepting the cup of tea.

"Just wanted to talk about a few things."

Victoria propped herself up on the arm of her chair. "What, is it January?"

Cold fingers walked up her back when she heard the name. Distracted, she hadn't thought about him the whole time they'd been in New Orleans. "Yes. A little bit."

"What happened with him? I mean, I'm pretty sure he didn't die. You couldn't have loved that prick."

"Ha ha. Too soon, Vic."

"For him? Not too soon. What did he do?"

She thought about her sister's ability to read people. Victoria certainly had been right about January, his no-good ass. He'd come home one morning after work and said he was going back to his ex-wife — the heathen. "He acted typically."

Victoria took a long drink of her tea. "Don't let that affect you. They aren't all typical."

"Some are atypical?"

Her sister smiled, pausing to consider this. "Yes." She reclined, then sat back up. "Actually, no. January is atypical. He's not the norm, Willow. I don't want you to think that way."

She didn't think that way, not really. Men like January just reminded her that she needed to be careful. Anyway, she was done with the losers. It was time to look for a catch, her family willing to give a guy a chance if she brought one home. They were done with the curse thanks to Nickie. She realized that what happened with Jimmie had kept her from falling in love, had stopped her from finding anyone worthy like him, worried that he'd be taken away. "Enough about him. What I wanted to talk to you about is my business plan."

"You couldn't just bring this up at dinner? Or after dinner? Or any other time besides my workday?"

"You're always tired after your workday. And I wanted you to take me seriously. This is a business proposal I'm offering you." Willow swung her legs around onto the sofa, leaning back on the armrest, the way people did while in their therapist's office. "In time, after I process everything, I want to write a book and publish it. It would be about spells and the loa and such."

"A book?"

"Yes. Something for people who want to get started with hoodoo work. Like *Hoodoo for Dummies*. A 101 kind of approach."

Her sister nodded, humoring her, it seemed. "I see. Accessible hoodoo."

Willow snapped her fingers and sat up. "Exactly. That's it. Maybe that's my title right there. See, I was right about that workmind of yours. Once you leave this office, it goes to mush."

Willow continued, sharing what she'd learned about self-publishing, her ideas for selling her book online and through social media. She considered herself a wonderful saleswoman. "Not that I have to be great. The book will sell itself."

"Okay, that's fine. But what do you need from me?"

"Not a lot. Just a place to stay. I'll help Madelyn with the cooking, as long as you provide a nice amount for groceries, of course. And a stipend, for my day-to-day expenses. And then, some business line items — supplies, an initial print run, all of that."

"And what's in it for me? What do I get out of it?" Victoria asked.

"Well, I could pay rent, for once. And maybe I could help you get some of your clients back." Victoria's face drooped, and Willow quickly felt bad for her words, though she'd said them in earnest. She genuinely thought the book would help both of them.

Willow considered the project a good investment, and that's what she wanted it to be. She hoped her sister would agree. She could even teach Nickie a few spells along the way, a skill she could use to make a few extra bucks in college.

"I need a specific budget for the next six months for all the book expenses. And I'd like you to do some marketing for the practice. And train Madelyn on the tax stuff. And if you decided to do any special services for my clients, like Maya Ackbar, I don't want to know about it. Don't tell them about it either."

Shit. She should have figured Victoria would find out about her work somehow. But she couldn't believe what her sister was implying — that she wouldn't mind if she kept it up. Willow wanted to gloat, sure her sister had only said so because she realized her impact on the business. Why else had she lost so many clients since Willow had been gone? Then again, perhaps Victoria was such a talented therapist that clients only required a few sessions for her help to become effective. Or they moved or lost their insurance coverage. There were dozens of reasons for the drop in clients, but Willow wouldn't name herself, her leaving the practice, as one. "You got it. Spells only in secret. And what else?"

Victoria lifted her chin in consideration. "And that's it. Well, maybe you can take me to the place where you get your eyelashes done. And your nails."

"It's a date," Willow said, surprised that it had been so easy to get her sister's support. "I'm not gonna let you down, Vic. I'm going to get started right away. Maybe there will even be a series. Or a class I can teach online. Maybe Madelyn could be my assistant too."

Victoria cocked her head. "Oh no. You're not taking Madelyn from me."

"Oh, it's like that? She wouldn't even be here if I hadn't brought her out." The words jetted from her mouth before she could catch them. She hoped they went by fast enough for Victoria to miss them.

No such luck. "Wait a minute," her sister said. "You called Madelyn out here?"

Not as explosive as the Jimmie secret, but this was another big one. She explained herself, that she thought Madelyn could help out with Nickie, and the timing had seemed right. She eventually admitted to fronting Madelyn the money their mother had used to pay Victoria back. "But what does it matter now? Everything worked out, right?"

Victoria had had enough of her for the day. She rested her head on her palm but mustered a smile. "Just write this damn book, Will."

Willow stood, relieved, stretching her arms high as she yawned. She pointed at her sister, shook her finger. "It's going to be a bestseller. You watch." She turned away from Victoria, but her sister called her name. When Willow faced her, her eyes had lost their tension.

"I do appreciate you, Willow. Always have. Still do."

Willow tipped her head to the side, happy to hear such words from Victoria. She reached for the door handle, paused before turning it. "Hey, question, Vic. How is Russell going to see you with your new lashes and fancy nails if you refer him to a new therapist?"

Victoria tucked her feet underneath her in the chair. "I swear, Willow. You are the absolute worst with that eavesdropping. Go on and leave, Ms. . . . Say? What kind of name you put down?"

Willow blew her sister an air kiss as she left.

That night after dinner, as Willow sat between Madelyn and Augusta watching *Jeopardy!,* Nickie asked to speak to her in the kitchen. She smiled, wondering what trouble this could be and said, "Sure."

On the kitchen counter lay a faded, tattered paper. Another sheet from the book. It was the Much Better potion, something Bela Nova had noted that Mr. O'Brien had stolen. "This was under my bed. It must have come out of the book at some point when I had it there."

Willow scrunched her eyes, curious how that particular page had been the one left behind. She picked it up to get a better look. "I remember this page. Never used it. It didn't seem like the most potent combination. This is all stuff we have around the house. A potion gets its strength from how hard you work to make it." The Much Better potion. Boiled sugar water, the juice from four limes and two oranges (catch those seeds), enough rum to make it burn. No wonder they'd ignored it all these years.

"What about that passi . . . edulis? That doesn't seem like something we have."

Willow smiled. "Passiflora edulis. We've got some in the garage."

"Can you make it? I really want to know if it can make things much better," said Nickie.

She frowned, curious what in particular Nickie wanted to improve, but didn't question the girl.

Maybe it would help her feel better. Willow still felt fragile, though their experience in New Orleans had helped her see her grandmother's revelations in a new way. Eventually, she'd ask Nanagusta hard questions, come to terms with what she'd learned about her father so far. She had a new family to connect to, an aunt named

Ramona, for one. Though she'd looked, she hadn't found an obituary online or any proof that Harlowe Decuir had died. She wanted to meet him, but for some reason, the prospect of connecting with her aunt excited her more. Hopefully, Ramona would be as wonderful an aunt as she hoped she'd been to Nickie. In the meantime, she'd keep watching out for her niece, and together they'd make sure to enjoy life to the fullest.

"I won't make it, but you can. You the one whipping up secret infusions in the kitchen and shit. Come on."

46
AUGUSTA

Victoria elbowed Augusta awake. Sleep was a deep place that Augusta knew eventually she'd settle into and never leave, but not for many years, she'd decided. If she was going to beat Bela Nova in age, it meant she still had more than a few decades to survive. What Victoria had shaken her from was a dream space, an area she liked to visit a few times a day. She met Dudley Lee there sometimes. Benjamin too, the version of him who'd come across her on the workshop floor, not the one she'd discovered online, although he'd become quite distinguished, had held onto his handsomeness. Over the years, she'd wrestled with her feelings for Benjamin, how quickly she'd fallen for him, her naive heart so easily struck, making her a dangerous woman. But he'd escaped in time. Maybe he could sense what was happening back then, a whisper in his gut telling him to follow his dreams. Or maybe he hadn't loved her back. It didn't matter. She wouldn't watch any of his movies, but she would always dream about him, this man who had come along right when she'd needed someone most.

She'd been yanked from her sleep to try a drink, some sort of punch that Nickie and Willow had made. Victoria handed her a glass, the sweet flowery scent familiar to Augusta. She sat up on the couch and took a sip, almost coughed it up, not anticipating the burn. Still, it was tasty. She treated herself to another.

Her taste buds weren't as discerning as they'd once been, but the drink reminded her of old times, of her days at the shop. She tilted her head to the side, considering what was beyond the citrus flavor and the dark rum.

"It's that Much Better potion, the one Bela Nova claimed Mr. O'Brien had stolen. Made with passiflora edulis," Nickie came out to explain.

"Passa, what?" Madelyn said.

Passiflora edulis. Yes, Bela Nova used it in many ways. For love potions and attraction formulas. And for stirring in with her mug of spirits late some evenings when her spirits were low.

"Passiflora edulis," Willow said. "It's the passionflower, Mom."

Augusta recalled the night she first saw Bela Nova mix up the solution, her draped attire musty with smoke and sweat after getting in a fight, the woman's lip busted and bleeding. "Augusta, we have any passion fruit juice? If not, go on downstairs and rustle some up for me. Hurry up, I ain't got all night." As she spoke to herself and to Augusta, Bela Nova opened and closed cupboards and pulled items off shelves, clanging and banging away, bumping her body into chairs and the stove.

Augusta had been able to find passion fruit juice at the bar downstairs. Bela Nova poured it into a tall glass already filled with murky liquid that she held as she sat in bed. "Go on and get me something to stir this with."

Augusta left and returned with a long, metal spoon from the kitchen, but Bela Nova hadn't needed it anymore — she'd already downed the entire concoction. "Thieving rat," she said before handing her empty glass to Augusta. She burped and closed her eyes, blue shadow still iridescent on her lids.

When she came back to the workbench,

Augusta saw that the book was open to the Much Better potion with the note that it had been stolen by Mr. O'Brien during the terrible storm of 1944. Word was she'd sent him home with a glass of it after his restaurant became flooded, also sharing with him instructions for how to make more for himself. "Mix a little of this up whenever you're feeling down, you hear?" It was her go-to pick-me-up, something she used to take the edge off. Bela Nova's version didn't have any rum in it, but she'd added it to the list of ingredients once she'd learned that Mr. O'Brien had done so, selling the drink at his Club Tipperary the following summer, a fast hit in the Quarter. He'd been the one to turn it into a cocktail, but Bela Nova still felt slighted, wanted both credit and the cash he brought in from selling it to locals and visitors alike. And she'd probably hold on to that grudge until the end of her days.

Madelyn called Nickie over to refill her glass, garnished with two cherries and a slice of orange. Augusta quickly slurped down what was left of hers so Nickie could pour her some more too.

Madelyn relaxed into the couch, letting her head fall back as she closed her eyes.

"Just like that, I'm back in New Orleans. On Bourbon Street. You know, this tastes just like a Hurricane."

Nickie set the pitcher down. She didn't think Victoria noticed, but Nickie had poured herself a glass as well, sipping when her mom wasn't looking, then placing it on the floor by her foot. "That's exactly what it is. Auntie and I figured it out. I looked it up while we were making them. Apparently, they became popular during the war or something like that. There's a restaurant in New Orleans famous for them called —"

Pat O'Brien's. Augusta slapped the coffee table as she said the name in her head, believing for a second that her family had heard her, each turning her way.

Willow said it for her. "Pat O'Brien's, over on St. Peter."

He wasn't exactly a thieving rat, he'd just made the recipe into his own, but Bela Nova certainly hadn't seen it that way.

"So he took her potion and turned it into a business?" Victoria asked. "I guess you weren't the only one to wrong Bela Nova, Nana. You think she cursed him too?"

Apparently not, with Pat O'Brien's one of the busiest spots in the Quarter. But now that the woman had her book back, that place had better watch out.

■ ■ ■ ■

While Augusta had surely come far with her computer skills, she didn't mind asking for help. Though Nickie was the youngest in the house, she believed Willow the most suited for the mission at hand. She'd be over soon, having temporarily passed out on the couch after her fourth Hurricane. Until then, Augusta would do a little surfing.

Reckoning Week, as Augusta now called it, had shaken loose so many answers for her, solutions that had been sitting in front of her for so long, while at the same time prompting new questions. And regrets. She knew she had some making up to do. She had changes to make. They all did.

For one, she could return to being proactive. That had been the problem before, but now she wouldn't be so reckless about it. She could build on lessons, on experience, on heartache. And she would help her mentor in the process. Truth was, the woman had saved Augusta from a future that wasn't right for her, and for that she had to be grateful. Augusta had come to understand that she and Bela Nova had acted from the same place, out of love for Dudley Lee. After all these decades, she'd finally forgiven the woman who'd cursed their family, and she hoped that, by returning the book, Bela Nova had forgiven her too.

From the table, she picked up a wide black candle, one she'd adorned with knock-off gemstones she'd purchased years before at a craft store. Keeping her hands as steady as she could, she used a ballpoint pen to etch the name of the person she planned to bless: *Loa Bela Nova.*

All the woman had wanted was to live on after her death the way Lanora had, revered and powerful, someone future generations would call on to intercede on their behalf for help. When Augusta had stolen Bela Nova's book, she'd made that outcome impossible for her old mentor. She would burn the candle all night, all the next day, and the next until nothing remained, and she'd write a new song about the wondrous and magnificent Bela Nova, and she too would become immortalized as a loa.

The idea didn't make her feel better, but maybe, she thought, Dudley Lee had been born to die young anyway. Some people's fates were chosen that way, so that others could do things they wouldn't otherwise do. If he'd lived, if he hadn't fallen victim to the curse, she wouldn't have met Benjamin, and she wouldn't have had Madelyn, Victoria, Willow, and Nickie. She could say the same for Victoria, who would never have been motivated to go back to school without Jimmie's untimely death. Without the story of Lanora, her granddaughter would never know the power, the beauty of the gift, of getting others through tragedies of their own.

Her life couldn't be understood except in the way Augusta chose to make sense of it. But she still had living to do — not as much as what had already gone by but enough to have a little fun.

Willow finally woke up and walked over to the dining room. "Nana, check you out, boo. You looking nice. Got that hair slicked. Wearing some lipstick. You got a hot date coming by?"

Augusta pointed to the aperture on the laptop.

"That's the camera, Nan. What, you want to take a picture?" Augusta nodded, and Willow jumped right into director mode.

After a few dozen shadowy shots, they moved locations, setting up in the front room, the orange light filling in Augusta's contoured face. "Let's use my cell phone." Willow had brushed gloss on Augusta's lips and bronzer over her cheeks. Her hair was in a low braid, but Willow had brought it over one shoulder so that anyone who looked at Nan's picture would see that she still had more than a fair share of hair. "Don't smile so much, Nan. You can't look like you're trying too hard."

Augusta frowned at the girl, always thinking she knew everything, but soon enough she relaxed her way into a bit of a smile, but not too wide. They took five shots, the last of which Augusta added to her new Facebook profile. Then she used it again for a datemate.com account. She didn't know if she'd ever meet anyone in person, but just the chance to befriend a man or two. Or three . . . Beyond seeing these women flourish in the house and watching her shows, that would be something worth waking for each day.

Epilogue:
Victoria

Victoria went through the security line first, her hardside spinner riding on the conveyor belt without issue. She'd grabbed it and started walking, turning to tell Nickie how she and Willow used to carry travel items in clunky suitcases, even garbage bags on long road trips the rare times they took them. But Nickie, she noticed, was still back at security. As was the rest of the family, their bags not moving, an agent called over for further inspection. She went back toward them, adrenaline upping her temperature at least a degree. "What's the holdup?"

Nickie shook her head, a soft roll of her eyes. "We're only allowed one bottle of wine or champagne in our bag per person, and —"

"*You're* allowed zero bottles of wine or champagne." Despite looking the other way at Nickie's new fondness for Hurricanes, she didn't want to enable her drinking.

While she'd relaxed the house rules, her daughter still needed parenting.

"I wasn't going to drink it. Willow asked me to fit one in. And then she had each of us pack a second bottle. Nana's got a four-pack of canned Moscato in hers."

Victoria eyed her sister. "Willow, really?"

"Well, I was just trying to save you some money. You know, everything gets charged to the room."

"I know, Willow," she lied.

On the train ride back from New Orleans, she'd promised the women that they could go on a cruise during Nickie's spring break, but she'd only skimmed the website on how cruises worked. But it was fine. They deserved the trip for putting up with her all these months. And how much damage could they do in four days? She'd taken off a full week, even though her schedule was beginning to fill up again, which Victoria credited to their new social media accounts, not any special add-ons of Willow's.

She and her sister had come a long way. Both of them had been abandoned by their mother, raised without fathers. They could all stand to give each other a little grace.

Victoria had forgiven herself for Jimmie. She'd done something simple — fallen in love. Really, they'd all done it, even Madelyn at some point, her mother regaling her with stories from New Orleans, her past life, one she missed but didn't seem to want to go back to.

"Just tell them to toss the wine. I know you prefer a cocktail anyway, right, Madelyn?"

"Shoot — beer, wine, margarita, Zima, Tequila Sunrise, I don't care. As long as someone cute and under thirty brings it to me, I'll be alright."

They managed to get aboard the ship, get to their suites, and not get kicked off before departure. While Augusta napped and Nickie tried to connect to Wi-Fi and Madelyn and Willow went down to the tequila bar, Victoria sat out on the balcony, taking in the view of Long Beach, its gleaming buildings, oil islands, the picturesque Queen Mary. She wasn't sure why, but emotion overcame her, so much so that she had to use her arm, then her shirt, to soak up the tears. She wept quietly, not wanting to wake her grandmother, a great woman who had fears but had stepped out from their shadow to do better for herself and for her family.

"What's wrong, Mom?"

Victoria jerked in surprise. A breeze tousled her hair as she straightened up. She wondered how horrible she looked, if all the crying had further darkened and sagged the skin under her eyes. Finding a quick smile for Nickie, she told her nothing was wrong. "I'm just feeling a little . . . overwhelmed, I guess. And happy."

Victoria always envied her daughter's ability to lift one eyebrow, a trait she must have inherited from Jimmie, the right one always triggered by half-truths and hogwash. Not good for a future therapist, though it might work if she considered becoming a lawyer. Or a cocktail artist. Or the owner of a rare books shop. There were infinite ways for Nickie to use her gift. Nickie had told her about the sensations she'd been having, with temperature and itchiness. Soon enough, she'd learn what her body was trying to tell her. Nickie would figure it out, and Victoria would be there with guidance if she wanted it.

"This is happy?"

"Yes, this is, Nick." Nickie sat down beside her — not on the chair next to her but on the wooden balcony floor as the buildings and mountains of California slowly shrank away from them while she took pictures with her new camera. Ayida Wedo's eyes from the charm against Nickie's neck caught the midday sun.

"You decide which school yet?"

Nickie shrugged. "I don't know. Long Beach State's a great school. But it would be fun to leave. A new state, Arizona's not too far. But you'd miss me."

Victoria smiled, no longer shocked at the ways her daughter had been able to maneuver around all the obstacles Victoria put in her way. For years, Nickie had been a passenger on a dizzying carnival ride, wondering when the operator would stop it. In the meantime, she'd wisely applied to another school. It was always smart to have options. "Real estate's good in the Phoenix area. I'll just buy another house over there. No need for the dorms," she joked.

Someone knocked. Probably Willow and Madelyn, back from the bar. The two of them were staying in the room next door, free to get into their own kind of trouble. "I got it," she told Augusta who had been woken up.

"Hey-ey," her sister and mother sang when Victoria answered, both holding the type of tropical drinks required for vacation pictures, Willow in a tankini, Madelyn wearing a matronly bathing suit and topped with a wide-brimmed yellow hat.

"You got kicked out the bar already?"

"No, but we did run into someone." They

both looked down the hall, Madelyn grinning, Willow with a proud smirk.

"Who?"

"Russell! Come over here, Big Russ."

She felt faint. This was it with her sister. The meddling had gone too far this time. "Willow," she said roughly under her breath, "you couldn't give me some kind of warning? I look a mess. And why would you do this to me?"

Irked as she was, in the pit of her stomach, she located a tickle. Small, but very present. She wouldn't talk to her sister the rest of the trip and would make her and Madelyn pay for their own drinks and anything else they found to charge to their room. But maybe, it might be nice to hang out with Russell. She'd been curious about a comedy show on Night 2 listed on the handout left on their bed. Maybe he'd want to join her . . . as friends. He had a new therapist, and the clock had started on the ethics waiting period if something were ever to become of them. And anyway, no one had to know he'd been a client. It's not like her family would rat her out to the State.

"You're good, Vic." Willow and Madelyn were still peeking down the hall, footsteps coming nearer. All Victoria had time to do was wiggle her nose and sniff, hoping nothing was sticking out from her nostrils, and smooth down her hair. The grays were out, the eyes were puffy, the outfit was practical. This was her.

Madelyn stepped back to make room. But the person who arrived between the two of them wasn't someone she knew. It was a man dressed in cruise-ship blue, holding a tablet. "Nice to meet you, Ms. Montrose. My name is Russell. I'm the ship's activities director. Having a wonderful time so far?"

The two hadn't brought this Russell in on their joke. He turned to look at each of them as they fell into laughter. Madelyn made such a big deal of it that she spilled some of her drink. "You see her face?"

"Oooh, that was a good one, Mama."

"Is everything okay?" His concern was focused not on the two women behind him but on the one on the bed in the red cotton sundress who was slapping the covers, her body jerking in heaves. He surely thought the older woman was having an attack, but that's just how Augusta cracked up.

"She's fine. They're all fine." Feeling bad for the guy, Victoria listened to his spiel, signing Augusta up for a hula class, herself and Nickie for guitar.

For a brief moment, her chest felt empty. Had she really hoped Russell might join the family on their cruise? But the feeling soon transformed back into joy. At least it wasn't pain. Indeed, there was no reason to be disappointed. She and Russell would certainly talk again when they returned. He'd wanted to share about his experience with his new therapist, check on her dracaena. And she supposed she could stand to buy a few pairs of jeans, something for a casual Friday every once in a while. Even if her list of clients fully ramped up again, she vowed not to keep herself booked the way she once had. Favored one or not, she had to take care of herself as well.

For now, for this trip, she'd enjoy her family, the ones most precious to her. She'd say a prayer, thanking God for them. Things would eventually change. Nickie would move out soon, no matter which college she chose. Maybe she could tell her about the time she and Jimmie had toured the *Queen Mary,* how he'd been more knowledgeable than the tour guide, answering a few questions on the ship's history for other guests in their group. Nickie had surely gotten her smarts from him. Willow would meet someone, a good guy this time. Or she wouldn't meet someone, content to focus on her new career. She had books to sell, the first already being edited, the second one to be outlined as they sat in lounge chairs this week. Madelyn might stick around for a while, and that wouldn't be so bad. Her mother was quite amusing and an excellent assistant, and Victoria was learning to see more than her mother's past mistakes. She'd never admit it to Willow, but Victoria was glad her sister had called the woman. And with Nanagusta, she hoped to soak in every drop of time they had left with the woman. Their matriarch, the one who had sacrificed everything for them.

Victoria couldn't guarantee that their family had been freed from the curse placed on them by Bela Nova so many decades ago, but she vowed not to operate as if it still clung to them. Bela Nova's words had haunted their family for far too long, and now they had to be bold enough to live without it.

Maybe she'd find the guts soon to reach out to Jimmie's mother, who'd stopped talking to him once they married, not interested in meeting Victoria even after learning she was pregnant. He'd written her off as ridiculously old-fashioned. It scared her to do so, but she had to try for Nickie, who surely had cousins, other relatives who'd love to meet her. Just like Willow had reconnected with her aunt Ramona (who'd claimed Victoria as a niece as well), and had exchanged emails with Harlowe, living in Brazil with his third wife and two cats.

Maybe someday soon they could take a real vacation back to New Orleans, back to the Quarter. They'd eat oysters, and jambalaya, and even more beignets, and shrimp Creole. They'd visit Marie Laveau's House of Voodoo on Bourbon Street, a place she'd read about online. They could attend Mass at St. Louis Cathedral, light votives for Jimmie, for Dudley Lee. And they could visit several of the city's cemeteries, looking for relatives — the Laurents and the Heberts. The possibilities were plenty. What would *not* be an option, in New Orleans or anywhere, was operating out of fear. Her hands were clean and dried of that muddy water. And it didn't matter how long it had taken her to get to where she now was, to the stateroom, braiding Nana's hair, soothed by the low hum of the music leaking out from Nickie's earphones.

Funny — it sort of sounded like DeBarge.

ACKNOWLEDGMENTS

I'm thrilled to have enjoyed the experience of writing and publishing *Black Candle Women* with so many people. I'm very blessed by my Creator, my collaborators, my friends, and my family.

I share this book with my amazing editor, Melanie Fried, who took a hundred-thousand-word idea and helped shape it into something worth sharing. I'm so happy that you took a chance and believed in me, and am grateful for all of your wonderful ideas for bringing the Montrose women so vividly to life. I also appreciate the contributions of the wonderful team at Graydon House/HTP, including Kathleen Oudit, Diane Lavoie, Ambur Hostyn, Randy Chan, Pamela Osti, Sophie James, and Justine Sha. Bokiba, thank you for your dazzling cover and vision of the Montrose women.

I have such a funny and fabulous agent in Cherise Fisher. Working with you has been a dream. How cool it is to have a "home" with you and the rest of the team at WSA, including Wendy Sherman and Callie Dietrich. You ladies rock.

A big thanks to Kimberly Davis and Robert Lebsack at Chance Artworks for the wonders you did with my author photo.

There are dozens of people who take care of me, hug me, make me laugh, take me out to eat, buy me drinks, check on me, and send me funny videos. Parts of you are infused in *Black Candle Women.* You know who you are: the Day Ones (Tanya Spurgeon, Erika Thomas, Juanita Craft), my Bruins (Tami Herrera, Barbara Denianke, Janine Gonzaga, Kenda Blakeney, Mandla Kayise, and the talented and gracious Ava DuVernay), my Trojans (Jeannine Cofield, Callie Burnley), the "fam" (Kristina Ratthanak, Eddie Ramirez, Logan Ramirez, Sandy Wedgeworth, The Longs — William, Molyka, Leo, Theo), my Ladies/PHEMsters (Jenn Gonzalez, Mario Gonzalez, Emily Holman, Gabriela Hurtado Ivonne Alarcon, Veronica Morales, Julio Rodriguez, Belinda Prado, Shawna Stevens, Nora Balanji, Amairani Cortez, Julia Couto, Cindy Grajeda), the Queens of the Hill (Melody Osuna, Liz Weithers, Cynthia Gerhart, and Rebecca Bustamante), the LLCF West Media Team

(Shawn Jones, Sam Warren, Alex Lee, Bob Cralle, Ken Bleich, and Darrell Simms), and simply, my people (Teliscia Moore, Vanessa Solorzano, Darlene Maye).

Some people had no idea the beautiful deed they were doing when they asked how my writing was going, called me an author, or otherwise showed an interest in my pursuits. There are several of you but those I haven't already mentioned include Pastor Charles Latchison, Felicia Royster, Valerie Roberts, Nelson Kerr, Emily Duval Ledger, Radha Pema, Lisa Sefe Uini, Beatrice Holman, Jody Forter, and Tilane Jones. Also, I appreciate the assistance and advice I received from Nina Shaw early in my publishing journey.

I owe the deepest gratitude to Denise Alvarado and the illustrious Zora Neale Hurston for their wisdom and words on Voodoo, the ways of the loa, tricks, spells, curses, blessing oils, incantations, cures, and more.

My writing community also bears much responsibility for this book: my teachers and unofficial mentors (Janet Fitch, Gabby Pina, Judith Freeman, Brighde Mullins, Janet Ghio, Sandra Tsing Loh), fellow MPWs (Erin LaRosa, Yvonne Georgina Pugh, Amy Meyerson), author friends (Elana Arnold, Karen Winn, Lisa Williamson Rosenberg, Betty Yee, Nicole Vick, Sarah Enni, Elise Bryant), and my insightful and nurturing writing group (Olga Jobe, Kim Gittens, Amber Butts, Cecilia Esther Rabess, Carolyn Edgar, Melissa Desa, and Shea Owens). You've all blessed me in incalculable ways.

Special shout-out to Alice Castellanos, Cyan Wedgeworth, and Alyssa Lopez for being my Book Ladies. So glad to have you on board this ride with me.

My family has allowed me to ignore them from time to time so I could write, edit, go to school, jump on chats with other writers, attend conferences, and read. Please know how much I love and appreciate each one of you for supporting my dream of authoring books. I feel the prayers of my mother-in-law, Anna Brown, and the warmth of my sisters, Jataundalyn Brown, Shona Love, and Carrie Brown, and my brothers, Michael Brown, Harold Love, and William Sims, in addition to all of my sweet and fabulous nieces and nephews. I always appreciate the love from my Hebert cousins — in the Bay and beyond — as well.

Dad, I'm grateful for your love and support. Without it, my dreams would have been much smaller. I hope you know how much you mean to me.

I wrote this story about mothers and daughters because I am a mother of daughters — four of them. Kelsey, Alaysia, Chanel, and Kourtney, you are my inspiration. My favorite times in life are when we're all together. And now, we have David to join us, too — America's favorite son-in-law.

And you're right, Brownie. You're my little girl, also, and the best writing companion in the world, even when you interrupt my flow by pawing me to demand a walk.

Kasey, you're my partner in life and a partner in this book's journey. You are always looking out for us and our family. I probably don't tell you enough how much I love you, but when I forget, you can pull open this page and read it over and over again.

My mom, Deloris Hebert, was the most creative person I ever knew. She always believed in me, and was the biggest fan of everything I did. She is the soul of this book, and everything I write. She would have loved all of this.

AUTHOR'S NOTE

Black Candle Women began as an exercise in reminiscing about the summers I spent at my uncle's house in New Orleans. My mother taught elementary school and had the summers off, and since she didn't fly, we always traveled from northern California to Louisiana by train. The journeys by train were just as exciting for me as our destinations. During my many trips, I met my pen pal for life, Christina, and had my first kiss. My mother started sharing fascinating information about our family tree, including my parents' own journey from Louisiana to the Central Valley in California decades before. At the time, I'd been writing snippets of this story in my creative writing program at USC and getting nowhere, and the more I learned about my own family history — including my mother's petitions to Catholic saints — the more excited I became about my own storytelling. Soon, the Montrose women were born.

But as I continued writing the novel, trying to work out more of the Montrose women's story, it felt like something was missing. I found the inspiration I needed while visiting my parents over the holidays. One afternoon, I pulled out a bunch of cookbooks in search of a recipe for the Okinawan doughnuts I used to make as a kid (in addition to visits to my uncle's, I regularly attended a Japanese cultural camp in Stockton that, one year, distributed a cookbook of all the dishes we made). To this day, I still can't find the recipe, but I did come across a tattered folder holding all sorts of pages — a Cajun/Creole catalog from the New Orleans School of Cooking, recipe cards written in my mother's school-teacher script, cooking tips torn out from old magazines and newspapers, along with notes here and there from my mom — to herself, and to her only child — me. The collection of papers was such a beautiful documentation of her life, one I could share with my own daughters, and I thought I could use a book in a similar way to connect the women in the novel.

While *Black Candle Women* has evolved over the years, I feel great joy that my mom read an early version — one with the book

— before she passed away a few years ago. Hopefully, it transported her back to our summers in New Orleans and warmed her with those nostalgic, irreplaceable memories of family, food, and home, as writing it did for me. And I hope the story of these women warms you, reader, as well.

BLACK CANDLE WOMEN
PLAYLIST

"Controlla" — Drake
"All This Love" — DeBarge
"Love's Train" — Con Funk Shun
"The Power of Love" — Huey Lewis & the News
"Shame" — Evelyn "Champagne" King
"Poison" — Bell Biv DeVoe
"B.U.D.D.Y." — Musiq Soulchild
"Just Like a Star" — Corinne Bailey Rae
"Give Me the Night" — George Benson
"Anotherloverholenyohead" — Prince
"Black Magic Woman"— Santana
"You Make Me Wanna . . ." — Usher
"Some Kind Of Lover" — Jody Watley
"A Night to Remember" — Shalamar
"All This Love" — DeBarge
"Meeting In the Ladies Room" — Klymaxx
"Boo'd Up" — Ella Mai
"I'm Every Woman" — Whitney Houston/ Chaka Khan

"Murder She Wrote" — Chaka Demus & Pliers
"The Payback" — James Brown

Find it on Spotify: https://tinyurl.com/bd emdtm5

READING GROUP GUIDE

1. Victoria has structured her life in a way that supports her and her family's isolation. Did you understand why she chose to live that kind of life? If the household hadn't been shaken up by Nickie's interest in Felix, Madelyn's arrival, and Willow's relationship with January, do you think Victoria would have been able to maintain this way of living forever? Why or why not?

2. Although Willow doesn't believe in the curse, she has still kept herself from being in a relationship, at least until she meets January. Why do you think she behaves this way? Why does she change her behavior when January comes into her life?

3. After learning about Victoria's relationship with Jimmie, Augusta doesn't inter-

vene. How would you have acted if you'd been in Augusta's position?

4. Like Augusta's mother, Victoria envisions a certain future for her daughter and tries to control her. What other patterns are passed on among the generations? Discuss how traditions and behaviors, both useful and harmful, can continue within families.

5. At several points in the story, there are four generations of Montrose women living in the same household. What impact does this living arrangement have on their lifestyles? Is it more of a hindrance or a help to have so many generations under one roof?

6. Why do you think *Black Candle Women* was selected as the title for this book? How are the Montroses black candle women? Is Bela Nova also a black candle woman?

7. Which Montrose woman was your favorite? Why?

8. Discuss the family curse. Do you think Bela Nova was justified in cursing genera-

tions of Montrose women? Does your family have any superstitions?

9. The Montrose family documented much of their history in the book that originally belonged to Delilah. Why was Augusta willing to return it to Bela Nova with so much of their story inside? Is there an item that your own family passes down between generations? How does your family share and celebrate its history?

ABOUT THE AUTHOR

Diane Marie Brown is a professor at Orange Coast College and a public health professional for the Long Beach Health Department. She has a BA and MPH from UCLA and a degree in fiction from USC's Master of Professional Writing Program. She grew up in Stockton and now lives in Long Beach, California, with her husband, their four daughters, and their dog, Brownie. *Black Candle Women* is her debut novel.